In a Family Way

Book I of
"The Commitment" Series

Lee —
May we always
be "In A Family Way"!
Enjoy the book!
Happy New Year
Karen D. Badger
1/1/2014

BLUE FEATHER BOOKS, LTD.

Mr. Webster defines the word "matriarch" as "a mother who is head and ruler of her family and descendants." I dedicate this book to the matriarch of my family—my mom, Ellie Atherton. To say my mom is our family's matriarch is putting it mildly. She sacrificed everything for us. As a single mother in the 1960s, she raised five children nearly single-handedly with very little money, but a with a treasure chest of love. Anyone who can handle five teenagers at the same time is a saint in my eyes. She is the bond that holds our family together to this very day. Her fighting spirit has been inherited by her five children, fifteen grandchildren, and at the time of this writing, five great-grandchildren (and one more on the way). This book is about family and commitment. My mom embodies the true meaning of family. Her strength and perseverance through hard times was an inspiration to me. No matter how dire our circumstances, she held her head high with pride and never wavered in her commitment to give us the best life possible. She is the yardstick against which I measure myself as a wife, mother, daughter, sister, aunt, and friend. She inspired me never to walk away from a challenge. She made me believe I could do anything I set my mind to. I only hope that someday, I am half the woman she is. I love you, Mom. You are my hero. This book is for you.

In a Family Way

A BLUE FEATHER BOOK

by

Karen D. Badger

This is a work of fiction. All characters, locales and events are either products of the author's imagination or are used fictitiously.

IN A FAMILY WAY: BOOK I OF "THE COMMITMENT" SERIES

Cover drawing by Kyren L. Badger, age 5.
Cover design by Ann Phillips

A Blue Feather Book
Published by Blue Feather Books, Ltd.
133 Merck Rd
Cleveland, GA 30527

www.bluefeatherbooks.com

ISBN: 978-0-9822858-6-2

First edition: March, 2010

Printed in the United States of America and in the United Kingdom

Acknowledgements

I wrote this book more than ten years ago as an online series of stories. I knew that revising and editing them would be a huge undertaking. I never imagined, when I started this process, that I would go through three editors before the book was ready for publication. I must confess that for a while, I thought this book had very bad Juju. It reminded me of that big Venus flytrap in *Little Shop of Horrors* because it kept making my editors disappear.

Joan Opyr provided initial feedback before Miss Venus gobbled her up. Then Jane Vollbrecht put me through five months of hell and rewrites before it bit her on the wrist. Fortunately, we managed to polish the first half of the book to spit-shine perfection, and in the process, I learned a thing or two-thousand about writing... so much so, I was able to clean up the second half of the book well enough that Nann Dunne was able to escape Ms. Flytrap's grasp altogether. Nann—I said a prayer for you each evening to keep you safe from the infamous Ms. V. I'm glad to see it worked. Each of you contributed to the final product, but I can't thank Jane and Nann enough for your patience, dedication and diligence that finally brought this book to publication... a little later than I wanted, but much better for the effort. Thank you, fine ladies (sorry, Jane) for all your hard work.

Thank you Emily for insisting over and over that this book *will* get out! You never once gave up on me, even when I was close to giving up on myself. You are the best. Thank you for being my publisher and my friend. I'm crossing all my fingers and toes that the next book in this series has a much smoother ride.

Each time I pick up this book, the cover brings tears of pride to my eyes. Many, many thanks to my five-year-old grandson Kyren for providing the cover art. You did a super job, Ky! Nona loves you very, very much. Way to go, Bubba-Dude!

Last, but certainly not least, I would like to thank my partner, Bliss, for being my rock. She was my sounding board for ideas and kept things in perspective while I ranted and raged about how blunt Jane was being. She spent many evenings unscrewing me from the ceiling, encouraging me to keep working at it and reminding me that Jane had my best interests at heart. Little did I know at the time that she was also providing support and encouragement to Jane who was in the unenviable position of having to provide an education on editing to a good friend. No worries, Jane—I know now that it was for my own good. I can't believe I'm saying this, but I am sincerely grateful that you were so tough on me. I really did learn a lot. Anyway, thank you, B. I love you and I appreciate you. How'd I get so lucky to have found you? Turnabout is fair play though... its my turn to alternately encourage you and kick your butt to get your book finished.

Part I:

The Commitment

Chapter 1

"Damn construction!" Billie inched forward in a long line of traffic backed up on I-90 just short of the Albany, New York, cloverleaf. She glanced at her watch. Four forty-five p.m. "Great. I'm going to be late again. I'll be lucky if they don't fire my ass this time." Billie ran her fingers through her long, dark hair and fought the feelings that threatened to overwhelm her. "I don't know how much longer I can do this. I'm being pulled in a hundred directions at once... my paralegal job, my second job at the gym... and Seth. I don't have enough energy for all this. And now I'm talking to myself."

She cursed. "Come on, damn it." At last traffic began to move. "It's about time." She spent the rest of her drive to the gym remembering the events that had thrown her life into chaos.

On the last day of kindergarten, a car hit her son, Seth, as it illegally passed the school bus he'd just exited. He didn't have a chance. The impact threw him twenty feet into the air, and he landed on his head. He was rushed to the hospital where a team of trauma specialists worked on him for hours. The doctors said it was a miracle he hadn't died at the scene. A few days later, he had emergency surgery to drill a hole into his skull to relieve pressure on his brain. That was six months ago. He'd been in a coma ever since. What should have been the joyous start of summer vacation transformed into a traumatic turning point in their lives.

Seth's accident changed nearly every facet of Billie's life. Her days were filled with work; first her job at the law firm and then her early evening stints teaching aerobics. She spent the rest of each evening at the hospital, where she held Seth's hand and talked to him for hours. Even though he was unresponsive, she read to him and smoothed his hair. When visiting hours ended, she drove home and fell, exhausted, into bed.

Every day at the hospital presented a challenge. Billie stared at Seth's face and hoped for a glimmer of recognition, but day after day she was greeted with nothing more than an occasional facial twitch. Still, she held out hope and believed her vibrant six-year-old son wasn't doomed to spend the rest of his life in a vegetative state. Despite the doctors' dismal prognosis, she was sure he was still in there. They strongly encouraged her to place him in an institution, but she refused. She couldn't do that to him. It felt like giving up. In a nursing home, the doctors would make no effort to help him. He'd be discarded, forgotten. As long as she could afford to keep him in the long-term care facility at the hospital, she would.

Which was why she was hurrying to the gym to work her second job. She hated stealing the time away from Seth's bedside, but she needed extra income to pay for the portion of his long-term care her family insurance plan didn't cover.

Billie had high hopes that Seth was on the road to recovery. She thought he'd moved his little finger while she sat with him the previous night. She summoned the on-call doctor, but unfortunately, Seth didn't do it again. She hoped to coax another response from him at tonight's visit. She sighed deeply, and the December air seemed even chillier.

She arrived at the gym and rushed to change into her leotard. As she dressed, she caught a glimpse of herself in the mirror. She'd lost weight due to the constant stress, and her face betrayed her chronic exhaustion. "You look like hell, Charland," she said to her image. "After Seth is well, you need to take better care of yourself."

Billie entered the aerobics room and counted a dozen of her regulars there. She mumbled an apology for her tardiness as she slipped a workout CD in the stereo and took her position at the front of the class. Her students began to stretch and warm up. Billie tied back her hair and kicked off the dance routine with some mildly taxing moves.

About ten minutes into the warm-up, someone opened the door. "Class has already started," Billie shouted above the music. "You'll be better off to come back on time tomorrow."

Billie gave the newcomer her most intimidating look, but the new student appeared unfazed and joined the class anyway. Billie took advantage of the mirrors at the front of the room to study the persistent imp. She was a slight woman, whose height put her at chin-level to Billie. She had long, red-gold hair and a well-toned body. Billie studied her face and saw the most startling emerald green eyes she'd ever seen. *My God, I wonder if she knows how stunning she is?*

Suddenly, the new arrival fell flat on her face.

"I'm all right," she said as she held out her hand to ward off others who rushed over to help. "It happens all the time."

She scrambled to her feet and tried to fall back into step with the rest of the class. Billie cut the music and ended the warm-up early.

As the class took a short breather and water break, Billie walked over to the woman and touched her shoulder. "Are you sure you're all right? You know, you should've stretched first. You can hurt yourself if you don't warm up."

"I know, and I'm sorry I was late," she said. "I had to stay at work—again. My free time seems to be shrinking."

Billie chuckled and extended her hand. "I know exactly how you feel. By the way, I'm Billie Charland."

"Nice to meet you. I'm Caitlain O'Grady. Cat for short."

Billie felt a spark pass between them as her hand enveloped Cat's. "Welcome to my aerobics class, Cat. I'd love to chat, but I've got to get the class moving again before we lose our momentum." Billie walked back to the front of the class, selected the next track, and pressed Play on the stereo.

"Let's get started. We have a new member tonight, so we'll spend a little time with basic steps before we do our regular workout." Billie ran the class through the fundamentals that would be used in the dance routines. She kept a close eye on how Cat handled the footwork. Billie grimaced inwardly. Cat was totally uncoordinated. She should've known there'd be a flaw in that beautiful package somewhere.

Billie led the class through the regular workout and carefully watched Cat in the mirrors. Had it not been for the real possibility of injury, Cat's performance would've been laughable. It was almost painful to watch as she bumped into the other students and tripped over her own feet. Finally, the class was over. Billie stopped Cat on her way to the door.

Cat wiped the sweat from her brow. "I'm hopeless, right?"

"I wouldn't say hopeless," Billie lied.

"You're too kind. I've always had two left feet. I hoped aerobics would help me learn a little coordination. I guess I shouldn't waste my time or yours, huh?" Cat looked at the floor.

"Don't sell yourself short. All it takes is time and practice. Don't give up on yourself after only one class."

"You wouldn't be interested in giving private lessons, would you?" Cat asked. "I'd be willing to pay for them."

Billie wasn't sure whether it was a sincere inquiry or asked only in jest. "Private lessons?" Serious question or not, the idea intrigued Billie, but the part of her brain that dealt with everyday realities knew her life was already overloaded and she wondered where she would find time for Cat's training.

She really didn't want to say no. She considered Cat's offer and made one of her own. "What are your mornings like? My real job starts at eight. Maybe we can meet for an hour before we go to work."

"Mornings would be great. What time?"

"How does six sound? We can meet right here at the gym."

"Six is fine. When can we start?"

"No sense putting it off. Why not tomorrow?"

"Terrific." Cat picked up her towel and water bottle. "I'll see you in the morning." She took two steps toward the door. "I'll bring coffee. How do you drink it?"

"Black and strong."

"Somehow I knew you'd say that." Cat waved her hand in the air without looking back.

Billie watched her go and thought about the commitment she'd made. "Like I have time for another obligation," Billie said to the empty room. She gathered her gear and pondered what on earth had prompted her to agree to Cat's offer.

*   *   *

The next morning, Billie woke with a feeling of happy anticipation, and it both frightened and pleased her. It amazed her how helping a new student become more agile created such excitement. Or was it because the new student was Cat?

Billie arrived at the gym bright and early. She removed the top of her Tae Kwon Do uniform and stood in front of the mirrors in her black muscle T-shirt. She stared at her reflection. Most folks call this kind of shirt a "wife beater," she mused. How appropriate, given what I endured from Brian.

Two years in therapy had taught her how she enabled his violence. Every day, she congratulated herself for realizing the only way to take his power away was to leave him. Looking back, she knew it was the right decision, both for her and for Seth.

Oblivious to everything but the need to celebrate her freedom, Billie began her warm-up drills.

Cat slipped into the room and sat in the corner to watch Billie run through her routine. The loose fabric of her karate gi snapped as she kicked out with her bare feet at her invisible opponent. Her black hair flowed around her shoulders but was tinged with sweat along the hairline. Billie's well-toned muscles rippled as her arms circled in defensive moves. Her eyes were closed and her face frozen in a mask of total concentration as she made her way around the room, apparently by instinct.

A short time later, she stopped and stood at attention, feet together and arms at her side, as she bowed slightly from the waist to pay homage to her invisible master.

As she emerged from her trance, she opened her eyes. Cat's and Billie's gazes locked on one another.

Cat broke the spell, yelling when she spilled the coffee she was holding.

"Damn it." She danced around to shake the hot liquid from her leg. "I'm the clumsiest person on the planet."

Billie grabbed her towel and wiped off the hot coffee. "Come sit over here and let me take a look at that." She led Cat to a chair. "I have some salve in my gym bag if you need it."

She took the coffee from Cat and put it on a table. Lifting the lower edge of Cat's spandex gym shorts, she examined the scalded area.

"It looks a little pink, but I don't think it's burned. You'll be good as new in no time."

"Thanks." Cat pulled the leg of her shorts back down. "And thanks for making time for these lessons. I hope I'm not taking you away from anything... or anyone."

Billie toyed with the idea of telling Cat about Seth but, instead, put on her shoes and made her way toward the sound system. She stood with her back to Cat as she felt the blush rise to her cheeks. "Happy to do it. If you're ready, let's get started." Billie dared not look directly at Cat. She knew her face was as pink as Cat's leg.

Cat stripped off her sweatshirt. She was wearing an abbreviated spandex sports bra. The bra, combined with the shorts that hugged her well-toned legs and exposed her abdomen, left nothing to the imagination.

Billie's breath caught in her throat. She'd seen dozens—no, make that hundreds—of good-looking women in skimpy sportswear. Why the hell was this one making it impossible for her to breathe?

Billie pushed Play on the stereo. As the music began, she fell into her typical warm-up routine. Cat tried to follow her every move but failed miserably. Billie put a stop to it after about ten minutes of struggling to keep Cat in step.

"Cat, this approach doesn't work for you. We need to try something else." Billie saw Cat's forlorn expression in the mirror.

"I can't do this, Billie. It's a waste of your time. I'm ready to quit. Thanks for trying, though."

Billie rested her hands on her hips. "I don't think so, Red. I haven't exhausted my bag of tricks yet. I'm not ready to call it quits."

"If you think it's worth another try, I'm game, but I still think you're wasting your time. I'm pretty sure I'm hopeless."

"We'll see about that."

Billie reset the CD. The music filled the room as she stood behind Cat. She felt Cat tense. Billie put a hand on each of Cat's shoulders.

Billie's eyes met Cat's in the mirror. "Reach back with your arms and put your hands on the outside of my thighs. I'll hold your shoulders. You need to attach yourself to me so that we can move as one."

Billie saw Cat's eyes grow large. "I won't bite you. Come on, do as I say. One way or another, we're going to teach you how to be graceful, even if it kills us both."

"That's not outside the realm of possibility."

"Close your eyes. Relax," Billie whispered in Cat's ear.

Billie waited for a sign from Cat, who let out a deep sigh. "I think I'm ready."

Cat rested her trembling hands on Billie's thighs. Billie began to sway in time with the music, and Cat followed along.

"Relax," Billie repeated. "Lose yourself in the music."

They continued the rhythmic sway.

"Step touch. That's it. Right leg over, left toe tap. Left leg over, right toe tap. Good. You're doing fine." Billie spoke each instruction softly. "On the count of four, we're going to take two steps to the right followed by two steps left. Here we go. Four, three, two, one—two steps right," Billie said. Cat went left while Billie went right. In the process, Cat stepped on Billie's foot and nearly caused both of them to tumble to the floor.

Cat clenched her fists at her sides as Billie shook off the pain in her foot. "I'm such a klutz. I'll never get this. And I'm really sorry I stepped on you."

"I'm all right. Don't be so hard on yourself. We'll try it again, only this time, I'll hold on tighter." Billie once again stood behind Cat.

"Tighter?"

"Close your eyes. Listen to the music. Feel the flow." Billie took Cat's hands and put them back in place. Once again, they swayed side to side.

Billie removed her right hand from Cat's shoulder and encircled her waist. She pulled Cat backwards until she molded against Billie's frame.

"Remember, relax and follow my lead. That's it," Billie said.

Soon, they were moving back and forth across the floor, in step with each other and with the music.

Billie lowered her head to Cat's ear. "You're doing fine. Right leg over, left toe tap. Left leg over, right toe tap. Lose yourself in the moment." Billie looked at the two of them in the mirror. She liked what she saw.

Cat let her head fall back onto Billie's shoulder. Soon her eyes closed as they floated back and forth across the room.

Billie was in heaven. Cat was so appealing—way more appealing than Brian had ever been. Seth was the only good thing that came from her marriage to Brian.

Seth. She needed to focus on him, and until he regained his health, she barely had time for herself, never mind a partner. She wasn't even sure Cat was a lesbian. The last thing she needed to do was hit on a straight woman. Heaven knew she'd made that mistake in the past.

Billie put some distance between them. "Hey, Ginger, time's up. I need to get to work."

"Okay, Fred." Cat withdrew from Billie's arms.

"You did really well. We'll pick this up again tomorrow at six—unless you want to come for class tonight."

Cat smiled as she collected her towel from the corner and wandered toward the door. She stopped. "No, I'll pass on making a fool of myself in front of the class again, but would you like to get a drink after work tonight, or maybe dinner?"

Billie's heart was in her throat. "I'd love to, but I can't. I have a standing commitment after my aerobics class every night. I'm really sorry." Billie saw a look of disappointment cross Cat's face, only to be replaced by an awkward smile.

"I understand, really I do. Maybe some other time? I'll see you in the morning."

Cat opened the door.

"Wait," Billie said. "My evenings are booked, but that doesn't mean we can't meet earlier, say for breakfast. How does that sound?"

"Terrific. How about Rose's Diner at five tomorrow morning? It's a truck stop, but they have great food. After breakfast we can come over here and still have our class around six. Does that work for you?"

"It sounds fine. I know Rose personally. You're right, the food's good there. I'll see you in the morning. And by the way, you really did do well this morning. You'll be an expert in no time."

"Thank you, I couldn't do it without your help. See you in the morning."

The door closed behind Cat. "Bye, Ginger," Billie said, her heart racing with the possibilities.

Chapter 2

On that cool December morning, Billie sat at a small table in the corner of Rose's Diner sipping her coffee. During the messy breakup with Brian, she'd learned to position herself so that she had a clear view of the entire room. More than once, she was able to make a hasty retreat when Brian arrived in a drunken rage. Old habits died hard.

Her vantage point also allowed her to observe Cat's arrival. The sight of her raised goose bumps, despite the warmth of the diner. She rubbed her hands up and down her arms and marveled at the effect Cat had on her.

Cat smiled when she spotted Billie in the corner. "Good morning. This is a big sacrifice for me. I'm not much of a morning person, so it takes something pretty special to get me out of bed this early."

"Good morning." Before Billie said anything more, the waitress interrupted her.

"'Morning, Billie-girl. You're here early. Who's your new friend?"

"Darlene, this is Cat. Cat, Darlene. Cat's one of my aerobics students."

"Nice to meet you, Cat." Saccharine laced her words. "What can I get you gals this morning?"

Billie didn't look up from her menu. "I'll have a fruit cup, toast, and orange juice."

Cat said, "I'll have the big breakfast and a side of cottage cheese, please."

"How on earth can you eat like that and stay so trim?" Billie asked.

Darlene grabbed the menus and stomped away.

"I've always had a fast metabolism. I guess my body needs a lot of fuel. I've never thought much about what I eat. I suppose it'll catch up with me someday." Cat gestured at Darlene. "What's her problem?"

"Let's just say that she's been trying to sell me something that I'm not interested in, and now she thinks I'm shopping elsewhere."

"Shopping?" Billie noted the look of confusion on Cat's face. A moment later, Cat's eyebrows rose high on her forehead as Billie's meaning became clear. She blushed profusely.

Billie tried to ease Cat's discomfort. "So, tell me about yourself."

"What do you want to know?"

"Everything. How old you are, where you live, what you do for work. You know, the usual stuff." Billie propped her elbows on the table and rested her chin in her hands.

"I'm twenty-six, I live in a condo on Western, near Gilderland, and I'm an anesthesiologist. I also work in the ER. Let me see— what else can I tell you? I have three sisters, two older, Amy and Bridget, and one younger, Drew. Unfortunately, they're pretty scattered across the country and they're all pretty busy with kids and jobs, so I don't get to see them often. Between them, I have five nieces. My parents winter in Florida and summer here in Albany."

"You're a doctor? You're kind of young for that, aren't you?"

"In most circumstances, yes. I mean, at my age, most doctors-in-training are beginning their residency, but I knew I wanted to be a doctor pretty early in life so I entered an advanced pre-med program in high school and was able to apply my credits to college. That allowed me to graduate college when I was eighteen and med school at 22. I finished a three-year residency program last year."

"Cat Howser, MD, huh? A regular child prodigy."

Cat looked away.

"All right. Enough teasing. Tell me, what do you do in your spare time?"

"Two nights a week, I volunteer at the Crisis Management Center, and in my spare time, I write."

"You write? You mean stories?"

"Yes, stories and poetry. It's been one of my hobbies since I was little. It brings me peace, and it helps me relax after a trying day. But enough about me. Your turn."

Before Billie spoke, Darlene arrived with their food. Billie noted a sly look on Cat's face. Without warning, Cat put her hand over Billie's on the table. Billie froze, not sure what Cat was up to. Darlene took one look and trounced off.

Cat chuckled. "I'm sorry. I couldn't resist. Her attitude got to me. Forgive me?"

"It serves her right. Maybe she won't be so obvious the next time you're around."

"Maybe not." Cat picked up her fork. "Now, spill it. Tell me all about you."

"All right. I'm twenty-seven, almost twenty-eight, divorced. I live in a loft on Fuller Road near the hospital, and I'm a paralegal. I work in a law office in Colonie. I need one more year of college to complete my law degree, but that's on hold right now. As far as siblings go, zip. Nada. I'm an only child. Sad to say, my parents are gone. Oh yeah, and I teach aerobics five nights a week at the gym on Central, but you already knew that."

"You've only got a year left for your degree? If you don't mind me asking, why put it off?"

"I… ah… I have some… uh… other priorities that demand my time and financial resources. I'll finish my degree later, when things straighten out." Billie felt her eyes stinging with unshed tears.

Cat reached out again to cover Billie's hand with her own. "You've known me for less than a day, but if I can help, I'd be happy to do anything I can."

Billie wiped away the tears that rolled down her face. "I appreciate your concern, but there's not much anyone can do to help me with this particular problem. Everything that can be done has been. At this point, it's mostly a waiting game."

"Sometimes it helps to have someone to wait with. Don't wait alone if you don't have to."

Billie turned her hand over and grasped Cat's. "Thanks. I'll keep that in mind." She looked at her watch. It was nearly six. "We'd better finish up if we're going to have time for your lesson."

"If you're not up to it…"

"The workouts help to relieve stress. I'd rather do the lesson, that is, unless you've eaten too much to move."

"Don't you worry about me, Billie-girl. I can move fine. Just you watch me."

Little did Cat know, Billie intended to do exactly that.

Chapter 3

Three months later, Billie and Cat still met for lessons every morning, with the occasional early breakfast prelude. Billie rested against the back wall of the aerobics room and watched Cat glide across the floor. "That's it. Great job! On your next turn, add a cha-cha."

Cat did as instructed and winked seductively at Billie as she passed by.

"Show off."

Cat stuck her tongue out on her next pass across the room.

"You'd better be careful what you do with that tongue."

Cat lost her footing, but instead of becoming frustrated as she might've done in the past, she lifted her arms and twirled like a ballerina.

Billie laughed out loud. "Nice dance step, but not quite what the music calls for." She tossed a towel to Cat. "Enough for today, Red. I've got to get to work."

"Drat. It's just starting to be fun." Cat wiped her brow.

Billie draped her arm around Cat's shoulder. "It amazes me how far you've come in twelve weeks. You've picked up the dance routines nicely."

"I have a great teacher," Cat said. She stumbled for a step or two and clutched at her side. "Oh my God!"

"Cat, what is it?" Billie led her to a chair.

"I don't know."

"Are you all right?"

Cat stood and twisted at the waist. "Yes, I think so. Whatever it was appears to have passed."

"Are you sure?"

Cat put her hand on Billie's face and smiled. "I'm fine, but thank you for being worried about me."

"Can't lose my dancing partner, can I?"

"Not a chance."

"Good. I'll see you at Rose's on Monday, right?"

"Any chance you're free for dinner sometime over the weekend?" Cat asked.

"I'd love to, but…"

"You can't break your commitment," Cat finished for her.

Billie nodded.

"All right. See you on Monday."

As Billie watched Cat leave, she acknowledged the nagging feeling in the pit of her stomach. She knew she should tell Cat about Seth, but she was unsure how Cat felt about her, let alone how she'd feel about accepting a disabled child into her life. Billie hated not being honest with Cat, but she decided to wait to see if their relationship progressed to the next level before she told her about Seth.

* * *

On Monday morning, Cat failed to show up for breakfast. Six o'clock came and went, but still no Cat. Billie went to the gym and looked up Cat's address in the membership registry. Her gut told her something was wrong, and she'd learned never to doubt her intuition.

She fought the rush hour traffic to get to Cat's condo. She scanned the wall of mailboxes in the lobby until she located the one with Cat's name. Billie pushed the elevator call button but lost her patience and raced up the stairs two-at-a-time to the third floor. She found unit number four and knocked. A woman wearing a shortie nightgown opened the door. In the background, Billie saw a small girl sitting at a table, a bowl of cereal in front of her.

"I'm sorry. I must have the wrong unit, but the mailbox in the lobby says Caitlain O'Grady lives here."

Without so much as a glance at the child, the woman said, "Tara, go wake up your mom and tell her she's got company." She fixed a cold stare on Billie. "You've got the right place."

The girl ran from the room. While they waited, the woman continued to eye Billie up and down.

Cat has a daughter? Billie's wonderings were cut short.

"So, are you the one she's been spending so much time with lately?"

From the woman's appearance, Billie surmised she'd recently gotten out of bed. She wondered whose bed that would be. Cat no doubt had a good reason for not telling her about Tara, and this woman was probably another subject better left unexplored.

"What's the matter? Cat got your tongue?" the woman asked. She laughed at her own comment.

"Look, tell Cat that Billie stopped by. I'll catch up with her later."

Billie felt a tug on her jacket. She looked down into the face of a miniature Cat, complete with green eyes and reddish-blonde hair.

"Mama's sick and can't get out of bed. She wants to see you. She said your name is Billie. My name is Tara, and I'm four years old. How old are you?"

Billie crouched down in front of Tara. "Your mom is sick?"

"Mama's been puking all night. She said to bring you to her." Tara took Billie's hand. The woman sneered at Billie as Tara led her to Cat's room.

At the door, Tara let go of Billie's hand, scampered onto the bed, and perched herself on Cat's lap. Billie saw Cat cringe in pain. Tara held Cat's face between her hands. "Here she is, Mama."

"Thank you, sweetie. Why don't you go finish your breakfast? I need to talk to Billie for a while."

"Okay." Tara bounded off the bed and ran out of the room.

Billie closed the door and rested her forehead against it with her back to Cat. She was angry but realized Cat owed her no explanation. Her relationship with Cat had thus far been based only on friendship, but still, not telling her she had a child… Billie pushed aside her anger. Cat needed her help now, not her recriminations.

Billie pivoted to face Cat. She looked like hell. Her hair was dull and matted, and her face, usually so bright and animated, was pale and pasty. Her lips were cracked, and her eyes held none of their typical sparkle. Instead, they were red-rimmed and darkened with circles.

Billie crossed to the bed in two long strides. She sat on the edge and felt Cat's forehead.

"Damn, you're burning up. What's wrong? What are your symptoms?"

"I'm fine."

"Like hell you are. Why aren't you in the hospital? For Christ's sake, woman, you're a doctor."

Billie saw that Cat was avoiding her gaze. "Damn it, talk to me."

Cat met Billie's eyes. "The symptoms indicate appendicitis."

"Appendicitis? Are you out of your mind?" Billie jumped to her feet. "Jesus Christ, Cat. We need to get you to the hospital."

"Calm down. I said it might be appendicitis. It might also be gallbladder."

"Does it hurt anywhere in particular? Like here?" Billie pressed down on Cat's stomach but got no reaction. "Or here?" Billie pressed midway down on Cat's right side. She watched Cat's face carefully for signs of discomfort but didn't see any until she released the pressure.

"Ow!" Cat clutched at her abdomen as she drew her knees up.

"That's it. I'm taking you to the hospital. If this is appendicitis, it could burst and kill you. You know that. I don't want an argument. Do you understand?" Billie looked directly into Cat's eyes as she spoke.

Cat's eyes closed tightly. Billie suspected it was another wave of pain.

Cat gasped. "Oh God. All right, help me up. I need to get dressed."

"No time for that. I'll wrap a blanket around you and carry you to my car. I don't want to waste another minute." Billie yanked the cover from the bed and folded it around Cat.

"Wait. What about Tara? We have to take her with us."

"That woman who answered the door can stay with her. We need to get going."

"No, that woman, Gail, is leaving me today. She's moving out."

Billie threw her hands out to the sides. "What did you plan to do if I hadn't come by this morning?"

"My parents are on their way. They're flying in around two this afternoon."

"You could be dead by this afternoon." Billie's frustration intensified.

"It couldn't be helped, Billie. My sisters live farther away than they do. All three of them offered to come stay with Tara, but my parents can get here the fastest."

"Aren't there friends or coworkers you could have left her with?"

"I'm not going to leave her with just anyone. She'll be most comfortable with my parents."

"Where are they coming from?"

"Florida. I called them last night."

"Oh, for Christ's sake, Cat. You should've gone to the hospital hours ago."

"I can't leave Tara alone. Please. Either we wait for my parents, or we take her with us. My parents will take her from you when they get here."

Billie caught the look of sheer panic that crossed Cat's face. "All right. We'll take her. What's the closest hospital?"

"Albany Medical Center."

"That's on Commercial. I know exactly where it is." She should know. Seth had been there for the past nine months.

"Right, but the closest branch is on New Scotland. I work there."

Billie scooped one arm under Cat's knees and the other behind her back, then lifted her from the bed and carried her down the hall into the living area.

She laid Cat on the couch and squatted down so she was face-to-face with Tara, who was curled up in an overstuffed chair in front of the television. "Tara, I need you to get dressed right away and come with me and your mom."

"Where are we going?"

"We need to take Mama to the doctor. Like you told me, she's sick. Show me where your room is, and I'll help you get your clothes on."

A few minutes later, Billie returned with a fully clad Tara, complete with rag doll hugged tightly to her chest. Billie looked around for Gail who was nowhere to be seen.

"Gail disappeared in a hurry," Billie said louder than she intended.

Tara looked up at Billie. "Gail is gone. Mama and Gail had a big fight yesterday. Mama told her to leave."

Much as she might like to explore what Tara's comments meant, the fact that Cat was nearly unconscious dictated prompt action. Billie grabbed what looked like a set of house keys from the kitchen table and retrieved Cat from the couch.

Not willing to waste time waiting for the elevator, Billie carried Cat down the three flights of stairs with Tara clinging to the back of her coat. Billie did her best to settle Cat comfortably in the front seat and buckled Tara into the back. She sped to the hospital and pulled into the emergency lane. She quickly got out of the car and reached into the backseat to unbuckle Tara then ran around to the front passenger seat and lifted Cat out of the car.

"Tara, come here and stay close to me," Billie said.

Tara once again grasped the hem of Billie's coat and followed Billie into the emergency room.

"Help! I need help here." Billie gently laid Cat on a gurney then stepped away to allow the ER crew to assist her. She lifted Tara into her arms and approached the admissions desk. "Don't worry. The doctors will fix Mama up good as new."

Tara clung even more tightly to Billie. "I'm scared."

"I know you are, sweetie, but your grandma and grandpa will be here soon to take care of you."

"Name," the admissions clerk said.

"Billie Charland."

"And what's wrong with little Billie?"

"No, the child isn't sick. It's her mother."

"So the mother's name is Billie Charland?"

"No. *I'm* Billie Charland. Her mother's name is Cat. I mean, Caitlain O'Grady."

"And what's the nature of Ms. O'Grady's illness?"

"Appendicitis. At least I think so. Hell, I don't know! I'm a paralegal, not a doctor." Billie's strident tone over her annoyance with the admission's clerk appeared to frighten Tara. Billie felt her tiny body tense.

"I need Ms. O'Grady's full name, social security number, home address, phone number, next of kin, and insurance information." The woman held her hands poised over the keyboard.

Billie adjusted her hold on Tara. "Look, I don't have any of the information you're asking for. This is a medical emergency. We kind of left the house in a hurry."

"You'll have to go home and get the information. We can't create a billing record without it."

"Oh, for Christ's sake." Billie didn't want to leave Cat there alone and wondered where she'd find the necessary information. She put Tara down on the floor and asked for a piece of paper and a pen. "Give me that list again."

The woman's exasperated sigh made Billie want to slap her. "Full name, social security number, home address, phone number, next of kin, and insurance information. Oh, and we need the name and address of her employer, as well."

"Employer?" She handed the pen back to the receptionist. "I think you already have all the information you need. She's an anesthesiologist at this hospital."

Billie took Tara's hand, stormed away from the flabbergasted receptionist, and led Tara to the ER waiting room. They claimed two of the uncomfortable chairs, ready to wait for however long it might take to get news of Cat's condition.

As the morning dragged on, Tara drifted off to sleep with her head resting on Billie's shoulder and her rag doll clenched under her arm. With nothing to do but think, Billie replayed the morning's events. She couldn't believe Cat hadn't told her about Tara, but at least it made her feel justified in not mentioning Seth. Seth's condition was a very personal issue for her, and one she divulged only to significant people in her life. Her relationship with Cat hadn't yet reached that level. She thought next about Gail and wondered how she fit into Cat's life. Billie shook her head as she cautioned herself against becoming involved with a woman who apparently already had a partner—even if it was a partner with whom she'd just had a major fight, according to Tara.

Tara stirred in Billie's arms, evoking memories of the times she and Seth shared such moments. She was overwhelmed by a sense of loss as she thought of Seth, helpless and unresponsive in his hospital bed. She sighed out loud when she realized she'd spent nearly her entire adult life losing the people she loved. First her parents, and then Seth. Seth was still alive, but one could hardly characterize his life as living. She'd lost the little boy who left for school that morning.

Billie looked at Tara and was struck by how much she resembled her mother. A wave of maternal tenderness washed over her, followed by an epiphany. Her heart beat wildly as she tried to reason with herself. She couldn't possibly be in love. She didn't have time for that complication in her life and pondered whether she was ready to be romantically involved with Cat when she had no idea if Cat would be accepting of Seth.

Billie rested her head against the wall and closed her eyes. A sob caught in her throat, as she feared she could lose Cat before she had the chance to find out if they might build a relationship. Billie felt tears running down her cheeks.

Tara awoke. She lifted her head and looked into Billie's face. She rubbed the sleep from her eyes then wiped the moisture from Billie's cheeks. "Are you sad about Mama?"

"Yes, I am."

"Mama says when you get sad about someone its 'cause you love them. Do you love Mama?"

"I think I do. I hope she gets better soon, so I can tell her that."

"Mama loves you, too. I heard her tell Gail, and then they yelled at each other." Tara squirmed on Billie's lap. "Is Mama gonna be okay?"

Billie noticed tears in Tara's eyes. She hugged her. "She'll be fine. Please don't cry." Billie wiped the tears from Tara's face. "That's a good girl. How about we go to the gift shop and buy a book to read?"

"I'm hungry. I want Mama."

"It'll be fine. I promise. Come on. Let's go buy a book and some snacks. And as soon as we know how Mama is, we'll get some lunch."

When Billie and Tara returned from the gift store, she settled Tara into a chair beside her with her doll, a package of cookies, and an orange juice from the vending machine. Billie rested her head against the wall once more and thought about how different her life would be if she'd met Cat instead of Brian seven years ago.

Brian was a mistake, especially since Billie had always known she was attracted to women. He was a mistake she made to please her parents. In their eyes, he was the perfect catch, well suited for their only child. He was educated, came from a wealthy family, and had a good job. Little did her parents know that he was emotionally unavailable, and as their relationship progressed, so did his drinking and abusive behavior.

Billie and Brian made a striking pair. Brian was blond, with Adonis good looks, while Billie was olive-skinned with long, flowing black hair and features beautiful enough for a model, or so she'd been told. But good looks on the outside can hide a world of ugliness on the inside. During her marriage, Billie was constantly at war within herself. Her head tried to convince her heart that her public image and financial security held more importance than happiness, and that her parents' happiness was more important than her own. For nearly three years, Billie listened to her head instead of her heart. All it got her was Brian's emotional indifference and abuse, which increased in frequency and severity with each passing year.

Billie's parents had no idea where her heart wanted to lead her, and they took that innocence to their graves. Ironically, it was their deaths in an auto accident when Seth was two that prompted Billie to take stock of her life. She discovered she didn't want to be on her deathbed, filled with regret for the bad choices she'd made. She didn't want to die never having known true love, never having experienced what it would mean to live her life with someone who touched not only her body, but also her soul.

Billie shook off her daydreams and reflected on her present predicament. She loved Cat, of that she was sure, and if what Tara said was true, Cat loved her, too. In the three months Billie had known Cat, she found her to be a caring, considerate person. She was convinced that Cat couldn't possibly be the kind of person who'd reject a handicapped child. She resolved to tell her about Seth, and she prayed Cat wouldn't run. In spite of her romantic inclinations, Billie had no illusions about her choices. If Cat did reject Seth, it would mean giving up the love of her life. When all was said and done, she'd choose Seth over Cat. She wouldn't run the risk of Cat breaking his heart, even if protecting him broke her own heart.

Billie recalled the dates she'd had over the past two years. Not one of them made Billie smile at the mere thought of her. None of them filled her with delirious anticipation and fluttering butterflies when she entered a room. None of them made her feel like spending the rest of her days drowning in her eyes, never wanting to come up for air. None of them had that effect on her. None, until Cat. Tara's comment about Cat loving Billie made her smile. She took a deep breath and her heart raced with excitement.

Billie noticed the time. Eight o'clock. "Shit! I forgot about work. I need to call in." Billie clamped a hand over her mouth as she realized she'd cursed in front of Tara. She walked a few paces away to use her cell phone and reached her boss's voice mail. "Hi, Art. It's Billie. I'm sorry for the short notice, but I need to take the day off. Possibly tomorrow as well. A friend of mine is seriously ill and is in the hospital. I'm at the ER waiting for word about how she's doing. She has a young child, and there's no one to look after her until her grandparents fly in this afternoon, so I hope you understand. I appreciate the time off. Call me if you need me. Thanks."

Over the next four hours, Billie alternated between reading to Tara and making trips to the vending machine and bathroom. Several times, she soothed Tara's fears about her mother. She also made multiple inquiries about Cat's condition, but to no avail. After a change of shift in the nursing staff, she spoke to the new nurse at the desk.

"Excuse me. My friend has been in there for over four hours. Can you check on her and give me some idea of how she's doing?"

"What's your friend's name?"

"Caitlain O'Grady."

"Cat? Cat is here in the emergency room?"

"Yes. We brought her in this morning. She disappeared into that room over there, and we haven't seen her since."

The nurse rose to her feet. "Wait right here and let me see what I can find out."

A short time later, the nurse returned. "I'm sorry, I didn't catch your name."

She extended her hand to the nurse. "Billie Charland. How's Cat?"

"She was taken to surgery several hours ago, and she's still there. That's all I was able to find out. If you go to the family waiting room on the third floor and pick up the phone in there, you'll be connected to the nurses' station in the OR. They should be able to tell you more."

Billie and Tara made their way to the third floor, where Billie inquired about Cat's status. The nurse in the OR told them the doctor would be with them shortly.

"Can't you at least tell me how she's doing?" Billie asked nervously.

"As I said, the doctor will be with you shortly."

A sense of doom filled Billie's heart as she hung up the phone. She found one empty seat in the crowded waiting room and sat with Tara on her lap. By the time the doctor appeared, she'd all but persuaded herself that Cat had died on the table.

"I'm looking for the family of Caitlain O'Grady."

Billie was immediately on her feet. She picked up Tara and cradled her on her hip as she met the doctor.

"That would be us." Billie extended her hand to the doctor. "Billie Charland," she said as she shook his hand. "How's Cat?"

"Are you the person who brought her in?"

Billie nodded.

"Then she has you to thank for saving her life. She's a lucky young woman. If she'd been brought in any later, the hospital would've lost one of its best anesthesiologists."

Billie wobbled backwards and sank to the couch, her knees weak with relief. Tara snuggled in closer to Billie and laid her head on her shoulder as she eyed the doctor warily. Billie kissed the top of Tara's head as she moved her onto her lap.

The doctor explained. "Her appendix burst as soon as we touched it, spilling toxins in the abdominal cavity. We flushed it clean, though. She has an excellent chance of a full recovery. She's sedated and will be in the post-surgical unit until tomorrow morning." He paused. "You look exhausted. Why don't you go home and get some rest? Like I said, she'll be unconscious until about this time tomorrow. Leave your number with the receptionist, and we'll call you if her condition changes."

Billie thanked the doctor as she held Tara closer.

Under other circumstances, Billie would've objected to leaving Cat in the hospital alone, but she had Tara to think about—and Seth.

"Tara, Mama's going to be fine. You heard the doctor say so. But she's going to be asleep for the rest of the day, so she won't be able to talk to us. How'd you like to go out for a nice lunch?"

"Can we go to McDonald's?"

That was Seth's favorite place to eat, too. "Sure, McDonald's it is. Come with me while I give my cell phone number to the receptionist, and we'll go."

*   *   *

After lunch, Billie went back to Cat's condo. She hoped that familiar surroundings would help ease Tara's worry over her mother's illness. Tara was asleep within blocks of leaving McDonald's.

Billie parked the car and carried Tara into the building. Fumbling with the keys she'd grabbed earlier, she found the one that unlocked the door. She tucked Tara into bed and returned to the living room. The light was blinking on the answering machine, and she resisted the temptation to listen to Cat's messages. The apartment was in disarray, so she decided to pass the time cleaning. An hour later, the apartment was spotless.

Billie checked the time when she finished cleaning the house. It was two o'clock. "If I remember right," she said out loud, "Cat said her parents' flight would be landing about now. Since they think Cat's still at home, I'm sure they'll come directly here from the airport."

An hour later, she was putting the last load of laundry away in Cat's bedroom when she heard the patter of little feet coming down the hallway. She pretended not to notice and let Tara sneak up behind her. At the last second, she scooped her up in her arms, flung her down on Cat's bed, and tickled her.

After an appropriate amount of tickle warfare, Billie rolled onto her back and entwined her hands behind her head. Tara climbed on top of Billie and straddled her stomach. She wrapped her hands around Billie's elbows.

"I've got you, bad guy. Surrender to Tara the Great."

"Please, Tara the Great, please don't hurt me. I surrender. Take me prisoner if you want, but please don't hurt me."

Tara sat up and crossed her arms. "I wouldn't really hurt you. I'm only playing."

"I know that." Tara's attitude reminded her of Seth. "Your grandparents should be here soon. What would you like to do while we wait?"

"I don't know. What time is it?"

Billie looked at the clock on the bedside stand. "Three o'clock."

"Three o'clock!" Tara bounced up and down. "Time for *Barney*. Quick, turn on the TV."

She scampered off the bed and ran into the living room, and Billie followed.

For the next hour, Billie and Tara watched the purple dinosaur sing and skip his way across the screen. At least Tara watched. Billie spent the hour in another zone as she contemplated what the future might hold for her and Cat. Ideally, they'd live as one big happy family, two parents, two children, happily ever after. The American Dream. Unfortunately, a child in a coma was more like a nightmare.

The minutes ticked by, and Billie wondered what was keeping Cat's parents. If they didn't arrive soon, she wouldn't be able to teach her aerobics class that evening.

The phone rang. Billie froze and hesitated long enough for the answering machine to pick it up.

"Cat, this is Dad. Honey, I'm afraid we've been delayed."

Billie grabbed the receiver. "Hello?"

"Cat? Thank God you're still home. We've been calling your cell phone and leaving messages on your machine at home all day."

"No, this is Billie. I'm afraid Cat..."

"Billie? We've heard a lot about you. This is Doc, Cat's father."

"Mr. O'Grady. I'm so glad you called. Cat's in the hospital. Her appendix—"

"Is she all right? When she called last night, I had a hunch she was worse off than she led us to believe. How is she?"

"Her appendix burst, but the doctor said she'll make a full recovery."

"Wonderful. How's the little one doing?"

"Tara? She's okay. I'm amazed she's as relaxed as she is. I'm virtually a stranger to her, after all."

"Cat wouldn't leave her with someone she didn't trust. We'll be there sometime tomorrow afternoon to take over with Tara and check on Cat. The weather's been pretty bad here in Orlando, so most flights were cancelled, including ours. We're scheduled to land around two tomorrow afternoon."

"Two o'clock. Got it. Tara and I will probably be at the hospital. Albany Medical Center on New Scotland. The one Cat works at."

"We'll go directly there from the airport. I'll call the hospital and tell Cat about our delay as soon as I hang up with you. Thank you for being there for both Cat and Tara. If you're half as wonderful as Cat's told us you are, you'll make a great addition to our family."

Addition to the family?

"All right, sir. We'll see you tomorrow."

Billie hung up the phone and rubbed her face as she tried to digest what Cat's father had said and figure out what to do for the next twenty-two hours. She inhaled deeply to steady her nerves. With no other options, she decided to take Tara along that evening.

"Hey, Tara, I've got a question for you. I need to do some things today, and I wondered if you'd like to come along."

"Where are we going?"

"First, I have a class to teach at the gym. The gym has a place for kids, filled with lots of toys and books. You'll stay there while I'm in class. Do you think you'd like that?"

Billie saw a look of uncertainty cross Tara's face. "Will you come back to get me?"

"Of course I will, you silly goose. I'll only be gone an hour, and I promise to come back for you."

"Where else are we going?"

"I thought maybe we'd pick up a quick pizza and go visit someone. What do you think?"

"Who?"

"A very special young man named Seth. Seth is very sick. I visit him every day. I love him very much, and I hope you'll like him, too. Someday, he'll get better, and I'll be able to take him home. Would you like to visit Seth with me? Maybe you can help him feel better."

"Do you think he'll like me?"

"He'll love you, but he won't be able to tell you. He looks like he's sleeping all the time. I read to him and talk to him because I believe he can hear me, even though his eyes are closed."

"After we go see Seth, are you going to come home with me?"

Billie gathered Tara into her arms and held her close. "I'd never leave you here all by yourself. I promise."

"Pinkie swear?" Tara crooked her right pinkie and held it out to Billie.

"Pinkie swear," Billie replied, as she locked her pinkie with Tara's.

Tara threw her arms around Billie's neck and hugged her. "Will you come live with Mama and me when she comes home?"

"Let's take this one day at a time, okay?"

"Okay. Can we go now?"

Chapter 4

Billie had a hard time convincing Tara to leave the child-care facility at the gym. "Time to go. We still need to visit with Seth."

"Can I come back tomorrow?"

"Your grandma and grandpa will be here tomorrow, so you won't have to come back."

Tara lowered her chin to her chest and pouted. "But I want to."

Billie knelt on one knee. "I'll tell you what. I'll talk to your mom about it."

"Really? Oh boy. I can color some pictures for my new friends. I can't wait."

"Slow down, there. I said I'd talk to your mom about it. That doesn't mean she'll say yes. Now, how about we get some dinner?"

Over dinner at the pizza parlor, Tara played *Twenty Questions* with Billie.

"How old is Seth?"

"He's six."

"Is he your brother?"

"No, he's my son." Billie watched Tara for her reaction.

Tara's eyes opened wide. "You're his mommy?"

"Yes, and he's special to me. I love him very much. It makes me sad that he's in the hospital."

"Does Seth have a daddy?" Tara chomped down on her pizza slice.

Billie wiped a drop of pizza sauce from Tara's chin with a napkin. "Yes, Seth has a daddy, but he doesn't see him very often."

"Why not? Doesn't Seth's daddy live with you?"

"No, he doesn't live with us. Seth's daddy and I don't love each other anymore, so we decided not to stay married."

Tara put her pizza down and folded her arms across her chest. Her pixie-like features contorted into a scowl. Billie reached across the table to touch Tara's cheek. "Is something wrong?"

"I don't have a daddy," she said softly.

Tara's fatherless state was a subject that Billie decided not to tackle at the moment. "How about we take the rest of this pizza and go visit Seth?"

Tara scooted from her chair. "Maybe Seth will want some pizza."

If only he could, Tara. If only he could.

* * *

Billie belted Tara in the backseat for the ride to the hospital. "How did Seth get sick?"

"He was hit by a car that passed his school bus. He hit his head real hard, and it hurt him inside his brain."

"Mama says cars aren't s'posed to pass buses when the lights are on."

"You're right, but the man who hit Seth was drinking, and he made a bad decision because of it."

"He's a bad man. Did the p'lice put him in jail?"

"He isn't really a bad man. He's sorry for what happened to Seth and wishes he could make him better. He made a bad choice that day, that's all." Billie believed in teaching children compassion, but in this case, she wanted to rip the guy's head off.

"Here we are." Billie pulled into the parking lot of Albany Medical Center's Commercial Avenue branch. "Remember, you need to be quiet in there so that we don't disturb the sick people." As they walked across the parking lot, Tara slipped her hand into Billie's.

Billie was a familiar sight around the hospital. She hadn't missed a nightly visit with Seth since his accident. In the early days, she took a leave of absence from work and stayed with him around the clock. When it became apparent that recovery would be slow in coming, the doctors convinced her to go home at night. Soon, the threat of losing her job and her dwindling savings account meant she needed to return to work full time. Nearly nine long months had passed since the awful day he was hit by the drunk driver.

Billie led Tara through the maze of hallways to Seth's room. As was true every time she walked through the door, Billie saw her precious son lying unmoving in his bed, his face like a cherub's. He had his father's light hair, the color of corn silk, and long eyelashes that brushed his cheeks.

Tara climbed into the chair beside the bed. Billie bent over and kissed Seth's forehead.

"Hi, scout. How are you doing today? I've got lots to tell you, but first I want you to meet someone." She motioned for Tara to move closer to Seth.

Billie waited for Tara to follow her instruction. "Seth, this is Tara. Tara, this is Seth."

"Hi, Seth." Tara's voice was little more than a whisper. After a few seconds with no response, she said loudly to Billie. "I don't think he can hear me. His eyes are closed."

"Close your eyes," Billie said. "Can you still hear me?"

"Uh-huh."

"Well, I think Seth can hear us, too. Here, climb up onto the bed and help me read to him." She patted the bed.

Tara dropped out of the chair and scampered onto the bed, but was careful not to crowd Seth's legs. Billie read out loud and Tara explained the pictures. After story time, Billie told him about Cat's illness, and how they'd rushed her to the hospital that morning. Over the three months that she'd known Cat, Billie often spoke to Seth about her, including her sincere but often inept attempts at dance and aerobics. She was certain she saw his mouth twitch into a slight smile when she told him about Cat falling on her face in the middle of class.

By the end of the visit, Tara had snuggled in beside Seth and talked to him with such conviction that Billie feared her heart might burst from the sheer joy of watching the tableau. Tara told him the name of every doll she owned, described in detail all of the characters on Barney and what they'd done in today's episode, listed the names of her cousins, aunts, and uncles, and explained that her Grammy and Grandpa lived in Florida in the winter but came home in the summer and that they would come to see her very soon. She asked him several questions, but when he didn't respond, she went on to supply answers of her own.

The visit flew by, and soon it was time to leave. It appeared to Billie that Tara's nonstop chattering to Seth elicited responses from him. The signs were small: a slight movement in his little finger, a flutter of his eyelashes, a sudden quirk at the corner of his mouth, and Billie left the hospital that night with more hope than she'd had since the accident.

"Can I visit Seth again? Can I?" All the way back to Cat's condo, Tara begged Billie to let her visit Seth the next night.

"I'll talk to your mom about it. I think Seth enjoyed having you there tonight."

"I'll color some pictures for him at the gym tomorrow."

Billie opted to remind Tara that she might be spending the afternoon with her grandparents instead of accompanying her to the gym.

"I'll color pictures for him anyway," Tara said. "Maybe I can give them to him later."

"He'd love that. He really likes race cars."

It was almost ten when they got home. Billie gave Tara a piggyback ride up the stairs and deposited her on her bed.

"There you go."

Tara bounced up and down on the bed.

"Whoa. That's enough. Time to get ready for bed. Here, let me help you." Billie reached for Tara's nightclothes and helped her into them. "Under the covers you go."

"But I haven't said my prayers yet." Tara scrambled out of bed and knelt on the floor. When Billie remained standing she said, "Will you say them with me?"

Billie reluctantly knelt beside Tara.

Tara rested her elbows on the bed and clenched her hands together. "God, please make Mama feel better real fast so she can come home. Please help Seth open his eyes. I want him to be my big brother. Thank you, God. Amen." Prayers over, she climbed into bed and Billie tucked her in.

Billie kissed her on the cheek. "That was a really nice prayer. Thank you for thinking of Seth. Good night."

"Good night."

Billie shut off the lights and closed the door behind her. She slumped against the door and fought to control her tears.

Wearily, she headed toward what she presumed was the guest room, stripped down to her T-shirt and underpants, crawled between the clean sheets, and sank into a deep sleep.

Chapter 5

During the night, Billie had vivid dreams. She saw herself in a hospital operating room, where she stood at the head of a table and looked down at Cat's face. Cat was pale and lifeless. Tears spilled down Billie's face.

Billie whispered into Cat's ear, "I love you. Don't you dare leave me. Fight! Do you understand me? Fight!" As she spoke, a tear fell from her eye onto Cat's cheek, landing with a splash.

Cat's eyes opened, startling Billie.

"Take care of her. Promise me you'll take care of her," Cat pleaded.

The look of desperation in Cat's eyes was so intense it made Billie feel as though the air was being sucked out of her lungs.

"Promise me," Cat rasped again.

Billie nodded as she watched Cat drift away.

* * *

Billie bolted upright in bed and looked around in wide-eyed confusion. At first, she didn't recognize her surroundings. She composed herself and closed her eyes as the events of the previous day returned to her. Drenched in sweat from her nightmare, she reached for her cell phone on the bedside table.

"Hi. This is Billie Charland. I'm calling to check on Caitlain O'Grady." She dreaded what she might hear about Cat's status. "Yes, I'm here. She is? Good. I'll see her in the morning. Thank you."

Billie released a sigh of relief. She drew her knees to her chest and wrapped her arms around them. A sudden movement under the blankets startled her. Cautiously, she lifted the corner of the spread to see Tara asleep in a fetal position. It was nearly time to rise, so it made no sense to move her back to her own room.

Billie got out of bed, showered, and realized she didn't have any clean clothes to change into. "I knew I should've stopped by my place for a change of clothes last night. I wonder if Cat has something I can borrow."

Billie rummaged through Cat's dresser and found a pair of panties, socks, and a T-shirt that fit all right. After she slipped on her jeans and shoes and combed her wet hair, she went to wake Tara.

"Tara. Tara, sweetie. Time to get up."

"I'm still sleepy."

"I know, but you need to get up if we're going to visit Mama in the hospital."

Billie left the child to get herself out of bed while she went to make coffee. A few minutes later, she looked in on Tara who was still fast asleep.

By the time Tara was dressed and fed, it was nearly nine. Billie had hoped to leave earlier, but since she was running late, she decided to postpone a trip to her apartment for clothes until later when she went to teach her aerobics class. She settled Tara into the backseat and handed her the bag of coloring books and crayons they'd brought to keep her entertained while visiting Cat.

When they arrived at the hospital, Billie pulled into a parking space and climbed out of the car to open Tara's door. "Here we are. Out you go."

Tara jumped out of the car and took Billie's hand.

"Are you excited to see Mama?" Billie grabbed the bag of books and crayons before closing the car door.

"Yes. Can she come home with us today?"

"Probably not, but she should be home in a few days."

As soon as they entered Cat's room, Tara released Billie's hand and ran toward the bed. Billie caught her from behind just before she pounced on top of Cat. "Easy does it. Mama has a very sore boo-boo on her belly, and you need to be careful not to bump it."

"Billie's right. You need to be gentle. Now come here and give me a hug." Cat extended her arms. Tara eased onto the bed, gently folded herself into Cat's arms, and covered her mother's face with kisses.

"I missed you," Cat said to Tara.

"Mama, I've been having so much fun. We went to Billie's gym and I made some new friends and we went to McDonald's and we went to eat pizza and we watched Barney and we colored and we had a tickle fight and..."

"Whoa, slow down," Billie said.

"Sounds like you had a great time. I bet you didn't even miss me."

"No, Mama, I missed you, too. I woke up last night and I was afraid, but I went to sleep with Billie. When can you come home?"

"The doctor came in this morning and said I may be able to go home in about three more days."

Tara asked Billie for the bag of coloring books and crayons. She climbed off the bed and took the books and crayons over to a chair in the corner of the room. Billie wheeled the moveable bedside table over and lowered it for her to use as a desk.

After Billie helped Tara settle in, she returned to sit on the edge of the bed. She took Cat's hands in hers but avoided Cat's eyes as she composed herself. She had so much to say to Cat. She lifted Cat's hand and coupled it palm-to-palm with her own. Her hands were so small. Like a child's. Billie glanced at Cat and was captured by her gaze as warmth spread through her abdomen.

"Cat, about Tara. Why didn't you tell me?"

Cat yanked her hand away from Billie's. Billie noted the consternation on Cat's face.

Cat stammered her answer. "Wow. That's not what I expected you to say."

Billie folded her hands in her lap and lowered her voice so Tara couldn't hear their conversation. "What did you expect me to say? How do you expect me to feel about this? I mean, I came looking for you yesterday because you stood me up at the gym. I was worried about you. Next thing I knew, there's a child and a half-dressed woman in your condo. Why, Cat? For the moment, I'll overlook the half-dressed woman, but why didn't you tell me about Tara?"

Cat's answer sent Billie reeling. "I didn't tell you because I needed to protect her from you."

"What the—"

"No. Let me finish. I refuse to expose my child to someone who's not willing to make a life-long commitment to her. She's been deserted before. We both have. But when her other mother left, I swore I'd never put her in a vulnerable place again just to satisfy my own desires."

"Her other mother?"

"It's a long story, and one I don't wish to discuss with Tara in the room."

Stunned, Billie stared at her hands in her lap. At length, she looked at Cat. "I'd never hurt a child. I'm sorry you don't trust me."

"I didn't say I don't trust you. Hell, you've had my kid for the past day and a half, and the two of you come waltzing in here this morning like you've been best friends for life. She doesn't even seem to care that my parents' flight was delayed by a day. My dad called and left a message on my phone last night. He said their flight was delayed and that you were with Tara at my condo. You're obviously good with her, and it's clear she's more than comfortable with you."

Cat sucked in a breath. "What worries me is what'll happen tomorrow, or the day after, or a month from now. Unfortunately, my plan to ease you into her life is completely blown out of the water now. I'm terrified that she may become collateral damage if we decide to end our friendship. Tara is the most important person in my life, Billie. She'll always be my first priority."

"And what about Gail?" Billie asked.

"I hired Gail as a live-in day-care provider for Tara. She'd been with me for about six months before I met you. What I didn't know when I hired her, was that she was more interested in me than in Tara. Like you said about Darlene that first morning we had breakfast at Rose's, she was trying to sell me something I wasn't interested in buying."

Billie tried to wrap her brain around all that Cat had told her. Her heart thumped so strongly she was sure Cat saw it beating right through her shirt. All these revelations from Cat, and she still hadn't choked out one word about Seth. The enormity of it almost overwhelmed her.

"I really wish you would've told me about Tara earlier."

Cat raised her eyebrows. "Why on earth does it matter?"

"Because I love you. There, I've said it. I love you." Billie fought to keep her chin from quivering as she waited for Cat's reaction.

"You love me?"

Billie nodded. A parade of emotions passed over Cat's face. Billie had no choice but to wait until Cat was ready to speak.

"Are you saying you'd feel differently about me if you'd known about Tara? Do you even like children, Billie? Has the time you've spent with Tara these past couple of days been a ruse to win me over? If that's the case, forget about it. I don't have room in my life for someone like that."

Billie rose and walked a few feet away to stand in front of the window, her back to Cat.

Silence permeated the room for several long moments.

Billie felt a tug on her shirttail. She looked down to see Tara holding several pages from her coloring book toward her. She kneeled and accepted the pages. "Wow, you did a super job coloring these pictures. Are they for me?"

Tara nodded her head vigorously. "Do you like them?"

"I love them. Thank you for coloring them." Billie hugged Tara.

"I can color some more if you want."

Billie was touched by the look of sincerity on the little girl's face. "Would you? That would be really nice."

Tara skipped back to the corner and resumed coloring.

Billie stood and backed up against the windowsill. She looked at Cat. "Do you have room in your life for more children?" She crossed the room to stand beside Cat's bed.

"That's an odd question." Cat frowned. "To be honest, I hadn't planned to have more children. I pretty much have my hands full with Tara."

"I see." Billie sighed and lowered her chin to her chest once more.

"Billie, look at me."

Billie raised her eyes to meet Cat's and saw tears washing down Cat's face.

"I'm so sorry," Cat said. "I hate that I'm the cause of the fear I see in your eyes right now."

Billie's chin quivered. She tried to speak, but words failed her.

After what felt an eternity later to Billie, Cat spoke. "I'm sorry if my words seem harsh to you, but Tara is my child and I need to do whatever it takes to protect her. Surely you can understand that." Cat paused. "I should've said this when you told me how you felt a few minutes ago. I love you, too. You own my heart. I think you've always owned it, even before I met you. I've always known that someday I'd find you. But if you can't accept my child, our relationship would be doomed from the start."

Billie swallowed hard. "I do accept your child, but can you accept mine?"

Cat's eyes opened wide. "What are you saying?"

"I have a son."

"You have a son?"

Billie saw the fire raging in Cat's eyes.

"How dare you sit there and judge me about keeping Tara a secret from you when you've done the very same thing to me?"

"The circumstances are different."

"I fail to see how keeping your son a secret is any worse than my keeping Tara's existence from you. What makes him so different?"

"What makes him different? Tara is alert, healthy, inquisitive and playful, loud and rambunctious, endearing and flirtatious. She's a joy to be around. Seth is none of those right now. Seth has been lying in a hospital bed in a coma for the past nine months." A look of horror crossed Cat's face. "Yes, Cat. My child is little more than a vegetable right now."

"Oh my God, Billie. I'm sorry."

"Yeah, well, so am I. I'm especially sorry you don't want more children, but like Tara is for you, Seth is my first priority. I'll protect him and nurture him with everything that I am. For the rest of my life, if necessary."

"Can't something be done for him? I mean, what are his doctors saying?"

"They aren't saying anything very encouraging. He could stay like this forever, for all they know. I, for one, choose to believe he's still in there. I see small signs that he's aware of his surroundings. Last night when Tara and I went to visit with him, he appeared to be aware of her presence."

"You took Tara to see him?"

Tara tugged on Billie's hand and handed her two more pictures. "Here are the race car pictures I colored for Seth. I want to give them to him when we go visit him. I had fun when we went to see him. When can we go again?"

Billie looked from Tara to Cat. "Yes. I'm sorry if you don't approve, but it's not like I had a choice. Your parents were delayed, and I couldn't leave her alone. And I sure as hell wasn't going to miss a visit with Seth."

"Your commitment," Cat said softly.

"Yes, my eternal commitment."

* * *

Cat clicked through the channels looking for something interesting to watch while she waited for Billie and Tara to return from lunch. Bored with the choice of programming, she shut the television off and pressed her head into the pillow. The thought of raising a handicapped child scared her. The demands of a healthy child overwhelmed her enough, never mind those of a child needing constant attention. She felt horrible that she hadn't assured Billie she'd love and accept Seth as her own, not that Billie had asked her to. But if Billie ever did, she knew she'd have to make that commitment if she wanted Billie as her life partner.

The ringing of the telephone jolted her from her reverie.

"Hello?"

"Hey, Cat. How are you feeling?"

"Amy, I'm so glad you called. I'm feeling much better."

"I assume Mom and Dad finally arrived? Mom was panicking when she called me from the airport to say their flight had been cancelled."

"They're actually scheduled to land at two this afternoon. I'm really glad Billie was able to watch Tara while they were delayed."

"You've got that right. I'm anxious to meet her. She sounds like a real gem."

Cat fell silent.

"Cat?" Amy said. "Cat? Are you there?"

"Yes."

"You were quiet for a moment there. What's up?"

"Nothing."

"Don't give me that crap. I'm your big sister, remember? You've never been able to keep anything from me."

"Well..."

"Fess up. I know something's bothering you."

"Things were great until Billie dropped a bombshell on me."

"I'm listening."

"She has a son."

"And you have a daughter. So what's the problem?"

"Her son is a vegetable. He's in a coma."

"God, Cat. How?"

"She didn't say. I don't know how to deal with it. I mean, what if he stays that way for the rest of his life?"

"Do you love her?"

"Yes, I do. Very much."

"Well, I can't tell you what to do, but you need to decide if your love for her is strong enough to overcome the difficulties that come with it. True love doesn't come along every day, sis. Think long and hard about that before you let her go."

Cat pressed her head into the pillow and closed her eyes. "I will. Thanks, Amy."

Cat's attention was drawn to the doorway as Billie entered with a sleeping Tara on her shoulder. "I have to go, Amy."

"Okay. I'll give Bridge and Drew a call with a status report. Don't be surprised if they give you a call later as well. Take care of you. Hugs and kisses for Tara. Love you."

"I love you too. Bye."

Billie glanced at Cat as she laid Tara down next to her mother. "Amy?" she asked.

"My sister. She called to see how I'm doing."

"It's nice that you have siblings. Having no family around is a real downer sometimes."

"I can imagine. I talk to my sisters a couple times a month. I wish we had more opportunities to see each other, but they all have families—except Drew, that is, but she's pretty busy with school."

Billie nodded and brushed the bangs from Tara's forehead. "She's a beautiful child, Cat."

"Thank you. I've always thought so. Billie, tell me about Seth. What happened to him?"

Billie stared out the window. "I'll tell you all about that, but it'd be like starting a story in the middle. I haven't exactly been forthcoming with you about my life before we met. I should probably begin with my marriage to Brian."

"Okay, start with that."

"I married Brian seven years ago. I was almost twenty-one and had completed a two-year paralegal degree, and before you ask, yes, I knew when I married him that I preferred women. The marriage was more for my parents' sake than my own. I never told them about my preferences. I always assumed they'd be devastated if they knew I was a lesbian. They treated me like a princess. I loved them dearly, and I couldn't stand to disappoint them, so I married Brian. They adored him. When Seth was born, they doted on him even more than they had on me. From their perspective, my marriage was happy, loving, and secure."

"But it wasn't?"

"The first year and a half of our marriage was all right. I didn't love Brian, but he treated me decently, that is, until he found my diary. It was the one place I spoke my heart without fear of retribution—at least I thought it was safe. His reaction when he found my diary taught me to never put my feelings on paper again. I haven't kept a diary since. Anyway, as you might guess, he discovered my preference for women. He was livid. He threatened me with bodily harm, but I was pregnant with Seth by then, so I was relatively safe."

"But that changed after Seth came along, didn't it?"

Billie nodded. "Brian started drinking after he discovered my secret. Things worsened considerably after Seth was born. Brian kept my diary and threatened to give it to my parents. As if that wasn't enough, he used physical abuse to, as he put it, keep me faithful. It was relatively tame in the beginning, a slap across the back of the head, a shove here and there, but as his drinking increased, so did the severity of the abuse. All along, he held my parents' love and trust over my head as a weapon to keep me in the marriage."

"How was he with Seth?"

Billie walked back across the room and sat next to Cat. Cat took Billie's hand, which she cradled between her own.

"When he was sober, he tolerated Seth. On occasion, he even showed a bit of affection, but when he was drinking, which was most of the time, his tolerance vanished. Don't get me wrong, he never physically abused Seth, but his emotional neglect was just as harmful."

"How did you break free of him?"

"That's the ironic part. It took an event more devastating than my own abuse to end the downward spiral of my life. The day my parents died changed everything. It was both the worst day of my life and the happiest day of my life, because I knew he couldn't hurt my parents or me by telling them I was gay. It was also the day I discovered how badly he neglected Seth."

"What do you mean?"

"I'd gone out for dinner with a friend. When I got home, Brian was all but passed out on the couch in a drunken stupor. Seth was two years old. He was standing in his crib screaming at the top of his lungs. His diaper was a nasty mess. I managed to rouse Brian and demanded to know what the hell he'd done for the past several hours. He confessed that he'd spent the entire evening drinking and yelling at Seth because he wouldn't stop crying. Of course the baby was crying—Brian hadn't fed or changed him.

"I told him I'd put up with his drinking and his neglect of Seth for the last time. We argued and screamed for an hour or more, and then it was like something inside him snapped. He beat me so severely that I had to call a taxi to take me to the hospital. No way was I leaving Seth there with that maniac. I packed a diaper bag and took Seth with me, even though I was barely able to see out of one eye and I had bruises all over me. And then, in what has to be one of the saddest coincidences ever, while I was in the emergency room being treated for the injuries Brian had inflicted, an ambulance brought my parents in after a horrible car accident. DOA."

Cat began to cry. "My God, Billie, you've been through so much. I had no idea. I'm so sorry."

Billie wiped a tear from the corner of her eye. "It amazes me how much it still hurts, even after all this time. From the hospital that night, Seth and I went to my parents' empty house. The very next day, I filed for divorce and then pressed charges against Brian for assault. His well-to-do parents struck a deal with the prosecutor, and they talked me into dropping assault charges in exchange for an uncontested divorce and custody hearing, as well as a trust fund in Seth's name. Brian pretty much disappeared from our lives at that point. I'm not even sure he knows Seth has spent most of the past year in the hospital."

"Okay, that tells me how you got to be a single mother, but what about Seth? How did he come to be in a coma?"

"Nine months before I met you, Seth was hit by a drunk driver. He was getting off his school bus when the car hit him. He flew through the air and landed on his head. He's been in that bed ever since." Billie closed her eyes and cried.

"Come here." Cat opened her arms to Billie.

Billie allowed herself to be enveloped in Cat's arms. "Cat, he's only six years old. My poor baby. He can't spend the rest of his life like this. He just can't."

* * *

At three that afternoon, Cat's parents arrived at the hospital. Cat's mother went to the bed to hug her daughter and granddaughter.

"Sir," Billie said as she stood and offered her hand to Mr. O'Grady.

"Doc. Call me Doc," he replied as he shook Billie's hand. "Ida and I want to thank you for taking care of Tara and Cat the past two days."

"It's my pleasure, Mr... er, I mean, Doc." Billie noted the time. "Cat, I should get going. I need to swing by my apartment before I teach my class."

"Do you have to go so soon?"

"Yeah, I should."

Tara, who'd been snuggled near her mother, stood on the bed and launched herself at Billie. Billie barely caught her before she fell off the bed. "Take it easy there," Billie said.

"Billie, did you ask Mama if I can go with you tonight?"

Cat raised her eyebrows at Billie.

"She really wants to visit with Seth tonight. You heard her say she enjoyed last night's visit, and I'm positive he enjoyed it as well. Last night, she played in the day care at the gym while I taught my class before we went to visit Seth."

Cat looked at Tara. "Why don't you stay with Grammy and Grandpa tonight? You haven't seen them in a while, and they came home just to take care of you. You can go with Billie tomorrow night. How does that sound?"

"But, Mama, I really want to go," Tara whined.

"I'll tell you what, Tara," Billie said. "What if I pick you up early tomorrow and we'll go to McDonald's before the gym?"

Tara continued to pout. "All right."

Billie tickled Tara's neck. A smile broke out across Tara's face.

"There's that pretty smile," Billie teased. "Tomorrow will be here in no time." She looked at Doc and Ida. "My class is at five, so I'll pick her up around three-thirty tomorrow."

Billie hugged Tara and kissed Cat on the cheek. She extended her hand to each of Cat's parents. "It's so nice to meet you both. I'll see you tomorrow."

Chapter 6

"How'd you like to go with me to get a snack?" Ida asked Tara.

"Okay." Tara took Ida's hand and pulled her toward the door.

"Hold on, there. Before we go, pick up your coloring books and crayons."

Tara gathered her toys and shoved them into the plastic bag. She put the bag on the foot of Cat's bed.

"Good girl," Ida said. She turned to her husband. "Doc, are you coming with us?"

"No. You two go and enjoy your snack. I've some things I need to discuss with Caitlain."

After Ida and Tara left the room, Doc sat on the edge of Cat's bed and held her hand. "Who's Seth?" he asked.

"Seth is Billie's son." Cat told him what she knew, which wasn't much, about Seth's accident and current condition. "I don't know what to do, Daddy. I love her so much. I don't want to lose her, but I don't know if I want to tie myself down with a handicapped child."

"I'm surprised at you, Caitlain. Every child needs love and acceptance, regardless of their level of ability."

Cat sank into the pillow and closed her eyes. "I know. It's just that it took me by surprise. I know so little about his condition— about how long he'll be destined to live like this. My heart breaks for Billie. I can imagine how I'd feel if it was Tara lying in that hospital bed."

"So what's the problem?"

"My life is so busy with work and Tara. I honestly don't know if I have the time or energy to take on a disabled child."

"You wouldn't be doing it alone, you know. Tell me again exactly what's wrong with Seth."

"He was hit by a car nine months ago. From what Billie has told me, his head hit the pavement pretty hard. It looks like a serious brain injury."

"You said he's been in a coma for the past nine months, correct?"

"Yes. Billie said his doctors believe his chances are slim to none that his condition will improve. She has such hope that he'll recover. She says she sees signs that he's aware of his surroundings. I want so much to believe her, but it sounds like his doctors have pretty much closed the book on any possibility for recovery."

"Where is he?"

"He's at the Commercial Avenue branch of the AMC."

Doc stood and squeezed Cat's foot through the blanket. "Get some sleep, Cat. I've some business to attend to this afternoon. Your mother and I will bring Tara for a visit tomorrow morning. Sleep well, kitten."

"All right, Daddy, and thanks for listening."

"Anytime, honey. Anytime."

* * *

Billie left the hospital and went to her apartment. She stopped in the lobby to pick up her mail, which she threw on the kitchen table. Fifteen minutes later, she'd watered her plants and sat down at the table to sort through her mail. At the bottom of the pile was a letter from the Albany Medical Center. With a knot in her stomach, she tore it open.

> *Dear Ms. Charland,*
>
> *We're sorry to inform you that the clinical staff has reached the unanimous conclusion that your son is in a persistent vegetative state and that no further improvement in his condition is likely. We'd like to meet with you at your earliest convenience to discuss his future care. Please contact our office as soon as possible to schedule that meeting.*
>
> *Sincerely,*
> *Dr. Wayne Wyckart*
> *Director, Albany Medical Center.*

"Oh my God. Oh my God." Billie paced from room to room and scanned the letter several more times.

She composed herself and called the phone number on the hospital letterhead. There had to be some mistake. She found the doctor in his office. "Hello, Dr. Wyckart, this is Billie Charland. My son, Seth, is under your care at AMC. Yes, he's the young boy in a coma from a car accident. I received a letter asking for a meeting to discuss Seth's future care. Can you tell me what this is all about?"

"The letter was rather clear. The clinical staff has concluded that your son is most likely in a permanent vegetative state and further care within the hospital facility may not be the best option."

"What the hell is that supposed to mean?"

"We'll discuss this in more detail when you schedule the meeting."

"But you can't do this. He's only a child."

"Ms. Charland, its time you faced the truth. Your son will likely remain the way he is for the rest of his life."

"No. How dare you say that? This is my child we're talking about, and I won't allow you to treat him this way. He's in there. I know he is. I can see it."

"I'm sorry, Ms. Charland. Please call my receptionist to schedule the meeting, and I think the sooner we discuss this, the better. We shouldn't need more than fifteen or twenty minutes of your time. Good day."

Billie paced furiously across the room. "What am I going to do? How can they give up on him?" She stopped to calm herself. "Get a grip. Call the receptionist and make the appointment. Maybe it won't be as bad as it sounds."

Billie called and arranged to meet with the staff the following Thursday at 3:00 p.m.

She closed her eyes to quell her rising panic. "Calm down. Hysterics won't help. Go to the meeting and see what they have to say." She packed her bag with clean aerobics clothes and left for the gym. She'd discuss this with Seth's primary care physician during her visit that evening.

* * *

Billie left the gym at six. When she arrived at the hospital, she stopped at the front desk and was told Dr. Richmond was still on rounds. "Please let Dr. Richmond know that I need to see him before visiting hours end this evening. I'll be in Seth's room. Thanks."

Billie went to Seth's room and greeted him in her usual manner. "Hey, scout. How ya doing today, my love?" As always, Seth lay in his bed with his eyes closed. Billie sighed. It discouraged her that day after day, she received no response from him. She wondered how much longer she'd be able to handle his condition before she totally broke down emotionally. She taped the pictures Tara colored for him to his wall then sat down next to the bed and took his hand.

"Cat's doing well. She's sore, but she'll make it. She's pretty tough, you know." Billie paused to see if there was any reaction. None was evident. "Cat is a very special person. I know you'll love her as much as I do. She's Tara's mom. You remember Tara, don't you? She came with me to visit you last night."

Billie opened her eyes wide. She was sure she saw his eyebrow lift. She had a hunch about something. "Cat's parents arrived today to take care of Tara. Cat thought she should spend some time with her grandparents tonight, so I'll bring her with me to visit you tomorrow. Tara can't wait to see you again."

This time, the corner of his mouth twitched. Seth appeared to react every time she said Tara's name. She tried again. "Tara colored some nice pictures of race cars for you. I've hung them on your wall over there. I wish you'd open your eyes to see them, love."

His eyelashes fluttered but remained closed. *That's it. It's Tara. She's getting through to him.*

Billie needed to be sure Seth's apparent reaction to Tara's name wasn't a fluke, so she didn't speak it again. Instead, while she waited for the doctor, she read to Seth, held his hand, and stroked his hair.

After a time, she paused and looked at him. Although she knew she wasn't truly objective, in her opinion, he was, indeed, a beautiful child. Yes, he'd inherited a few traits from Brian: the color of his hair, the spattering of freckles across the bridge of his nose, the cleft in his chin. The rest of him, however, was more like Billie. The most obvious characteristic he inherited from his mother were his eyes—the same light sky-blue—and from what Billie could tell, they had the power to melt any heart they set themselves upon. How Billie longed to see those eyes, to see herself reflected in them.

The doctor interrupted Billie's daydreams. "Excuse me, Ms. Charland. You wanted to see me?"

Billie stood. "Yes, Dr. Richmond. I received a letter from the director of the hospital, and I'd like to discuss the contents of it with you in private, if we could." She indicated with her eyes that she didn't want to talk in front of Seth.

"Of course. Please follow me to my office."

Billie kissed Seth on the forehead. "I'll see you tomorrow, sweetheart. I'll bring Tara with me again. How does that sound?" Billie saw the corner of his mouth move.

Billie had an uneasy feeling as she followed the doctor. He gestured for her to enter first and closed the door firmly behind him.

The doctor leaned against the edge of his desk and crossed his arms. "What can I do for you, Ms. Charland?"

"Let's cut the bullshit right up front, shall we?" Billie put one hand on her hip. She pulled the letter from her pocket and grasped it in the other hand. "This letter indicates that your team of doctors reviewed Seth's case and that you don't believe there's any hope of recovery. Is that a correct assessment?"

"That's correct. As much as we'd like to ignore the truth, it's been evident for the past"—he checked Seth's chart—"let's see, nine months."

"This letter says the staff wants to discuss further care for him. What does that mean?"

"It means we've followed standard protocol relative to the care and treatment of traumatic head injuries, and we're now suggesting the final course of action."

"Protocol?"

"Yes. When your son first arrived, he was treated in intensive care, followed by care in a step-down unit on the neurosurgical ward. Once he was stable, he was transferred to the sub-acute unit of our facility, and then to LTAC."

"Yeah, I know. LTAC—Long Term Acute Care. He's my son. I've been paying attention, you know."

"Certainly, Ms. Charland. I didn't mean to imply otherwise." The doctor cleared his throat. "After LTAC, he was transferred to the rehabilitation inpatient treatment center. All of this was done without any apparent improvement in his condition. The final step in the process is to move him to an independent off-site rehabilitation hospital or nursing home. Look, Ms. Charland, we don't anticipate any significant improvement for him in the near future. We also don't see any reason he should be here taking up a bed when his needs could be better met in a nursing home."

"Nursing home? Are you insane?" Billie heard the edge of hysteria in her voice. "Would you do that to your child?"

"We're not talking about my child."

Billie was sure she heard sarcasm in the doctor's voice. "No, we're not, but I thought I was talking to someone with a heart. Apparently, I was wrong. I can see that I'm wasting my time with you. I'll take this up with the director." Billie put her hand on the doorknob.

"Ms. Charland," the doctor said.

Billie spun around to face him. The leering look on his face turned her stomach.

"Maybe we can discuss this over dinner?"

"What are you suggesting, Dr. Richmond?"

"I'm suggesting that maybe we can work something out concerning your son." As he spoke, Dr. Richmond stepped right up next to Billie, pinning her against the door. He pressed her into it. He reeked of cheap cologne.

Billie brought her knee up and caught him sharply in the groin. He sank to the floor.

"I don't think so, Doctor. I've scheduled the meeting, and I'll have my say with the staff. Until then, Seth will receive the very best treatment possible right where he is, or your superiors will hear about this little encounter. You got that?"

His only response was a groan.

Billie grabbed his scrotum and squeezed hard. "I said, you got that?"

"Yes… yes, please leave."

"Gladly. But I'll be back tomorrow to see Seth, and you'd better not have given me any reason to be unhappy with his treatment. Good night, you sorry piece of shit." Billie stomped out of his office and slammed the door behind her.

By the time she walked to her car, her anger had subsided enough for her to drive within the speed limit. Too keyed up to go home, Billie went to the hospital to say good night to Cat. Although visiting hours had ended, Billie convinced the nurse that she could be permitted to say good night.

Billie entered Cat's room and crouched down beside the bed so that her head was very close to Cat's. Gently, she brushed a stray lock of hair from Cat's forehead. She kissed the spot where the hair had lain. Billie gazed lovingly at her. When it was clear Cat was lost in slumber, Billie walked out of the room and softly closed the door.

*   *   *

Before going to work the next morning, Billie dropped by the hospital for a short visit. Cat was awake when she entered the room. She didn't look happy to see her.

Billie stood beside Cat's bed and lowered her head for a kiss, but Cat turned away. "Are you feeling all right?" Billie asked as she felt Cat's forehead.

Cat brushed Billie's hand away. "I'm fine."

Billie pulled a chair up close. Cat refused to meet Billie's eyes. Billie grasped Cat's chin. "Enough is enough. Talk to me. Tell me what's wrong."

Cat wrenched her face out of Billie's grasp. "You smelled like men's cologne last night."

"What do you mean?"

"I was awake when you came into my room."

"You were awake? Why didn't you say something?"

"I didn't know what to say. You smelled like men's cologne. You'd obviously been with a man."

"Yes, I was—"

Before Billie explained that the man was Seth's doctor, Tara scampered into the room.

"Mama!" Tara climbed onto Cat's bed and kissed her mother.

"Good morning, sweetheart," Cat replied. As she hugged Tara, Cat shot a meaningful look in Billie's direction.

Billie took the hint. "I'll be late for work if I don't get moving." She almost ran into Doc and Ida as they entered the room.

"Good morning, dear," Ida said as she hugged Billie.

"Good morning." Billie shook Doc's hand. "I hate to be rude, but I'm running late and need to get to work."

"Billie, can I still go with you to see Seth tonight?" Tara asked. "You promised."

Billie looked expectantly at Cat. "I should be able to pick her up around three-thirty. We'll go the gym and then visit with Seth. I can have her home around nine. Is that okay?"

Cat nodded.

Billie dropped to one knee and opened her arms. Tara ran into them. "It's a date." She looked at Doc and Ida. "Will you be here or at Cat's condo this afternoon?"

"Probably here," Doc said.

"All right then. I'll be back this afternoon."

Chapter 7

On Thursday, Billie arrived at the hospital promptly at 2:50 p.m. for her meeting with the clinical staff. The receptionist escorted her to a conference room, where she sat alone. At 3:15, she looked around the empty room. Just as she reached for the doorknob, the door flew open. A middle-aged man with graying hair bustled into the room. He carried a thick manila folder bearing Seth's name on the tab. He nearly collided with Billie.

"Ms. Charland, I presume?"

Billie extended her hand. "Yes. And you are?"

"Wyckart. Dr. Gerald Wyckart. Please have a seat." He remained standing as Billie sat. "Please excuse my tardiness. This hospital is a very busy place."

Billie nodded. "Will others be joining us?"

"Actually, no. We all have busy schedules, and I drew the short straw."

Billie leaped to her feet. "You drew the short straw? How dare you use a remark like that to describe my son's situation? You make it sound like you've been sent on a distasteful chore."

Dr. Wyckart closed the folder and dropped it onto the table. He put his hands on the back of a chair and leaned forward. "To be truthful, it is. It's never pleasant to convince a family member that a situation is hopeless."

"Seth isn't hopeless." Billie spoke each word crisply, barely able to keep her loathing in check.

"I'm afraid I disagree with you on that point." He retrieved Seth's folder and thumbed through several pages. "Your son has shown relatively no improvement since he was admitted nine months ago. The staff's opinion is that he's unlikely to recover anymore than he already has. Because of that, we feel it's no longer appropriate to keep him in this hospital."

"And what am I supposed to do with him?"

"You need to find alternative care for him. We realize that process can take several weeks. We encourage you to relocate him as soon as possible, preferably within the next month."

"And if I can't relocate him that soon?"

"Then we'll discharge him from this facility, and you'll have to take him home until you can find suitable accommodations."

"What? Seth needs professional care. He can't come home. Not yet. He's not ready. We can't give him the care he needs there." Despite her distress, she surprised herself by her choice of pronoun. We? What was she saying? She and Cat hadn't decided to be a couple yet, never mind establish a family.

Dr. Wyckart bundled the papers together and stuffed them back into the folder. "I'm sorry, Ms. Charland, but the staff has made its decision. Dr. Richmond will continue to be his primary physician while you're making alternative arrangements. Please direct all of your questions to him."

"I realize it may not matter in the few weeks Seth has left here, but I'd prefer you assign someone other than Dr. Richmond for his primary physician. I'd rather not have a doctor attending my son who offers preferential treatment in exchange for sexual favors."

The color drained from Dr. Wyckart's face. "Are you accusing him of making inappropriate advances toward you?"

"That's exactly what I'm saying, and he offered to change his recommendation in regards to Seth's care, in return."

"I see. I assure you your allegations will be investigated. Have a good evening." He swung around and left the room.

Billie dropped into the chair, speechless, as the enormity of what awaited hit her.

* * *

Billie struggled to concentrate during her aerobics class that afternoon. She was preoccupied with Seth's situation and wanted to talk to Cat about it. After her and Tara's visit with Seth, Billie returned to the hospital. She pulled into the parking lot and sat in the car for several moments. She was unsure about how to mend the misunderstandings from two days earlier. "Okay," she said to herself, "you can't go in there with guns blazing. After all, you did smell like men's cologne Tuesday night. Just be calm and explain what happened." Satisfied with her plan, Billie went inside.

Billie pushed the door open to Cat's room. "May I come in?"

Cat closed the book she was reading and laid it on her lap. Billie took that as permission to enter. She walked across the room and pulled a chair close to Cat's bedside.

"How are you feeling?"

"I've been better."

"I thought I'd stop in to see you before I went home. I've already dropped Tara off with your parents. We had a good visit with Seth this evening."

"That's nice."

Billie rubbed her face then rested her hands on her thighs. "Look, why don't we drop the small talk. I came here tonight to defend myself."

"I don't want to hear it."

"I'm sorry you feel that way, because I'm going to say it anyway. You said I smelled like men's cologne last night. You're right, I did, but believe me, it wasn't by choice."

"What do you mean?"

"Let me start from the beginning. I received a letter from the hospital requesting a meeting. I called the director, and in a nutshell, he told me Seth would probably stay the way he is for the rest of his life and that the clinical staff wanted to meet with me to discuss further care. I met with Seth's primary physician, Dr. Richmond, Tuesday evening to see what he knew about the letter, and he pretty much told me I had to make plans to relocate Seth to a nursing home. I can't believe he was so heartless. Whatever happened to the Hippocratic oath? Or maybe it's really the hypocritical oath. To make matters worse, he suggested he might be able to modify his recommendation if I put out. Can you believe it? He even went so far as to pin me against his office door. That's why I smelled like men's cologne."

"My God, what did you do?"

"Let's just say his equipment will be out of order for a while."

"You need to report him. If you don't, I will."

"I already did. Look, the point is, I came here last night hoping to talk to you about it because you're a doctor, but when I entered the room, you appeared to be sleeping. It turns out you weren't. I wish you'd said something last night instead of blindsiding me this morning."

"Stop right there. You dropped a pretty big bombshell on me yesterday when I learned about Seth and his condition. Talk about blindsiding. I was caught off-guard by that news, so I wasn't exactly at my best when you came in here last night smelling like you'd been with a man."

"I'm confused. Was I asleep when we agreed to be a couple? Don't get me wrong, I'm in no way, shape, or form interested in being with a man, and I truly love you, but we've made no promises to one another. Don't you think your jealousy is a bit misplaced?"

"I don't know what you mean. I told you yesterday that I loved you, too."

"Yes, you did, but you also said you didn't have room in your life for more children and that you had your hands full with Tara. That statement spoke volumes."

"That's not fair. You asked that question before I knew Seth existed."

"Would you have allowed yourself to fall in love with me if you knew I had a son?"

"Of course. What kind of question is that?"

"Okay, then would you have allowed yourself to fall in love with me if you knew about Seth's condition?"

"Its kind of late for that, don't you think?"

"You haven't answered my question."

"Billie, I really don't want to discuss this."

"Answer the question, Cat."

Cat threw her hands in the air. "I don't know. Is that what you want to hear? I need time to adjust. I just found out about Seth. I know so little about his condition. I haven't even seen him yet. I think it's unfair of you to back me into a corner like this."

Both fell silent for several moments. Cat broke the stalemate.

"Look, I do love you. I've never felt this way about anyone before in my life. Yes, I want to be your partner. I want that more than anything I've wanted in a very long time. I won't deny that Seth's condition scares the shit out of me, but I'm willing to go into this with an open mind."

"What if Seth remains this way for the rest of his life? Do you think you can handle it?"

"I don't know. I honestly don't know. Please don't condemn me before I have time to adjust to this."

Billie inhaled deeply. "Fair enough."

"When's the meeting?" Cat asked.

"The meeting with the clinical staff?"

"Yes. When is it?"

"It's already happened. It was this afternoon."

"And what was the meeting about?"

"For starters, it was supposed to be a meeting with the staff, but Dr. Wyckart, who happens to be the director, was the only one who showed up. As far as I'm concerned, their professional courtesy sucks. According to Wyckart, the entire staff recommended I find an alternative care facility for Seth. They've urged me to do that in the past, only this time they aren't giving me a choice. They're evicting him from his bed. I have one month to find him a new home."

"I can't believe that. First that sleaze bucket Richmond feels you up, then they evict your kid."

"I don't know what to do. If they'd spend more time with him, they'd see how he responds to certain things, especially to Tara." Billie swallowed in an attempt to control the quiver in her voice before she continued. "He's such a wonderful child. One look from those baby blue eyes and you're hooked. If they make me put him in a nursing home, I may never see those eyes again."

"How exactly is he responding to Tara?"

"Every time I say her name, he reacts in small ways, like raising an eyebrow or twitching the corner of his mouth. I told him that she colored pictures of race cars for him, and he fluttered his eyelashes, almost like he was trying to open his eyes to see them. When I took her with me, she talked to him nonstop, and that seemed to prompt a lot of reactions from him."

"Huh. And his diagnosis is a persistent vegetative state?"

"That's what his records say."

"Something about this doesn't sound right. I know a prominent neurosurgeon. Maybe I'll have a talk with him about it."

"At this point, I'll take any help I can get."

Cat yawned.

"Time for you to get some sleep." Billie kissed Cat on the forehead. "I do love you. I so hope you can come to accept Seth and learn to love him as much as I do."

"I love you, too."

"Good. Now scoot down under the covers. I'll see you sometime tomorrow. Have pleasant dreams."

"You, too. Good night."

Chapter 8

The next morning, Billie sat at her desk with the telephone receiver wedged between her shoulder and her ear. A tall, dark-skinned man appeared in her office doorway. "Hey, Charland, do you have that brief ready? I need to be in court in an hour."

Billie waved her supervisor into the room. "Art. Come in. I'm on hold." Billie sorted through the stack of papers on her desk. She extracted a two-page memo and held it out. "Here it is. Do you need me to go to court with you? I know this case inside out. I'd be happy to present it for you."

Art grinned. "You'll make a good lawyer one day. You need to get your butt back to school and pass the bar. You know you have my support."

"You know what's holding me back. In fact, he's the reason I'm on hold. Seth is being evicted from the hospital, and I'm trying to find a convalescent home that will take him."

"He's being evicted? Are you serious? That's cold."

"Cold is putting it mildly. I don't know what I'll do if I can't find a place for him in the next few weeks."

"What does Cat have to say about it? She's a doctor, right? Maybe she has connections."

"I haven't asked her for help."

Art raised an eyebrow. "Why not?"

"She hasn't even met Seth yet. Our relationship is so new, I hate to put such huge demands on her so soon."

"Does she know Seth could remain the way he is for the rest of his life?"

"She knows, and quite frankly, she said it scares her, but she's agreed to approach it with an open mind."

Billie saw the frown on Art's face. "What are you thinking?"

"It seems to me that if she loves you, she'd be willing to make it work regardless of Seth's condition. If she's having doubts about him, you might want to ask yourself if she's the right woman for you."

Billie stared at Art, unable to formulate a reply. A voice in the earpiece saved her from thinking more about it. "Oh, hello. Yes, my name is Billie Charland and I'm looking for accommodations for my son."

* * *

"Good morning, my love." Cat opened her arms to Tara.

Tara hugged her then sat back on her knees on Cat's bed. "Grammy is taking me ice-skating today."

"That sounds like fun." Cat looked at her mother. "Good morning, Mom. Is Tara behaving for you?"

"She's an angel. I thought we'd go to the indoor skating rink and then to lunch. My plan is to tire her out so she's napping when that Barney character comes on the television this afternoon." Ida chuckled.

Cat laughed. "I hear you." She looked around. "Where's Daddy?"

"He stopped at the nurses' station. You know what a worrywart he is. He's probably reading your chart to be sure they're caring for you properly."

"I did no such thing."

Cat and Ida directed their attention to the doorway. "Good morning, Daddy," Cat said.

"Grammy, can we go now?" Tara asked.

"Tara, be a good girl and listen to Grammy. And be sure to wear your knee pads and helmet while you skate."

"I will, Mama."

"All right then. Have a good time."

After Ida and Tara left, Doc crossed the room to sit on the edge of Cat's bed.

"Were you really reading my chart?" Cat teased.

"Actually, I stopped at the nurses' station to call the director at the Commercial Avenue branch of the AMC. Wyckart is his name. I called to let him know I'd be visiting his facility this morning to review a patient's records."

"Seth's?"

"Yes. I'd like to see for myself what the diagnosis was nine months ago and what type of rehabilitation program they have him following, or not following, as the case may be."

"Billie came to visit me after she left Tara with you and Mom last night. She's convinced Seth is more aware and reacts to his environment more than the doctors are giving him credit for."

"What evidence does she have?"

"She said that he raises his eyebrows, flutters his eyes, and moves the corners of his mouth, and sometimes moves his fingers."

"Those could very well be involuntary movements."

"That's what I thought as well, but apparently, they occur when she mentions Tara's name. Also, the couple of times Tara visited, they happened more frequently. Is it possible that he's reacting to her?"

"Anything is possible. As you know, the brain is a very complex organ. There's so much we still don't know about it." Doc rose from the bed. "So, I'm off to Commercial Avenue. I'll be back after I review Seth's records. If I'm not satisfied with what I learn, I may ask Billie for permission to examine him myself."

"Oh, while you're there, you might want to speak to Dr. Wyckart about Seth's stay in the hospital."

"Why's that?"

"Billie received an eviction letter this week. Dr. Wyckart believes Seth is in a persistent vegetative state and will most likely stay that way, so in his opinion, further time in the hospital is pointless."

"Hmmm. Let me look at his records. It could be Wyckart's right, but I'll reserve judgment until after I've seen for myself."

"Oh, and one more thing. There's a Dr. Richmond on staff, and he's in charge of Seth's primary care. It might be prudent to have another doctor assigned instead."

"And the reason for that is...?"

"Let's just say Billie objected to the proposition he made to her in order to rescind Seth's eviction. You'll know him when you see him. He'll be the one walking funny. I'd hate to have him take out his misdirected frustrations on Seth."

Doc's eyes narrowed. "I'll discuss that matter with Wyckart as well. I'll be back this afternoon."

* * *

Billie stopped at the hospital before her aerobics class for a brief visit with Cat. She held her right hand behind her back. "Hi. These are for you." Billie produced a bouquet of roses.

"They're beautiful. But you didn't have to do that."

"I know, but I kind of felt bad about our confrontation last night. I wanted to apologize for being so abrupt with you. It's just that I get worked up when it comes to Seth."

"No apology necessary. Come, sit down." Cat patted the bed.

"I've only got a few minutes."

"This will only take a minute. I have news for you."

"What is it?"

"I talked to that neurosurgeon I know, and he's going to look at Seth's records."

"Who is this guy? Can we trust him?"

"I know him intimately. And I do trust him. He's my father."

Billie's head snapped back. "Doc?" Realization hit her. "Duh, Billie, put two and two together. Doc—doctor? I didn't know he was a neurosurgeon."

"Not only is he a neurosurgeon, but he's well connected with the American Medical Association. He carries a lot of clout around here."

"But doesn't he live in Florida?"

"He's semi-retired. He and Mom are snowbirds. They generally go to Florida just after Christmas and come home in late March. While he's in Florida, he's a consultant to the hospital there and performs surgery when necessary, as well. When he's here, he works full time at Albany Medical Center."

"So, he's looking at Seth's records?"

"Yes. I expected him to be back by now. I'm eager to see what he has to say. Oh, and he may ask your permission to examine Seth."

"Of course. If he thinks it will help, by all means. I don't know what to say. He hardly knows me. What makes you so sure he'll be willing to help?"

"My parents have known about my sexuality since I was a teenager, and they're totally supportive and accepting. I've told them all about you. They know that I love you. That's enough for them to accept you. And Seth. Seth's quality of life is on the line here. I wouldn't ask Daddy to help if I didn't have complete confidence in him... and in us."

*　*　*

Doc returned to Cat's hospital room minutes after Billie left for the gym. He got right to the point. "Cat, I've reason to believe Seth has been misdiagnosed."

Cat's hand flew to her mouth. "What?"

"His records are inconsistent with Billie's observations. If his condition truly were that of a persistent vegetative state, he wouldn't be reacting to outside stimuli. Furthermore, his Glasgow Coma scores are all greater than one. It appears our friend Dr. Richmond has a less-than-stellar reputation in the medical community, and his misdiagnosis may have cost Seth valuable recovery time. Needless to say, he's no longer Seth's primary physician."

"I spoke with Billie about the possibility of you examining Seth, and she's willing to do anything that might improve his condition."

"I'll arrange to examine him tomorrow then."

"I think you should take Tara with you so you can see for yourself how, or if, he responds to her."

"Good suggestion. You're to be released tomorrow, aren't you?"

"Yes. I can't wait. Four days feels like forever, especially with hospital food. I'll ask Mom to take me home while you're examining Seth."

"I'll tell you what. I'll schedule Seth's examination late enough in the day so you can be there as well. You haven't met him yet, have you?"

"No, I haven't. I didn't learn about him until after I was in the hospital."

"I'll put together a regime of diagnostic tests tomorrow morning while Mother takes you home, then I'll pick both you and Tara up before going to the Commercial Avenue branch. Do you have Billie's cell phone number? I'll call her tonight and ask what time is best for her to be there."

* * *

Doc offered Cat his arm as they slowly made their way down the hall toward Seth's room. Tara jumped up and down beside them.

"Hurry, hurry. I want to see Seth."

"Be patient, princess, your mom is moving a little slower than normal because of the cut on her belly."

"We'll get there soon enough," Cat said. "Come, take my hand."

Doc stopped outside of Seth's room. "Let me spend a few minutes alone with him. I want to see if his demeanor changes when

Tara comes in." Doc retrieved a chair from inside Seth's room so Cat could sit in the hall.

Doc stood beside Seth's bed. "Hi, Seth. My name is Doc, and I'm Cat's dad. You don't know me, but I'm a doctor, and your mom asked me to take a look at you. Is that all right with you?"

Doc noted on Seth's chart that he was unresponsive.

"Your mom tells me you like race cars. I see pictures of race cars on your wall. Tara colored them, didn't she?"

Seth's eyes fluttered.

"Would you like to see Tara again?"

Doc observed a slight twitch at the corner of Seth's mouth.

"You're in luck. She's waiting in the hall with Cat. Wait right here and I'll go get them."

Doc motioned for Cat and Tara to enter the room. Tara ran to the bed and snuggled in next to Seth while Cat waited by the door.

"Hi, Seth. Do you like the race car pictures I colored for you? I missed you. When can you come home and be my big brother?"

Doc watched as Seth's eyebrows rose high on his forehead and his eyes fluttered once more.

"Billie's right. It's incredible how responsive he is to Tara. Persistent vegetative state, my ass." He looked at Cat. "He's a very handsome young man. Come over and have a look for yourself."

Cat walked to Seth's bedside and sat in the chair Doc had pulled close for her. She looked into his face. "He's beautiful." A powerful rush of maternal emotion filled her chest. "How did I ever doubt that I'd love this child?"

"I'm sorry I'm late," Billie said as she rushed into the room.

Cat saw the look of surprise on Billie's face.

"Cat. I didn't know you'd be here," Billie said.

Cat extended her hand to Billie. "He's beautiful. Introduce me, please."

Billie sat on the edge of Seth's bed and kissed him on the head. "Hey there, love. It looks like you've got lots of company today. Tara is here to see you. Cat and Doc are here, too. Doc is Cat's dad, and he's a surgeon." Billie lifted Seth's hand and put it inside one of Cat's. "Scout, this is Cat. She's Tara's mom. She's the one I've been telling you about. Cat, this young man is my son, Seth."

"Hi, Seth. You're even more handsome than your mom said you were. I'm very happy to finally meet you." Cat felt Seth's fingers flex inside her hand. She looked quickly at Doc. "His fingers are moving." She addressed Seth once more. "Seth, I'm going to turn the television on so you and Tara can watch cartoons while your mom and I talk to Doc. After that, Doc wants to examine you."

* * *

Billie and Cat sat in chairs across from Doc. Billie's hands shook nervously.

Doc squeezed Billie's shoulder. "Relax. I'll explain what I found when I reviewed Seth's charts and what my exam told me, and then I'll go over the tests I think we should run." Doc released his grip on Billie's shoulder and sat back. "All right. There's no easy way to say this, so I'll be direct. I've reason to believe Seth was misdiagnosed nine months ago."

Billie jumped to her feet. "What? Those bastards."

Doc folded his arms across his chest. "I understand your anger. Sit, and I'll tell you how I came to that conclusion."

Billie sat down and folded her hands in her lap to hide the tremors that ran through them. "I'm sorry."

"No reason to be sorry. I'd feel the same way if it were one of my girls in Seth's position. Like I said, I think he's been misdiagnosed. I base this on a couple of things. First, just as you described, we've seen his response to Tara. Second, his records contain the results of testing which measure responses to applied stimuli. The first test is called the Glasgow Coma Scale. It's based on a fifteen-point scale. The lowest score a patient can receive is zero and the highest is fifteen. It estimates the outcomes of brain injury in the areas of motor response, verbal response, and eye opening. A score of one indicates no response. The higher the score, the more interactive the person is. With a diagnosis of persistent vegetative state, one would expect a score of less than three, which means absolutely no reaction to stimuli. Seth's score was a five."

"Five doesn't sound like a very high score."

"It isn't, but it's significantly better than I expected. What this ultimately means is that Seth isn't in a persistent vegetative state. Before we discuss that in more detail, let me tell you about one other test result that supports the misdiagnosis theory. It's called the Ranchos Los Amigos Scale, which measures the levels of awareness, cognition, behavior, and interaction with the environment. There are eight levels of awareness, beginning with no response at level one, to purposeful and appropriate response at level eight. Again, persistent vegetative state would be an accurate diagnosis for level one. Seth's test results nine months ago indicated a level two, which meant he had generalized response."

"So what does this mean relative to his recovery?" Billie asked.

"Unfortunately, it means we're starting over. If he'd been properly diagnosed nine months ago, his doctor would've ordered a more appropriate rehabilitation program than the one he underwent. Since brain injuries can become worse with time, we've lost the benefit of early treatment. Because of the nine-month delay and the improper treatment program, it's possible he's sustained damage that's now irreversible."

"Are you saying his doctors are right, that his condition has no chance of improving?"

"No, I'm not saying that at all. His treatment plan was appropriate for someone with persistent vegetative state. However, he's demonstrated response to stimuli that clearly shows that's not the case. The fact is, he is responding to stimuli. Where there's response, there's hope for treatment."

Billie smiled through her tears. "I don't know what to say. I haven't had any real hope for nine months."

"Hope is one thing we definitely have," Doc replied. He rose to his feet. "I'll order the appropriate tests before I leave today."

Cat labored to her feet. "Obviously, we need to re-baseline him with a repeat of the Glasgow and Ranchos Los Amigos tests. I'd also recommend an EEG as well as a CT scan and MRI," she said.

"My thoughts exactly," Doc said. "The best scenario would be to uncover a specific reason for his lack of consciousness that is correctable rather than general brain damage that may require more extensive rehabilitation. I'll go order the tests for tomorrow morning. I should be back shortly to do a physical exam."

Doc left to set up Seth's tests.

Billie took Cat's hand in her own and squeezed it lightly. "Thank you."

"Billie, I don't know what I was thinking. I took one look at him and realized there was no way I could resist falling for him. Tara wants Seth to be her big brother. And I want him to be my son."

"Yeah. Can Seth come home to live with us?" Tara asked from her position on the bed.

Billie fought the tears that threatened to fall as she smiled at Cat. "Do you mean you want us to be a family?"

"I'm saying I want us to be whole, all of us, beginning with Seth."

* * *

Late the next day, after he received the results from the tests he'd ordered, Doc did another quick exam of Seth, then stepped back from the bed and instructed Billie to dress him while he went to get Cat and Tara from the solarium at the end of the hall. A few moments later, they returned.

"Have a seat, and I'll tell you what I know."

Cat and Billie once again sat opposite Doc. Tara climbed onto the bed with Seth. Doc turned on the TV in hopes of keeping Tara occupied while he spoke with Cat and Billie. He grinned as his granddaughter explained to Seth in detail everything that was happening in the cartoon.

Satisfied that he had Cat and Billie's uninterrupted attention, Doc addressed the matter at hand. "The tests I carried out this afternoon indicate he has strong reflexes and reacts to pain. His muscle tone is poor, but I think that's due to months of inactivity. If the diagnosis on record were accurate, there would be no reflexes and no reaction to pain. This supports my theory that he was misdiagnosed. Even though the injury is old enough not to effectively react to a treatment regime, we can pursue other radical steps, but those steps may require brain surgery. Of course, what I'm saying is preliminary. Because of what I've seen thus far, I've ordered additional tests to help me develop a proper course of action. The lack of reaction the pupils of his eyes have to bright light concerns me. I saw this condition before, in another small child in the hospital in Florida, and in that case, I was able to reverse the damage with surgery."

Doc heard a sharp gasp of breath escape Billie's throat.

"Unless I miss my guess, Billie, you see a conflict of interest in that approach."

Billie nodded.

"If I'm right about your concern, I think I can overcome it on a technicality. While surgeons operating on their own families is generally frowned on, since the two of you aren't married, you and Seth aren't members of my family." He paused and smiled reassuringly. "Not yet, that is." He patted Billie's hand before continuing. "I have surgical privileges in this hospital, and we have one of the most advanced neurosurgery units in the country here. It may take some time to arrange it, but if these additional test results support surgery as a treatment, I'm willing to do the procedure."

Chapter 9

Doc made the necessary arrangements for Seth's tests and returned to Seth's room to collect Cat and Tara before joining his wife for dinner.

"Are my girls ready to go?"

"I don't mind taking them home," Billie said.

"Don't you have an aerobics class to teach?" Cat asked.

"I couldn't possibly concentrate on teaching a class when so much is happening with Seth. I called the gym while Seth was being tested and put myself on indefinite leave. I'll just have to figure out some other way to supplement the payments for his long-term care facility."

Doc squeezed Billie's shoulder. "Don't worry about the financial end of things right now. I hope we can find a way for Seth not to need long-term care."

He waited as Billie composed herself. "I was going to suggest that Ida and I take Tara for the next few days. Since we're going to be staying here instead of going back to Florida for the rest of the winter, she can help us feel at home at our place." He caught the look on Cat's face. "We'll only spoil her a little, I promise, and it'll give you time to heal before going back to work and having to take care of both Tara and yourself."

"Can I, Mama?" Tara asked. "I like to stay at Grandpa and Grammy's."

"Of course you can, but only if you promise to be a good girl."

"I promise." She grabbed her grandfather's hand. "Let's go, Grandpa."

Cat kissed her father. "Thanks for taking her."

* * *

Billie held the car door open as Cat slowly lowered herself into the passenger seat.

Out on the road, Billie took a quick look at Cat. "I can't thank you enough for asking your father to examine Seth. I hope he can help him."

"Daddy will do everything he can. The test results will help determine how much can be done. He's hoping the tests will tell us why Seth isn't able to do more than the slight movements we've witnessed."

Preoccupied with what the future might hold for Seth, Billie fell silent for the rest of the ride to Cat's condo. Before exiting the car, she looked at Cat. "Do you really think he'll need brain surgery?"

"Most likely, yes."

"The thought of it scares me to death."

"That's understandable."

Tears rolled down Billie's cheeks.

"Come here," Cat said.

Billie leaned across the console and put her head on Cat's shoulder. She closed her eyes and felt a gentle kiss on her forehead.

"It'll be all right. You're not alone. I'll be by your side every step of the way."

* * *

Cat walked into the condo in front of Billie. "I don't remember leaving this place so clean."

"I found myself at loose ends the day of your surgery, so I cleaned while Tara napped."

Cat rubbed Billie's arm. "That was very sweet of you."

Their gazes locked on one another. Billie shuffled from foot to foot. "I should head home and let you get some sleep."

Cat took a step closer and touched Billie's face. "I was hoping you'd stay tonight."

Billie pressed her forehead to Cat's. "I'd like nothing better than to hold you in my arms while you sleep."

"Then stay. Please."

Billie pulled her head back. "I will." She kissed Cat then pulled back once more. She kissed her again, this time with increased ardor. Cat's hands moved to her hips, pulling her closer.

Billie released Cat from her embrace, stepped back, and held her an arm's length away. "I so want to make love to you, right here and now, but we need to be patient and wait until you're healed."

"You're right, of course. How about I draw a tub and we soak for a while?"

"What about your incision? Should you be getting it wet?"

"It's held together with a waterproof dressing—no stitches."

While the tub filled, Cat went back into the living room and slipped into the circle of Billie's arms. She felt a slight tremor run through Billie. "Are you all right?"

Billie nodded. "I'm a little overwhelmed, that's all."

"We have the entire evening to figure out how to relax you." Cat took Billie's hand and led her to the bathroom. "How does a glass of wine sound?"

"Sounds great, but only if you join me."

Cat stepped in close and kissed Billie. "Of course I will."

Billie kissed Cat's jawline and neck. "Umm, you taste so good."

"If you keep that up, neither one of us will get that bath." Cat's actions belied her scolding tone as she leaned her head back to give Billie better access to her neck. She pulled herself out of Billie's grasp. "Wait right here."

She returned carrying a bottle of wine and two glasses. She put the wine down and faced Billie. "This has got to go," she said. She pulled Billie's T-shirt over her head and discarded it on the floor beside them.

Still without breaking her gaze, Cat snaked her hands behind Billie and released the clasp on her bra. A visible wave of relief crossed Billie's face as the bra fell away. Billie's bra followed the T-shirt to the floor. Cat was terribly distracted by the erect peaks inches away from her face; however, she stood her ground as she slid her hands into the back of Billie's shorts and pushed them downward past Billie's hips. Unable to resist, she squeezed Billie's flesh as the shorts and panties made contact with the floor.

"Oh God." Billie grasped Cat's arms.

Cat kissed the vee between Billie's breasts and smiled as she felt Billie shudder once more.

Billie lowered her face to Cat's. Cat closed her eyes and expected a kiss, but instead, Cat felt Billie's tongue tracing the outline of her mouth before it delved deep inside.

Cat moaned as she grasped Billie's naked hips for support.

Billie released the buttons on the front of Cat's shirt and slipped it from her shoulders. Cat found her arms trapped by her sides. She nearly lost her balance as she relinquished her handhold on Billie's hips.

Billie moved behind her and trailed her fingertips across Cat's abs.

"Billie," Cat moaned and pressed herself back into Billie's chest.

Cat's shirt was the next piece of clothing to join the steadily growing pile on the floor after Billie pushed it from her shoulders. Cat felt her desire mount, and she guided Billie's hand into the waistband of her shorts. She gasped as Billie's fingers slipped into her moist crevice, but was frustrated when her shorts denied Billie free access. Cat pushed them past her hips, where they fell to the floor. She kicked the offending garment away from her ankles and stood before Billie clad only in bra and panties.

Billie circled to the front of Cat, and her fingertips traced a path around Cat's waist. "Like you said about my shirt, these have got to go." Billie tossed Cat's undergarments across the room.

Cat's desire escalated as she felt Billie, totally naked, beneath her fingertips. She used her hands to explore Billie's breasts, back, and buttocks, while her mouth traced a path along Billie's neck and shoulder.

Cat managed to get a few words in between kisses. "Billie, we need to get into the tub."

"Let me take a look at your incision first." Billie knelt down and kissed the area around the transparent dressing.

Cat shuddered as intense waves of desire coursed through her. "Oh God." Cat pulled Billie's head closer.

"I can smell your arousal. God, what you do to me," Billie said.

"Billie... the tub," Cat reluctantly reminded her again.

Billie stood to her full height and scooped Cat into her arms. Cat felt the exquisite softness of Billie's skin as Billie slowly lowered her into the warm water. Billie then stepped into the tub and settled in behind her. Cat nestled against her, with her back resting against Billie's chest. She poured two glasses of wine and handed one to Billie, then relaxed into her arms to savor the moment.

Cat rested her head on Billie's shoulder as Billie's fingertips drew lazy circles around her left nipple. She pressed her head into Billie's shoulder and moaned. "Hmmm, that feels good. Damned appendix. I finally get you alone and naked, and I can't do anything about it."

Billie kissed the side of Cat's head. "I know. I've been waiting for this moment almost since I laid eyes on you. You're so beautiful. You've no idea what you're doing to me right now."

"Sorry."

"How long did your doctor say you had to wait?"

"He said four to six weeks before engaging in strenuous activity."

"Four to six weeks? You're killing me here."

Cat chuckled. "You're not the only one dying."

"You're right, of course. As hard as it'll be to wait, I want our first time to be without restriction. We'll just have to wait until you're fully recovered to make our dream come true."

Cat shifted slightly so that she saw Billie's face. "Thank you."

"For what?"

"For everything. For being so understanding, for being willing to risk your heart, for making time for me and Tara in your life."

"You're worth any risk I may have to take. I love you."

"I love you, too."

Cat settled in once more with her back to Billie and her head resting on Billie's shoulder. For several moments, neither of them said a word.

"Billie, I never thanked you for watching Tara when I was sick. Hell, I never even asked you to stay with her, but I'm so glad you did. She's rather taken with you."

"It's funny how she wriggled her way into my heart." Billie chuckled. "I have to admit I was shocked when Gail opened your door that day."

"Gail. Ugh. That's a mistake I'll never make again."

"Tara said that you had a fight with her, over me no less, and that you asked her to leave."

"That daughter of mine sure has a big mouth. I'll have to talk to her about that." Cat paused. "Yes, we did have a fight, and yes, it was about you. She threatened to leave me in the lurch without day care if I continued to see you. You can imagine how that pissed me off. No one tells me how to live my life. Not even my parents. She was stupid enough to pull this on me after I'd spent a day-and-a-half throwing up and doubled over in pain with appendicitis. It didn't take me long to tell her to pack her bags and get the hell out."

Billie laughed. "I wish I'd been there to see that."

Cat chuckled and held her empty glass toward Billie. "Do you mind?"

Billie grabbed the bottle of wine and refilled their glasses.

"Speaking of your parents, I can't believe how incredibly accepting they've been of Seth and me. They don't even know us, yet they're treating us like family."

"They know you better than you think. Heaven knows they've heard enough about you over the last few months. While they were in Florida, I talked to them two or three times a week. Hell, they knew I loved you before you did."

"It's obvious they don't have a problem with our relationship. Your dad was pretty blunt about it."

"Billie, my dad means well, but don't let him push you into something you're not ready for. I heard his comment about the marriage thing and…" Cat wasn't sure what more to say.

"I didn't say his talk of marriage bothered me."

"Billie Charland, are you proposing to little ole me?" Cat asked in a fake Southern accent. Cat looked over her shoulder and saw the fear of rejection in Billie's eyes. Her heart shattered at the sight. "Billie, I love you with all my heart. Nothing would make me happier than to be your wife."

"I think we'd better wait to see what happens with Seth before you commit yourself. I know you said you wanted us to be a family, but if your father can't help him, the future may not be so rosy."

Cat swiveled around. Her sudden movement splashed water out of the tub and onto the floor and spilled her wine into the tub. "What did you say?"

"I said that you need to go into this with your eyes open."

Cat pinned Billie to the back of the tub by her arms. Their faces were a mere breath's width apart. "Is that what you really think of me? Do you think I'd turn tail and run as soon as things got rough? Damn you."

Cat pushed backward and retreated to the other end of the tub as tears cascaded down her face. "Heaven forbid, but if something ever happened to Tara, would you want out of our relationship?"

Billie averted her gaze. "No, I wouldn't."

"I know I've given you reason to question my feelings toward Seth, but I've also asked for time to adjust, and adjust I will. I'm made of a lot tougher stuff than you give me credit for. If I wasn't, Tara wouldn't be with us today."

"What do you mean?"

Cat fell silent.

"Cat?"

Cat grabbed the sides of the tub and slowly rose to her feet. She stepped out onto the bathmat and grabbed her towel.

"Where are you going?" Billie asked.

"I'm not sure I'm ready to talk to you about Tara." Cat dried the moisture from her body, donned a robe, and left the room.

Billie sat in the tub of cooling water and tried to make sense of what had just happened between Cat and her. An anxious feeling settled in the pit of her stomach as she worried her careless words had driven Cat away. Unable to shake the feelings, she climbed out of the tub, toweled herself dry, and tied the robe closed around her waist. She went in search of Cat and found her lying on the bed, the sheet pulled up to her chest and her robe draped over the coverlet at the foot of the bed.

Billie stopped in the doorway and rested her shoulder against the frame. "I'm sorry. I don't know what else to say except I've been taking care of Seth on my own for so long that it's difficult for me to accept help. I didn't mean to imply you weren't able to handle Seth's condition."

Cat extended her hand. "Come here," she said.

Billie discarded her robe and slipped in beside Cat. Cat went willingly into her open arms and nestled her head in Billie's neck.

"I'm sorry I overreacted. I know I'm protective of Tara, but I'm all she has."

Billie tightened her hold around Cat. "What did you mean, earlier, about why you weren't sure you wanted to talk to me about Tara?"

"Haven't you ever wondered why I'm a single mother?"

"Yeah, but I... I..."

"You assumed either I'd been married and divorced or I got myself into trouble. Right?"

"When I first learned about Tara, that's exactly what I thought. But you said something about her other mother leaving. I have to admit that I'm curious. I've wanted to ask, but it's never felt like the right time to bring it up."

"Tara is the result of in vitro fertilization with a sperm donor. Shannon and I went through hell to get pregnant."

"Shannon was Tara's other mother, I presume?"

"Shannon was my partner, and yes, she was Tara's other mother. We met when I was twenty and still in med school. She was twenty-six and had just started her three-year residency program. We were together for two years before she talked me into having a child."

"So, what happened?"

"The first attempt ended with a miscarriage. It was very hard on both of us. Luckily, the second insemination was successful, and as Tara's birth approached, we had everything to look forward to. We both had promising careers, we loved each other, and we had this child who would bind us closer than we ever imagined." Cat's voice cracked.

"You loved her very much, didn't you?" Billie tensed as she waited for Cat's reply.

"I loved her more than life itself, and I thought she felt the same toward me. I guess hindsight is twenty-twenty." Cat paused to collect her thoughts. "Like I said, conceiving was Shannon's idea. The timing wasn't great. I was only twenty-two and just starting my residency, but there was nothing I wouldn't do for her." Cat wiped the tears that had formed in the corners of her eyes. "I can't believe it still hurts after so long."

"So Tara was born when you were just beginning a three-year residency, and Shannon had only one year remaining in hers, right?"

"She actually had less than a year to go by the time Tara was born. Needless to say, it was a big sacrifice on my part. Juggling motherhood and a hospital residency is nothing I ever want to do again."

"With so much schooling still ahead of you, why didn't Shannon offer to carry the baby?"

"Shannon couldn't have children. She had a hormonal disorder that prevented her body from producing ova."

Billie frowned. "Did your relationship end before or after Tara's birth?"

"After. In fact, she's only been gone for two years."

"Two years? So, what happened? If things were so good between you, why isn't she here now?"

"Honestly? I don't know what happened. Things were wonderful after Tara was born. Shannon was a very loving and attentive mother. New York allows same-sex co-parents to adopt their partner's children, so she legally adopted Tara when she was about six months old. Things between Shannon and me were good, too. She turned thirty a few months after Tara's second birthday. I took her on a surprise dinner theater cruise, and we had a wonderful time. That night, she told me over and over that she loved me, and she promised we would be together forever. A week later, she called from the airport and said she wouldn't be coming home. She was on her way to Chicago with a coworker."

"So, just like that, she calls and says she's not coming home? No warning? No explanation?"

"None. I was caught completely off guard. I honestly don't know what went wrong. When she returned from Chicago a week later, I confronted her, but she refused to talk about it, so I still don't know why she left. I have no closure. I've come to terms with the fact that I may never know what I did to drive her away. I can only hope that whatever mistakes I made, I don't repeat them with you."

"You know, it might not be anything you did. It appears to me that she needs to take the blame for your breakup. It pretty much sucks that she refused to even talk to you about it. That isn't fair at all. My guess is she was cheating on you, probably with whomever she ran off to Chicago with."

"You might be right."

"Do you still love her?"

Cat thought for a moment. "I'm not sure I can describe how I feel about Shannon now. She broke my heart. I didn't know heartache could hurt so much. Do I still love her? I don't think so. What bothers me most is not knowing why she left. When I think of her, I don't feel love. I feel hurt, betrayal, sadness, and of course, anger. Her refusal to talk to me about the breakup has made me doubt myself, and believe me, that's a very uncomfortable feeling."

Billie lowered her chin to her chest and closed her eyes. She inhaled a deep breath before she asked her next question. "Is she still around?"

"For the first few months after she left us, we continued in the same residency program. After that, she transferred to a hospital in Texas. I've since lost track of her."

"And what about Tara? Is Shannon still legally her parent?"

"When she returned from Chicago, she filed for custody of Tara."

"Obviously, the courts ruled in your favor," Billie said.

"Not entirely. Shannon adopted her. She had legal rights, like any estranged parent in a divorce."

"Did you marry her?"

"No. I thank the heavens every day for that. I didn't marry her, but that didn't change the fact that she was legally Tara's parent. We went to court, and they awarded us joint custody. About a month after the court's decision, the unimaginable happened. She picked Tara up for her weekend visit but didn't bring her back."

"Oh my God. What happened?"

"At first, the police wouldn't do anything. When they asked me if I thought Tara was in danger, I had to honestly answer no. Anyway, she brought her back three days later, and I threatened to have her arrested for kidnapping. Had she been convicted, she'd have lost her residency and her career. She chose, instead, to transfer her residency and to drop out of Tara's life. We haven't seen her since. I won't say it's been easy raising Tara alone, but I'd do it again in a heartbeat."

"I'd do the same for Seth. He's the most important thing in my life."

Cat touched Billie's arm. "Billie, I was wrong about Seth. I admit I was scared when you told me about him, but to be honest, if it were Tara in that condition instead of Seth, I'd want you to love her, just like you want me to love him. I know I'm strong enough to accept him and all of the potential consequences that go with him. The question is, will you let me?"

Billie lifted tear-filled eyes to Cat and nodded.

"What are you thinking?" Cat asked in little more than a whisper.

"I'd be lying if I said this thing with Shannon doesn't bother me. I'm both angry and jealous and more than a little afraid that you might still be in love her. I'm afraid to have my heart broken, and I'm afraid Seth could be hurt in the process, too."

Cat caressed the side of Billie's face. "Billie, believe me when I say I love you with all my heart. Yes, I loved Shannon once, and maybe I still need to work out the closure issue, but I promise that I'll never give you reason to doubt me. Please give me a chance to prove my love to you."

Billie took Cat's face between her hands and kissed her. "I love you, Cat."

"I love you, too."

Cat burrowed closer to Billie. She released a sigh of contentment. "Sleep, my love."

Billie kissed the top of her head. "Pleasant dreams."

Chapter 10

Two days later, Billie met Cat in the hallway outside Doc's office in the Albany Medical Center. She kissed Cat. "Sorry I'm late. Traffic was pretty slow." Billie looked around nervously. "God, my stomach is a mess."

Cat rubbed Billie's back. "I understand. The test results could mean a turning point for Seth."

Billie ran her hand through her hair. "What if it's bad news, Cat? I don't think I could deal with the disappointment."

"It's possible that Daddy won't be able to do anything for him, but I'm crossing my fingers and hoping for the best. Are you ready to go in?"

Billie smoothed the front of her jacket and forced a smile onto her face. She nodded, and they walked through the door.

"The test results are in," Doc said. He opened the folder in front of him and extracted a graph, which he slid across the table. "We completed a twenty-one-point EEG at intervals of fifteen minutes for three hours. As I suspected after my physical evaluation of Seth three days ago, the results indicate normal brain activity."

"The results are normal? Then why is he in a coma?" Billie asked.

Cat picked up the graph and studied it. "What about the MRI and CT scans?"

"Good question." Doc extracted two films from the folder and walked to the far side of his office. He snapped the two films into the clip of the light bar. "Come look at these. They're films of the CT and MRI scans."

Cat stood with her hands on her hips as she scrutinized them. Billie stood beside her, frowning.

Doc said, "I don't expect you to know what you're looking at, Billie, but I promise it will all become clear after I explain the results to you." He addressed Cat. "Do you see anything abnormal?"

"Radiology isn't my specialty, but if you want my opinion, I see something out of the ordinary right here." Cat pointed to a specific area of the film.

"You're right. That's called the reticular activating system, or RAS for short."

"The reticule... what?" Billie asked.

"Reticular activating system," Doc repeated. "It's the part of the brain believed to be the center of arousal, wakefulness, and motivation. It's crucial for maintaining consciousness. The nuclei located there receive input from the body's sensory systems, such as sight, smell, taste, and so on. It's the part of the brain that makes the body aware that a lemon is sour or that sugar is sweet or that fresh popcorn smells wonderful."

Cat pointed to the film again. "So is this cloudy area scar tissue? It'd make sense to me that if the RAS was inhibited in some way, say by scar tissue, the link between being aware of outside stimuli and the ability to react to it might be impaired."

"Nice call, Dr. O'Grady. You're exactly right. I knew my money was well spent when I sent you to medical school."

"Wait a minute, here," Billie said. "Are you saying the scar tissue is like a door locking Seth inside, and that he can see and hear from behind the door, but it's in the way of him expressing his awareness?"

Doc nodded.

"So how do we open the door?" Billie asked.

"We do it surgically," Doc replied.

"Isn't that risky?"

"All operations carry a certain amount of risk," Cat said. "The question is, what are the odds it will be successful?"

"I give it better than fifty-fifty odds," Doc said.

"That's not very high," Billie replied.

Doc squeezed Billie's shoulder. "It's better odds than he's facing without the surgery."

Billie looked plaintively at Cat. "What do you think?"

"I have confidence in Daddy. He's an excellent surgeon."

Billie closed her eyes for a moment. When they opened, two small tears escaped. "Do it."

* * *

Billie wept uncontrollably as she watched the nurse wheel Seth down the hall on a gurney.

"Have faith. Everything will be fine," Cat said.

"He's just a baby. He's so vulnerable. I'd give anything to trade places with him."

"I know you would. I would, too. Come on, let's get some coffee. We're in for a long wait."

"You go ahead. I'm staying right here." Billie took a seat in the surgery ward waiting room.

Cat wrapped her arms around Billie and kissed her head. "I'll be right back."

It was two weeks since Doc had set the wheels in motion toward Seth's surgery and potential recovery. During that time, Doc and Ida returned to Florida and closed their seasonal home and moved back to their summer home, not far from Cat's condo. Before he left, Doc ordered an additional battery of tests that would help him formulate a surgical approach in hopes of reversing the damage done both by Seth's accident and the ineffective treatment he'd received.

Billie rested her head against the wall and closed her eyes. The last two weeks had passed by in a blur. Between the demands of her job, visits with Seth, and spending time with Cat and Tara, Billie barely had time to think. Despite lying in Cat's arms each night, she slept fitfully, as her mind never wandered far from her son. She felt exhausted. She was almost glad that Cat was still recovering from her own surgery. As much as she wanted to make love to Cat, her focus was elsewhere. Hope and worry about Seth's future filled her mind.

"Here you go," Cat said as she offered a coffee to Billie.

Billie opened her eyes and sat up straighter in her chair. "Thank you. You're a lifesaver. I really need this."

Cat sat next to Billie and sipped her coffee. "You didn't sleep well last night, did you? You were very restless."

"No, I didn't. I'm sorry if I kept you awake."

"I wouldn't have it any other way. We're in this together. I want to share every moment of this with you. I want to be there for both you and Seth."

Moisture filled Billie's eyes as she smiled. "I love you."

Cat took her hand and held it. They sat outside the operating suite during the entire surgery. For ten grueling hours, Billie paced off-and-on and refused to eat or sleep. Finally, Doc emerged from the OR. He looked tired but sported a satisfied smile on his face.

"Everything went fine. I was able to remove the scar tissue in the damaged area of the brain and repair some of the electrical connections that were severed." Billie's knees buckled; Doc caught her before she fell. "Whoa, there. Here, sit down." He guided her to a chair. "Like I said, the surgery went well, and I'm very hopeful we'll see some improvement in Seth's condition. He has a long path to recovery in front of him, including some pretty intense physical therapy. If the surgery worked, he should make a full recovery."

Billie looked at him through her tears and nodded.

"When'll we know if the operation was successful?" Cat asked.

"This type of procedure either works or it doesn't. If it worked, we'll know as soon as he wakes up sometime tomorrow morning. He's being stitched up and will be transferred to recovery in about a half hour."

Billie took Doc's hand. "I don't know how to thank you."

"I already have all the thanks I need. You've given me what none of my natural children have been able to. A grandson! Do you believe it? I have six beautiful granddaughters, but no grandsons, until now that is. For that, I thank you. Now, if you'll excuse me, I need a bath, a good stiff drink, and my bed. Not necessarily in that order."

Cat looked at Billie. "We need to get you home. You heard him say Seth will be out of it at least until tomorrow morning. You need some sleep, or you'll be of no use to him tomorrow."

*   *   *

A 6:00 the next morning, the phone rang. Billie jumped to her feet and grabbed it. *Please, God, don't let it be bad news.*

"Hello?"

"Mama?" a little voice said.

"No sweetie, it's Billie."

"Is Mama with you?"

"Yes, she is. Hold on." Billie nudged Cat. "Cat, wake up. It's Tara."

Cat raised her head from the pillow. "Huh?"

"Tara's on the phone."

Cat accepted the phone and a quick kiss. "Hi, honey, what's up? Yes, Billie and I will be going to the hospital soon. What's that? You want to come with us?"

Billie nodded her head.

"Sure, we'll pick you up in about an hour, so be ready. All right. I love you, too. See you in a bit. Bye-bye." Cat hung up the phone and lay back down. "C'mere," she said as she opened her arms to Billie.

Billie went into Cat's arms and held her close. "Good morning."

"Good morning to you, too. How did you sleep?"

"Not well. I couldn't get Seth out of my mind. You, on the other hand, wasted no time. You were out like a light."

Cat kissed Billie on the nose. "Thank you for loving me."

"Loving you is easy. I should be thanking you for taking Seth and me into your heart."

"I had no choice. You captured my heart the moment I laid eyes on you." Cat traced her fingertips across Billie's forehead. "You're going to need help with Seth when he comes home. Why don't you move in here with Tara and me?"

Billie furrowed her brow.

"What are you thinking?" Cat asked.

"I'm thinking that life is about to change for all of us. It won't be easy. We don't know how bad Seth's disabilities will be."

Cat tucked a strand of hair behind Billie's ear. "Whatever his *abilities* are, we'll deal with it. We'll give him a loving home and the best care possible. But whatever happens, he'll know he has two moms who love him unconditionally."

Billie closed her eyes and the mist that had gathered there squeezed between her lashes. "Thank you," she whispered softly.

* * *

An hour later, with Tara belted in the backseat of Billie's car, they set off for the hospital. On the way there, Tara asked, "Billie, will Seth wake up today?"

"I hope so, honey."

"Me, too. I want to ask him to be my big brother."

"I'm sure he'll like that." Billie's voice choked with emotion. She glanced at Cat and saw tears in her eyes as well. *Look at us. We're a couple of mush balls!*

Doc met them coming down the hall toward Seth's room. Billie stopped short when she saw the look of excitement on his face.

"I don't want you to get your hopes up yet, but there are some definite signs of animation from Seth this morning," he said.

"Oh my God." Billie fought to hold back the burst of emotion.

"Breathe, Billie, breathe," Cat said.

Billie grabbed Cat's hand, scooped Tara up onto her hip, and ran the rest of the way to Seth's room.

As they entered the room, Billie handed Tara to Cat. She stood beside Seth's bed and noted how small and pale he looked with white bandages wrapped around his head. She sat on the edge of the bed and kissed him on the cheek. She whispered in his ear, "Come on, baby, open your eyes for me."

After a brief flutter, blue met blue.

"Mom?" a weak little voice said.

Billie released the tenuous hold she had on her emotions. She lowered her head to Seth's chest and cried. Soon, Cat was beside her as tears coursed down her face as well.

Tara went around to the other side of Seth's bed and climbed up beside him. "Hi, Seth." She picked up his hand to hold it in her own.

"Hi, Tara. I remember your voice."

Billie jerked her head up and looked pointedly at Cat. "I knew he was in there. I knew it."

"Mom?"

"Yes, my love?" Billie wiped the tears from her face.

"I'm kind of hungry. Can we get McDonald's?"

Tara seconded the motion as she scooted off the bed.

Part II:

A Family in Blood

Chapter 11

Doc O'Grady cleared his throat and drew the attention of everyone in the room. Billie enveloped Doc in a warm hug. "I don't know how to thank you," she said.

"No thanks necessary."

Cat wrapped her arms around them both. "Thank you, Daddy. I knew you could do it."

Doc brushed the moisture from Cat's cheek. "I only did part of the work, kitten. Seth did the rest, and he's not out of the woods yet. We have a lot of work to do before he's fully recovered." Doc looked over to Seth. "Speaking of which, don't you think it's time you introduce me to the young man?"

Billie wiped her face with the back of her hand, took Doc's hand in hers, and led him to the bed. Cat circled the bed and lifted Tara into her arms.

Billie sat on the bed and brushed Seth's cheek with her hand. "Hey, scout, here's someone I want you to meet."

Seth looked at Doc and said, "Hi, Grandpa."

Billie's eyebrows arched high on her forehead. She shook her head and looked back and forth between Seth and Tara. "So, I see you two have already planned everything, huh?"

Tara extended her arms out to both sides and tilted her head. "I want Seth to be my big brother, so Grandpa has to be his grandpa, too, right?"

Doc took Billie's hand and directed her off the bed. He sat in the space she vacated and leaned close. He gave Seth a conspiratorial wink and said under his breath, "Just like a woman—always trying to control things."

Seth giggled and held a hand to his mouth to hide a smirk.

Doc took Seth's small hand into his own and shook it in a gentlemanly fashion. "Seth, my name is Doc, and I'm Cat's dad. Since Tara has already decided that I'm your new grandpa, I'd be proud to be so. What do you say, partner?"

"Can I really call you Grandpa?"

"What would you like to call me?"

Seth appeared to contemplate the question for a minute then looked over to Tara. She cupped her hands around her mouth like a megaphone and mouthed the word Grandpa. Seth smiled and nodded his head. He looked back at Doc. "I think I like Grandpa best."

"Grandpa it is." Doc glanced over his shoulder at Cat and smiled. He looked back to Seth. "Tell you what. I'm going to let you spend some time with your new family, but I'll be back to examine you, all right? We have a lot of work to do before you can go home, and I'll need you to be strong and brave through it."

"I will, Grandpa." Seth's arms shook as he reached up to give Doc a hug.

Doc tweaked Seth's nose. "After all, partner, when you're better, we have a lot of catching up to do, you and me... fishing, football games, you know—guy stuff."

Seth grinned from ear to ear. "Yay! I can't wait."

"All right. I'll be back soon." He kissed Seth's forehead then took Tara from Billie's arms to give her a big hug. "Seth will need a lot of help from you, princess. Do you think you're up to it?"

"Oh boy. Can I really help?"

"Not only can you help, but you'll need to help. Your mom and Billie are going to need someone to play with Seth and stuff like that."

"I can do those things, Grandpa."

"Good. I'm sure Seth is going to love having a little sister." He kissed her and gave her back to Billie. "I'll be back later."

After Doc left, Billie took Cat's hand and stood beside Seth's bed. She put Tara down at the foot of the bed and motioned for Cat to join her at the head. It didn't take long for Tara to scamper to the top of the bed and position herself next to Seth.

Cat reached out for Tara. "Be very careful for Seth's head. He has a very big cut there that will hurt if you bump it. Why don't you come sit over here with me?" Cat motioned to a chair by the bedside.

"No, leave her there. She's fine," Billie said. She addressed Tara. "Mama is right. You need to be careful of his cut."

"I'll be careful." Tara lay down next to Seth.

Seth looked at Tara and grinned.

Billie sat on the edge of the bed and pulled Cat down in front of her. She felt Cat tense. Billie whispered in her ear, "Relax, he's going to love you, just like I do."

Billie took Seth's hand. She raised it to her lips and kissed his knuckles.

Seth rolled his eyes.

Cat whispered to Billie, "I think you're embarrassing him."

Billie chuckled and released his hand. "I think you're right," she replied as she noted the pink tinge on Seth's cheeks.

Cat elbowed Billie in the ribs.

Billie made an 'ooomph' noise. "All right, all right. I get the point." She cleared her throat. "Seth, this is Cat. I told you all about her when I came to visit, remember?"

"Mom said you fell flat on your face in her aerobics class. That must've been funny." He looked at Tara and both of them giggled.

Cat swung around and raised her eyebrows at Billie.

Billie tried to recover as gracefully as possible. "Um, err... oh, hell. I've never kept anything from him. I wanted him to know and love everything about you."

Cat kissed Seth's cheek. Before she raised her head, Seth circled his arms around her neck for a hug. She returned the hug and kissed him again on top of the head and laid Seth back down onto his pillows. She traced the side of Seth's face with her fingertip. "Seth, Tara and I would love for you and your mom to come live with us when you leave the hospital. Like a real family. Would you like that?"

"Do I get my own room?"

"Absolutely."

"Can we, Mom?" Seth asked.

Billie looked at Cat. "This will mean a lot of changes for all of us, you know."

"I know," Cat replied. She leaned back into the circle of Billie's arms.

Billie wrapped her arms around Cat. "It won't always be easy," she said.

"I don't want easy. I want you... I want us... I want our family."

"Mom?" Seth said.

Billie looked at Seth and Tara lying side by side on the bed, sporting identical puppy-dog faces.

"Well..." Billie rose from the bed and paced back and forth. "This is a pretty serious decision. One that shouldn't be taken lightly." She fought to suppress a grin as she saw the worried look on Seth's face. She continued to pace. "I'll have to take some time to think about it." She stopped in front of Seth and Tara and put her hands on her hips. "Time's up." With enormous effort, she adopted a stern look. "I have one question for you, Seth,"

"What?"

"What color do you want your new room to be?"

Everyone was silent for so long, Billie was concerned that her teasing had gone over their heads until she saw realization dawn on Seth's face.

"Do you mean it, Mom?"

"I mean it."

"Tara, I'm gonna be your big brother," Seth said.

Tara rose up onto her knees and clapped her hands. "Yay! Can Seth come home today?" she asked Billie.

"Not today, but very soon."

"Oh boy, I can't wait. Seth, you're gonna love our house. We have a really cool TV to watch Barney on, and I have lots of dolls and books, and…"

Cat dragged Billie to the far side of the room while Tara gave Seth a blow-by-blow description of what life would be like in the Charland-O'Grady household. She wrapped her arms around Billie's waist. "You're so bad, Billie Charland."

"Who, me?"

Cat turned around in her embrace so that they both faced the bed. They looked over to see two small heads together.

Billie whispered into Cat's ear, "I think we're in trouble."

* * *

As he'd promised, Doc came back a short time later to examine Seth.

"Okay, let's take a look at you."

"What are you looking for?" Cat asked.

"I need to assess his current strength and limitations so we can formulate a plan for physical therapy."

"That would be our cue to head out." Cat kissed Seth on the cheek. "Tara and I are going to run out while Grandpa does your exam. We'll be back soon with a surprise for you."

Billie followed them into the hallway. "Is everything okay?"

"I don't think Seth would appreciate Tara and me seeing him in his underpants during the exam, so I'll take Tara to the bookstore to pick out something for him to read and maybe some activity books, too. I'll get Tara some lunch while we're out as well. Can I bring something back for you?"

"No, I'm fine. I'll get something from the cafeteria later." Billie handed Cat the car keys and kissed her and Tara.

"Thanks. We'll be back in a couple of hours."

When Billie returned to the room, Doc was shining a light back and forth across Seth's eyes.

"What can I do to help?"

Doc looked up at her. "Not much right now. This is only a preliminary exam. We'll need to wait a day or two to give the swelling in his brain a chance to go down before taking him to the physical therapy lab."

"Swelling in his brain? What do you mean?"

"As with any surgery, there's a little swelling. That's expected, but with brain surgery, the swelling can affect the quality of test results. We need to give the patient extra time to recover before we can accurately determine the degree of physical therapy that will be required." Doc shut the light off and slipped it into his coat pocket. "Everything looks fine. I'll order a few tests to monitor his progress, but most of them will have to be repeated when the swelling has diminished to determine the true nature of the disability."

"Disability? I'm not sure I like that word."

"Don't let the word bother you. It's just a measure of his current impairment. The degree of disability should diminish fairly rapidly once he's doing physical therapy."

Doc entered a few notes on Seth's chart, put the clipboard aside, and helped Seth to sit on the edge of the bed to test his reflexes. "Your balance is a bit off because you've been lying down for so long, so I'm going to ask your mom to sit next to you and help you sit up. Is that okay with you?"

Seth nodded. "Will I be able to stand up by myself, Grandpa?"

"Maybe not right away, but we'll do everything we can to make you better fast. After all, some fish are out there waiting for us to catch, remember?"

Doc checked all of Seth's reflexes with a rubber hammer and noted the results on his chart. Next, he helped him back into bed to check his pain thresholds. He took Seth's chin in his hand and raised his head until his eyes met his own. In a soothing voice he warned Seth about what was to come. "This next test might hurt a little bit. You can cry if you need to, but you have to let me finish all the tests so we'll be able to tell how much help you'll need to get better. Do you understand?"

Seth nodded.

"Billie, why don't you climb onto the bed behind him and rest him against your chest." He spoke to Seth. "Hold on to your mom's hands and squeeze them tight when it hurts. And try to stay as still as possible."

Billie positioned herself as directed and wrapped her arms around Seth. She offered her hands for him to hold on to. "Be brave. It'll be over soon," she whispered in Seth's ear.

Doc took Seth's arm, pricked his skin at various intervals along its length, and recorded his reactions on his chart. He repeated the procedure on Seth's legs. The muscles in Seth's arms flexed every time he squeezed Billie's hands. "You're doing a great job," Doc assured him. Finally, the testing was over.

Billie held Seth close while Doc wrote the final entries onto Seth's chart. "I'm proud of you, sweetie. You did really well."

Doc picked Seth up and hugged him warmly. "You were very brave. Nice job." Seth yawned. "Before you take a nap, I need to have your feeding tube removed. Do you think you can stay awake for a while longer?"

"Can I have McDonald's for lunch?"

Doc gently lowered Seth to the bed. "You haven't had solid food since your accident so we'll have to start you out slowly with some soft foods. Maybe in a couple of days, we'll see about McDonald's."

Seth looked disappointed.

"It's all right, love," Billie said. "The time will go by quickly. Look, when Grandpa says it's all right, we'll all get McDonald's and bring it here to have a picnic with you."

"Really?" Seth's frown quickly disappeared.

"Really."

"Will you come, too, Grandpa?" Seth asked.

Doc chuckled. "You bet. Try to keep Grammy and me away. It's a date." Doc addressed Billie. "I'll stop at the nurses' station to order the PEG removal."

"PEG?"

"Percutaneous Endoscopic Gastrostomy. The technical name for his feeding tube."

"Is it a difficult procedure?" Billie asked.

"It's rather simple. It's usually pulled out by external traction."

"Will it hurt him?"

"It might make him a little uncomfortable, but it's not really painful. If he has a sensitive gag reflex there may be a little vomiting, but no real pain. We can give him medication to relax him prior to the procedure."

"I think that might be best."

"I'll go order the procedure as well as a bland lunch he can have after the meds wear off. I'll go over the results in my office while the PEG is being removed, and try to summarize them for you. During his nap, we'll talk."

Billie ran her hand through her hair.

Doc smiled and said, "It's early yet. Don't worry. I've seen significantly worse results in the preliminary tests, with full recoveries. Rest assured, we'll do everything we can for him. He's young, and more often than not, children respond to therapy much faster and more effectively than adults. He has an excellent chance of full recovery."

* * *

Removal of the feeding tube was accomplished without incident. Lunch, however, was a bit of an ordeal.

"I'm not eating baby food, Mom."

"Honey, it's not baby food. Look, you like mashed potatoes, right? Well, this is just mashed bananas and corn. Same church, different pew. See what I mean?"

Billie hid a smile as Seth furrowed his brow and frowned at the food on his tray. "It still looks like baby food to me. How about I eat the pudding?"

"How about you eat half the bananas and corn before eating the pudding?"

"Aw, Mom."

She quickly countered his complaint. "You could eat all of the bananas and corn before your pudding."

"Oh, man!" Seth picked up his spoon.

Billie had an overwhelming urge to guide the spoon to his mouth as she watched Seth struggle to eat. His coordination was poor after several months of inactivity. The more effort he put into it, the steadier his hand became, but he still ended up with more food on his shirt than in his mouth.

After lunch, Billie cleaned him up and returned his tray to the nurses' station. When she returned to Seth's room, he was fast asleep. She lowered his bed into the flat position, maneuvered him down under the covers, and sat back in the chair to wait for Doc and the test results.

* * *

Some time later, Cat and Tara returned. Tara climbed into Billie's lap and laid her head on her shoulder. Soon, she was fast asleep. Billie rubbed her hand up and down Tara's back.

Cat took Tara out of Billie's arms, laid her on the bed next to Seth, and pulled the covers up to her chin. Cat sat on Billie's lap in the very spot Tara had occupied.

"Are you all right?" Cat asked. "How did Seth's tests go?"

Billie snapped out of her trance. "Doc said he'll have the results summarized for us soon. I expect him at any moment, in fact. He says he's seen worse preliminary results, with full recoveries. He's hopeful."

"Remember, my love, no matter what, Seth has come back to us. He's alive and alert and totally beautiful. No matter what happens... no matter if he makes a full or partial recovery, we'll love him and protect him together. Right?"

"Right."

Several tender kisses later, they were interrupted by a voice in the doorway. "You two need to get a room."

Cat jumped at the sound and looked up. Billie noticed the blush that rose to Cat's cheeks as she scurried off her lap and smoothed her jeans and shirt.

"Oh for heaven's sake, Caitlain, stop your fussing. You were only kissing," Doc said.

"Daddy, I know what we were doing. Oh God. This is so embarrassing."

"Well, my dear, get over it. I've got some news for the two of you." He pulled up a chair, sat down in front of them, and opened the folder in his lap. "Before we put any stock in these test results, we need to keep in mind that Seth has been inactive for the past nine months or so. He'll need a lot of rehabilitation to improve his overall muscle strength, tone, and coordination. What we don't know yet is how much of his disability is related to the injury versus the inactivity."

"There's that disability word again."

Doc continued. "Billie, you were there during the tests. You saw that he has a low pain tolerance, which is good. This means that the pain centers in his brain aren't blocked."

"Did you use the pinprick test?" Cat asked.

"Yes. The results are noted on this chart."

"I see you used the visual analogue scale to determine the intensity of the pain. Are the noted results direct inputs from Seth, or do they reflect your observations?"

"A little of both. Mostly, I assigned the assessment based on his reaction. In nearly all cases, he registered a moderate to severe reaction."

Billie looked at the chart in Cat's hand. "You two are talking Greek. Help me understand this chart. What's an analogue scale?"

Cat said, "It's called a visual analogue scale, or VAS. VAS is an instrument that measures a characteristic or an attitude that ranges across a continuum. The values are generally observed rather than actually measured. For example, with the pinprick test that Daddy used on Seth, he recorded the amount of pain Seth apparently felt based on his reaction to the pinprick. The possible reactions range from no pain to severe pain. The VAS is simply a linear representation of that reaction, marked on a horizontal line. More simply put, if someone drew a line on a paper and indicated the left-most extreme represented one, and the right-most extreme represented ten, then asked you to indicate on that ten-point scale, how you felt today, you'd point to a spot on the line that correlated to your feeling. Feeling really good would prompt you to point to a spot on the right side of center."

"I get it," Billie said. "So, for Seth's test, no reaction to the pinprick would be plotted on the left side of the scale and a moderate to severe reaction would be on the right side."

"Exactly," Doc said. "We want all of the results to be as far to the right as possible, which they were."

"In a nutshell," Cat said, "Seth's VAS results indicate no blockage of the sensory neuro-pathways. That's a good thing."

"That's putting it mildly," Doc said. "What it essentially means is that there's no reason Seth can't regain most, if not all, of the sensory functions he had before the accident."

Billie sat back and sighed in relief.

"Anyway," Doc continued, "his pain tolerance is low, his pupils react well to light stimulation, and his involuntary reflexes are good. I also understand the lack of muscle strength and tone, considering he's been inactive for so long. That'll improve with time and strength training. I'm concerned about his lack of coordination, but I need to know how coordinated he was prior to the accident."

Billie grimaced. "Seth was extremely coordinated. In fact, his father, Brian, used to tease him about how he liked to draw and dance. He used to call him a sissy boy and threaten to sign him up for ballet lessons." Billie's eyes filled with tears at the hurtful memories.

Cat began to pace. "That bastard," she said under her breath.

"That's an understatement."

"His own son?" Doc said. "How could he treat him like that?"

Billie heard the disgust in Doc's remarks. "Brian was an abusive drunk. When he discovered I preferred women, he blamed me for what he saw as Seth's flaws. In his mind, my fag genes, as he called them, were the reason Seth was such a talented dancer. He never missed an opportunity to throw it in my face. Brian had many ways of expressing disgust for me, and some of them make the abusive name-calling look like a walk in the park."

"That ignorant son of a bitch." Cat resumed her trek back and forth across the room. Billie addressed Doc once more.

"To answer your question, Seth was very coordinated. Is his current lack of coordination a big problem?"

"As I said, the tests we did today are preliminary. We'll redo some of them and do some new ones in a few days when we're sure the swelling is gone. However, our concerns aren't without merit. If he continues to lack coordination, it may be a problem."

"What could it mean?"

Doc looked up from his clipboard. "Again, the tests are preliminary, but at the very worst, he could come away from this with some degree of permanent brain damage and minor physical disabilities."

"Brain damage?" Billie felt shaken to her core.

"I said that was the worst that could happen. He's awake, alert, and cognitive, and his VAS scores were high, so that's probably not the case, but it's a possibility you might need to prepare yourself to accept."

Billie contemplated Doc's explanation. "Doc, is coordination something that a person's born with, or can it be learned and improved?"

"Most of the time they're born with it. Either they're coordinated, or they're not."

"Yeah, like my superb performance in the first aerobics class I attended," Cat said.

Billie laughed.

"Aerobics class?" Doc asked.

"It's a long story," Billie replied. "You were saying?"

"I was saying that a person can learn to become less clumsy, but it requires constant effort and attention. It's difficult to teach your body to become graceful if you aren't already. On the other hand, if a person loses natural grace through a traumatic injury like Seth's, healthy portions of a damaged brain have been known to compensate and to relearn skills no longer manageable by the damaged portion of the brain. Why do you ask?"

"When Seth was eating his lunch, he had a hell of a time guiding the spoon to his mouth. He had food all over himself, but by the time he got to his pudding, he'd improved remarkably."

Doc rose and put his hand on her shoulder. "That, my dear, either means it's very good pudding, or there's reason to hope. Considering it was hospital food, I tend to believe the latter." He stopped at the door on his way out. "By the way, I'll instruct the nursing staff not to disturb you for the next couple of hours." With a wink, he was gone.

Billie chuckled as Cat covered her pink face with her hands.

As soon as Doc left, Cat resumed her position on Billie's lap. She nuzzled her face deep into Billie's neck and began to nibble on the tender flesh there. Billie moaned and dropped her head to the side to give Cat better access.

"God, you smell good. I love you," Cat said.

"Mmm, love you back."

Billie ran her fingers up and down Cat's arm. "I'm looking forward to making love to you. How much longer before your incision is healed?"

"The doctor said to give it four to six weeks. It's been what—a little more than three?"

"I'm sorry for being so impatient, but I so want to show you what you mean to me."

"Soon, love, soon."

Billie tightened her hold around Cat. "Hmmm, this feels wonderful," Billie said.

"I agree."

"Life is about to take a dramatic turn. I hope you're prepared for that," Billie said.

Cat lifted her head. "I can take whatever life throws at me as long as you're there to help me deal. Speaking of dramatic turns, did Daddy say how much longer Seth would be in the hospital?"

"No, he didn't. But if he's going to do more extensive testing after the swelling goes down, I'm guessing another three or four days at least. Why do you ask?"

"The day after tomorrow is Monday, and if I'm not mistaken, both of us will need to go to work."

"Correction, I need to go to work. You have to get permission from your doctor before you go back. You need to be careful not to push yourself too hard."

"I'll take that under advisement. Like I said, our schedules are about to change significantly."

"You're right. It's an awful thing to say, but after so many months of the same routine, I'm not used to thinking about managing my work schedule around Seth. It was always a given that I'd spend time with him after work and aerobics. It's going to be rough to manage time off for his therapy sessions."

"I swear you've got the shortest memory on the face of this planet," Cat said in a chiding tone.

"What?" Billie wondered what she'd said to get herself into trouble.

"Do the words 'we're in this together' strike a familiar chord? I can arrange to work evenings for the next few months so I'll be able to cover the days with Seth, and you can cover the nights. My job is a lot easier to manipulate than yours. I'll even take him to his therapy sessions. What better way for us to bond? I'll see if the PT clinic can schedule his sessions mid-morning so I can help with his therapy."

"What would your schedule look like?"

"I'd work the four-to-midnight shift. The hospital will be thrilled to have an anesthesiologist available in the emergency room in the evenings for the next several weeks. I'd get home around twelve-thirty. If I get right to bed, I should be able to get up with the kids around eight. I'll drop Tara off at Mom's on the way to Seth's PT sessions and pick her up on the way back home. Of course, that means you'll have to be home around quarter-to-four, so I can get to work on time."

"That shouldn't be a problem. If I have to, I'll bring briefs home with me and work on them in the evenings. Art's a very understanding boss. I'm sure he won't mind."

"It's all set then. I'll check with the PT lab about mid-morning sessions for Seth before we head home today."

"You amaze me, Cat."

"What do you mean?"

"You don't mind completely upending your schedule for Seth?"

"Not at all. I'd do exactly that for a biological child, and if I'm going to be a mother to him, I need to treat him like my son. Let me help you take care of him like you cared for Tara when I was ill."

Billie was at a total loss for words.

"When Seth's out of therapy, I'll switch back to normal hours. After that, we'll need to address the problem of full-time day care, at least until he's ready to go back to school. I certainly don't want to end up with another Gail situation."

"We should think about the day care at the gym," Billie said. "Tara seems to like it there. They have an after-school program, so we might want to consider that as well, once the kids are in school."

"It's settled, then. The only part I don't like about this plan is that you and I will have limited time together until Seth's well," Cat said. "Except for the weekends, that is."

"At least we'll still be able to sleep together," Billie pointed out.

She wrapped her arms around Cat and buried her face in her neck. She sighed contentedly. A slight shudder ran through her as she fought to keep her emotions in check.

Cat pulled out of the embrace and took Billie's face between her hands. "I thought you liked the plan."

"I love the plan. And I love you for thinking of it."

"I'm confused. Why the tears?"

"Seth's father would never make the sacrifices you're about to make on his behalf, yet here you are, practically a stranger to him, and you're willing to turn your life upside down for him. I think Seth and I are the two luckiest people in the world." Billie tucked a strand of hair behind Cat's ear. "I love you more than I've ever loved another human being, besides Seth. I hope I never disappoint you or give you cause to stop loving me."

* * *

Seth's physical therapy baseline assessment was scheduled for four days later. That afternoon, Billie met Cat at the hospital. Together, they helped Doc and the therapists put Seth through a series of tests.

Seth held onto the walker in front of him. His white knuckles indicated how tight he was grasping the aluminum bar. His legs shook as he struggled to remain standing. Billie held fast to the restraining belt around his waist to keep him upright. With each step he took, Billie used her hold on the belt to compensate for his lack of balance.

"It hurts, Mom." Seth began to cry.

Billie knelt down in front of him and brushed the bangs out of his eyes. "I know, love, I know. But if we don't do this, you won't get better, understand?" She wiped the tears from his cheeks and continued, "Please be strong, little man, I know you can do it."

Seth pulled himself up to his full height. "Okay, Mom. I'll try." Determination settled on his face as he pushed the walker to the other side of the room where Cat waited for him. When he reached her, Cat pulled him into her arms.

"Great job. I knew you could do it. I'm so very proud of you."

For the next couple of hours, Seth was poked, prodded, contorted, and manipulated in an attempt to measure his agility level. It was after 11:00 a.m. when Billie carried him back to his room. He fell asleep in her arms on the walk down the hallway.

"He's a beautiful child," Cat said as she tucked the covers around him.

Billie nodded. "At times, he was my only reason for living. Knowing he depended on me was what kept me going."

"Was it really that bad?"

Billie opened her arms to Cat and reveled in the contact as Cat wrapped her arms around Billie's waist. "Someday I'll tell you about it. I promise."

"Hmmm. I wish I could stay like this forever, but I need to spend some time with Tara before I go to work this afternoon."

"Oh, I almost forgot. Doc said it's all right to have our McDonald's picnic today. Do you think you can take a break from the ER around six-thirty? I'll leave to pick Tara up from your mom's around five and swing into McDonald's on the way back. Heck, I think I'll ask Ida to come along. Doc will order a light snack for Seth mid-afternoon, and that should hold him over until dinner."

Cat grinned. "You're such a soft touch, Billie Charland. I've never seen someone wrapped so tightly around the little fingers of two small tykes. I can see who's going to have to be the tough parent in this family."

"Guilty as charged," Billie admitted. "Do you think you can get away for about an hour?"

"I wouldn't miss it for the world."

"Good. Go enjoy time with your daughter, and I'll see you tonight." Billie stole one more kiss and slapped Cat on the bottom as she left the room.

Chapter 12

Tara's eyes opened wide when Billie directed her car into the parking lot of the fast food restaurant and pulled around to the drive-up window. "We're having McDonald's tonight?"

"Grandpa says that Seth can have solid food, so we're going to have a picnic in his room. How does that sound?"

"Yay!"

Billie glanced at Ida in the passenger seat. "That granddaughter of yours has a bottomless pit for a stomach."

"Don't I know it," Ida replied. "Caitlain was the same way at her age. She used to ask for food everywhere we went, even from complete strangers. She used to embarrass me so."

Billie, Ida, and Tara entered Seth's room, arms loaded with burgers, fries, nuggets, sodas, and apple pies. Seth was on the bed clicking through the TV channels with the remote control. He shut off the TV when they entered with their treasure. "McDonald's!"

Billie put the bags of food on the dresser and gathered Seth into her arms. "I missed you, scout."

"Where do you want to eat?" Ida asked.

"Why don't I hand Seth off to you, and I'll spread that blanket across the bed?" Billie pointed to the blanket folded at the foot of Seth's bed.

Seth went into Ida's arms. "How's my favorite grandson today?" Ida asked. "Your mom told me about your therapy session this morning. I understand you worked very hard."

"Yeah. It was really hard to walk across the room, but I did it."

"You keep that up, and you'll be as good as new in no time."

"Can we eat now, Grammy?" Seth asked.

Cat came into the room just as Seth spoke. "It looks like our grocery bill is about to skyrocket with two eating machines in the house."

Billie's attention was drawn to the doorway when she heard Cat's voice. She raised her eyebrows high onto her forehead.

"Two?" she questioned as she remembered the extensive breakfast Cat ate on their first visit to Rose's.

"All right, three. Let's eat. I'm starved," Cat said.

"Me, too," the children chimed in.

Billie spread the blanket across the bed and sat against the headboard with Seth between her legs. Doc arrived in time to help Cat move the food from the dresser to the blanket. Cat sat in a chair near the foot of the bed.

"I have good news for you. It appears the road to recovery isn't as long as I originally anticipated."

"Really?" Billie asked.

"Really. The results of yesterday's assessment are better than expected." Doc looked at Seth. "It looks like you can go home in a week or so, but first we need to put together a therapy schedule for you. Cat, I understand you've rearranged your work schedule so you can help with Seth's therapy sessions. While he's still here in the hospital, it might be a good idea for you to learn the massages and routines so you'll be ready for him when he goes home." Doc reviewed the information in Seth's folder. "It says here his sessions will be at ten in the morning."

"I know. I asked the clinic to schedule them at that time so I could help," Cat said.

"Will he be able to go to school next fall?" Billie asked.

"I don't see why not. I expect he'll make rapid progress once his therapy begins."

"Will we be focusing on strength building and balance, or will his exercises include stretching, joint control, and muscle re-training?" Cat asked.

"All of the above. As to when they're introduced into the PT routine, that all depends on his progress. He'll need to do his routines daily at home, and he'll still need to come to the hospital three days a week for specialized therapy."

Doc addressed Seth once more. "So, scout, are you up for the challenge? I won't lie to you. It will be hard work, but I'm betting you're one tough trouper."

Seth nodded around a mouth full of French fries. "I'll work hard, Grandpa. I promise."

By the time their picnic was over, they had a plan and several willing players.

Doc rose and kissed Ida on the check. "I must excuse myself. I'm covering for a colleague and have rounds to make. Seth, I'll check in on you before I go home."

"What time to you think that'll be, dear?" Ida asked.

Doc looked at his watch. "I should be ready to go within the next hour. If you think you'll still be here, I'll swing by to collect you. That will save Billie a detour on her way home."

"That'll work," Ida replied.

After Doc left, Billie transferred Seth into Cat's lap so she could collect the food wrappers and discard them in the trash. She returned to Seth and Cat and put her arms out to take Seth from Cat's arms.

"No, let me walk to the bed" he said.

Billie looked at Cat over Seth's shoulder. "Should he be doing this yet?"

"If he's willing and able, we should let him. His effort to walk is no more traumatic than what he went through in the PT clinic this afternoon." Cat looked at Seth. "Don't let go of Mom's hands. You'll need to stand for a while to re-learn your balance."

Seth lowered his feet to the floor and slowly shifted himself into a standing position. Cat remained behind him with her hands on his hips.

"Grammy, look at me," Seth said. "I'm standing up."

Ida clapped her hands. "I'm so proud of you."

"Yay!" Tara cheered as Seth stood on his own two feet. "Are Seth's booboo legs fixed, Mama?"

"Not yet, honey, but they're definitely getting better."

Billie grasped his hands and held them as he steadied himself. Her smile was infectious as she noted the look of pride on Seth's face. "You're one awesome kid, Seth. I'm so proud of you. Let me know when you've had enough, and I'll carry you to the bed."

"No. I want to walk."

Again Billie looked at Cat, who nodded her approval.

Tara scurried onto the bed and stood in the middle of it. She clapped her hands as Seth walked slowly across the room.

With Billie taking mini steps backward and Cat holding onto Seth's hips from behind, the trio made their way to the side of the bed. It took nearly five minutes to travel a distance of about six feet. Seth was shaking by the time he sat on the edge of the bed. As soon as he sat down, Tara wrapped her arms around his neck from behind. Seth grinned ear to ear.

"Way to go, dude." Billie put her hand up for a high-five.

Cat sat on the bed beside him and wrapped her arm around his shoulder. "You're very brave to do that so soon. You did a super job."

Seth yawned.

"Wow, it's almost eight o'clock. It's been a long day for you," Cat said.

"Scout, why don't we tuck you in and you can watch cartoons with Tara for a bit," Billie said. "I want to visit with Cat and Grammy for a while."

Doc stepped into the room. "That didn't take as long as I thought. It looks like we can call it an early evening."

"Rounds over already?" Ida asked. "I guess we can head home, then."

Doc and Ida kissed both grandchildren good night, then bid Cat and Billie good night as well.

While the children lay side-by-side, Billie and Cat cuddled in a chair together. Within minutes, Tara drifted off to sleep. A short time later, Seth's eyes began to droop.

"Poor thing," Billie said. "He's done more in this one day than he has in nine months. I'm afraid he's going to be pretty sore tomorrow."

"Perhaps. You know, you should probably get Tara home to bed. I need to get back to the ER."

"Hopefully you'll have a quiet evening."

"I don't know about that. There's a full moon tonight. That's when all the nuts and squirrels come out. It never fails. Emergency room cases appear to increase when the moon's full, so who knows what my evening will be like."

"What do you do when you don't have surgeries to anesthetize?"

"I help out where I can. I'm an anesthesiologist by training, but I'm also qualified for general medicine. Staying busy makes the nights go by faster, and it never hurts to have an extra doctor available when there's an emergency." Cat looked at Seth and realized he was on the edge of sleep. "I want to say good night to Seth before he falls asleep."

Cat tucked the blanket around Seth's chest and kissed him on the cheek. "Be a good guy tonight. I'll stop in later and check on you." Cat wrapped her arms around Seth and hugged him. "I love you, big guy," she whispered in his ear.

"I love you, too, Mama," he whispered back.

Cat kissed Tara on the cheek then took Billie's hand and led her out into the hall where she leaned against the wall. She pressed her hands into her chest over her heart and looked up into Billie's eyes through unshed tears.

The tears overflowed and rolled down Cat's cheeks. Alarmed, Billie put her hands on either side of Cat's face. "What's wrong?"

"Nothing's wrong. Everything is oh, so right."

"Why the tears?"

"Did you hear him? I whispered that I loved him, and he answered, 'I love you, too, Mama.' He called me Mama. He said he loved me, too. God, this is such an incredible feeling."

Billie pulled Cat into a tight embrace and held her before they pulled apart. She wiped the tears from Cat's face. "I want you to wake me when you get home tonight so we can celebrate this milestone together."

"Okay."

Billie kissed Cat one more time and wiped the final remnants of tears from her face before Cat left to return to work.

Billie kissed her sleeping child. "I'll see you after work tomorrow. Sleep tight. I love you." She gathered Tara in her arms and headed for home.

Billie looked into the rearview mirror at Tara in the back of the car as she waited for the light to change. The sight of the vulnerable sleeping child touched her heart and made her realize that Tara would probably be taking a backseat to Seth for the next several months. She imagined how that might hurt Tara, so she resolved to include her in all aspects of Seth's recovery and to make special time for her—time that would belong to her alone.

Billie carried Tara into the apartment and to her room where she put her to bed.

*   *   *

A little after midnight, Cat let herself into the apartment. She'd spent the entire evening filled with anticipation about her time alone with Billie. She dropped her keys on the coffee table and her coat on the couch and quietly entered Tara's room. She tiptoed over to the bed and sat on the edge. "You're going to be a wonderful little sister to Seth," she whispered. Cat kissed her cheek. "Sleep well, little one. I love you."

In the hall, a soft glow showed under the door of her own room. As she walked closer, she heard the faint strains of music. Wild anticipation filled her as she reached for the doorknob. She pushed the door open and scanned the room. Several scented candles, positioned around the room, cast a seductive glow over everything. Classical music played softly from the stereo on the dresser, and two partially filled wine glasses sat waiting on the nightstand. Of all the amenities the room had to offer, none was more appealing than the central figure that caught Cat's eye, a beautiful vision in a see-through black negligee, sleeping on the bed. Cat leaned against the doorframe and crossed her arms in front of her. She sighed and felt a rush of love fill her heart.

As quietly as she could, she closed the door and walked toward the bed. Her entire body throbbed with desire for the sleeping beauty before her. For many reasons, including her own recovery from surgery and outright exhaustion at the end of each day, she and Billie had yet to make love. She removed her clothing and climbed onto the bed. She gently lowered herself on top of Billie and felt her stir under the pressure of her body.

"Cat," Billie said. "You're home."

Cat loved how raspy sounding Billie's voice was when she first awoke.

Billie ran her hands over Cat's back and down across her bottom. "Hmmm, you're naked. You should've let me help you with that."

"I wanted to surprise you. What better way than with naked flesh?"

"You're an evil woman," Billie said. "You're home early."

"Yes. Things weren't as busy as they normally are during a full moon. It appears the gremlins stayed home all night having wild monkey sex instead of enticing the crazies to be out and about hurting themselves."

Billie chuckled. "You're very funny. Unfortunately, my plans to wait up for you fell victim to a long and emotionally tiring day. I'm sorry, love. I wanted to surprise you with music, wine, and seduction, but I pooped out."

Cat kissed the end of Billie's nose. "Well, the music is still playing, and the time is always right for seduction," she said as she lowered her mouth to Billie's.

Billie's lips parted at the insistence of Cat's tongue. One of Billie's arms wrapped around Cat and pulled her close as the other hand sought the back of her head.

Billie pulled back, ending the kiss. "Your hair's wet."

"Messy surgery. I showered at work. Now shut up and make love to me."

"Yes, ma'am."

Cat pushed the spaghetti straps of Billie's negligee off her shoulders. "Take it off. Please."

Billie shifted from under Cat, brought her knees under her, and knelt over Cat, straddling her naked body. Cat's breathing became ragged as she watched Billie peel the negligee off her body and throw it to the floor. Billie threw her head back and ran her hands over her own breasts and abdomen. Her right hand slipped into the curls guarding her treasure.

Cat sat up and wrapped her arms around Billie's body. "God, I've wanted to do this from the moment I laid eyes on you. You're so beautiful. I need you," she said and took one of Billie's nipples into her mouth.

"Ah! God. That feels so good." Billie captured Cat's head between her hands.

Cat quickly shifted her attention to Billie's other breast where she feasted hungrily. Her own desire was raging nearly out of control as she struggled with herself to be gentle with the tender morsel between her teeth. She felt tremors run through Billie as she slipped two fingers into the folds hidden by the dark brown triangle. Billie doubled over and grasped Cat's shoulders for support. She pushed Cat away.

Cat looked at her questioningly. "Billie?"

Billie pushed Cat back onto the bed. She stretched her long frame out over the length of Cat's body and looked directly at her. "I love you, Cat."

"Why did you stop me?"

"Because it's happening too fast. I'm so turned on I wouldn't have lasted another minute. This is our first time. I want it to last forever."

Billie kissed her, and Cat moaned as Billie's mouth broke contact and roamed lower. Cat's desire grew into a state of sexual madness as Billie used her mouth to tease, bite, and caress Cat's skin. Later, pushed almost over the edge by Billie's foreplay, Cat demanded fulfillment. "Now, Billie. I need you now."

Billie filled Cat to the core as she plunged deep into her while continuing to suckle Cat's engorged bud. Suddenly, the room was filled with loud cries of release as Cat climaxed. Cat felt Billie's hand cover her mouth to stifle cries loud enough to raise the dead.

Billie enveloped Cat in her arms while the trembling subsided.

"You, my dear, will have to learn to tone it down," Billie said.

Cat grinned at Billie. "It's your fault, you know." With an evil look, Cat shifted her weight so that she was lying on top of Billie. "Let's see if I can make you scream."

Cat had the upper hand as she nipped at Billie's neck. Billie's hips raised in response, lifting Cat right off the bed.

"I'm not sure how long I can hold out. I nearly fell over the edge along with you," Billie said.

"Be patient, my love. I want to savor every moment." One at a time, Cat caressed Billie's swollen nipples with her tongue and sucked them into her mouth over and over. Billie arched her chest. A spasm caused her pelvis to flex. "God, Cat. I need you."

Cat saw the raw emotion in Billie's eyes and almost lost her resolve to make her wait as long as possible. "Not yet, my love." Cat's voice was husky as she lowered her mouth to Billie's breasts once more.

Billie pushed downward on Cat's shoulders.

Cat smiled at Billie. "Patience, love. I promise it will be worth the wait."

Cat ran her tongue around Billie's navel while she cupped Billie's womanhood. Her tongue meandered across Billie's abdomen to a tender spot above her hip. Cat bit down hard as she drove three fingers deep into her, bending them upward as she massaged the sponge-like spot. Billie succumbed to the orgasmic waves. Her body convulsed as Cat pressed into her. After what seemed like an eternity to Cat, Billie's body slowly relaxed and became still, save for her ragged breathing.

Cat climbed on top of Billie. "Is it safe to uncover your mouth?"

Billie nodded her head as Cat removed her hand. "Touché, love… touché."

Chapter 13

For the next week, Cat helped with Seth's physical therapy routine during the mornings, spent time with Tara in the middle part of the day, and worked in the evenings. Billie worked during the day and spent her evenings caring for Tara and visiting with Seth. On Friday, Seth was discharged from the hospital. Billie took the day off from work to celebrate the momentous occasion with her new family.

She stepped out of the shower that morning and towel-dried her hair in front of the bathroom mirror while Cat finished rinsing. She gazed into the mirror. *You look happy, Charland. Is that a sparkle in your eyes? I haven't seen that for months.* She smiled and a wave of happiness washed over her.

As Billie dragged a comb through her hair, she addressed Cat. "You know, so much has changed in my life over the past few months. So many good things have happened. I met you and fell hopelessly in love. I have Seth back, and now he's coming home. There's so much to be grateful for, and it's all because of you."

"You give me more credit than I deserve." Cat turned off the shower and slid the door open.

Billie handed her a towel as she stepped onto the bathmat.

"Thank you." Cat quickly wiped the moisture from her face and hair. As she dried herself, she looked at Billie. "What, may I ask, is that grin for?"

Billie's grin broadened. "Damn, you're cute, especially stark naked with your hair arranged so beautifully."

"What do you mean?"

"Take a look. It's sticking out at several odd angles. Very cute indeed."

Cat looked into the mirror. "Ha, ha, very funny."

"Yes, it is. I can see that smile you're trying to hide. Tell me it isn't funny."

Cat snapped the towel across Billie's bottom.

"Why you little imp!" Billie said as she chased Cat out of the bathroom.

* * *

Cat and Tara followed Billie into Seth's room. Billie took one look at him and knew he was ready to go home. He sat on the edge of the bed and held himself erect by a firm grasp on the footboard. A bag of personal belongings he'd accumulated over the months in the hospital, including stuffed animals and the pictures Tara had colored for him, was tucked under the other arm. Tara climbed onto the bed and sat next to him.

"I'm ready, Mom. Let's go," he declared.

"Right after I check with Grandpa for any special instructions."

"Aw, Mom."

Cat ruffled his hair. "She's right. I'll tell you what, I'll go look for Grandpa to see if he has time to speak with us."

Billie knelt on one knee in front of Seth. "Are you excited to go home?"

"Yeah. It's pretty boring here. I can't wait to see my new room."

"Do you want to play dolls with me when we get home?" Tara asked.

"I don't play with dolls," Seth said. "That's girl stuff."

Cat returned with Doc in tow. "Look who was already on his way to see you."

Doc shoved his hands deep into his lab coat pockets and looked over the rim of his glasses. "I understand there's someone in this room who's anxious to go home. You wouldn't happen to know who that is, would you?"

Seth raised his hand and waved it rapidly, as though he had the answer to a particularly easy question at school.

Doc laughed. "I can't imagine why you'd want to leave. Why, it's only been, what—nine months?"

Seth threw his hands out as if to make a point. "Grandpa, that's like, my whole life." They all laughed.

"I suppose we can let you out on good behavior, but you still have a lot of hard work ahead of you before you're fully recovered. Are you up to it?"

Seth nodded. "I am. I am."

"Cat, Billie, here are a list of rules Seth will have to follow if he's to have a full recovery." Doc handed them a package of papers that contained Seth's therapy schedule and routine, along with his discharge papers. He lifted Seth into his arms and gave him a bear hug before he handed him over to his mother. "You and I, young sir, have a fishing date. Let's give a couple of weeks of therapy a chance to get you stronger. When you're ready, we'll see about drowning a few worms."

"Can I go, too, Grandpa?" Tara asked.

Doc looked down at Tara and extended his arms to her, which she quickly entered. He tweaked her nose. "Are you kidding? Scout and I plan to use you for bait."

"Grandpa!" Tara whined as laughter broke out around her.

Cat retrieved a wheelchair while Doc went over Seth's discharge paperwork with Billie. Lying in the seat of the wheelchair was a child-sized aluminum walker. "Here are your wheels, champ."

Cat removed the walker and wheeled the chair to Seth's bedside. "How long will he need to use the chair?"

"It will depend on how fast he recovers. If you're going any great distance, shopping for example, he should use the chair, at least for the next couple of weeks. If he's making good progress, he can migrate to the walker. He'll need some sort of four-point support until he regains his sense of balance."

"And at home?" Billie asked.

"At home, you can let him get around in any manner he prefers... the chair, the walker, holding on to furniture. He can even crawl around, if he likes. Any and all movement will enhance his muscle tone and speed his recovery."

Cat locked the wheels on the chair, helped Seth to his feet, and settled him in the large chair.

"Can I ride, too?" Tara asked.

Seth slid over to make room for her.

With Doc's help, checkout was accomplished quickly, after which, they went to the park to enjoy a picnic lunch. Cat and Tara ran ahead to spread the blanket and lay out the food under a big oak tree while Billie retrieved Seth's wheelchair from the trunk and helped him transfer into it. Billie discovered how difficult it is to push a wheelchair across the grass but thought the alternative of carrying him across the park would embarrass him, so she put her back into the chore and pushed their way to the blanket.

Billie slid her hands under Seth's arms to help him out of the wheelchair.

"Mom, I want to do this myself."

Billie stood by and anxiously watched as Seth climbed out of the chair and fell onto the blanket. She darted forward to help, but Cat stopped her.

"No, let him do it," Cat said.

Billie saw that Seth was unharmed, so she stepped back and released the breath she was holding.

Cat whispered into Billie's ear, "Relax. He needs to feel independent. Let him do as much as possible for himself."

Tara dug the bag of coloring books and crayons out of Cat's duffle and knelt on the blanket beside Seth. "Wanna color with me?"

"Sure."

Tara dumped the coloring books and crayons onto the blanket. Both children lay on their stomachs and chose a book.

"I'll color a picture for you to put on the fridge," Seth said to Billie.

"Me, too," Tara said.

"That'll be great." Billie nodded to them.

"Let us know when you get hungry, okay?" Cat said to the kids.

"Okay, Mama."

Cat rested her back against a tree while Billie reclined on the blanket and laid her head in Cat's lap. They opened the books they'd brought with them and settled in to read.

* * *

After their picnic lunch, Cat and Billie took the children shopping to purchase new clothes for Seth. In preparation for their move to Cat's condo, Billie went through all of Seth's clothing and realized he'd grown enough during his hospitalization that most of it no longer fit him.

While they shopped, Cat noticed a man staring at them. She made eye contact and thought there was something familiar about him before she panicked and quickly looked away. Cat located Tara and assured herself that she was near by. "Tara, don't wander off. Stay close." She tugged on Billie's arm. "Billie, that man over there is giving me the creeps."

Billie looked in the direction Cat pointed. "What man?"

Cat looked again, but he was gone. "Oh well, it must've been my imagination."

As they continued shopping, Billie made sure Tara received as many items as Seth to prevent her from feeling left out. They loaded the bags into the back of the car, and Cat touched the side of Billie's face. "Thank you, love."

"For what?"

"For thinking about Tara. You're quite a softy, you know."

"I don't want her to feel displaced. It's going to be tough enough having to share us with Seth. It'll even be harder when she realizes Seth will require our attention more than she will for the time being."

"Regardless. Thank you for thinking of her."

"You're welcome."

* * *

It took two trips from the car to the apartment to take in all their packages. Cat waited in the car with the children while Billie made the trips inside. Finally, it was time for Seth to see his new home. Billie pushed his wheelchair into the apartment and locked the wheels to allow Seth to safely climb out of it. She stood behind him and held him up as he slowly walked around and looked at everything. Tara jumped up and down next to him as Billie showed him the bathroom, her and Cat's bedroom, and Tara's room. She saved his room for last. Tara scampered inside Seth's room ahead of them and climbed onto the bed while Cat stood in the doorway and leaned against the door casing.

Seth looked around his room. The walls were mint green and decorated with a race car motif. A racetrack border circled the room at chair-rail height, and matching curtains and bedspread completed the decor. All of his toys and books from their old apartment lay neatly placed around the room.

Seth's eyes grew wide. "Oh wow! I love race cars, Mom. This is great."

Billie helped Seth sit down on the bed, facing the doorway. "You have Mama to thank for this. She spent a lot of time making this room special for you."

Seth extended his arms to Cat. Cat crossed the room and hugged him. "Thanks, Mama."

Cat sat on the bed beside him. "You're welcome. We're going to work on Tara's room next weekend, if you'd like to help."

"Yeah, Seth," Tara piped in. "We're putting Cinderella on my walls."

"Yeah, cool," Seth replied.

Billie chuckled to herself as his tone of voice and rolling eyes made it clear he thought Cinderella was pretty dumb.

For the rest of the afternoon, the children played in each other's rooms or watched cartoons on TV while Billie and Cat put their new purchases away. Seth moved from room to room mostly by crawling around the floor, with Tara on all fours right behind him.

Cat commented that it was time for her to get ready for work. "I'd so rather be home tonight with my new family. I'm pretty jealous, you know. I'm glad today's Friday. At least I'll get the next two nights off."

Billie lowered her forehead to Cat's. "I know. But it will only be for a few more weeks."

"Yeah, you're right." Cat looked at her watch. It was nearly three o'clock. "Geesh, I'd better get dressed. You're going to the gym tonight, right?"

"Yes. It's my first night back. It's going to feel odd taking the aerobics class instead of teaching it, but I couldn't expect them to hold the teaching position for me when I wasn't sure when I could recommit myself to it."

"What are you going to do with the kids?"

"I'll drop them off in the day care at the gym."

"Do you think Seth is up to it? It's been a pretty busy day for him."

"He'll be fine. It's only for an hour, and it will give him a chance to socialize with other kids. Trust me, it'll be fine."

"All right."

"Now, go get dressed or you'll be late for work."

Cat saluted Billie. "Yes, ma'am."

Billie closed the bedroom door behind Cat and looked at the two children on the floor in front of the TV. "We don't need to leave for the gym for another two-and-a-half hours. What do you two rug rats want to do until then?"

The children shouted in unison. "Watch Barney!"

Billie groaned. "Oh great. Purple monster time."

* * *

Billie dropped Tara and Seth off at the gym's day care. Before leaving for her class, she spent several moments with the day-care provider to discuss Seth's condition.

"Hi, Becky. This is my son, Seth."

Becky extended her hand to him. "Hi, Seth."

"Seth is my big brother," Tara said.

Becky raised her eyebrows. "Really?"

"Seth doesn't have any restrictions. He'll probably climb out of his chair and get around mostly by crawling. He's pretty independent, so you should let him do for himself unless he asks for help."

"Got it. Don't worry about him. I'm sure things will be fine."

"Seth, Tara, have a good time and behave for Becky. I'll be back to get you in an hour."

After class, Billie went to collect the children. Tara was sitting in a chair, holding a cloth with ice in it to her lip. Seth was on the floor playing with race cars. Billie went to Tara to inspect the damage. She had a slightly split lip. She asked Becky what had happened.

Before Becky answered, Tara piped in. "It's his fault, Mom." She pointed to a boy who sat in the opposite corner with his hands crossed in front of his chest.

Billie noted the pouty look on his face and the bruise around the boy's left eye.

"He was mean to Seth. He called him a cripple, so I punched him, and he punched me back," Tara said.

Billie looked at Tara. *Did she call me Mom?* "Tara, I'm very proud of you for defending your brother, but hitting isn't always the answer. The next time something like this happens, promise me you'll tell the teacher."

Tara pouted. "All right, I promise."

Billie lifted Tara's chin and kissed her on the cheek. "Why don't you get ready while I see to Seth?"

Tara nodded and went to get her shoes on. Billie tried to hide her mirth as she saw Tara scowl and raise her fist at the boy in the corner on her way across the room.

Billie bent down and picked Seth up. He wrapped his legs around her waist and held onto her neck.

"Hey, scout. Are you all right?"

"Yeah, I'm okay. But I wish I'd have punched the guy out myself instead of Tara. It's kind of embarrassing to have your little sister fight for you."

"You know it's because she loves you, right?"

"I know, but it's still embarrassing."

"Seth, very soon you'll be as good as new and you'll be able to take care of yourself. In the meantime, be proud that you have people who are willing to stand up for you. Who knows, some day you may be able to return the favor."

"Okay." Seth kissed her on the cheek and hugged her hard.

Billie sat Seth in a chair and handed him his shoes while she got his wheelchair ready. Seth climbed in and made room for Tara beside him.

Billie loaded the children into the car. "How does spaghetti sound for dinner?"

She heard a chorus of cheers as she headed to the nearest Italian restaurant.

* * *

Cat was never so happy to see the end of her shift. She'd had an especially traumatic evening with several emergencies that required surgery, including a small child who'd been critically injured in a car accident. None of her medical training prepared her for dealing with the heartbreak of seeing a small child in such desperate need. As an anesthesiologist, she could only assure the child was in no pain and that her vital signs remained stable during surgery.

She hung around a little longer than necessary to check on the child's progress and, as a result, left the hospital more than an hour after her shift ended. As she made her way through the dark parking lot to her car, she felt she was being watched. Halfway through the parking lot, she stopped and looked around. Fear crept up her spine like a caterpillar. The hair along the back of her neck stood on end as she quickly climbed into her car and pushed the lever to lock all the doors. As she left the parking lot, she scanned the area to make sure she wasn't being followed and drove home as fast as she dared.

She parked behind the condo, ran to the building, and bolted up the three flights of stairs to her unit. She didn't feel safe until she'd slipped inside and locked the door. She threw her keys on the kitchen table and went straight to the bathroom where she splashed water on her face. That was the creepiest feeling. Someone was watching her. She was sure of it.

After she checked on the kids, she tiptoed into her bedroom. She peeled off her clothes and got into bed beside Billie. As she wrapped her arms around Billie's waist, she couldn't keep herself from shivering. Billie stirred beside her.

"Go back to sleep, love. I'm sorry I woke you," Cat said.

Billie gathered Cat into her arms. "You're shivering. What's wrong?"

Cat didn't want to alarm Billie with her overactive imagination. "Nothing. Everything's fine. I'm just cold."

Cat felt Billie's arms tighten around her.

"Better?" Billie asked.

"Oh, yeah, much better. How was your evening?"

"Everything was fine until Tara decided to punch out a bully at the day care," Billie explained. Cat heard the mirth in her voice.

"What?"

"Yeah, there was this boy at the day care who made fun of Seth's disability, so Tara punched him." Billie chuckled.

"That isn't funny." Cat fought to keep a grin off her own face.

"Well, he punched her back, and he split her lip a little bit, so I think she's learned her lesson about fighting, but I'm pleased that she's so protective of Seth."

"What am I going to do with the lot of you?"

"Don't worry about it. Things like this have a way of working themselves out. In no time, the three of them will be playing like they're best friends." Billie paused. "So, how was your evening?"

Cat sighed. "Long and traumatic. We had emergency surgery tonight on a little girl who was injured in a car accident. The parents should be put in jail for not having her in a car seat."

"I hear you. I've assisted in court cases similar to that where parents have been prosecuted for reckless endangerment."

"It makes me sad for that little girl to know it could've been avoided."

"You have such a soft heart. That's one of the things I love most about you."

Cat snuggled into Billie's embrace. "Hmmm... I'm not the only softie in this family. By the way, how was Seth tonight?"

"Exhausted. I took them out for spaghetti after my aerobics class, and he fell asleep on the way home. He's not used to so much activity."

"You took them out for spaghetti? Man, they're going to hate to see me return to normal hours."

"They'd hate it even more if they had to eat my cooking. Oh, and we brought some home for you. It's in the fridge. You can have it for lunch tomorrow, or should I say today?"

Cat yawned.

"You're tired, poor baby. Sleep well, my love. I love you."

"Love you, too."

Billie drifted back to sleep, and Cat lay in her arms feeling safe and warm but very much awake. She couldn't get the feeling of being watched out of her mind. She lay awake all night, wondering what, if anything, she should do. She feigned sleep when Billie rose at seven a.m.

* * *

Thank God for the weekend, Billie thought as she awoke. Cat was curled up beside her. She carefully climbed out of bed and used the adjoining bathroom. She'd intended to rejoin Cat, but noises coming from the kitchen gave her cause to investigate. Billie slipped a football jersey over her head then closed the bedroom door behind her on her way out. In the kitchen, she found the two kids sitting at the table, enjoying a breakfast of cookies and potato chips.

Billie learned against the doorframe and crossed her arms.

"Hi, Mom," the kids said together.

"Come have some breakfast with us," Seth added as he shoved several chips into his mouth.

Billie sat down and grabbed a cookie. She shook it at them in mock sternness. "You know, Mama will kill me for letting you guys eat this junk for breakfast."

"We won't tell her," Tara said.

"Won't tell me what?" a voice asked from behind them.

"Busted," Billie said as the kids giggled.

Billie looked guilty as Cat reached over her for the bag of chips.

"We'll talk about this later," she whispered in Billie's ear.

The kids moaned in unison. "Aw, Mama."

Cat frowned at them. "I don't want to hear it. You're both old enough to know better." Cat put the chips into the cupboard then faced the kids. "How about some pancakes?"

"With blueberries?" Seth asked.

"Blueberries it is."

Billie chuckled as she came up behind Cat at the counter and wrapped her arms around her. "Now who's the softy?"

"Don't you think for one moment that sweet-talking me is going to get you off the hook."

"Can't blame a girl for trying." Billie planted a kiss on Cat's cheek and scooted away in time to avoid a wet dishcloth across the face.

"Missed me!" Billie set the coffeepot up while Cat prepared pancake batter. "I thought you were sleeping when I got out of bed."

"I've tossed and turned since I got into bed last night. Maybe I'll be able to nap after breakfast."

Billie felt Cat's forehead. "Are you all right?"

Cat nodded. "Yeah. Apparently, last night's trauma with that little girl keyed me up. I'll be fine after I get some sleep."

* * *

After breakfast, Cat reminded Billie that it was time for Seth's therapy session.

"Cat, you need to get some sleep. We can do his therapy later in the day."

"No. The caffeine has kicked in, and I'm wide-awake now, so we might as well get it out of the way. And besides, it's Saturday and I can sleep in tomorrow."

"You're the boss," Billie said.

"And don't you forget it. Seth, time for PT," she called into the living room.

Seth groaned. "Do we have to?"

Billie felt sorry for him and took Cat aside. "Maybe we can cut him some slack and skip the therapy for today."

Cat massaged her forehead with her hand. "Billie, he hates his therapy, and I don't blame him, but if we don't do it, he won't get better. I'm sorry if this sounds harsh, but if we give in to his pouting, it will only get worse."

"But it hurts him."

"Don't you think I know that?" Cat replied in a loud voice.

Cat saw the kids react to her harsh tone. She turned her back to the living room and invited Billie to join her at the sink.

"Look," Cat said. "I know it hurts him. Do you think I enjoy doing it? I've spent a lot of time trying to harden my heart to his protests. I hate it. My heart breaks every time he cries."

Billie sighed and closed her eyes. "I'm sorry. I didn't realize how much it takes out of you. You're right, we can't give in." Billie kissed the top of her head. "I want you to show me how to do the therapy. There's no reason you have to do this on your own. It's bad enough you have to deal with it all week. The least I can do is take over for you on the weekends."

"Are you sure you want to do this? It isn't pleasant."

"I'm sure."

Seth's therapy was segmented so that the first hour focused on upper body exercises and the last hour on lower body. Near the end of the session while Billie massaged the kinks out of Seth's legs, Cat went to fill the whirlpool tub with warm water. She returned carrying Seth's and Tara's bathing suits. She dropped Seth's trunks onto his chest. "Hey, big guy, how about a dip?"

Seth looked astonished and his eyes grew big and round. "Dip? Where?" he asked.

"You get that suit on, and let me worry about where." She turned to Tara. "Hey, scamp, do you want to join your brother?"

As soon as the words left her mouth, Tara was naked.

"Tara O'Grady. Do you have any modesty at all?" Cat asked.

"I see her appetite isn't the only thing she inherited from her mother," Billie said.

Cat faced Billie with her hands on her hips. "Is that a complaint, Ms. Charland?"

"Oh, no, don't get me wrong. I'm kind of partial to exhibitionists. Honest, I am." Billie scooped Seth up and took him into the bathroom to help him change.

Seth and Tara sat in the tub, up to their chests in warm water.

Cat poured a few drops of bubble bath in front of each whirlpool jet. "Ready?"

Cat saw the anticipation on Seth's face as he waited for what was to come.

"Count it down with me... four... three... two... one." They all counted together as Cat hit the jet-stream button. The water came to life and churned around the two small bodies. Seth and Tara shrieked with joy as the mountain of bubbles began to grow. Billie and Cat stood in the doorway and grinned at their excitement.

Cat stood on tiptoes and whispered in Billie's ear, "How about a nice hot cup of coffee?"

Billie wrapped her arms around Cat's waist and kissed her forehead. "Sounds great."

"You did really well with Seth's therapy," Cat said. "I know it's hard for you, but really, you did well."

"Thanks."

Cat looked at the children. "I'm going to make lunch while you're enjoying the water. You've got about a half hour to play. Try not to get water on the floor."

"Okay, Mama," the children replied.

Later, at the lunch table, Billie nudged Cat. "Look at them."

Both struggled to stay awake.

"Poor things. I think playing in the tub tired them out," Cat said.

"Not to mention Seth's therapy."

"Nap time," Cat announced.

At Tara's insistence, Billie tucked them both into Seth's bed, where they quickly fell asleep. After a busy morning, Cat and Billie enjoyed some much-needed time alone in each other's arms.

Chapter 14

On Monday morning, Billie dragged herself out of bed to get ready for work. Before she left, she made the rounds of the bedrooms, kissed each of the kids, and slipped out the door. Halfway to her car, she stopped and looked around. She had the odd sensation of being watched. She chalked it up to paranoia and set off to work.

Billie called home midday to check in with Cat. "Hey, love. How's your day going?"

"Not bad. The kids just finished their bubble bath and are having lunch. I think I'll take advantage of their nap time to catch a few winks myself. I'm beat."

"I wish I could be there with you. But there wouldn't be much sleeping."

Cat snickered. "You're incorrigible. Do me a favor and don't ever change."

"I've been this way for nearly thirty years, not much chance of change at this point. I'll take a rain check on that nap if that's all right with you."

"I'll have to check my schedule to see when I have an opening," Cat joked.

"I'm sure your secretary can clear your schedule for me."

"I think that can be arranged."

"Off to bed with you. I'll see you when you get home after work. I love you."

"I love you, too. Bye."

The phone rang as soon as Billie returned the receiver to the cradle.

"Hello?"

"It's been awhile."

Billie froze. Old tapes played as fear followed by disgust overwhelmed her. "Brian?"

"That's right. How've you been?"

Billie's voice dropped an octave. "What do you want, Brian?"

"Don't be so crass. I'm only calling to say hi."

"I don't believe that for a minute. What do you want?"

"Well, if you insist, I'm a little low on cash. How about helping an old friend?"

"Friend? You've got to be kidding."

"Hey, why not let bygones be bygones? Truce?"

"Truce my ass! You've no leverage anymore, Brian. Crawl back under your rock and leave me alone."

"Come on. Is that any way to treat your son's father?"

"Some father you are. I told you nine months ago that Seth was in the hospital in a coma. Did you even once bother to visit him? No!"

"I've been out of town."

"Bullshit. You don't care. You never did."

"I don't need this shit. I only need some cash."

"Why don't you get it from Mommy and Daddy? Heaven knows they can afford it."

"I can't. It's a gambling debt. My parents told me long ago they wouldn't bail me out of careless debt."

"So you've come to me instead."

"These guys don't fool around. My life's in danger if I don't pay them back."

"I don't see where that's my problem."

"Damn you, Billie. Are you going to cough up some dough or what?"

"No. Go find some other sucker."

"Don't make me do something you'll regret."

"Go to hell."

"Have it your way. Oh, by the way, you're wrong. I do have leverage. Later."

The line fell silent. She hung up the phone. Billie was light-headed and nauseous as dread filled her heart. "Damn it! Why now?" she muttered aloud. "My life's finally back on track. I've found the perfect person to share it with. Seth's on his way to being healthy again. The future couldn't look better. Why does that asshole have to show up now? He said he has leverage. I wonder what that means? What are you up to, Brian?"

* * *

Soon after Cat put the kids down for their nap and retired to her own bed, she heard a noise in the living room.

"Billie? Is that you?" She waited for the reply that didn't come.

Cat threw off the covers and crept to the bedroom door. She opened it a crack and peered out. *Oh my God!* A man was dismantling the stereo system. In reflex, she jerked the door closed, and it made an audible thud. She ran to the bedside table and grabbed her cell phone.

Cat flipped open the phone just as the door to her bedroom crashed open. The phone fell to the floor by the side of the bed.

"Make one sound, bitch, and I'll slit your throat. Then I'll kill the kids. You got that?"

Cat climbed onto the bed and pressed herself against the headboard. "Who are you?"

"Let's say I'm an old acquaintance of Billie's."

"What do you want?"

"Your stereo system for one. I should be able to get a pretty penny for it. Oh, and by the way, you can thank Billie for this little visit."

"Billie?"

"Yeah. I asked her for help, and she told me to go to hell. I ask you, is that any way to treat her son's father?"

"Brian?"

"Brian Charland, in the flesh." He sat on the edge of the bed and leaned in toward Cat. "Now you know where Seth got his good looks."

The smell of alcohol on his breath made Cat's stomach queasy. She stalled for time. "What do you want?"

"I told you. I want your stereo, and anything else I can walk out of here with that will make me some money."

"Take them. Take anything you want and leave. Just don't hurt my kids."

"Your kids? At last count, one of them is mine. That little girl of yours is pretty. Very pretty. I've been watching you. That's how I knew you were at home. I've been watching all of you for a while."

Oh God, she should've told Billie about this when she first sensed it.

Brian touched the side of Cat's face.

Cat recoiled.

"You asked me what I want. What I really want is to teach Billie a lesson. She treated me like shit earlier today. That was a mistake."

Cat's growing anger overcame her fear. "From what I understand, you did your share of treating her that way for several years."

Brian backhanded Cat across the face. "Shut up, bitch! Billie's going to pay for how she treated me, and if you end up as collateral damage, that's tough luck for you."

Brian ripped the shirt from her back.

Cat fought back. "No. Don't do this. Please."

Brian hit her again, spraying blood from her split lip all over the bed. He grabbed her around the neck and pinned her to the bed. "Resist me, and I'll kill you... and the kids."

Cat had to accept that he meant what he said. She closed her eyes and nodded as the tears escaped.

Brian grabbed her breasts with one hand as he unfastened his belt and trousers with the other. She tried her best to pull a mask over her consciousness as he entered her and savagely took her against her will. He bit and clawed at the flesh on her chest and face as he thrust into her over and over again. Then it was over. He rolled off, sweaty and covered in her blood.

Cat hung over the side of the bed and threw up the contents of her stomach. "Oh my God. Oh my God," she moaned. Her cell phone lay on the floor within reach, and she grabbed it. She flipped the phone open and speed-dialed Billie's cell number.

Brian rolled over and touched her arm.

She pushed him violently away. "Don't touch me, you filthy son of a bitch. Get away from me."

Brian grabbed her neck. "She should've given me the money, then none of this would have happened."

Intense feelings of hatred overcame Cat. "Take your hands off me and get out of here."

"I'll go when I'm damned good and ready, and you'd better start treating me better if you care about those little kiddies in the other room."

"If you touch them, I'll kill you."

"Not if I kill you first."

*   *   *

Billie was typing a letter into her computer when her cell phone rang. She flipped the cover open and held the receiver to her ear. "Hello?" No one answered and she pulled the phone away from her ear and looked at it. She still had a signal. "Hello?" she said again into the mouthpiece. She was about to hang the phone up when she heard voices... two voices, one male and one female.

"Cat? Cat? Is that you?" She held the phone to her ear again and listened to the conversation on the other end of the line. Her eyes opened wide as the nagging fear she felt earlier in the day returned. "Cat! Baby... say something. Please."

Billie grabbed her car keys and ran for the door. She ran red lights and stop signs as she raced through traffic. While she fought her way through the maze of cars on the highway, she called 911.

"Nine-one-one. What's your emergency?"

"My partner needs help."

"Is you partner with you?"

"No, she's home. At least I think she is. My cell phone rang a couple of minutes ago, and I can hear a scuffle on the other end of the line."

"What's her address?"

"1163 Western Boulevard. I'm on my way there now."

"I'm dispatching an officer to that location right now. What's your partner's name?"

"Caitlain O'Grady."

"Do you know who she's struggling with?"

"No. All I know is that the other person is a man."

"Is there anyone else in the house with Ms. O'Grady?"

"Our children."

Distracted by the phone call, Billie slammed on her brake to avoid hitting the car in front of her as they approached the traffic signal. "Damn it!"

"And how old are the children?"

"Six and four. I need to go. I shouldn't be on the phone while driving."

"I'd prefer you stay away from the scene until the officers get there."

"I can't do that. Cat and my children are in danger. I need to go. Goodbye."

Billie screeched the car to a halt in the parking lot and ran into the building. She scaled the stairs, three steps at a time. The apartment door was ajar. Her first thoughts were for the children. She ran to each of their rooms but found them asleep in their beds.

She raced toward their bedroom. "Cat! Cat, where are you?" She pushed the door open. The scene before her overwhelmed her senses as an uncontrollable rage filled her heart and mind. She pounced on Brian, who was in the process of zipping his trousers.

Billie landed a roundhouse kick to Brian's chin. He slammed into the wall but stayed on his feet. "You bastard! You son of a bitch! I'll kill you!" She slammed her elbow into his solar plexus. He gasped for air and retched the contents of his stomach all over the floor. He made a break for the door. She swung her leg again and hit him squarely on his nose. He was airborne briefly, then smacked into the bathroom door and sank to the floor, unconscious.

"Billie! No!"

Billie's eyes were wild with anger as she wheeled to face Cat.

Cat extended her arms. "Billie... please."

Billie abandoned her assault on Brian and pulled Cat into her arms. Tears ran down both their faces.

"Mom?"

Billie looked toward the door and saw Seth standing just outside the room.

"Go to him," Cat urged.

Billie went to Seth and ushered him away from their bedroom as she closed the door behind her.

"Mom, what happened? I heard a loud noise."

Billie wiped the tears off her face with the back of her hand. "Mama had an accident."

"Is she hurt?"

"Yes she is." Billie knelt in front of Seth. "Could you please go back to you room? I need to call Grandpa and Grammy to come stay with you while I take Mama to the hospital."

"I'm worried about Mama."

"She'll be okay, but I need you to go to your room right now, and don't come out until Grandpa and Grammy get here. Can you do that for me?"

Seth nodded and returned to his room.

A knock on the door drew Billie's attention away from Cat once more.

"Police. We received a nine-one-one call to this address."

Billie opened the door and admitted two officers. "In the bedroom at the end of the hall."

Billie called Cat's parents. "Hello, Mom? This is Billie. Mom, there's been an incident. We need you to come stay with the kids for a few hours."

"An incident?" Ida asked. "What happened, dear?"

Billie tried to compose herself. He voice choked with emotion as she answered. "Mom, Cat was raped."

"Oh my poor baby. No!"

Billie heard the phone clatter to the floor. "Billie, this is Doc. What's going on?"

"Doc. I'm so sorry. Cat... Cat was raped."

"What do you mean, Cat was raped?" he demanded. "By whom?"

"I'll give you more details later. The police are carting his ass off to jail as we speak. I need to get Cat to the hospital, but we need someone to stay with the kids."

"The kids? Where were they while this was happening?" Billie heard the anger in his voice.

"Napping. They both slept through the actual attack. I'm afraid Seth woke up while I was beating the shit out of the asshole who did this to her, but I don't think he saw anything. He's in his room right now waiting for you to get here. We need you to come over as soon as possible."

"Yes. Yes, of course. We'll be there right away."

* * *

Billie sped to the hospital with Cat sitting in the seat beside her. She parked her car in the emergency care lot and walked Cat inside, where the emergency room staff took over. Cat lay on the gurney with one arm thrown over her eyes.

"What do we have here?" the physician on duty asked as he approached the gurney.

"Rape victim," the paramedic replied.

The physician took Cat's wrist and moved her arm away from her face. "Cat!" He addressed the ER nurse. "Move her into room one and order a rape kit, STAT." He extended his hand to Billie. "I'm Mike Carson. You must be Billie. Cat talks about you all the time. It's obvious you two have a very special relationship."

"Yes, Dr. Carson," Billie replied as she shook his hand.

"Mike," he said. "Call me Mike. Can you tell me what happened?"

Billie fought to hold back the tears. "I'm sorry," she said. She took time to compose herself.

"No problem. Take your time."

"Ah... I'm not really sure what happened. I wasn't home. I got there just as the bastard was getting dressed."

"Do you know the assailant?"

"All too well, I'm afraid. He's my ex-husband."

A technician entered Cat's examination room. "That'll be the rape kit I ordered," Dr. Carson said.

Billie grabbed Dr. Carson's arm. "Mike. Can I…"

"Sure. Considering what she's been through, I think she'll appreciate having you there."

Billie followed Dr. Carson into the examination room. He stood by Cat's gurney and examined the bruises on her face. "Hey there, Cat. I'm real sorry you have to go through this, but you know the drill. We have a standard rape kit, and we need to take samples from your genitals, rectum, and mouth, as well as head and pubic hair samples. Oh, and of course, scrapings from beneath your fingernails." He glanced at Billie before continuing. "Billie tells me the assailant is in custody, but as you know, we need these samples to convict him in a court of law."

Dr. Carson addressed the attending nurse. "Please ask the receptionist to get the photographer here to document any cuts, bruises, or other injuries. Also, you'll need to provide Cat with a set of scrubs to wear home. The police will want her clothing for evidence. Thanks." He spoke to Cat. "I know how painful this must be for you, so I'll try to get this over with quickly. First I need to ask you a few questions. Did you bathe or brush your teeth after the attack?"

Cat shook her head no.

"Good. Do you suspect that you were given a rape drug? If so, we'll need to take a urine sample as well."

Cat looked away but again shook her head no.

Dr. Carson put his hand on Cat's shoulder. "This isn't your fault. You may be feeling a whole range of emotions, all of which are normal considering what you've been through, but this isn't your fault. We'll do everything we can to help you get through this. As you know, we have an excellent counseling facility here. I recommend both you and Billie see a counselor."

Cat nodded.

"Good." He looked at the attending nurse. "Let's get the samples we need so she can go home."

* * *

During the drive home, Cat sat silently in the passenger seat with her head resting against the side window. Billie touched her arm.

Cat jerked away. "Please, don't touch me."

Billie hit the steering wheel with her fist. "Damn him. I should've killed the bastard."

Cat closed her eyes and compacted herself into an even tighter ball.

Billie didn't trust herself to speak for fear her rage would consume them both. When they arrived home, she opened Cat's door and helped her out of the car. Cat pulled away from Billie's touch.

Inside, was a note from Cat's parents. Billie read the note aloud. "We've taken the children home with us to give you some privacy. They don't know what actually happened. Seth knows Cat is injured but doesn't know how. We've assured him she'll be okay. Please call us and let us know how you are. We love you. Mom and Dad."

Billie squeezed Cat's upper arm. "Thank God for your mom and dad."

Cat once again pulled away from Billie. "Please. Don't touch me."

"Cat, please talk to me."

Cat headed straight for the bathroom, where she spent the next half hour under the spray of the shower. Billie called Cat's parents and filled them in on Cat's condition and asked them to keep the children overnight.

Billie held a towel to envelop Cat when she stepped out of the shower. She half-expected Cat to pull away once more, but she stood eerily still and silent as Billie towel-dried her skin and applied salve to the bites and scrapes left on her face and neck by Brian's assault. "Wait right here," Billie said as she went to retrieve a clean pair of panties, shorts, and T-shirt from their bedroom and helped her put them on.

Billie opened her arms. The pain she saw tore at her heart. "This doesn't change how much I love you. Nothing will change that. Please let me hold you."

Cat relented and stepped into the circle of Billie's arms. Billie held her close for several moments and then gathered her up and carried her to the rocking chair in the living room.

The apartment was totally quiet as Billie rocked Cat back and forth. Billie felt Cat tremble uncontrollably. All Billie could do was hold her and soothe her with words of love and assurance. "I love you so much. Please believe that. I need you. I want to spend the rest of my life with you and the children."

Billie felt Cat relax in her embrace. Cat yawned.

She kissed the side of Cat's head. "I'm going to put you to bed. You're exhausted."

Cat's eyes opened wide. "I won't go in there. Please don't ask me to go into our bedroom."

Billie understood Cat's revulsion. "Baby, no, not in there. We'll sleep in Seth's room tonight."

Cat nodded and allowed Billie to lead her to Seth's room and lay her gently on the bed. Billie removed her own clothing and slipped in beside Cat. She gathered the emotionally shattered woman in her arms. "I love you. Please believe that."

Cat sobbed loudly and apologized over and over to Billie. "I'm so sorry. I couldn't stop him. I let him do it. I let him do it. Oh God! I was so afraid he'd hurt the children. He threatened to hurt them. I had to let him do it."

Billie tightened her arms around Cat. "No, sweetheart, please don't apologize." The emotion in Billie's voice made it difficult to speak. "You didn't ask for this. It's not your fault. Baby, it's not your fault." Billie began to cry as she buried her face in Cat's hair. "I would've done the same thing in your shoes."

"You don't understand. For several weeks, I've felt like I was being watched and followed, but I didn't tell you about it. I didn't want to worry you. If only I'd said something, maybe none of this would've happened. Maybe I wouldn't have put the children and myself in danger. I'll never forgive myself."

Billie was silent for several minutes. "Cat, if anyone's to blame, it's me. Brian called me at work and asked for money. I told him to go to hell. He said I'd be sorry I didn't help him, but in my wildest dreams, I never thought he'd do something like this. Damn him." Billie shook with fury. "Damn him to hell."

"I should've told you," Cat said again, her voice barely a whisper.

Billie resisted the urge to fly into another rage. Cat needed comfort and support, not a partner who was out of control with anger. "It's not your fault. Please believe that."

Cat offered no response as she pressed herself closer to Billie and closed her eyes. Exhaustion claimed her as she fell asleep. Billie lay awake well into the night.

Chapter 15

Despite Billie's efforts to clean and repaint their bedroom, Cat refused to sleep there and chose instead to sleep with Tara. Cat arranged to have two additional dead-bolt locks installed on the front door and had an electronic security system installed on the door and all of the windows. She refused to stay in any room alone and even left the bathroom door slightly ajar whenever she was in there.

"Cat, we need to get help. You can't go on avoiding the situation."

Cat turned her back on Billie and walked across the room. "The last thing I need is to be reminded of what happened. You've no idea how painful it is. I don't want to relive it over and over again in a shrink's office."

"We can't go on like this. You've become a stranger to me. You're angry all the time. You cry at the drop of a hat and jump at every little sound. This isn't healthy."

"Can you blame me? Tell me you wouldn't be angry if it happened to you. You're the fortunate one."

Billie released a long sigh. "I don't need you to constantly remind me of who the victim is here. I feel guilty enough about it already. But if the truth be known, you're not the only victim."

Cat crossed her arms. "What the hell is that supposed to mean?"

"Our relationship has been victimized as well. You won't let me touch you. We haven't made love since it happened. We don't even talk anymore. Hell, I'd be happy just to hold you at night while you sleep, but since that first night, you won't allow that either."

"This isn't about you, Billie."

"You're right. This isn't about me. It's about us, or at least what used to be us."

Cat stormed away and stood in front of the living room window with her back to Billie.

"Cat…"
"No. I don't want to talk about it."

* * *

Billie dealt with her guilt by immersing herself in the case against Brian. She used her knowledge and connections within the law firm to push her case into the courts. Brian's influential family used their leverage to erect roadblocks at every turn. Billie dreaded the day Cat would have to face her attacker in court.

Billie was frustrated by Cat's indifference to her feelings. Outwardly, Cat appeared to be functioning as though nothing had happened. She was affectionate with the children and was still dedicated to helping Seth complete his physical therapy. She also spent a significant amount of time on the phone talking to her mother and sisters. Cat returned to work shortly after the attack and it appeared to Billie that she was functioning well in a professional capacity. Everything appeared normal except when it came to her relationship with Billie. She could not show affection to the woman she'd committed her life to.

On the day the court scheduled Brian's trial, Billie came home with an armful of roses and a bottle of champagne. She'd asked Ida to take the kids overnight so she could celebrate with Cat when she arrived home that evening from work. Billie positioned the roses and candles strategically around the living room and put on soothing music. She wanted to provide a safe and unassuming atmosphere for Cat. It was her hope that Cat would see the gesture for what it was—one of love and affection

The anticipation in Billie's chest grew when she heard a key slip into the lock. As Cat entered the condo, Billie hoped news of Brian's trial would trigger a new beginning for Cat and provide her with a chance to heal from the emotional wounds he so brutally inflicted on her. The anticipation quickly turned to concern as Cat looked around the room and sank to her knees in tears.

Billie helped her up. "Cat… Cat, honey… come sit on the couch. Tell me what's wrong." Billie wrapped an arm around Cat and led her to sit on the edge of the couch.

Cat continued to cry. "I don't know what's wrong. I'm so sorry. You've been so good to me over the past few weeks, and all I've done is treat you badly." She looked around at the candles. "You did all of this for me. Here I am, a blubbering idiot, and I can't even tell you why."

Billie waited for the tears to subside.

"Why do you do such wonderful things like this when I'm so awful to you?"

Billie knelt in front of Cat and took Cat's hands in hers. "I did all of this for you today to celebrate some good news. We have a date for Brian's trial. We're one step closer. I wanted to celebrate that with you, but I also did this because I love you. I love you with everything that I am, and I hoped this would help to heal the pain that has been such a significant part of our lives for the past several weeks."

"I'm sorry."

Billie took Cat's face between her hands. She gently kissed the corner of Cat's mouth. "Let me love you," she whispered.

Cat began to cry. "I... I can't. I'm sorry. I'm so sorry."

Billie sat back on her heels for a moment then rose from the floor to take Cat into her arms. "It's all right, love. It's all right. At least let me hold you while you sleep."

"I won't sleep in our room."

Billie held Cat by the shoulders. "I know. I know. The kids are at Mom and Dad's for the night. We'll sleep in Seth's bed."

Later, Cat slept soundly while Billie stared at the ceiling. She thought about how much she loved Cat, but acknowledged that they'd never get through the trauma unless Cat was willing to face her demons. Otherwise, their relationship was doomed.

* * *

The next morning, Billie awoke to find Cat had already risen. She climbed out of bed and walked into the hall. "Cat?" The bathroom door was closed. "Cat? Cat are you in there?"

"Yes. I'll be out in a minute."

Billie paced back and forth in front of the door, trying to decide how to broach the subject of couples' therapy with Cat. Several more minutes passed without Cat emerging. Billie called through the door. "Are you all right?"

"I'm fine...aahhh. Oh God... aahhh."

"You don't sound fine. I'm coming in." Billie pushed the door open. Cat was kneeling in front of the toilet. Billie stepped forward and held Cat's hair back while she emptied the contents of her stomach into the bowl.

Cat sat on the floor and leaned against the wall opposite the toilet. "Oh my God, I feel horrible."

Billie extended her hand. "Come on. Let me help you up. You need to go back to bed. I'll get you a glass of water after I tuck you in." Billie led her back to bed. As Cat sat in bed with her water glass in hand, Billie picked up the phone.

"Who are you calling?"

"I'm calling your doctor. Something isn't right here."

"It's only a stomach bug. I'll be fine."

"I'm calling your doctor anyway. Things haven't been right for several weeks. You need to be looked at."

"Billie..."

Billie grasped Cat's hand. "No. Enough is enough. You need help. No, strike that. *We* need help. You're withdrawn, you won't let me touch you, and now you're throwing up. You're seeing a doctor, and I don't want an argument about it."

Cat's only answer was to stare into the water glass she held in her lap.

* * *

Billie leaned against the examination table as she watched Cat get dressed. "I'm surprised at how thorough Dr. O'Brien's examination was. I mean, blood tests, urine sample, throat culture seems like a lot to me. I know I just met her today, but I liked her personality. She really put me at ease."

"Patty's a good doctor. As far as the tests are concerned, she wants to cover all the bases. Any doctor worth their weight would do the same. She's been my doctor for several years."

"You'd know better than I." Billie became uncomfortable with the tension in the room as Cat finished dressing and began pacing the room. "Cat, we need to talk to Dr. O'Brien about our relationship."

"What do you mean?"

"I mean she needs to know that things haven't been good between us since the rape."

"Billie, I'd rather not air our dirty laundry in public."

Billie stood and intercepted Cat's trek across the room. "I think the dirty laundry is part of why you feel the way you do. I want to talk to her about it."

"Billie..."

"No, Cat. I'm tired of hoping it will resolve itself. Work with me here, okay?"

"All right. Have it your way."

"Thank you."

Billie's attention was drawn by a knock on the door.

"Come in," she said.

The nurse pushed the door open and stepped inside. "Dr. O'Brien will see you in her office now."

Billie and Cat stepped through the door opened by the nurse and into Dr. O'Brien's office. Dr. O'Brien glanced up from the paper she was reading and rose to her feet. "Please, come in and sit down." She gestured to a pair of chairs in front of her desk. She remained standing until they were seated.

Dr. O'Brien looked at Cat over glasses perched at the end of her nose. "Cat, Billie, tell me what life has been like in your home since the rape." Cat visibly cringed at the word "rape".

"Getting through each day has been a struggle," she replied.

"That's an understatement," Billie said.

Dr. O'Brien sat back in her chair and looked at Billie. "Care to elaborate?"

"I don't want to sound like an insensitive clod. I can only imagine that what Cat went through was horrible, but quite frankly, Dr. O'Brien, Cat has been listless and withdrawn, especially when it comes to her relationship with me. She seems fine with Seth and Tara, and I assume she's doing okay at work, but things haven't been good between the two of us since the attack."

Patty wrote a few notes on Cat's chart. "How so?"

"Like I said, she's withdrawn. I'll find her staring off into space. She sleeps all the time, and she cries at the drop of a hat. This morning, she was in the bathroom vomiting." Billie hesitated. She opened her mouth to speak but fell silent.

Dr. O'Brien tilted her head in Billie's direction. "I sense an unfinished thought, Billie. What else do you have to tell me?"

Billie struggled to remain in control of her emotions.

"She, ah…" Billie cleared her throat. "She appears to find my touch repulsive these days. We haven't made love since the attack."

"Cat, is that right?" Dr. O'Brien asked.

Cat nodded.

"Any idea why?"

"I don't know."

Dr. O'Brien sat back. "I may be able to help you with that. People react and cope differently after being raped. That includes the victim of rape and the family of the victim. You need to know that these emotions are common. They can be upsetting and confusing, but they're normal."

"Confusing is putting is mildly," Billie said. "I don't know what I've done to cause her anger."

"You haven't done anything. Anger is a healthy emotion, and it's crucial to the healing process. It's not uncommon for rape victims to be angry with the rapist, themselves, the people they love, and even at the world. Anger is one of the easier emotions to understand in a situation like this. Guilt is another emotion that makes relative sense. Society tends to blame the victim of rape, and the victim always regrets not seeing it coming and preventing it. They also feel guilty about the effect of the rape on their family. It's important to understand that no one deserves to be raped, even if they drink to excess, dress in revealing clothing, or flirt with their attacker prior to the rape. Being raped is never the victim's fault."

Billie took Cat's hand in her own and squeezed it. "Listen to her, love."

Dr. O'Brien looked at Cat. "What else can you tell me about how you're feeling, Cat?"

"I don't know. Everything is so much more intense than before. I don't like being alone. If I'm alone in public, every man I see becomes a suspect. I've lost all confidence in my own sense of judgment. I wonder if I wasn't cautious enough of strangers before the rape. I feel so out of control all of the time. You know... powerless."

"Do you mean violated?" Billie asked.

"It's more than that. I feel like I've lost control over my own body. He waltzed right into our home and took what he wanted from me. I was powerless to stop him. I feel like such a coward."

Billie squeezed Cat's hand tighter. "That's not true, love. You made a very courageous decision to sacrifice yourself to protect the children."

"Sacrifice?" Dr. O'Brien asked.

"I let him do it," Cat replied.

"She let him do it because he threatened to hurt the kids if she struggled," Billie said.

"Billie's right," Dr. O'Brien said. "It took tremendous courage to do what you did."

Cat wiped the tears that rolled down her cheek. "I'd do it again in a heartbeat."

"Spoken by someone who truly loves her children," Dr. O'Brien said. "So, has anything else changed since the incident? How are your sleeping habits?"

"I don't think I've slept through the entire night since it happened," Cat said.

Billie raised her eyebrows. "Really? I didn't know that."

Dr. O'Brien frowned. "Billie, you've mentioned that you haven't been intimate since the attack. Are you even sharing a bed?"

Billie shook her head. "No. Cat has been sleeping with our daughter, Tara, but in her defense, I can understand her not wanting to sleep in our room."

"Maybe it's time you consider moving to a new home." Just then, the door opened and a nurse entered to hand a slip of paper to the doctor. Dr. O'Brien read the note "This changes things a bit."

Billie leaned forward. "What is it?"

Dr. O'Brien took her glasses off and put them on top of Cat's chart. "It's apparent to me that Cat is suffering from post-rape syndrome, also known as post-traumatic stress syndrome. I was going to prescribe an anti-depressant and recommend sessions with a therapist for both of you, but considering the test results I've just seen, I need to rethink the medication." She looked back and forth between the two. "Cat... Billie... according to this test result, Cat is pregnant."

*　*　*

Billie stole several glances at Cat as they drove back to the condo. Cat sat in the seat beside her and stared out at the scenery. Neither spoke. Billie was worried about Cat's mental state and about what this new child would mean to their lives. She struggled with how she felt about this turn of events and was very concerned that she'd ultimately resent both Cat and the child for putting her in this situation. Most of all, she worried that she might not be able to love the child knowing how it came to be.

When they arrived home, Billie encouraged Cat to rest, and directed her to Tara's room where she watched Cat curl in a fetal position. Billie called Cat's parents and asked them to keep the children for an extra day. She didn't tell them about the baby. She decided to leave that decision to Cat's discretion. Billie worked through the mental stress with Tae Kwon Do routines throughout the day and checked on Cat periodically. Each time, she urged Cat to talk to her about this new turn in their lives. Each time she was met with silence or tears.

As night fell, Billie found herself sitting alone in the darkened living room, no closer to answers than she was earlier in the day when Dr. O'Brien delivered the news. She spoke the words aloud that were eating her up inside. She was sure the walls would listen even if Cat wouldn't. "I don't know how to deal with your pain, Cat. I don't know what to say. I can't tell you that everything will be all right, because I'm not convinced of that myself. It isn't my place to tell you what to do about the child. I'm so afraid that you'll blame me for what's happened. I don't know what to do. I need you to talk to me." When the living room fell victim to the shadows of night, Billie decided to confront the issue head on.

Billie entered Tara's bedroom and closed the door. "Cat, we need to talk about this."

Cat sat with her back against the headboard and sighed. She looked at Billie and extended her hand. Billie's heart skipped a beat as she took this gesture as a positive sign. She crossed the room and took Cat's hand.

"Billie, please sit with me."

Billie sat on the bed in a cross-legged position in front of Cat. She rested her elbows on her knees and gave Cat her full attention.

"Billie, my heart hurts so. I'm so sorry you have to go through this."

Billie's forehead furrowed as she reached out for Cat's hand. She kissed Cat's knuckles. "Don't worry about me. It's you I'm concerned about."

"It's us I'm concerned about. Why did this have to happen? We were beginning to build a life together." Cat began to cry anew.

"This was so unexpected. I mean... they did a pregnancy test at the hospital, and another one two weeks later. Who would've thought they'd be false negatives? I was unprepared when Dr. O'Brien gave us the test results," Billie said.

"Billie, I want to keep the child."

Try as she might, Billie was unable to stop the gasp of breath.

"I'm sorry if that isn't the decision you'd make, but this is my child, too, not just Brian's. I can't bring myself to terminate it or to give it away. I'm sorry."

Billie considered what this would mean and what her choices were. Could she walk away from it all? Did she even want to? She loved Cat so much, but could she call this child her own?

She paced the room. "I need to think about this. This decision has long-term consequences."

Cat bowed her head. "I understand," she said softly. "I understand that this baby will be a constant reminder of the painful years you spent with Brian. This is a big decision. I don't blame you for needing time."

Billie sat on the edge of the bed and lifted Cat's chin. "I do love you."

Tears welled up behind Cat's lids and rolled down her cheeks. "I love you, too."

After hearing Cat's decision, Billie needed time and space to think about what the child would mean to their relationship, so she went to the gym. For the next hour, she was alone in the weight room taking her anger out on the heavy bag.

She wiped the sweat off her brow as she threw her punches. "Umph! Umph, umph, umph." She grunted as the boxing gloves made consecutive rapid contact with the canvas bag. "Damn you, Brian!" she screamed, and her glove made hard contact once more.

Out of breath and weak with exhaustion, she sat on the closest bench and began to cry. "Why? Why now? Why Cat? I'm so afraid of what this will mean. We already have two children." She thought about Tara and Seth and the realization struck her that this child would be the biological sibling of both children. This child would literally tie the family together. Her biggest concern was whether she could love the child as her own. Would she want Cat to love this child if their roles were reversed?

*   *   *

Billie let herself into the condo and relocked the multitude of dead bolts. She looked down the hallway and saw the light was still on in Tara's bedroom. She opened the door. Cat was sitting up against the headboard. Her eyes were swollen and red, and many crumpled tissues littered the bed around her legs.

Billie saw the expectant and fearful look on Cat's face. She sat on the edge of the bed and took Cat's hand in her own. "I love you with all my heart. You complete me in ways I never imagined." Billie gently touched Cat's abdomen. A surge of emotion filled her heart as her fingertips made contact. She knew at that moment that she'd made the right decision. "I'll love and support this child like my own. This will be *our* child. This baby is part of you. It's part of Seth and Tara, and it will be part of me as well."

Tears flowed down Cat's cheeks as she wrapped her arms around Billie's neck and held her close. "I love you so much. This will be our child, my love... *our* child."

Part III:

Personal Preferences

Chapter 16

"Hi, Bridget," Cat said into the phone. "How are Kevin and the kids?"

"They're fine. We went to the cutest concert at Heidi's pre-school yesterday."

"A concert with preschoolers? That must have been entertaining."

"It was. I've never heard so many off-key voices in one place before, but it was adorable."

"I'm looking forward to attending Tara's and Seth's concerts when they're in school. In fact, Seth starts school in the fall, so that may happen soon."

"It'll be great when we can finally get our kids together. Heidi isn't old enough to really remember Tara, it's been so long since we've seen her. We haven't even met Billie yet, except to talk to her on the phone. And Seth is so cute, but you can only see so much in photographs. I'll bet Daddy is busting with pride at finally having a grandson. And then there's the new baby. Maybe it will be a boy as well. It's due in what… four or five months?"

"Four. And you're right. We need to find the time for a get-together. We haven't had a family reunion in quite some time."

"Heidi, don't climb onto that chair, you'll fall and break your neck. Look, Cat, I've got to run. I swear that girl will be the life of me. I'll talk to you later."

"Okay, Bridget. Love you."

"Love you, too."

Billie carried a cup of coffee to the kitchen table and put it down within Cat's reach. "Decaf," she said.

Cat grimaced. "Decaf? What's the point?"

"Limited caffeine while you're pregnant. You know that."

"Nag, nag, nag."

"Which sister was that?"

"Bridget. I think that woman can have a conversation all by herself. It's tough to get a word in edgewise."

"How is she?"

"Great." Cat looked wistfully at Billie. "I really miss my sisters. We need to figure out how to get us all together sometime soon."

"I agree." Billie sipped her own coffee. "See anything interesting?"

Cat turned to the next page of the classified ads she was looking at before her sister called. "This one here looks promising. Home for sale. Three bedrooms, two baths, dining room. New roof, carpet, and furnace, and it's relatively inexpensive."

"Where's it located?"

"Ugh. I can see why it's so cheap. It's not in the greatest part of town."

"We'll keep looking. We can't do anything until the condo sells anyway."

"Yeah, you're right."

Billie pulled a chair out and sat beside Cat. "I'll be glad to move into a new home. Not only does this place hold bad memories, but we're going to run out of room in four or five months."

"You got that right." Cat returned her attention to the classified ads. "Oh!" she exclaimed as she clutched at her side.

"Is the baby kicking again?" Billie asked. "Can I feel it?"

"Yes. Give me your hand."

Billie allowed Cat to position her hand on the side of her slightly distended abdomen. She concentrated intently as she strove to feel movement.

"There. Can you feel it?"

A broad smile covered Billie's face. "Yes. Just barely though."

"Movement at this stage of the pregnancy is pretty subtle, especially from the outside. In another few months, we'll actually be able to see the baby's elbow or foot through my skin."

"You're almost five months along now. If I remember right, that's about when I began to feel Seth kicking. I remember the first time it happened. I didn't know what it was, so I went to the doctor's, fearing I was miscarrying or something."

"I hear you. I was a nervous wreck when I carried Tara. I mean, I knew what to expect physically, we had covered that in med school, but I was totally unprepared for the emotional changes that accompany pregnancy."

Billie looked at Cat and smiled.

"What's the smile for?" Cat asked.

"I'm imagining what you'll look like when you're nine months pregnant. I'm betting you'll be very cute and sexy."

Cat pushed Billie's shoulder. "Sexy, my ass. I'm going to look like a cow."

"You'll always be beautiful in my eyes." Billie leaned forward and kissed her.

Billie felt Cat stiffen, but she didn't recoil as Billie feared she might. Encouraged, she took Cat's face between her hands and deepened the kiss, demanding entrance into Cat's mouth with her tongue.

Panic rose in Cat's eyes. She stood and walked to the opposite side of the room. "I'm sorry. I'm so sorry," she cried.

Billie rose from her chair and walked across the room. She took Cat into her arms and held her close. "It's time, Cat. Things can't go on like this. We need help."

*   *   *

"When you've been sexually abused," Dr. Connor said, "you suffer in more ways than the average mind can comprehend. When it's your partner who's abused you, your best course of action is to put some distance between you, but in your case, Cat, your abuser was a third party. One of the worst things you can do in a situation like this is to suffer in silence. Unfortunately, one of the hardest things to do is to talk to your partner about the abuse."

"You're right. It's been nearly impossible for me to talk to Billie about it."

"That's understandable, but withdrawing from your partner often leads to a failed relationship."

Cat and Billie both nodded.

"Cat, before we get into the details of how to reestablish a sexual connection with Billie, I need to ask you if you enjoyed what you and Billie had together before the rape."

"Of course I did. I love her," Cat replied.

Billie frowned. "Dr. Connor, what are you implying?" she asked.

Dr. Connor looked directly at Billie. "I'm trying to establish how important your former sexual relationship is to Cat. To be blunt, the decision to resume sexual relations with you has to be Cat's choice, not yours."

"I would never pressure her into something she didn't want," Billie said.

Cat took Billie's hand in hers.

Dr. Connor smiled. "I'm not saying you would. What we need to keep in mind here is that sexual abuse can take something that was once enjoyable and pleasurable and turn it into a nightmare. In theory, the more enjoyable and consensual your former relationship was, the easier it should be to heal the wounds Cat has suffered. I also believe, in your case, you have a distinct advantage."

"How so?" Cat asked.

"Your situation is somewhat different from what I'm used to counseling. In most of the cases I've dealt with, the victim has been a heterosexual female. Returning to a sexual relationship with a man after suffering traumatic abuse at the hands of a man is sometimes impossible. In your case however, Cat would be returning to a sexual relationship with a woman after abuse at the hands of a man. In my opinion, that gives you an advantage over most rape victims."

"So, what exactly does this therapy involve?" Billie asked.

"That's a great preface into the dos and don'ts of the therapeutic approach."

"Dos and don'ts?" Cat said.

"Yes. We'll discuss several methods for confronting your trauma, Cat, and several approaches to reintroducing yourself to an enjoyable sexual relationship with Billie." Dr. Connor addressed Billie. "Billie, many of these approaches apply to you as well. Cat needs your full cooperation and support if she hopes to overcome what she's been through."

"She has both. She always has," Billie said.

"Good. Let's begin." Dr. Connor sat back. "Rule number one is for you, Cat. If you feel uncomfortable, stop."

"Stop? Just stop?" Cat asked.

"Exactly. As I'm sure you know, post-rape syndrome is very similar to post-traumatic stress syndrome. It causes pain. Sometimes emotional, sometimes physical, and sometimes both. If you and Billie begin to engage in activities that make you uncomfortable in any way, stop immediately. Let Billie know what made you feel uneasy. Talk it out. Billie, you need to be willing to accept Cat's decision to stop any sexual activity regardless of how far it's progressed. Do you understand?"

"Completely."

"Good. Rule two—Cat, this one's also for you. Stay in control. Billie, you'll need to let Cat set the pace and take the lead. In no way should she be put in a subservient position. Cat, take charge. Be dominant. You may find that you'll even enjoy that role. I'm not saying you'll need to maintain these roles forever, but at least until Cat is able to enjoy a healthy sexual relationship without fear."

Billie crossed her arms and nodded.

"Rule three—keep it intimate. Obviously, rough sex isn't the way to get back into the game. Begin with romantic gestures... candles, massages, hugging, kissing. Do what's comfortable and follow the mood where it takes you. Rule four—stay in the moment. Cat, you need to keep your eyes open. Focus on you and Billie. Focus on what you're feeling. Use all of your senses to communicate with each other. Don't fall into the trap of allowing your mind to wander. It may wander to places you don't want it to be. Stop me if either of you have questions."

"No. Go on," Cat said.

"The final step—engage in counseling. There are many ways of doing this. One way is in this office. This office will be a place to discuss strategy as well as successes and failures. Another way is to maintain an open dialogue between you. Talk to each other about what you like and dislike sexually. Sexual abuse is unlike any other emotional disorder. You can't take a pill to fix it. You need to communicate."

Dr. Connor looked back and forth between Cat and Billie. She noticed a pink tinge covering their cheeks. "Cat, I sense you're somewhat embarrassed by this discussion."

"Maybe a little, but if it helps, I'm willing to continue."

"It's a plus to have a good attitude. Thank you. Billie, I sense you're disturbed and, possibly, angry."

Billie sat forward in her seat and looked at the doctor. "I confess you've put me on the defensive. I admit to being a little skeptical, but as Cat said, if it helps, I'll cooperate."

Dr. Connor smiled. "All right. I've saved the best for last. Hopefully the exercises I'm about to give you will lighten the mood somewhat and set the stage for restoring not only a fulfilling sex life, but an enjoyable one as well."

Dr. Connor held up her hand and counted off the exercises on her fingertips. "Here goes. First exercise—role-play. Dress up in lingerie. Get sexy."

"Not a problem," Billie said.

"Exercise two—play Naked-Twister."

Cat's eyes opened wide and she blushed.

"Exercise three—engage in any activity that you can participate in equally. Avoid being in a submissive position. Smear chocolate fudge on each other, or maybe whipped cream. Lick it off. Be sure to do it to each other."

Billie grinned. "Now you're talking."

Dr. Connor laughed. "These exercises are designed to put fun into the sexual act. Rape is anything but fun. Sexual activity needs to be the polar opposite of the sexual abuse experience. Any questions yet?"

Cat and Billie shook their heads.

"All right. The last thing we need to discuss is sexual positions. This is where we veer from the traditional therapeutic approach, solely due to the fact that you're both women. Sexual positions need to be neutral, or in such a way that Cat can be dominant. Woman on top is a good start. Face-to-face is another one that will allow you to be on equal terms and keep you focused on each other. Be bold and daring. Introduce a few yoga positions if you like, as long as Cat isn't in a submissive role. Cat, you need to avoid any position that makes you feel degraded or uncomfortable. Relative to the pregnancy, you'll need to modify your positions accordingly. I recommend your role-plays include the pregnancy. That can be an opportunity to be very gentle and loving toward each other."

Dr. Connor sat back. "A bit overwhelming, isn't it?"

"How long before I begin to feel sexual again?" Cat asked.

"That's up to you and Billie. You need to feel safe. Billie, you can help with that. Cat, your trauma was the result of an unsafe sexual situation. Once you feel secure and loved, you'll feel more comfortable expressing yourself in sexual ways. I won't tell you it'll all happen in a week, or a month, but it'll come in time. The pregnancy may affect when you begin to feel sexual. Some women lead very active sex lives during pregnancy, and some don't. I urge you not to lose hope. If you truly love each other as much as I think you do, things will come around. Be patient... and be persistent."

Chapter 17

Cat slipped her hand into the crook of Billie's elbow as they walked across the park.

"How are you doing?" Billie asked.

"I can't wait until this little bugger is born. This is rough on my lower back." Cat's weight shifted from side to side as she walked across the grass. "Not to mention I waddle like a penguin when I walk."

"A very cute penguin, I might add. Not much longer now. Dr. O'Brien says the baby is already dropping."

"By my calculations, I have maybe two weeks left, but this child has a mind of her own. She'll come when she's good and ready."

"I'm glad it's a girl."

"A boy would've been nice, too. At last, a place to sit down." Cat lowered herself onto the bench by their favorite tree.

"Are you comfy?"

"Yes, I am. Thank you, love. Would you mind laying the blanket out so the kids can have a clean place to eat lunch?"

Cat scanned the playground and located Seth and Tara playing on the jungle gym. "I can't believe less than a year ago Seth was barely getting around on his own. Look at him now, running and climbing all over the place."

Billie sat on the blanket in front of Cat. "I know. So much has changed in our lives. Before I met you, I never would have guessed I'd be part of a family again. And now, here I am with my best girl, watching our son and daughter play, and waiting for their little sister to arrive. I couldn't be happier, Cat."

Cat ran her fingers through Billie's hair. "Have I told you lately how much I love you?"

"You may have said it once or twice today, but I'll never tire of hearing it."

"Well, I do, you know… love you, I mean. You've taken on so much responsibility lately. Me, Tara, my child…"

"Our child, Cat. Our child."

"Our child," Cat said with a smile. "I can't tell you enough how much I love you."

"When we first learned about the pregnancy, I have to admit I was upset, angry, and jealous, but—"

"Jealous?"

"Yeah, jealous that I couldn't be the one to give you this child. Anyway, I had mixed feelings at first, but now, I'm so looking forward to this baby. Our baby. This child is a biological link between Seth and Tara. I don't care if the child isn't technically mine. It's mine in my heart, and I'll do everything in my power to be a good parent. Thank you for giving me this chance."

Billie watched Seth and Tara play on the swings. "Have you heard anything from the realtor this week about the condo?" she asked.

"Not yet. Don't worry. It'll sell soon."

"I sincerely hope so. It's been on the market for a long time."

"At this point, I don't think it'll sell before the baby arrives. We'll just have to make do."

"Thanks for moving back into our room. I know how difficult that was for you."

"Knowing it's temporary helps. Going to the therapy sessions has also helped a lot. Thank you for being so supportive."

"I'll do everything in my power to make this work."

Cat shifted her weight to one hip. "Wow, my low back really hurts today." She shifted again. "Oh, oh."

"Cat, are you all right?"

"We're in this together, right?"

"Together, love, together. I'm totally committed to you and our children. And I'm a woman who honors her commitments."

Cat grabbed her abdomen as pain doubled her over.

"Cat?"

"Get me to the hospital. My water just broke."

* * *

"Push," Billie said.

"Aaahhhhh."

"Come on, Cat. That's it. Push."

"Damn it! If you want this so badly, you push."

"Oh, no, no, no. Been there, done that, thank you very much. Not much longer, now. You can do it."

"Oh God, it hurts. I can't do this anymore."

"Yes you can. Breathe through it. That's it. Short breaths."

"The head is crowning," the doctor said.

Cat felt Billie behind her. "Can you see?"

"Just barely. It's a bit of a challenge to see over your stomach. You're doing great, Cat. Just a little longer."

"I was a bit worried we'd have to take her surgically, but things are finally moving," the doctor said. "It won't be long now."

"I can see her head, Cat. She has red hair, just like you. It'll be all over soon, I promise." Billie kissed her on the temple.

Cat clung to Billie's arms so tightly that her nails dug into Billie's skin.

"Oh my God!" Cat howled as the oscilloscope recorded the next contraction.

"Cat, on this next contraction, you'll need to bear down hard to get the shoulders out," the doctor instructed.

"Cat, brace your feet and push against me," Billie said.

Cat braced her feet behind the stirrups and pushed her head against Billie's chest. Her abdomen contorted as the contraction consumed her. A deep growl escaped her, and she bore down hard. Suddenly, relief filled her body as the child slid from the small opening. Cat slumped against Billie. A high-pitched wail filled the room.

"Well," the doctor said, "as you already know, it's a girl. One redheaded, very upset little girl from the sounds of it." She clamped the umbilical cord and lifted the child up for them to see before she laid the baby on Cat's chest.

"I guess she doesn't appreciate being pulled from her warm cocoon," Cat said.

She looked at the broad smile covering Billie's face as she stared at the wriggling creature lying on her chest.

"She's beautiful," Billie said.

"That she is," replied Cat.

"Are you ready to cut the cord?" the doctor asked.

The doctor's voice released Billie from the baby's spell. She took the shears in her shaky hand and reached over Cat's shoulder to cut the cord. "Yep, just call me Dad," she joked as she handed the scissors back to the doctor.

Billie returned her attention to Cat and the tiny infant still wailing in her arms. The child was perfect. Billie noted her red hair, delicate features, and dimpled elbows and knees. She bore a strong resemblance to Cat, however Billie readily saw traces of both Tara and Seth in her.

The sight of mother and daughter captivated Billie. Even with a sweat-covered face and stringy limp hair from the long and difficult labor, Cat never looked more beautiful to her. Emotion made speech difficult. All she could do was tighten her arms around Cat and lay her cheek on top of her head as they both gazed adoringly at their new daughter.

"Brace yourself, Cat. We need to deliver the placenta," the doctor said as she pushed down on Cat's stomach. In no time, it was over.

Billie squirmed her way out from behind Cat on the bed. She shook her legs to get the blood flowing again and regain feeling. A nurse took the baby from Cat to clean her up and take the necessary measurements as another nurse prepared Cat to be moved to her room. Billie took this chance to pull a chair next to the bed and speak to Cat face-to-face.

Billie took Cat's hand in her own and lifted it to her mouth. She kissed the back of each knuckle and pulled the hand close to her heart. "We have a beautiful daughter. She looks like you, red hair and all."

Cat looked at Billie. "I love you."

Billie couldn't keep the smile from her face. "I love you, too. Thank you for this gift. I promise I'll do everything I can to take care of her, and the rest of our family, too."

Billie followed close behind as the nurse wheeled Cat into her room and transferred her into the bed. Within moments, the baby was brought to her. Billie sat in the chair next to the bed and waited for the nurses to leave her alone with her family.

Billie could see Cat's eyelids droop. She took the baby from Cat's arms and kissed Cat on the forehead. "Why don't you take a nap? You look exhausted. I'll take care of the little one. All right?"

Soon, Cat was asleep. Billie walked to the window with the baby and allowed her gaze to wander out over the city. She looked down on the sleeping infant and hugged her close. "Your big brother and sister can't wait to meet you. Thank you for coming into our lives." Billie kissed the baby on the forehead and thanked every god in existence for giving her such wonderful gifts as Cat and her new family.

Billie didn't know how long she stood by the window before the sound of someone clearing his throat was heard. She'd fallen into a light trance as she hummed an old lullaby while she rocked back and forth. She pivoted toward the noise and saw Doc in the doorway.

Doc walked over to Billie and wrapped his arms around her and the child. "Another granddaughter." He planted a kiss on the baby's head. "Looks like Seth's monopoly still holds."

Doc took the baby from Billie's arms and tucked her into the crook of his elbow. He traced the side of her face with his free hand. "She looks like Caitlain."

"Yes, she does." Billie felt uncomfortable. As much as Cat scolded her for it, she still felt responsible for the rape.

Doc spoke to her without lifting his eyes from the baby's face. "It's not your fault, Billie."

Billie was shocked that he apparently read her mind.

"Look at this child. How can something so precious and beautiful come from such a vile act?" he asked.

"Her beauty comes from Cat," Billie said as she absently brushed the baby's hair.

Doc looked at Billie. "Cat told me he's behind bars for at least the next ten years."

"Yes. It took almost the entire pregnancy to make it happen, but he exhausted his appeals, and now he's locked away in prison for a long time. I'm thankful he was convicted without Cat having to testify. The DNA evidence was irrefutable."

"Does he know he has another child?" Doc asked.

"He knows."

Billie took the baby back from Doc and watched him walk to Cat's bedside and kiss her on the forehead.

Cat's eyes opened. "Another girl, Daddy."

"Yes, kitten, another girl, and what a beautiful one she is."

"How are Seth and Tara? Are they terrorizing Mom yet?"

Doc tweaked her nose. "You don't give your mother enough credit. After all, she raised you and your sisters, didn't she? None of you were exactly model children, and yet she survived. Don't worry about her. She can handle herself with two small tykes. But to answer your question, they're fine. They're anxious to come see their new sister, but otherwise, fine."

The baby began to protest in Billie's arms. Billie handed the fussing baby to Cat. "I think this little one is hungry. After we feed her, I'll go to Mom's and get the kids."

Doc cleared his throat. "Well, I think I'll leave you two alone while I make my rounds. I'll come back to check on you later." He kissed both Cat and the baby, winked at Billie, and was on his way.

"That was a smooth escape. I think the idea of watching me breast-feed scared him away," Cat said.

"You may be right. Here, let me get in behind you."

Billie climbed onto the bed to sit behind Cat, and she held her two girls in her arms as the baby breast-fed. It was the most amazing feeling in the world. She could stay like this forever.

Billie's gaze never strayed as she watched her new daughter take nourishment and fall asleep in Cat's arms. Billie dislodged herself from behind Cat and knelt on the floor beside the bed to watch in fascination as Cat changed the baby's diapers and took a physical inventory of fingers and toes.

"She's beautiful, isn't she, Billie?"

"I've never seen a more beautiful baby. She's perfect. Like her mom."

Cat looked at Billie. Billie saw the mischief in her eyes. "Which mom?"

"I'll leave you to think about that one, while I go collect the other two rug rats," Billie said.

∗   ∗   ∗

Fifteen minutes later, Billie pulled into the driveway of Cat's childhood home. She got out of the car and started up the walk when the front door opened and Seth and Tara raced out. Billie bent down on one knee to embrace the children, who ran toward her at full speed. The next thing she knew, she was flat on her back in the grass, with two giggling kids on top of her. Cat's mother, Ida, stood in the doorway with a smile from ear to ear.

Billie rose to her feet. She brushed the dirt and grass off her clothes and bent down to pick up the kids. With a child on each hip, she climbed the steps to the porch and kissed Ida on the cheek. "Hi, Mom."

"Come inside. Tell me all about my new granddaughter."

Billie followed her into the kitchen.

"Sit while I pour us some coffee," Ida said.

Billie set the kids down, and they ran into the other room to watch cartoons. Billie accepted the coffee Ida handed to her. "Mom, you're a lifesaver." She sipped the rich coffee. "This is wonderful."

"You're just in time for lunch. You must be starved." Ida pushed her toward the kitchen chair. "Tell me about my granddaughter while I get you something to eat."

Billie's face lit up as she thought about her new daughter. "She's beautiful. She has red hair and looks exactly like Cat. I suppose she's what Tara must've looked like when she was born."

Ida brought a bowl of homemade soup and a thick ham sandwich to the table and put them down in front of Billie. Billie's mouth watered at the sight. "Thanks, Mom." She picked up the sandwich and took a large bite. "God, this is good."

"I'm glad you like it. So, tell me, does the baby look at all like Seth?"

Billie knew this was Ida's way of indirectly asking if the baby looked like Brian. Billie's gaze fell to the table as she fought back the guilt that threatened to wash over her once again.

"I'm sorry. I shouldn't have asked that. It was very insensitive of me. Please forgive me."

Billie looked at Ida. "Mom, you don't have an insensitive bone in your body. I think Cat inherited that from you." She paused to collect her thoughts. "Don't apologize. You've a right to ask. I would have to say yes, the baby does resemble Seth a little. She mostly looks like Cat, but I can see traces of Seth and Tara in her as well."

Ida patted Billie's hand. "I'm sure she's a beautiful child. I can't wait to see her."

Glad to have that conversation behind her, Billie smiled and grasped Ida's hand. "You'll get your chance soon. It looks like Cat may be going home as early as tomorrow."

"She must've had an easy labor."

"Just the opposite. The labor was pretty long and intensive. I thought for a while that they'd have to deliver her by C-Section. About twenty-four hours after her water broke, the baby's head crested and soon after, it was all over. Cat was amazing. She only cursed me out about a dozen times." Billie smiled at her own joke.

"Only a dozen, huh? You're lucky. I cursed Doc far more than that, with each of our four daughters."

Billie looked unbelievingly at the gentle woman. "You? Curse? I don't believe it."

Ida stood up, walked behind Billie and wrapped her arms around her. Billie closed her eyes and leaned her head into Ida's arm. "Billie, my girl, believe it. You've gotten to know Cat's Dad.

He's the gentlest soul I know. So, where do you think Cat got her stubborn streak, huh?"

"I never would've guessed." Billie felt warm and safe in the older woman's arms. How she missed her own mom.

"What have you decided to name her?"

"We haven't yet. Cat wouldn't even discuss names while she was pregnant. She insisted on seeing the baby first."

Billie was startled by the sudden appearance of Seth and Tara who charged into the room and slid across the kitchen floor on their knees, barely missing Ida. "Hey, you two. That's enough of that."

"Aw, come on, Mom," Seth said. "It's fun."

"Yeah, Mom, it's fun," Tara echoed.

"Look, you almost took Grammy out at the knees. That's enough. Besides, you need to get ready to go see your new sister."

Seth jumped to his feet and brushed his knees off. "Can we go now?"

"As soon as you wash your hands and comb your hair," Ida said. "You want to look nice for Mama, don't you?"

The two kids ran to the bathroom to do as they were told. Moments later, Billie collected their overnight bag and backpack filled with toys and took them to the car.

Back on the porch, Billie bent down and hugged Ida. "We'll stop by on the way home from the hospital tomorrow."

"I'm counting on it."

"I love you, Mom. Thanks for taking the kids," Billie kissed Ida's cheek.

"I love you, too, sweetie. I'll see you tomorrow."

Billie got into the car and looked into the backseat. "Seat belts." The children complied as she put the car into gear. Billie and the children waved as they drove away.

Chapter 18

Seth and Tara asked several questions about their little sister on the way to the hospital.

"How big is she, Mom?" Seth asked.

"She's about twenty inches long. That's almost as long as two rulers. She weighs almost eight pounds, kind of like what your backpack weighs when your schoolbooks are in it."

Billie glanced in the rearview mirror and saw Seth try to estimate twenty inches between his hands.

"Wow. She's kinda small," he said.

"Not really. You were twenty-one inches when you were born."

"I was?"

"You were, and look at you now."

"How big was I when I was born?" Tara asked.

"I don't know, sweetie. We'll have to ask Mama."

"What does the baby look like?" Tara asked.

"She looks a lot like Mama, but she also looks like Seth and you, too, Tara. She has red hair just like you and Mama."

Billie barely had time to answer all their questions before she pulled into the parking lot. "Grab your toys," she said to the kids as they climbed out of the car.

Once inside the hospital, she took their hands and led them toward Cat's room.

Cat was breast-feeding when they entered the room. Billie carefully gauged Seth's and Tara's reactions to the child suckling at Cat's breast. Both seemed fascinated with what they saw. Tara climbed up to sit on one side of her mother. She intently watched the baby nurse. A little more timidly, Seth slowly made his way to the other side of the bed and looked up at Billie. She motioned for him to climb up, which he did very carefully.

"You can come closer," Cat said to Seth. She used her free hand to help him settle in next to her. She brushed the hair off his forehead and left a light kiss in its wake.

Tara was the first to speak. "Mama, does that hurt?"

"No, sweetie, it doesn't."

"That's 'cause babies don't have teeth," Seth said.

"Yes, that's part of the reason. The other part is that she isn't biting me, she's sucking, like you do when you drink from a straw. Understand?"

Both children nodded in response.

"All right, little one, I think you've had enough." Cat pulled the baby away from her breast and hefted her against her shoulder. It didn't take long for a loud belch to escape the baby's mouth.

Seth and Tara giggled.

"What a hog," Tara exclaimed.

"Yeah," Seth added. "We should name her Hogger." Seth's remark triggered peals of laughter from all of them.

"Let me take little Hogger while you get yourself back together," Billie said. She cradled the newborn in her arms like she was the most precious gift on the face of the earth while Cat retied her hospital gown.

"You know," Cat said to Billie, "the kids have a point. We do need to name her."

"You're right, but somehow, I don't think she'll thank us for naming her Hogger."

Cat wiped the tears of laughter from her eyes. "No, seriously, she needs a name."

"You're the one who didn't want to discuss names during the pregnancy."

"I know, I know. I explained that to you. I needed to see her before we named her. What if the name we picked didn't fit her face?"

Billie looked down into her daughter's face. "Yes, we're talking about you," Billie said to the baby as she stretched her arms straight up and yawned. Suddenly, she opened her eyes.

"Cat, her eyes are blue, like Seth's. Sky blue, in fact. Look." Billie held the baby close to Cat.

"Wow, they are blue. Most newborns are born with blue eyes. I hope they stay that color."

"Wait," Billie said. "That's what we can name her."

"Blue eyes?"

"No, don't you see? Her eyes are sky blue. We can name her Skylar."

"Skylar. Skylar." Cat looked at the baby. "It fits. I like it. I like it very much. She looks like a Skylar."

Billie looked at the two older children. "How about you two? What do you think?"

"I like it, too," Seth said.

"Me, too!" Tara said.

"Skylar, it is. Thank you, love. It's a beautiful name. In fact, I think we should name her Skylar Jean."

"You're giving her my middle name?" Billie asked.

"Yes. It's one way to make you a part of her. Is that okay?"

Billie kissed the baby's cheek. "It's more than okay. Thank you. I can't tell you what this means to me."

"Mom?" Seth interrupted. "Can I hold her?"

Billie looked at Cat and received a nod of approval. "Sure you can, honey. Here, scoot in closer to Mama and hold your arms out."

Seth did as he was told and opened his arms to receive his new baby sister. Billie noted that he held her in his arms like it was his favorite teddy bear. He looked at his two mothers and grinned, then lowered his face to hers until their noses touched. "Hi, Skylar. I'm your big brother, Seth."

The baby smiled and flailed her arms.

"Hey, she likes me!" Seth said.

"Of course she does," Cat said. "How could she not love her big brother?"

Billie didn't have the heart to tell him it was probably just gas.

"My turn. My turn!" Tara demanded.

Billie was so taken with her new daughter, she insisted on holding her almost nonstop for the rest of the afternoon, despite warnings from Cat that she was going to spoil her. Seth and Tara spent their time alternately visiting with the baby, and playing with their toys.

Soon, it was time to leave.

Billie reluctantly handed the baby over to Cat and addressed the older two children. "Time to collect your toys and get ready to go. We'll stop for pizza on the way home."

"Yay! Pizza!" they exclaimed.

Billie transferred Skylar into Cat's arms and kissed the baby's head. "I'll drop the kids off at Mom's tomorrow morning and be here bright and early to bring you home. Mom's very excited about seeing her new granddaughter."

"We'll have to pick Seth and Tara up, anyway." Before Billie got away, Cat whispered in her ear, "I can't wait to go home. I miss sleeping in your arms."

"I miss you, too. And I love you with all my heart. I'm looking forward to making love to you. It's been a long time."

Cat closed her eyes and nodded. "I know, but I think I'm ready. At least I will be after I recover from childbirth."

"You've been through hell and back over the last year. It's understandable that you need time to heal psychologically. Thank you for agreeing to go to the counseling sessions. I think they've really helped."

"I should be thanking you for being so patient with me."

"I love you. You're worth the wait."

Cat's eyes filled with tears. "You'd better get out of here before you turn me into a blubbering idiot."

Billie looked to the children. "Hey you two, how about kisses for Mama and Skylar?"

Both the children bounded to the bed and kissed their mother and little sister then ran back to the door. Seth took Tara's hand. "Come on, Mom. We're hungry."

Tara, being Seth's little echo, repeated, "Yeah, Mom, we're hungry."

Billie grinned and said to Tara, "If Skylar eats as much as you and your brother, we're going to be in *big* trouble."

Cat laughed and swatted Billie on the arm. "Get out of here before they wither away."

* * *

Billie arrived at the hospital the next morning to collect Cat and Skylar. She insisted on carrying Skylar as the nurse pushed Cat to the front door in a wheelchair where their car was waiting for them parked at the curb. After a short struggle with the car seat, they were on their way to Doc and Ida's.

Once there Billie snapped Skylar's car seat out of the base and removed it from the car. She took Cat's hand and walked toward the house. When they were halfway down the walk, the front door swung open.

"Here they come," Billie said as Seth and Tara ran down the stairs to meet them.

"Can I help carry Skylar, Mom?" Seth asked.

"I wanna help, too," Tara said.

"Okay. Okay. Both of you can help. Cat, this is going to be a bit awkward. You might want to go ahead of us."

Billie smiled as Ida fawned over her new granddaughter. "She looks like you did when you were born, Caitlain. I hope she doesn't make the poopy mess you did." Ida's comment drew the attention of Billie and the kids.

"Ma!" Cat's face reddened.

"Poopy mess?" Billie asked, unable to hide her amusement.

"Mom... Please."

"Oh yes." Ida addressed Billie without taking her eyes from her new granddaughter's face. "When she was about a year old, she was standing in her crib one morning covered from head to foot in poopy. I'm afraid the crib, the wall, and the floor suffered much the same fate."

"Oh, gross!" Seth said, and Tara made a face. Billie tried her best to contain the laugh that threatened to erupt from her chest.

"Geesh, Mom. Did you have to embarrass me?"

Ida looked at Billie and continued. "You know, to this day, I haven't figured out how she got her diaper off. We didn't have the nice disposable ones back then. She was wearing a cloth diaper with plastic diaper pants. She's lucky she didn't injure herself with the diaper pins."

Billie looked at her partner and grinned as Cat shook her head.

"So, Ida, do you like the name we chose for the baby?" Billie asked as she intentionally changed the subject to rescue Cat from further embarrassment.

All through the visit with Ida, Cat noticed that Seth and Tara had their heads together as they giggled and snuck sly looks at her. Several times, they asked Billie if it was time to go home. Normally when they visited Cat's parents, she and Billie had to drag them out of the house when it was time to leave.

After several yawns from Cat, Billie suggested they go home so Cat could rest.

On the way home, the children giggled back and forth across Skylar's car seat, which was situated between them. Cat frequently looked into the backseat to see what was so funny. She tried not to laugh when they not so subtly tried to be serious each time she turned around. Suspicious, Cat threw a sidelong glance at Billie. Something was up.

Billie carried Skylar to their apartment while Seth and Tara each took one of Cat's hands.

"What's this all about?" Cat asked.

"It's a surprise," Seth said.

Cat obediently allowed the children to lead her into the building and to the door of their unit.

"Mama, you have to close your eyes," Tara said.

"All right. They're closed."

Cat followed the children through the condo with her eyes closed.

"We're in the living room, Mama. You can sit down, but keep your eyes closed," Seth said.

Cat sat in the chair and listened to the scurry of activity around her. She heard Billie send Seth into her bedroom to fetch the baby's seat so she could put Skylar down safely, and she heard the general sounds of movement on the couch and in the kitchen. "What are you guys up to?"

Billie stopped by Cat's side and kissed her cheek. "One more minute, love."

Cat nodded and obediently kept her eyes closed.

A few minutes passed when Cat smelled something unusual. "What's that smell? Is something burning?"

"Nothing to worry about," Billie said. "Just keep your eyes closed."

"Okay, Mama," Tara said.

"You can open your eyes now," Seth said.

Cat opened her eyes. "Oh my goodness." On the coffee table in front of her, was a cake with a single lit candle and several presents wrapped in baby-shower paper. She looked around the room and saw decorations made of crepe paper and balloons, all in a baby motif. She took all of this in through moistened eyes, which finally fell on the occupants of the couch. All three children and Billie sat side by side, waiting for her reaction.

"How is it that I'm so lucky to have such a wonderful family?" Cat asked. "I love you all so much."

Cat's attention was drawn to the couch as a shriek came from the newest member of their family. "Could you hand her to me, Billie? My guess is she's hungry again."

Billie retrieved the baby from her seat and cradled her in her arms as she carried her to Cat.

Billie addressed Tara and Seth. "How about giving me a hand with the cake and ice cream while Mama feeds Skylar?"

The kids followed Billie into the kitchen while their little sister ate her fill at her mother's breast.

* * *

Billie was anxious to resettle in another home. Cat's condo not only held painful memories for both of them, but they were out of room. After what seemed like the hundredth time Billie ran into either the baby's swing or playpen in the middle of the living room, an acceptable offer came in on the condo. With a closing date scheduled, they set out to find a home that would be right for their growing family.

Billie worked with the realtor to schedule visits to a dozen houses before she and Cat found a cozy two-story home on a corner lot on the outskirts of town. Billie pulled into the driveway and parked in front of the two-car garage. "Let's look around the grounds before we go in," she said.

Billie waited for Cat to exit the car, then took her hand and walked around the house.

"Not bad," Billie said as they stood in the front yard and looked at the house. "It needs a little TLC, but it appears to be in good shape."

"I can picture a flower garden on each side of the front porch," Cat said.

"I also like that the backyard is fenced in. What do you say we go inside?" Billie suggested.

"I was hoping you'd say that. Do you have the keys?"

Billie pulled a set of keys from her pocket. "Yes. I picked them up from the realtor on my way home from work. She recommended we enter through the back door."

Billie led Cat around to the back of the house and onto a large screened-in porch.

"This would be nice on warm summer evenings. Can't you imagine us sitting here in our old age in twin rocking chairs?" Cat said.

Billie laughed. "Yeah, two old hags with one tooth between us, but I get the tooth first."

Cat shook her head. "You're insane."

"That I am. Crazy in love to be exact." Billie pushed open the back door. "After you." She stepped aside and allowed Cat to enter first.

"Wow, big kitchen," Cat said.

Billie spread the floor plan the realtor had given her out on the kitchen table while Cat walked through the room, opening cupboard doors.

"It says here that there's a family room in the basement." Billie picked up the floor plan and rotated it in front of her until she aligned it with the room they were in. "I believe that door over there leads downstairs. I'm going to check it out."

"Hold on, I'll go with you."

Billie flicked on the lights in the carpeted stairway and began to descend. Cat followed close behind.

Billie stepped into the family room. "This is nice. Look, there's a fireplace."

She wrote notes on the floor plan as they walked through the room. "I like this, Cat. The fireplace kind of does it for me."

Cat grinned. "Are you a closet pyro, or does the thought of making love in front of an open fire appeal to you?"

Billie wrapped her arms around Cat. "All of the above."

"You're incorrigible."

"That's me."

"I'm going to look around some more," Cat said. She broke free from Billie's embrace and walked to the far end of the room. "I wonder what's behind this door? Oh, it's the laundry. Very nice."

"There's a lot more to see. We should head back upstairs," Billie said.

Back on the first story, they found a large living room with another fireplace. The first floor also contained a guestroom and a bathroom. The living room exited onto a large front porch that overlooked a manicured front lawn, complete with a white picket fence.

"This feels like a fairy-tale house. Pinch me to see if I'm dreaming," Billie said. "It needs some minor cosmetic work—you know, a little paint and maybe new carpeting—but it's certainly nicer than any other we've looked at so far."

She pointed to the stairway at the far end of the living room. "I assume that leads to the second story."

She held Cat's hand as they ascended the stairs. They stood at the top of the stairs and looked around. Billie referred to the floor plan once again. "It says here this level contains four bedrooms and two bathrooms." She pointed to each of the rooms, beginning with those on her left. "Those two over there and the one at the end of the hall on the right would be the kids' rooms and the bathroom is there on your right. I'll bet the other bathroom is off the master bedroom."

"That door at the end of the hall must be the master bedroom," Cat said. "Let's go check it out."

"Okay, but I want to take a quick look at the other bedrooms as we go."

By the time they walked the length of the hall, Billie was all but convinced to purchase the house.

Cat turned the knob to the master bedroom and pushed the door open. "Oh my God. I love it. It's huge."

Billie walked through the room and stepped into the master bath. "Oh yeah," she said. "Nice big bathroom, and it has a double vanity. Now maybe I'll have room for my stuff."

Cat backhanded Billie across the stomach. "Hey, I need all my stuff to look good for you."

"Sweetheart, you'd look good in a potato sack and with no makeup at all."

"I love you, too."

Billie took Cat's hand and walked back into the bedroom. "So, what do you think?"

"This is perfect. It's everything we need. It's also closer to both our jobs, and it's right on the bus route for when Seth and Tara start school this fall."

"As far as I'm concerned," Billie said, "it's our dream house. I think we should buy it."

* * *

Billie and Cat made an offer on the house and submitted their financial application then waited anxiously for the bank's decision. After nearly two nerve-wracking weeks, their approval came through. A week later, they sat across the table from the owners to sign the final papers.

After the closing, Billie and Cat shook hands with the previous owners who wished them luck. The husband congratulated Billie on their new home while Cat exchanged greetings with the wife.

"Well, young lady," the older gentleman said. "Good luck with the house, I'm sure you'll be comfortable there, but a word of advice. Don't let your personal preferences be known in the neighborhood. They aren't accustomed to your kind, you know."

Billie narrowed her eyes and refused to let go of his hand right away. Instead, she squeezed it tight. She saw the man wince. "Why don't you let me worry about my preferences?" She released his hand and walked away to meet Cat who she intentionally embraced in an affectioate hug while the ignorant man stomped away, dragging his wife behind him.

Cat and Billie said their goodbyes and expressed thanks to the realtor as they collected their papers and prepared to leave.

"What was that all about?" Cat asked.

"Ignorance. Pure ignorance."

* * *

The next morning, Billie woke up before the alarm. She turned off the auto-alarm then threw the covers back. Careful not to wake Cat, she slipped out of bed, rummaged through her dresser until she found clothing suitable for working around the house, then slipped out of the room. About ten minutes later, she returned carrying two cups of coffee. She sat down on the side of the bed and set one cup down on Cat's nightstand.

Billie traced one of her fingers down the side of Cat's face. "Rise and shine," she said.

Cat draped her arm over her eyes. "What time is it?"

"Six o'clock."

"What? You said we could sleep until seven."

"True, but it's a beautiful day and I thought we could get an early start."

"Ugh."

"Come on, Cat. There's a nice hot cup of coffee waiting for you on your nightstand."

"Okay, you win," Cat sat up in bed and reached for her cup. "Good morning, cup of ambition." Cat cradled the cup between her hands. "Thank you, love."

"Don't mention it."

"Why are you up so early?"

"I was too excited to sleep. There's so much to do on the new house. I can't wait to get started."

"There's not that much work."

"It's in pretty good shape, but we have lots of minor touch-up work to do, you know, painting, minor repairs, deep cleaning. Stuff like that."

"I'm glad you decided to take a couple of weeks off," Cat said. "Between the two of us and the kids, we should be able to get everything done by the time you go back to work. Thank God I'm still on maternity leave. I couldn't imagine juggling a work schedule with moving into a new home."

"I hear you." Billie sipped her coffee. "I want to thank you for not fussing too much about the kids helping out with the renovations. I know it might be easier to leave them with your parents, but I really want them to feel at home right away."

"You're welcome," Cat said. "Oh, that reminds me. We need to remember the sleeping bags. The kids will need a place to crash if we decide to work into the evening."

"Good idea." Billie stood. "Why don't you finish your coffee and get dressed. I'll go wake them. Maybe we can stop for donuts on the way."

"You don't need to tell me twice," Cat said as she threw the covers back.

* * *

Billie stood in the new kitchen with her hands on her hips. She looked around the empty room. "I see a few places that need drywall repair, and we definitely need to repaint the walls."

"At some point, I'd like to replace the floor as well," Cat said.

"Yeah, I can see where it's worn in a few places." Billie looked toward the blanket she had spread on the kitchen floor when they first arrived. "Are you guys finished with your donuts? We have lots of work to do."

"What do you want us to do?" Seth asked.

"There's a woodpile on the side of the garage. Why don't the two of you bring some of the smaller pieces in and stack them next to the fireplace in the family room. Maybe we can have a fire tonight."

"Okay."

Seth and Tara ran out the backdoor. "All right then," Billie said, "let's get to work."

* * *

"Yes, we're located at fifty-seven Pine Terrace. Where are you now?" Billie asked the moving van driver. "You're only about a block away. Turn right just after the church. All right. We'll see you in a minute or two."

"Did they get lost?" Cat asked.

"A little, but they should be here right about... now."

"Mom, they're here. They're here," Seth said and ran out the front door.

Billie followed Seth and met the moving van just as it pulled into their driveway. She shook hands with the driver and volunteered to help unload their belongings. During several trips to the truck, she was acutely aware of the stares from her curious neighbors.

Within four hours, stacks of boxes and arrays of furniture littered every room. Billie waved as the van drove away. She turned to see Cat standing on the front porch.

"Now the fun begins," Billie said.

"The house looks like a bomb exploded in it. There's stuff everywhere. It'll take weeks to find homes for everything," Cat said.

"It'll be worth it in the end. I think we should set up the beds so everyone will have a place to sleep. Then we can begin in the kitchen so we can at least put dinner on the table tonight."

It took the rest of the day for Billie and Cat to unpack the kitchen. After dinner that evening, they worked to assemble the family room where the movers delivered the living room furniture. Billie started a fire and they sat around eating popcorn and playing board games on the blanket they'd laid out on the floor. Billie played with the older children as Skylar slept in Cat's arms.

Before long, the children began to nod off. One by one, Billie carried them to bed. She returned to Cat who was still in the family room, sitting on the blanket in front of the fire. She appeared to Billie to be deep in thought. Billie sat behind her and wrapped her legs around her. She pulled her close to her chest and buried her face in Cat's hair.

"A penny for your thoughts."

Cat sighed. "I'm thinking that I'm gloriously happy, and wondering what I did to deserve it."

Billie kissed her neck. "You deserve all this and so much more. You're the most wonderful person I've ever met. I count my blessings every day that you choose to love me."

Cat shifted in her seat and looked at Billie over her shoulder. "That choice was made a very long time ago, my love. We belong together. We always have. This is our destiny."

"You look happy. You can't imagine how that warms my heart. The past year has been rough on you."

"It's been rough on both of us, and I'm thankful that we've made it through intact. I wouldn't have blamed you if you'd decided to call it quits ten months ago."

"I couldn't do that. You and the kids are my life. I could never walk away."

"And now we have this beautiful new house."

Billie looked around at their new surroundings. "Do you think we'll be happy here?"

"I'll be happy wherever we are as long as we're together. But yes, I think we'll be very happy here. Why do you ask? Are you having second thoughts about buying the house?"

"No second thoughts. It's just that after the closing, the original owner warned me that we shouldn't divulge our relationship to our neighbors. Also, while I was helping the movers unload the truck, there were lots of curious stares in my direction. I even heard someone wonder out loud why they didn't see the man of the house among us."

Cat shifted again and faced Billie. "I heard them, too. But you know what? I don't care what they think. I'm not ashamed of our love. I refuse to hide it to please the neighbors. If they can't accept us as we are, they can go to hell. Pure and simple."

Billie smiled. *God, how I love this woman.* "You're right of course, but with that in mind, don't blame me if I put a few people in their places along the way."

Cat chuckled. "I trust you'll be nice about it?"

"As nice as the situation warrants, but I won't tolerate any attacks against you or the kids. I hope you understand that."

Cat wrapped her arms around Billie's neck. "I do, love. I understand. Let's see if we can start things off right by christening this room with loud, raucous monkey sex. That ought to get the neighbors wondering. What do you say?"

"It hasn't been long enough since the birth, has it?"

"Sky's almost seven weeks old. Enough time has passed. And besides, it's been an eternity since we've made love."

"Our therapist recommended we don't rush things until you're ready, Cat."

"I know, and I'm so very thankful for your patience, but there's something about this house—about this new beginning—that makes me want to put the rape behind me and move on."

"And you think that loud, raucous monkey sex is the way to do that?"

"Well, we could always play Naked-Twister."

Billie couldn't keep the grin from her face and the chuckle from her throat as she laughed heartily. "You, my dear, are a nasty woman."

* * *

Cat took advantage of her maternity leave to settle into their new home. When the work was finished on the inside, she planted flowers around the front of the house and along the edges of the walk to the driveway. Billie fixed gutters and repainted window trim and shutters. Seth and Tara helped both of their mothers repaint the picket fence around the front yard while Skylar played in her playpen.

Cat was on her hands and knees spreading mulch in the garden she'd planted in the front yard when a car drove by. Cat sat back on her heels and waved, but the driver either didn't see her or ignored her. Cat looked up at Billie, who was on the ladder painting. "Don't you think it's odd that no one has stopped in for a visit? I mean, the realtor made a point of telling us this neighborhood was particularly well known for its welcoming committees, charity fundraisers, and general friendliness toward each other. I was looking forward to friendly neighbors after living through those cold, business-like association meetings at the condo."

"You're right. We've been here all summer, and so far we haven't formally met any of our neighbors. At least the kids are making friends. Our backyard has become the hangout for the neighborhood children."

"They love the tree house and the hand-over-hand pulley elevator you rigged. The neighborhood kids are all over the tree house like ants."

"I love it when the yard is filled with kids. Being an only child, I missed out on all the fun that comes with large groups of kids playing together."

"Confess. What you like is the opportunity to join in the fun, especially the water balloon and squirt gun fights, not to mention the wrestling matches."

"I can't help it, Cat. It's fun."

"Yeah, I know. You get to have all the fun, and I get to hand out treats and drinks, and bandage scraped knees."

"Don't give me that line. You enjoy the games as well. You've developed a pretty accurate aim when it comes to throwing a water balloon, especially at me."

* * *

As much as the neighborhood children were openly friendly, their parents were not. Several times when the yard was filled with children, Cat noticed many of their parents pass by the fence. It appeared to her they didn't really want to restrict their children's fun, but she assumed they were somewhat wary of them as newcomers. Cat often wondered out loud to Billie whether the neighbors organized shifts to keep an eye on the children while at the Charlands'.

One day, during an intense water balloon fight, Cat decided to get in on the action. Soon, everyone was soaked, including Skylar. In one particularly good shot, Cat threw a balloon at Billie and hit her squarely in the face.

"Why you little imp!" Billie shouted as she charged Cat and tackled her to the ground. Billie straddled Cat's stomach and lowered her face close to Cat's. "Nice shot," she said.

Cat instinctively kissed her.

All hell broke loose.

Cat could only surmise later that the centurion on guard at that time had seen the kiss. Almost instantly, hordes of neighbors charged into their yard, grabbed their children, and stomped away.

Cat scrambled to her feet and tried to intercept them. "Wait. Wait, you don't understand." Her heartbreaking pleas were for the children, both hers and the neighbors'.

One particularly vocal parent stopped in front of Cat. "Oh, we understand fine, you pervert."

Billie was instantly at Cat's side. She grabbed the front of the man's shirt and dragged him in close. "Apologize to the lady."

"Billie, let go of him. It's all right," Cat said.

"No, Cat. He has no right to treat you that way." Billie looked at the man. "I said, apologize to the lady."

The man looked at her defiantly and said nothing.

Billie emitted a low growl.

"Don't make me hurt you in front of these children," she said.

The man looked at Cat. "My apologies. However, I don't approve of your kind, and I'd prefer it if you didn't allow your children to associate with mine in the future."

"Let him go, Billie," Cat said.

Billie released his shirt and pushed him backward. "Leave my property."

The man walked away, pulling his protesting son behind him.

Seth and Tara clung to their respective parents as they watched their friends being dragged away.

"What happened, Mama?" Tara asked.

"They're stupid," Seth said. "They don't think Mom and Mama should love each other. They're stupid."

Cat knelt down in front of Seth. "Sweetie, that's not a nice word to use. They don't understand how much we love each other, that's all. They don't understand that it's all right for Mom and me to love each other as much as they love their own husbands and wives." She looked back and forth between the children. "Feels pretty awful, huh?"

They both nodded.

"Remember this feeling, my loves. It's called prejudice. Prejudice is when you treat people badly because they're different from you. This feeling is exactly why prejudice is bad. Do you understand?"

They both nodded and hugged Cat, while Billie looked on.

Chapter 19

Cat and Billie stood at the end of the driveway and waved to Seth and Tara as the school bus drove away. Billie held three-month old Skylar in one arm.

"I can't believe summer's over and I have to go back to work," Cat said.

"I can't believe Tara is starting kindergarten already. I hope she remembers to get on the bus that drops her off at the gym at noon," Billie replied.

"You're such a worrier. The teacher's aide will see that she gets on the right bus."

"I'm also worried that Seth might feel awkward being in first grade. He'll be a year older than his classmates."

Cat rubbed Billie's back. "I'm afraid that couldn't be helped. He lost almost a whole year when he was in the hospital. I'm sure he'll be fine."

Billie kissed Skylar and handed her to Cat. "Here you go. I've got to run. Busy court schedule today."

"Okay. Remember that I'm returning to work today. Don't forget to pick all three kids up at the day care on your way home."

"I won't. Have a great day. I love you."

* * *

Forced into involuntary solitude by the prejudices of the neighborhood, Cat and Billie and their brood settled into a routine centered primarily on their family unit. The demands of work, school, and homework kept them busy during the week. On the weekends, they spent time with Doc and Ida or worked around the house and yard.

With the onset of fall came the colors of autumn and the cool night air. One Saturday afternoon, Billie, Cat, and the kids raked the colorful leaves into a pile nearly as tall as Cat.

"Watch out, Mom. Here I come." Seth ran across the yard and jumped into the middle of the leaves.

"My turn! My turn!" Tara jumped in behind him.

Billie and Cat joined them, and within minutes, they'd leveled the shoulder-high pile of leaves and crumbled them in their hands like dry parchment, as they laughed hysterically. Neighborhood children gathered a short distance beyond the fence and watched the horseplay.

Billie climbed out of the pile and offered her hand to Cat. They stood side by side and watched Seth and Tara bury themselves in the leaves. Billie nudged Cat. "Look at them." She gestured toward the children who stood on the other side of the fence that marked the forbidden zone. "It breaks my heart to see them standing there without being able to join in."

Cat shook her head. "I wish there was something we could do. Those poor kids are nothing more than victims of their parents' prejudices."

"I know I've grown tired of receiving the cold shoulder all the time and being stared at in the supermarket," Billie said. "At least the kids can still play with their friends at school."

"I hear you. Who would've thought school would provide a healthier environment for our kids than our own neighborhood?"

"Sometimes I wish I could just shake some sense into their parents. Can't they see how they're affecting their kids?"

"As much as I agree with you, Billie, confronting them would send the wrong message to our own children. I guess all we can do is hope something will happen to open their hearts. In the meantime, we need to give our kids as much love and attention as possible."

Billie tucked a strand of hair behind Cat's ear. "Do you ever wish things were different? I mean, life would certainly be easier in some ways if we were straight."

"Bite your tongue, Billie Charland. I happen to like who I am. I agree that some things in life are easier if you go with the flow, but swimming against the current is so much more interesting. Sure, we face more obstacles because of whom we love, but so far we've been able to get over every hurdle, and we'll get over this one as well, somehow. Besides, if we were straight, we wouldn't be together and that would be such a tragedy."

Billie grinned. "Consider my tongue bitten."

* * *

The holidays came and went at the Charland/O'Grady house with not one visitor except Cat's parents and the people they worked with. Even though they decorated their home gaily in holiday themes, the Trick-or-Treaters bypassed their house on Halloween, as well as the carolers did at Christmas.

They were thankful that the children still had their friends at school. At Christmas, Tara and Seth brought small gifts to school for their best friends, a little girl named Karissa, and a boy named Stevie. They learned later that these children belonged to Jen and Fred Swenson and lived a couple of houses down the street.

On Christmas morning, Billie barely had time to pull the blanket over their nakedness when Seth burst through the door and pounced on the bed.

"Mom! Santa found us at our new house."

"I told you he would. Where's your sister?" Billie asked.

"She's looking at the presents under the tree. There's a gazillion of them."

"Go tell her not to open anything yet," Cat said. "Mom and I will get Skylar up, and we'll be down in a few minutes."

"Okay." Seth scampered off the bed and ran out of the room.

Billie looked at Cat. "I'm not looking forward to the day they learn Santa isn't real."

"Me, either. We'll lose our leverage. It's great to hold Santa over their heads when they're acting up."

"You got that right."

"Mom and Dad should be here later this morning. They'll need to head home at a reasonable hour this evening. They've got an early flight out to Florida in the morning."

"I'm glad they waited until after Christmas to go," Billie said. "With my parents gone and Brian's pretty much divorced from Seth, Mom and Dad are the only grandparents he has."

"They love him like their own, you know."

"I know they do, and I couldn't be more grateful. I'm convinced you inherited your loving heart from them."

"Merry Christmas, my love."

"Merry Christmas to you too, Cat."

* * *

After the first big snowfall, Seth and Tara dragged Billie out of the house and enlisted her help to build a snow igloo in the front yard. It took them most of the day, but when they finished, it was big enough for Billie's tall frame to stand in. The neighborhood kids collected on the sidewalk outside their fence and marveled at the size of it.

"Wow, Mom. It's huge," Tara exclaimed.

"That's cool, Ms. Charland. Awesome. I wish we could play in it, too," one of the kids outside the fence said.

Billie walked over to the fence. "You know you're welcome to come in and play."

"My mom and dad won't let me" was the common response.

"Do me a favor, will you?" Billie asked. "Go home and tell your parents that just because Cat and I are gay, it doesn't mean that Seth and Tara are, and it doesn't mean that you guys will become gay if you're friends with them. Oh, and also tell them that I'm willing to talk to them if they want to discuss it. All right? Can you remember all that?"

They all nodded and ran off to deliver their messages.

Billie turned to Seth and Tara and rubbed her hands together. "What do you say we go sweet-talk Mama into making us some hot chocolate?"

"Oh boy," Tara said as she ran toward the house.

Seth walked up to his mother and took her hand. Billie saw the sadness in his face. She knelt down on one knee and took his face in her hands. "I'm sorry about all of this. I know you wish your friends could come and play. I hope this blows over soon."

"It's okay, Mom. I can still play with my friends at school. I was worried about you and Mama. Sometimes I hear Mama crying when you talk about it. It makes me sad to hear her cry."

Billie realized Seth was right. There were a few times when Cat had cried while they discussed the prejudice around them. She didn't realize that her sensitive son had picked up on it.

Billie pulled him in close. "Seth, you're such a wonderful boy. We love you very much. Don't you ever change. Deal?"

"Deal."

"Piggyback ride into the house?" she asked.

"Yeah!"

"Climb on, partner." Billie dropped to one knee and allowed Seth to climb onto her back.

* * *

Later that evening, when the children were asleep, Billie and Cat went downstairs into the family room and cuddled together on the couch in front of the fireplace. They wrapped themselves in a large blanket and sipped mugs of hot-spiced apple cider. The dancing flames of the fire captivated them as their gazes affixed on the red-yellow glow.

After a while, Billie broke the silence and told Cat about the confrontation in the front yard and about her conversation with Seth. As always, when they talked about how their children were hurt by the situation, Cat began to cry. Billie held her close. "Please don't cry, love. Sooner or later, they'll come around. Please don't give up."

"But we've lived here for six months, and nothing much has changed."

"I know." Billie snuggled close to Cat. "But this can't go on forever. Somehow it will get better. I know it will."

"How's your cider holding up?" Cat asked.

"It's almost gone."

Cat peered into Billie's near-empty mug. "Why don't you finish that last swallow, and I'll go check on the kids and refill our mugs."

Billie eagerly complied and handed her mug over to Cat then opened their blanket cocoon and allowed her to get out. While Cat went upstairs, Billie pulled her knees into her chest, wrapped her arms around them, and stared into the fire.

A short time later, Billie heard Cat call her from the top of the stairs. "Billie! Billie, come quick!"

Billie took the steps three at a time. She took Cat by the shoulders. "What is it? Are the kids okay?"

"The kids are fine. They're all sleeping." Cat led her to the window above the kitchen sink. "Look. The Swensons' house is on fire. I already called 911."

Billie saw flames dance along the roofline of the house down the street. "Holy, shit. We've got to do something. Where are my boots?" she asked frantically. She located them quickly and shoved her feet into them.

"Where are you going?"

"I'm going to help them. I have to. I wouldn't be able to live with myself if I didn't."

"I'm going with you," Cat said as she shoved her feet into her own boots.

"What about the kids?"

"They'll be fine. They're sleeping. They won't even know we're gone. And besides, I'll come back to check on them every few minutes."

"All right. Get your coat."

Cat and Billie ran down the snowy street. When they reached the front yard of the Swensons' house, they saw Jen Swenson burst through the front door and fall to her knees as she gasped for breath. Billie was instantly by her side.

Still coughing uncontrollably, Jen climbed back to her feet and lunged toward the door to her burning home.

Billie grabbed her arm. "Jen, you can't go back in there. You can hardly breathe."

"Let me go. My kids are in there. Let me go!" Billie saw the terror in her eyes. Jen nearly collapsed against Billie in tears. "Fred went in after them. He hasn't come out."

"Cat, I need you here!"

Cat ran to Billie. "Stevie, Karissa, and Fred are still inside. I need to go in after them. Jen needs your help. Please find her a blanket and look after her. Don't let her go back inside."

Cat put a hand on Billie's arm. "No, Billie. You can't go in there. The fire!"

Billie interrupted further protest from Cat. "I have to. They may be dead before the fire trucks get here. Cat, they're children."

Cat stared into Billie's eyes.

"They're children, Cat. We can't let them die." Billie's voice was choked with emotion.

"Go. Please come back to me. I love you," Cat said before Billie ran toward the house.

Billie pushed the front door open and rushed into the living room. She was nearly blinded by the darkness and smoke, which burned her eyes. She ran into an end table and released a string of curses before she dropped to her knees and crawled along the floor where the smoke wasn't as thick. She pulled the collar of her turtleneck over her mouth and nose to filter out some of the smoke as she crawled. She thanked God that the Swensons lived in a ranch style home so she didn't have to deal with stairs to the second level.

Billie groped around for what felt like an eternity before she found the hallway that led to the bedrooms. She crawled down the length of the hall as fast as she could until she encountered a body much larger than that of a child.

"Fred? Fred, can you hear me?"

She grabbed him under the arms and dragged him back in the direction she'd come, toward the front door. When she reached the door, she screamed for someone to take care of him then went back inside the house.

More familiar now with the layout, she quickly located the hallway again and crawled toward the other bedrooms. She heard muffled cries coming from the first door she came to. She pushed the door open and cautiously crawled into the room. "Stevie? Karissa? Honey, talk to me so I can find you."

"I'm over here," a small voice said.

"Keep talking, sweetie, I'm coming."

Within seconds, Billie located five-year-old Karissa. She put her on her back. "Hold on tight and keep your head down and eyes closed. I'll have you out of here in a minute."

Karissa did as she was told while Billie crawled back toward the front door. She knew she'd have to hurry if she had any hope of finding Stevie in time, so as soon as she saw the door, she stood, swung Karissa around into her arms and ran the rest of the way into the front yard. She put the crying child into Jen's arms and ran back into the house as the fire trucks, ambulance, and police cars arrived.

Billie didn't bother to crawl this time. Even more familiar now with the house, she held her breath and ran down the hall to the room at the end. She kicked the door open and was met with smoke that billowed out at her at an alarming rate. Once again, she dropped to her knees and prayed that she'd find him in time.

"Stevie! Stevie!" she yelled over and over again with no response.

Billie crawled forward as she groped for anything solid. Finally, she located the bed. She rose to her feet and felt around until she found Stevie. He was unconscious. She scooped him up into her arms and stumbled toward the door. She moved as quickly as she could down the hallway and into the living room. Billie was succumbing to the smoke as she stumbled and nearly dropped her precious burden. She steadied herself and soon burst through the front door as the strain of holding her breath nearly caused her to lose consciousness. She inhaled huge gulps of fresh air and coughed violently as she collapsed to her knees. A paramedic met her and took Stevie from her arms. Instantly, Cat was by her side.

"Thank God, you made it," Cat exclaimed through tears as a policewoman wrapped a blanket around Billie and helped her toward the ambulance.

"No," Billie said. "I want to go home."

* * *

"I don't want to go to the hospital."

Cat leaned against the bathroom sink and spoke to Billie through the shower curtain. "You need to go. Think of the smoke you inhaled. Christ, you went into that house three times. You need to go. I insist."

Billie poked her head out of the shower. "Cat..."

"No argument, Billie. I know what I'm talking about. I'm a doctor, remember? Look, you've been coughing since you came out of the house with Stevie, and your voice is raspy. Those are classic symptoms of smoke inhalation. Do as I say and get dressed. You're going to the hospital. I'll call Mom and Dad to see if they'll come stay with the kids."

"All right, I'll go, but there's no need to wake your parents. I can drive myself."

Cat narrowed her eyes, but accepted the compromise. "Okay."

Billie toweled herself dry, dressed in clean clothes, and grabbed her car keys. "I think after I get myself checked out, I'll see how the Swenson family is faring. I'm a little worried about Stevie. I sure hope he makes it."

Cat wrapped her arms around Billie's waist and laid her cheek on Billie's chest. "I'm so proud of you. You unselfishly risked your life for them. I was so afraid for you."

"I couldn't stand by and do nothing. I couldn't let those children die. I remember how I felt when Seth was clinging to life after that car hit him. I can't imagine how it would've felt to lose him. I wouldn't want any other mother to have to go through that."

"I know, love. I know." Cat squeezed Billie tight. "I want you to invite Jen to come back with you. We'll put her up here until Fred and the kids are out of the hospital, or until they have somewhere else to go."

Billie kissed Cat. "You're a remarkable woman, Caitlain Maureen O'Grady. These people have shown us nothing but contempt, yet you open your heart and your home to them at the first sign of need."

Cat stood on tiptoes and returned the kiss. "I think you need to include yourself in that description of remarkable, love. Go to the hospital. I'll have a big breakfast waiting for you and Jen when you come back."

* * *

Billie went to the emergency room and inquired about the Swensons. She was told Karissa had been treated and discharged and Fred and Stevie had been admitted. She went to Admissions and was given directions to Fred's and Stevie's rooms.

Billie strolled down the corridor and saw Jen sitting on a bench. Karissa was sleeping in her arms. As she drew closer, she could see Jen was crying. She sat down next to the distraught woman, wrapped an arm around her and allowed Jen to rest her head on her shoulder. Billie's heart was in her throat. She wasn't sure if Jen's tears were those of relief or grief.

After a few moments, Jen lifted her head from Billie's shoulder. "I don't know how to thank you," she said. "We've treated you and your family so poorly. How can you ever forgive us?"

Billie wiped the tears from Jen's cheeks as she realized she was no older than Cat. "Shhh, let's not talk about that right now. How are Stevie and Fred?" She prepared herself for the worse.

"They're both alive, thanks to you. Fred is resting comfortably and should be able to come home tomorrow. Stevie's in intensive care. He inhaled a lot of smoke, but the doctors think he'll be well enough to go home in about a week." Jen paused. "That is, if we have a home to go to."

"You have a home to go to. Ours."

Billie saw a look of confusion cross Jen's face.

"I'm under strict orders from the boss lady to bring you home with me. Our home is open to you and your family for as long as you need it."

"I don't know what to say... except thank you."

Billie gave her shoulders a squeeze. "That'll do."

Before they left the hospital, Billie called Cat on her cell phone to fill her in on Fred and Stevie's conditions and to let her know exactly when they would be home. An hour later, Billie, Jen, and Karissa pulled into the driveway of the Charland residence. Cat met Jen with a warm hug as they walked into the kitchen. Once again, Jen began to cry. Cat held her until she calmed down and asked Billie to organize the children around the breakfast table. Billie pulled a spare chair for Karissa next to Tara. The two girls held hands and talked excitedly.

"Where's Stevie?" Seth asked.

Cat saw the look of fear on Seth's face. She knelt beside his chair. "Sweetie, I told you the Swensons' house was destroyed by fire last night. Stevie's in the hospital because he breathed in a lot of smoke, but the doctors said he'll be as good as new in a little while."

"Is Grandpa fixing him?"

Cat smiled and brushed the hair off his forehead. "No. Grandpa and Grammy are in Florida right now. Stevie has his own doctor taking care of him."

"When can he come home?"

"In about a week, I think," Cat said as she received an affirming nod from Jen.

"Can I play with him when he comes home?"

Jen joined Cat and knelt on the other side of Seth. "You sure can."

Seth smiled.

Cat looked at Jen. "How about a cup of coffee?"

"Oh God, yes." Jen rose to her feet and followed Cat across the room.

Jen's hands shook so badly she nearly spilled her coffee.

Cat took the cup back from Jen and put it on the table. "Here, sit," she said as she held the chair for Jen.

"I'm sorry I'm such a mess," Jen said.

"That's understandable, considering what you've been through over the past twelve hours. You just relax and enjoy your coffee while Billie and I get breakfast on the table."

After breakfast, Jen helped Cat clear away the dishes while Billie bathed and dressed Skylar for the day. The three older kids retreated to Tara's room to play.

Jen was alone with Cat in the kitchen. "I don't know how to apologize for the way we've treated you," Jen said. "We allowed our prejudice to cloud our vision. All I know to do is say I'm sorry."

"Billie and I are used to being treated differently because of our relationship, but what we didn't anticipate was the effect it would have on our children. All of our children, yours as well as ours." She saw the guilt in Jen's eyes. "We've tried very hard to teach our kids tolerance and acceptance, and we think we've been successful, but when adults contradict those lessons it's difficult for them to understand."

Jen looked down at her cup again and nodded. Tears rolled down her cheeks. Cat rubbed her back.

Jen raised her face to Cat's. "I'm so sorry."

Cat smiled back and hugged her close. "I assume you've been up all night, so why don't you take a shower and get some sleep so you'll be fresh when you go back to the hospital this afternoon."

Jen wiped the tears from her cheeks. "I'd like that."

"You can leave Karissa here with us. Billie and I will take care of her for you. It'll give Seth a break from his pesky little sister," Cat joked as she led Jen to the upstairs bathroom.

"Wait here a minute." Cat left Jen in the hallway and went to her room to grab a clean nightgown and robe from her dresser. She handed the clothing to Jen. "You look to be about the same size as me, so these should fit. Leave your soiled clothes on the floor next to the tub, and I'll wash and dry them while you sleep."

"You don't have to do that."

"I don't mind, Jen, really. You've got enough on your mind without worrying about laundry. Jump in that tub. You stink, woman." Cat laughed to lighten the mood.

Jen returned the laugh and thanked Cat for her kindness. After a shower, she curled up in the middle of Cat and Billie's bed and fell asleep.

Cat emerged from the laundry room off the kitchen to find Billie using her inhaler. She went to Billie's side and felt her forehead. "So what did the ER doc say?" she asked. "Did they intubate you?"

"Huh?"

"Did they put a tube down your throat? Your voice is very hoarse."

"Hell no. They suggested it, but I didn't want any part of that. They made me breathe through this apparatus that measured lung volume, and they took a chest X-ray. And they put this thing on my finger with a light on the end of it. Beats the hell out of me what it is, but I felt like ET. Phone home... phone home."

Cat swatted her on the arm. "It's an oxygen sensor, you dufus. It measures the amount of oxygen in your blood. If it was abnormally low, they would've treated you for carbon monoxide poisoning."

"Well, after they looked at my throat and made me breathe into the machine, they gave me this inhaler and recommended throat lozenges and sent me home."

Cat wrapped her arms around Billie's neck and kissed her. "Thank you for going."

"You're welcome. I'll be back to normal in a day or two."

"Well, I think we're about to define a new normal. Your act of heroism had a huge impact on Jen."

* * *

Cat loaned Jen her car to return to the hospital that afternoon. She also loaned her a coat and convinced her to take one of Billie's for Fred just in case he was released early. While the children built snowmen in the yard, Billie went to investigate the damage to the Swensons' house. As she walked down the street, she once again felt curious stares from her neighbors, only this time when she stared back, she was met with smiles instead of hostility.

When she reached the Swensons' property, she saw rope-lines surrounding the house. She walked around the periphery. The house wasn't in as bad a shape as the smoke would've predicted. She hoped the Swensons had fire insurance.

As she investigated the damage, she felt a presence next to her and realized one of the neighbors had approached and was standing beside her with his hands shoved deep into his overcoat pockets. He rocked back and forth on his heels. She spared him a sideways look as their eyes met.

"Good morning," he said.

"Good morning," she returned in a raspy voice. She fell silent again and turned her attention back to the house. She'd be damned if she was going to start a conversation.

"Bad fire."

Billie's eyes remained on the damaged house. "Could've been worse."

"Yep, could've. If it wasn't for you, it would've been."

She looked at him. Before she replied, he extended his right hand.

"Name's Carl. Carl Thompson."

Billie took his hand within her own and smiled. "Billie Charland."

"The damage doesn't seem to be too bad," Carl said.

"I was just thinking the same thing."

"That was a brave thing you did, going into that house last night."

Billie shrugged off the praise.

"I hope Fred and the kids are going to be okay," he said.

178

"Actually, they're going to be fine. Jen and Karissa are at my house right now, and Fred should be released from the hospital later today."

"And their boy?"

"Stevie inhaled a lot of smoke, but his doctor thinks he'll recover in a week or so. The Swensons will be staying with us until they find another place to go."

"That's right neighborly of you."

"Cat and I couldn't live with ourselves if we didn't help. It's not in our nature to turn our backs on people in need."

"Maybe we can all learn a lesson from this," Carl said softly.

While Billie and Carl chatted about the damage to the Swensons' house, several more neighbors joined them, and soon they organized the neighborhood into a work force to help the Swensons recover from the tragedy. By the time Billie made her way home, a neighborhood meeting was scheduled in the elementary school gym for that evening.

Billie walked into the house, swept Cat into her arms, and swung her around in a circle.

"Want to tell me what this greeting is all about?" Cat asked.

Billie bent over and picked up Skylar, who was playing on the floor. She hugged her youngest child and sat down at the table. Skylar sat on her lap. "Give me a cookie for this little monster, will you please?"

While Skylar munched on her cookie, Billie explained to Cat what happened at the Swensons' home.

"That sounds more like the neighborhood the realtor told us about," Cat said.

"It's a pity our miracle had to come at the Swensons' expense, but as they say, it sometimes takes a tragedy to pull people together."

"At this point, I'll take the miracle anyway I can get it."

* * *

Jen returned around lunchtime with Fred in tow.

Billie took their coats as Cat enveloped Fred in a hug. His shoulders shook. "It's okay, Fred. Everything will work out. You'll see." She released him and stepped back.

"I don't know what to say. I was floored when Jen told me you opened your home to us. I can't begin to thank you enough, especially after the way we've treated you." Fred wiped moisture from his cheeks.

"There's no need to say anything. It's all in the past. Let this be a new beginning for all of us," Cat said.

Fred turned to Billie and extended his hand.

Billie's eyebrows rose high onto her forehead. "What? I don't get a hug, too?"

Fred grinned and wrapped Billie in his arms. When he released her, the tears began anew. "I'm overwhelmed at your bravery. Jen told me you went into our burning home three times. You risked your life for us. There's no way I can ever repay you."

Billie squeezed Fred's shoulder. "No payment necessary, Fred. I couldn't live with myself if I didn't help."

"Time for lunch," Cat said. "Sit. Is soup and sandwiches okay for everyone?"

"You don't need to go to so much bother for us," Jen said.

"No bother at all. Please sit."

"Fred," Billie said, "I met a neighbor named Carl this morning while I was looking at the damage to your house."

"Carl Thompson?" Fred asked.

"Yeah, that's the name. Anyway, Carl and I spent a fair amount of time talking about organizing a cleanup crew. We're meeting this evening at the school."

* * *

After lunch, the adults sat around the family room to discuss plans for the immediate future while the older children played outside in the yard. Skylar played with her blocks on the blanket in front of the fire.

Fred sat on the chair opposite the couch. Jen sat on the arm of the chair, lazily rubbing his back. Fred looked at Billie and Cat as they cuddled close together on the couch, and his eyes filled with tears.

Cat rose from the couch and leaned down in front of Fred. She took the weeping man into her arms. "Shhh, it's okay, Fred. It's okay."

Fred seemed to be trying hard to compose himself. His voice shook as he said, "I looked at the two of you just now and realized that your love is as deep and profound as mine is for Jen. How could I have been so shallow?"

He pulled out of Cat's embrace and dried his face with his hands. He rose to his feet and walked to the mantel, where he pivoted around to face the women. "I don't know how to thank you for your kindness, except to say that I'll work my ass off to see that this community accepts the two of you as equals."

Billie stood and extended her hand to Fred. "Works for me."

"Ditto," Cat said.

Billie put her hand on Fred's shoulder. "So, Fred, I think with a concerted neighborhood effort, your house should be ready to move back into in a few weeks. Until then, you and your family are welcome to share our home."

"In fact, we insist on it," Cat said.

Fred looked at his new friends and threw his hands into the air. "I'm at a loss for words. Thank you. Thank you from the bottom of my heart."

Soon it was time for Jen and Fred to return to the hospital to visit Stevie. They left, taking Karissa with them and promising they'd be back in time for the neighborhood meeting that evening.

* * *

As promised, the Swensons arrived home in time to eat a quick supper before they and their new friends went to the school. The meeting was well attended. Nearly every neighbor was there, wives, husbands, and children included.

Billie and Carl stood on the stage as they waited for the clamor to die down, while Cat, Jen, Fred, and their children sat in the front row. Billie felt as though she was on display, and she nervously shoved her hands deep into her pockets. When the room quieted, Carl stepped up to the microphone to start the meeting. Before Carl said anything, Fred rose and announced that he wanted to say a few words. Billie and Carl moved aside.

Fred climbed the steps to the stage and stood in front of the mike. "I'm so happy to be here with you tonight," he said as the room erupted into applause. "Thank you. Thank you all. Stevie should be home soon as well. It's a miracle we all survived." Fred waited for the clapping to die down again. "It is indeed a miracle. Angels came to live among us several months ago. Guardian angels. If they hadn't been there yesterday, I wouldn't be standing here before you right now."

Fred walked over to where Billie and Carl stood and took Billie's hand. Billie could feel her face flush in embarrassment as

Fred led her to the microphone. "Cat, Jen, please join Billie and me on stage, and bring the kids, too."

Billie was thankful she wouldn't be there alone as she watched Cat carry Skylar across the stage. She extended her hands to Seth and Tara as they, too, joined her. Jen went to Fred and wrapped her arm around his waist while Karissa grasped his hand. A hush fell over the audience at the display.

Fred stepped up to the mike. "Friends, before the meeting begins, I'd like to introduce you to the newest members of our community. As you all know, we haven't been very neighborly to this new family. We've all treated them with disdain and disrespect for the past six months, myself included."

Billie's discomfort increased as she watched several of the neighbors look away guiltily.

Fred continued. "Like I said, even though we haven't been very neighborly, that didn't stop them from risking their own lives and opening their home to us in our time of need. If it wasn't for this brave woman," he said as he pointed to Billie, "Jen would be at the funeral parlor grieving over three deaths, rather than here celebrating life, family, and neighbors."

The anxiety in Billie's stomach grew as she heard Fred's voice break. "Sitting in their home this afternoon, I looked at them and it struck me that they're no different from Jen and me, nor from you and Kathy, Jim," he said to another neighbor and his wife, "or from any of us who enjoy a loving marriage and family. It just so happens they're both women, but that doesn't diminish their love for each other, nor does it diminish their standing as good-hearted, warm, caring people. So, without further ado, I introduce you to Billie Charland, Caitlain O'Grady, and their children, Seth, Tara, and Skylar. And I might add, I think we owe them a huge apology and total acceptance into our community."

Billie looked at Cat nervously as Fred stepped away from the microphone and a silence fell over the crowd. She was about to lead her family from the stage, when a huge roar rose up from the audience, filled with cheers and clapping. She looked at Fred.

"Go meet your neighbors," he said.

Billie took Cat's hand and led them into the audience where they were greeted with hugs and welcoming handshakes for a full half hour. After a time, Billie felt a hand on her shoulder. She turned around and looked at Carl.

"We should probably get this meeting started," he said.

Billie agreed and followed Carl back to the stage.

Over the next two hours, they organized work crews and made plans to begin the next morning.

* * *

Cat organized a housewarming party for the Swensons, to be held on the day they moved back in. The snow-filled backyard was littered with kids in snowsuits, including Stevie, who'd come home from the hospital a week earlier. The adults crowded the interior of the ranch-style house. The feeling of true neighborhood revelry that permeated the air overwhelmed Cat.

She made a point of touching Billie affectionately with a hand on Billie's arm or her arm around Billie's waist as they personally introduced themselves to their neighbors. A few of them appeared curious about their relationship, but Cat was pleased at how positive the general reaction was. Countless neighbors stopped both her and Billie to comment on how beautiful their children were and to offer sincere apologies for their previous behavior.

Late into the afternoon, Skylar fell asleep on Billie's shoulder. Billie whispered in Cat's ear. "We've got a tired girl here. We should take her home to bed."

Cat readily agreed and went to the back door to call Seth and Tara in.

"Aw, Mama. We don't want to go home."

Cat stood in the doorway with hands on her hips, ready to scold the two children when she heard Jen's voice in her ear. "Let them stay. They can spend the night. Heaven knows you and Billie need some time alone after what we've put you through over the last few weeks."

Cat turned to Jen, a big smile on her face. "You mean it?"

"Absolutely. You go home with that gorgeous hunk of woman you have, and enjoy yourselves for the evening. I'll bring the children over sometime tomorrow afternoon."

Cat hugged Jen tightly. "You're a real friend. Thank you."

"No, Cat. It's the least we can do. As Fred mentioned on that stage two weeks ago, my life would be very different today if it wasn't for the two of you. I'll never be able to thank you enough." She kissed Cat on the cheek and hugged her once more.

"Jen, are you trying to move in on my woman?" Cat and Jen turned to see Billie standing in the kitchen doorway. Cat smiled when she saw the mischievous gleam in Billie's eyes.

Cat realized Jen saw the gleam as well as she watched her friend cock her eyebrow and slip her arms around Billie's waist. "I happen to know that your bark is worse than your bite, big guy. Go home and enjoy the rest of the evening with your lady."

"Yes, ma'am."

Cat called the kids into the house to let them know they'd be spending the night and to kiss them goodbye as Billie dressed Skylar in her coat, hat, and mittens.

"I'll run pajamas, toothbrushes, and a change of clothes over when we get home," Billie said as she hugged Jen.

Cat slipped her hand into the crook of Billie's arm, and they strolled home with Skylar cuddled in Billie's free arm.

* * *

While Billie was gone to deliver a change of clothes to the Swensons, Cat tucked Skylar into her crib and prepared their bedroom for an evening of seduction and romance. She lit several candles around the room, poured two glasses of wine, and loaded several soft classical CDs into the stereo. Knowing she had limited time before Billie returned, she stripped off all her clothing and pulled a clingy green slip over her head. She put spike heels on her feet and fixed her hair up into a bun at the back of her head. She stood in front of the bathroom mirror, freed several small tendrils of hair from the bun to lie along the fringes of her hairline, and applied ruby-colored lipstick. Cat cocked her head and looked toward the bedroom door when she heard noise coming from the first floor.

Cat listened at the bedroom door until she heard Billie go into Skylar's room. She must be checking on the baby. Cat left the door ajar until she heard Billie say, "Sleep well, sweet angel. I love you," then she scurried to the window and leaned against the sill. She waited with anticipation as the bedroom door slowly opened.

Billie stopped dead in her tracks. Knowing she had Billie's full attention, Cat reached for the wineglass she'd placed on the windowsill and raised it to her ruby-lined lips. She made eye contact with Billie, sipped her wine, then lowered the glass and traced her tongue around the periphery of her mouth. Cat saw that the seductiveness of her actions had the desired effect as Billie grabbed the doorframe for support.

"My God, Cat. You're beautiful."

Cat pushed herself away from the window and walked to the middle of the room. She crooked her finger at Billie. "Come here."

Billie crossed the room in two strides. Cat shivered as she felt Billie's hands run lightly up and down her sides and across her back.

"I promise to be gentle," Billie whispered. "Thank you for trusting me." Billie caressed Cat's curves as she nuzzled her face into Cat's neck. "Your skin tastes like sweet nectar. I could feast on you for all eternity."

Cat moaned and tilted her head to one side to give Billie greater access. She felt Billie respond with a more intense sense of urgency.

"I want you so much."

"Patience, my love, patience." Cat pulled out of Billie's embrace. "Stay right here." She put her wineglass on the nightstand next to the bed and returned to Billie in the center of the room. Slowly, she circled Billie, and lightly ran her hands over Billie's breasts and stomach. She saw Billie struggle to maintain control.

"You've got no idea what you're doing to me right now," Billie whispered.

"Oh, I think I do." Cat walked behind Billie and pressed herself against her back. She reached around to the front and unbuckled Billie's belt. Cat slapped Billie's hands away as it became obvious that Billie was trying to help.

Cat unzipped Billie's jeans and slid her hands into the front of Billie's panties until her fingers delved into the warm, moist crevice. Cat was inflamed by the deep moan she heard rise from Billie's throat.

"Oh God, you're so wet." Cat pushed the jeans off Billie's hips.

Billie kicked her jeans into the corner of the room as Cat's hands manipulated the buttons of her blouse. Soon, that garment joined the jeans as Cat nibbled on Billie's shoulders from behind.

Cat continued the slow torture, until she had every piece of clothing removed from Billie's body. Only then did she give Billie permission to turn around. As she turned, Cat danced seductively to the music. She swayed her hips to and fro and threw her head back to expose the length of her throat to Billie's eyes. Slowly, the dance continued while Billie stood totally exposed and vulnerable in the center of the room.

Cat erotically lifted her gown and torturously removed it an inch at a time. She could see the desire in Billie's face as her flesh was exposed to Billie's gaze. She darted away as Billie reached out to grab her, then she circled around and ran her naked breasts against Billie's back. She felt Billie shudder.

"Cat, I can't take this anymore. I need you."

Cat moved in front of Billie and guided her backward until her thighs contacted the mattress. She put her hand in the center of Billie's chest and pushed. Billie fell back onto the mattress. As soon as she was prone, Cat laid herself on top of Billie and kissed her passionately.

Cat felt Billie's tongue demand entrance. She pushed on Billie's chest. "Oh no, you don't. Not yet." Cat straddled Billie's waist. She saw the anticipation in Billie's eyes as she grabbed her wineglass from the nightstand. She took a large sip, returned the glass to the stand, and bent down and kissed Billie. During the kiss, she transferred the wine into Billie's mouth. Their mouths locked and soon their tongues entwined as they shared the taste of the sweet red wine.

Cat was startled when Billie flipped them over. She could only guess that the sensual kiss broke Billie's restraint. Cat became enflamed and a small moan escaped when she felt Billie's hands and mouth explore every inch of skin on her body.

Cat's eyes flew open when she felt Billie suddenly become still. "Billie?"

"I'm sorry, love. I didn't mean to be so rough. Forgive me?" Billie said.

Cat traced her index finger across Billie's brow and down her cheek. "I'm not made of glass. I won't break. I promise. I want you to love me. I'll let you know if I become uncomfortable. But right now, I want you to make love to me with everything that you are."

Cat reached the heights of ecstasy no fewer that three times. She begged Billie to stop before she ran out of strength to return the favor. She urged Billie onto her back and once again reached for the wineglass. She looked down into Billie's face and whispered, "Let the games begin."

The exchange was heated and intense. Cat struggled on more than one occasion to stay in control. After she threatened to tie her to the bedposts, Billie relented and allowed Cat total dominance. Cat took advantage of the opportunity and, for the next hour, proceeded to treat Billie to her own little corner of heaven… several times in fact, and even managed to join her on their last trip.

Thoroughly exhausted, Cat fell into a heap on top of Billie and slid herself into position at Billie's side. She snuggled her head into Billie's shoulder and draped her arm casually across her waist.

Cat soon realized that Billie was crying. She lifted her head. "What's wrong? Talk to me."

Billie smiled through her tears. "Nothing's wrong. I'm so overwhelmed that you've come to trust me. After what you've been through, I'm so thankful that you allow me to touch you, kiss you, and make love with you. Thank you."

"Only you, Billie. This would only be possible with you. I feel safe in your arms. You're my strength. You saved me from my fear. I couldn't imagine spending the rest of my life without making love to you." Cat snuggled again against Billie's shoulder.

"Sleep, my love," Billie said.

Both women fell into a deep sleep until their very hungry daughter awakened them the next morning with a piercing scream.

Chapter 20

Several days later, Billie and Cat returned home from taking the children to dinner.

"You two have about an hour to play before bath time," Billie called to Seth and Tara in the backyard.

While Cat took the baby upstairs to change her diaper, Billie walked over to the answering machine and saw the light was blinking. She pushed the Playback button. She listened intently as the message began to play. "Billie, this is Art. It appears your ex-husband has managed to convince the parole board to let him out on good behavior. Because we were the prosecuting attorneys, we got the call right after you left the office this afternoon. I thought you'd like to know before you came into work tomorrow and were surprised with it. Try not to worry. Hopefully, he'll play it smart and stay away from you and Cat. I'll see you at work tomorrow. Bye."

"Shit!" Billie yelled.

Cat ran down the stairs carrying a partially diapered Skylar. "Billie, what is it?"

Skylar dangled from her mother's arms, and Billie felt bad for startling Cat.

"Here, listen to this." Billie pushed the Playback button. She took Skylar from Cat.

While Cat listened to the message, Billie laid Skylar on the couch and finished diapering her.

When the message was over, Cat walked to the couch and sat down. "What are we going to do?"

"First, I need to contact Brian's lawyer and parole officer to see what the terms of his parole are. If they're doing their jobs, he'll be restricted from contacting you, Seth, or Skylar. Of course, being ordered to stay away and him obeying the order can be two different things."

"I'm scared, Billie."

"Yeah, I know. Me, too, but I promise to do everything I can to protect you and the kids."

"I know you will, love."

* * *

"What do you mean, he has no restrictions?" Billie shouted at Brian's lawyer, unable to believe what she heard. "For Christ's sake, he brutally raped Cat. What were you thinking?"

Art had gone with her, first to the parole office, then to Brian's lawyer to check the situation out. "Art, you'd better prepare a murder defense, because if he comes near Cat or any of my children, I'll kill him."

"Is that a threat, Ms. Charland?" the lawyer asked.

"You're damned right it is, asshole, and I mean it. If he comes anywhere near them..." Billie was furious.

"Well, maybe he offered your girlfriend something you can't. She had a baby from the ordeal, right? Did you stop to think that maybe she lured him on, or maybe she just wanted another kid?"

Billie lunged at the man in an attempt to grasp him around the throat and throttle him to within an inch of his life. She felt an arm around her midsection that held her back before she could reach him. She fell back slightly as Art pushed her away.

Art addressed Brian's attorney. "You're a very stupid man. I don't know how you managed to pull this off, but if anything happens to Ms. O'Grady or the children, it'll be on your shoulders and I'll see both you and your client go down. Do you understand?"

* * *

In the car on the way back to the office, Billie tried to make sense of Brian's release. "Art, how can this happen? The man's a convicted rapist for Christ's sake."

"You know Brian's family comes from money. A few well-placed donations can go a long way with the right politician. I'm not saying that's what happened, but I can't think of another explanation."

Billie chewed on her fingernails and looked out the window. "What am I going to do? How can I protect them?"

"I don't know. Without restrictions, we can't even slap a restraining order on him until he tries something."

Billie was nearly hysterical. "Until he tries something?"

"Maybe you should take your family away somewhere for a while."

Billie continued to stare out the window as she contemplated Art's suggestion. She looked at him and sighed. "I can't do that. Cat's job... the kids' school... our home. We can't just walk away from it all. No. There's got to be another way."

Art offered no further ideas, and they remained silent for the remainder of the ride back to the office.

As soon as Billie got to her office, she called Cat. She didn't believe for a moment that Brian would be smart enough to keep his nose clean, and she had to warn her. She tapped her pencil nervously on the desk as she waited for the hospital switchboard to put her call through.

Before long, a familiar voice came on the line. "Hello, Caitlain O'Grady speaking."

"Cat. Thank God."

"Billie? What's wrong?"

"He has no restrictions. There's nothing we can do unless he crosses the line."

"Oh my God. What are we going to do?" Billie could hear the pitch in Cat's voice rise with each word.

"I'm on my way home. I'll pick Sky up at the day care and swing around to collect Tara and Seth from school. We should be home at about the same time you get there. I don't want you at home alone. We need to figure out how to protect ourselves."

"Maybe he'll stay away."

"Maybe, maybe not. I'm not taking any chances. I don't trust him. Please don't argue with me about this."

"All right. I'll meet you at home in about a half hour."

"Please be careful. I love you."

"I love you, too. I'll see you at home."

* * *

Billie and Cat kept Seth and Tara home from school and inside the house for the rest of the week despite their complaints and whining. They did their best to entertain the bored children until Stevie and Karissa arrived home from school and came over to play.

On Friday evening, Jen and Fred joined them for a game of cards while the kids retreated to their respective bedrooms to play. Skylar had already been bathed and put to bed for the night.

Jen, in her usual bubbly manner, invited Cat to go with her to the mall the next day, an offer Cat declined.

Jen looked at Cat and Billie and back to Cat again. "Okay, give. What's going on here?"

Cat looked at the cards in her hand. "I... I... What do you mean?"

Jen pulled Cat's cards away from her face. "No self-respecting woman turns down a chance to go shopping. Something's wrong. I can feel it. Spit it out."

A look of silent communication passed between Cat and Billie, followed by Billie nodding her head.

"It's Brian," Cat said. "He's been released from jail."

Jen frowned. "Brian?"

"Maybe I should start from the beginning. Brian is Skylar's father... and Billie's ex-husband."

"Whoa, hold on there. Did you say he's Billie's ex-husband?"

Billie covered Cat's hand with her own. "Yes, and he's also Seth's father."

Jen glanced at Fred as his eyes yo-yoed back and forth between the two of them. "I can see you're as confused as I am." She put her playing cards on the table and held her hands up. "So, let me get this straight. Brian is Billie's ex-husband... *and* Seth's father... *and* Sky's father... *and* he's in jail... or at least he *was* in jail." Jen shook her head. "I must be having a blonde moment." She looked at Billie. "How did your ex-husband become Skylar's father?"

Cat and Billie exchanged an uncomfortable look. Realization dawned on Jen. "He was in jail. Oh my God." Her hand flew to her mouth. "God, Cat. I'm sorry. I didn't realize. Honey, I'm so sorry. I assumed Sky was the result of artificial insemination. What are you going to do?"

"He's a rapist?" Fred sounded alarmed as realization hit him as well. "How the hell does a rapist get out of jail?"

"Money," Billie said. "He bought his freedom. Or at least we think his family bought it for him."

"So you're going to allow him to scare you into seclusion?" Jen asked.

"I prefer to see it as protecting our family," Billie replied.

Jen touched the back of Billie's hand. "Honey, I didn't mean to offend you. It's just that you can't become hermits in case he decides to show his face. You can't let him do that to you."

Billie's back became rigid and her hands balled into fists.

"I failed to stop him the first time. I can't let it happen again," she said.

Jen looked at Cat. "How do you feel about this?"

"I'm scared as well, but part of me feels angry that we're allowing him to manipulate us. I mean, if he really wants to get to me or the kids, he'll find a way whether we live our lives openly or in seclusion."

Billie uncurled her fists and flattened her hands on the table. "I'm afraid."

"I am, too," Cat said, "but we can't stop living. If we do that, he wins. He wins and we lose. And you know how I hate to lose," Cat joked to lighten the mood.

Billie frowned. "Losing is exactly what I'm afraid of. Losing you and the kids."

* * *

On Monday, Cat convinced Billie to let the kids return to school. Brian had been freed almost a week earlier, and so far, there was no sign of him. She hoped he was using his head and making a conscious effort to stay out of trouble.

Midafternoon, the phone rang.

"Hey there," Billie said. "I'm calling to see how things are on the home front."

"Fine. Pretty quiet, in fact. The kids just got home and they're having their snack."

"I've been worried about you all day."

"Sweetheart, relax. Brian hasn't shown his face since he was released. He's probably learned his lesson."

"We can only hope. Still, I don't trust him."

"Really, don't worry. Oh, hold on a minute. I just heard a car door close. There's someone here." Cat looked out the window and saw a flower truck parked in the driveway. The deliveryman, who carried a large arrangement of flowers, was nearly at the kitchen door. A wide smile broke out across her face as she returned to the phone. "Oh, Billie, they're beautiful. You didn't have to send me flowers. Hold on, the delivery man's at the door."

She put the phone down, went to the door, and opened it wide.

"Delivery for Cat O'Grady," the man said behind the flowers.

"They're beautiful."

"Where'd you like to me to put them, ma'am?"

"Over there, on the table." Cat stepped aside and indicated the kitchen table. "Thank you so much."

The man set the flowers down and swung around to face her.

* * *

"Cat! Cat!" Billie shouted into the phone. She heard sounds of a struggle on the other end. Desperate for any contact, Billie yelled Cat's name again. Suddenly, the phone was picked up and a man's voice came across the line.

"Hey, Billie. Nice family you have here. From my count, at least two of them are mine, wouldn't you say?"

"You bastard. If you hurt them, I'll kill you. So help me God, I'll kill you." The other end of the line went dead. "God damn it!" Billie screamed.

She slammed the phone down and dialed Jen and Fred's number. After several rings, Jen answered the phone.

"Jen! Thank God you're home."

"Billie? Is everything all right?"

"No. Cat and the kids are in trouble."

"Oh my God. What happened?"

"Brian's in the house. He's in the house and he's done something horrible to Cat. I just know it."

"Call the police—"

"No. He's insane. If he sees the police, she doesn't have a chance. Do you understand? Don't call the police. Promise me."

"Billie..."

"Promise me."

"All right. All right. Tell me what you want me to do."

"I'm coming home. I'll call you on my cell when I get there. I need you to cause some type of distraction so I can get into the house."

"I'll do anything I can, Billie, but I still think you need to call the police."

"No. Trust me. I know what he's capable of. I still bear the evidence of it. Please, Jen. Just do as I ask."

"Okay. I'll be waiting by the phone."

Billie grabbed her car keys and ran out the door.

She parked her car half a block from the house and stole through her neighbors' backyards until she reached her own property. She broke a pane from a basement window, slipped into the basement, and called Jen.

* * *

Cat woke to find herself on the kitchen floor. Her jaw ached unmercifully. She looked around slowly and a feeling of terror grew in her chest as memories of the afternoon's events returned. In the distance, she heard Skylar crying.

Brian rushed into the kitchen from the living room as she pushed herself off the floor into a sitting position. He grabbed a handful of hair and dragged her to her feet.

Cat struggled to free herself. "Oww. Let go of me."

"It's about time you woke up. Shut that little whine-ass up before I do it for you. She's getting on my nerves. And don't bother calling the cops. I cut the phone lines while you were out." Cat stumbled as he released her.

Cat instinctively searched her back pocket for her cell phone.

"Looking for this?" Brian asked as he held her phone out for her to see. "I confiscated that, too."

Cat quickly composed herself and went in search of the kids. As she entered the living room, she saw a very frightened Seth sitting side by side with Tara on the living room couch. She made eye contact with them as she passed through the living room on her way to collect Skylar and silently urged them to be brave. She rushed up the stairs to retrieve Skylar from her nap. When she returned to the living room, she transferred the baby into Tara's arms.

"Be brave, my loves," she whispered. "Here, watch your sister for me." She wanted her hands free in case she had an opportunity to do something about their situation.

Brian paced across the room.

"Just what do you think you're going to gain, Brian? This is a no-win situation for you. The only place out of here for you is jail."

"I have no intention of going back to jail."

"Kidnapping is a serious crime. There's no way you're going to walk away from this."

Brian lunged at Cat and grabbed her around the neck. "Shut up." He pushed her to the floor.

Seth ran to her and covered her body with his. "Don't touch her!"

"Seth, please go sit on the couch with your sisters before he hurts you, too."

"I won't let him hurt you again, Mama."

Cat climbed back to her feet. "Please do as you're told. Your sisters are afraid, and they need you to be brave for them."

Seth went to Tara and Skylar on the couch. He took Skylar from his sister's arms and sat on the couch next to her.

"Brave little guy, isn't he? Just like his father," Brian said.

"No, you're wrong, Brian. His father is a coward. Seth's bravery comes from his mother."

Brian rewarded Cat's comment with a slap to the back of her head.

"Seth, no!" Cat said. Seth shoved Skylar into Tara's arms and flung himself at Brian.

Brian grabbed Seth's arm and twisted it hard enough that Cat heard an audible crack. Seth howled in pain, and Brian threw him to the floor next to Cat, who gathered him in her arms.

"No. His stupidity comes from his mother. She never knew when to back off either. You'd better shut him up before I really give him something to cry about."

Cat rocked Seth back and forth, trying to calm the hysterical child. "You've broken his arm, Brian. He needs help."

"He'll live." Brian resumed pacing.

"At least let me get an ice pack for him."

"Anything to shut the brat up. Make it fast, and don't try anything foolish or the kids will pay."

Cat went into the kitchen, poured several ice cubes into a plastic bag, and returned to Seth. "Here you go, sweetie. Just hold it on your arm, and it will help with the pain. I need you to be brave for me."

Cat turned back to Brian just as the doorbell rang.

He grabbed Cat by the hair and shoved her toward the door. "Whoever the hell it is, get rid of them."

Cat opened the door and was shocked to see Jen standing there. She was holding a large book in her hands.

"Good evening, ma'am. My name is Jen Swenson, and I wonder if I could interest you in purchasing this beautiful King James Bible?" Jen stepped into the living room and opened the front cover of the book.

Cat glanced quickly at the inscription. *Billie is in the house.*

Jen closed the book and handed it to Cat. "This book contains everything you need to know about living a good and just life. The advice within will assure you a place with the Holy One in the hereafter."

Cat sensed Brian's presence behind her and handed the book back to Jen.

"You must be the man of the house." Jen extended her hand to him.

"We're not interested," Brian said.

"You're not interested in spending eternity basking in the sunshine of our Lord? Here's your chance to redeem yourself. Wouldn't you agree that the fabric of society is deteriorating? Gambling and domestic violence are on the rise. Are you not concerned about those issues?"

"Look, lady, hit the road. I said we're not interested."

"Didn't your mother ever teach you not to interrupt a person when they're speaking? Talk about bad manners. You will surely spend eternity in hell if you continue along that path. It's not too late to save yourself. Just follow the advice in this Bible and you will find salvation."

Brian shoved Jen onto the porch. "If you don't get out of here, I'll show you how bad my manners can be."

"Well, there's no need to get huffy about it," Jen said. "Your mind is obviously the devil's playground. I urge you to reconsider."

Cat caught a motion out of the corner of her eye. She saw something pass by the kitchen doorway. She quickly returned her attention to Brian and Jen.

"Ms. Swenson," she said, "we appreciate your concern for our spiritual welfare. I assure you, help has arrived. In fact, a vision just appeared to me."

"Praise the Lord. I'm so happy you've seen the light. Salvation is absolutely a heartbeat away. Perhaps…"

Brian slammed the door in her face

While Jen distracted Brian, Billie slipped into the kitchen and moved as fast as she could to the other side of the archway between the living room and the kitchen. She pressed herself up against the wall and waited for her opportunity.

"Stupid religious bitch. Don't those assholes have anything better to do than harass people?" Brian said.

"Look who's calling the kettle black. I think what you're doing right now pretty much classifies as harassment. Exactly what do you plan to accomplish here?" Cat tried to provoke him into being careless.

"I want what's mine."

"And what would that be?"

"Well, by the looks of it, that would be one wife and two kids."

"They're not yours to take. They'd never go with you. You know that. What do you really want?"

Brian once more grabbed a handful of Cat's hair and bent her head back. "You think you're smart, don't you? You're right. I don't want them, but judging by this nice home you have here, I figure you and Billie have wads of money, and I intend to take some of it. That bitch owes me. Thanks to her, I've spent the better part of the past year in jail. She needs to pay for that."

"Billie's not responsible for you being in jail. You are. You're a filthy, vile, pig and you disgust me. You deserve what you got."

"Shut up!" Brian screamed and backhanded her across the face. Seth began to cry again.

Rage shuddered through Billie's body as she heard Brian abuse Cat. While trying to control her reaction, she accidentally knocked a small plaque off the wall she was pressed against and watched helplessly as it fell to the floor.

Brian's gaze shot toward the kitchen.

"What the hell was that?" he said.

Cat quickly recovered. "Maybe it's Billie. She's due home anytime now."

"I'm going to go check it out. If you even think of moving, I'll shoot you where you stand, is that clear?" Brian drew a gun from his pocket. "Billie's in for one hell of a homecoming."

Cat held her breath as Brian crept toward the kitchen.

"It's over, Brian," Billie said as he stepped through the archway.

Everything moved in slow motion for Cat. The food processor crashed down on Brian's head just as he fired a shot at Billie. He fell to the floor unconscious.

Cat screamed Billie's name and ran to her. Blood oozed from Billie's hairline and rolled down the right side of her face. She slowly slid down the wall and fell over on top of Brian.

Cat rolled Billie off Brian and cradled her face between her hands. "Don't you dare die." She looked toward the living room door. "Jen. Jen, are you still out there?" she shouted.

Jen pushed the door open. "Cat?"

"Jen. Thank God. Call 911. Hurry. Billie's hurt. Please hurry."

* * *

Jen soothed and quieted the children and got them immersed in coloring books. Now she paced across the living room, anxious for Cat to call with news of Billie's condition.

Finally, Cat called and Jen answered. "Cat?" she said, hoping for the best possible news.

"She's alive. The bullet caused minimal damage. She's going to make it."

* * *

Two months later, Jen stood in the backyard next to Cat. "What can I do to help?"

"Let me see. You can go fetch the cake from the kitchen and get the kids seated around the picnic table, if you would."

Jen organized the children as Cat carried Skylar to the place of honor at the head of the table and buckled her into the high chair. Seth and Tara sat on each side of the birthday girl to help her blow out the one candle on her cake and open her presents.

Cat had ordered a cake large enough to feed all the kids and another small cake specifically for Skylar. She put the smaller cake in front of her and pushed a candle formed in the shape of the number one into the icing. The children sang Happy Birthday to her while Seth and Tara blew out the candle.

"I'll take that." Cat grabbed the candle from the cake before Sky dove in and smeared chocolate frosting all over her. Cat looked at Jen. "Thank God for bleach."

Billie spoke from the far end of the table. "Come on, you two. Seth, Tara, move in closer so I can get all three of you in the video."

"Aw, Mom," Seth said.

"You, too, Cat."

"Aw, Mom," Cat teased.

"Don't you start in on me. After all, you assigned me the job of photographer and I do take my work seriously, you know."

Billie resumed filming. Overwhelming gratitude filled Cat as she realized Billie could've died from the gunshot wound two months earlier. She recalled how terrified she was when Billie sank to the floor on top of Brian. There was so much blood.

The X-rays confirmed the bullet had entered Billie's skull just above her hairline and lodged in the frontal lobe. Cat was beside herself with fear and heartache at the thought of losing the one person who made her life complete. She was certain the fates were looking down on Billie that day. The bullet could've done considerably more damage. She might've lost her sight, hearing, or sense of smell. Worst of all, she could've lost her memory, including those of their life together.

Over the past two months, with Cat's help, Billie engaged in intensive physical therapy to help her regain her sense of equilibrium.

"You're a pretty good photographer for a dizzy broad," Cat said.

Billie raised her eyebrows. "Dizzy, huh? I had no problem keeping my balance in those funky yoga positions you had us in last night, my dear." Billie spoke loud enough for Jen, who was standing next to them, to hear.

Jen looked at them and smiled.

Cat smacked Billie on the arm and blushed to the roots of her hair. "Billie."

"Ow. Hey, no fair, I can't defend myself here. I need to keep both hands on the camera."

Cat snorted. "You, defenseless? I think not."

"And what do you mean by that?"

Cat stood on tiptoes and kissed her. "What I mean, love, is that you have the power to knock me out with a simple look. And if I'm lucky, you'll be able to do that to me forever."

Billie smiled. "Forever?"

"Forever."

Part IV:

Fighting City Hall

Chapter 21

Brian's attack provided the authorities with more than substantial reason to rescind his parole, and he was ordered to serve the balance of his original sentence, plus two additional years for assault and battery. With their sense of security restored, Billie and Cat worked over the next several months to normalize their day-to-day activities and to minimize the trauma on the children.

One afternoon, Cat relaxed in the basement family room with her journal while Skylar napped in the playpen nearby. Just as she began to put pen to paper, Tara ran into the room and jumped onto Cat's lap.

"Mama, help! Seth is going to pound me."

Cat looked up in time to catch Tara and narrowly avoid Seth's elbow as he barged into the room and flung himself across Cat while he lunged at Tara.

"Whoa. Wait a minute. Stop it." Cat pulled the children down onto the couch, one on each side of her. "Time out here. What in the world is this all about?"

Each child pointed a finger at the other as they began to speak at the same time.

"She broke…"

"Seth wants to…"

"Stop. Both of you. One at a time. Tara, you go first."

Seth began to object. "You'll get your turn," Cat said. "Now sit still. Tara?"

"I was walking in the hall, and Seth ran right into me. It's not my fault his castle fell."

Cat turned her attention to Seth. "What have you got to say?"

"I spent all day building my Lego castle. I was bringing it to show you, and Tara ran right into me on purpose. It fell on the floor and broke into a gazillion pieces."

Cat stood up, creating another opportunity for Seth to lunge at his sister.

"Whoa, there. That's enough. Do you understand me?" Cat said sternly as she separated the children once more. She stood in front of them with her arms crossed and noted how they glared at each other. "Tara, were you running in the house again?"

"I wasn't running. I was walking fast."

"You were running," Seth said.

"I was not."

"That's enough," Cat said. "If you can't talk civilly to each other, you'll both go to your rooms. Do you understand?"

"Yes, Mama," they said together.

"Seth, do you think Tara really ran into you on purpose?"

"Well, maybe not."

"All right. What do you suggest we do about this?" She returned to her seat between the children.

"Use your imagination," she said when they shrugged their shoulders. "Your castle was destroyed, right, Seth?" Cat acknowledged the nod Seth gave her. "Well, what did the neighborhood do when the Swensons' house was destroyed by fire a year ago?"

Seth looked up at her. "They all pitched in and rebuilt it?"

Cat nodded her head and smiled.

"Hey," Tara said. "You and me can rebuild your castle, Seth."

"You and I," Cat corrected.

"You wanna help, too, Mama?" Tara asked.

"No, honey, I was correcting your speech. Oh, never mind. The two of you go rebuild the castle. When you're finished, you can bring it down together to show Mom and me. And, Tara, since you caused this by running in the house again, I want you to pick up all the blocks, understand?"

The children got up and went toward the stairs.

"And make sure to pick up all the pieces so your little sister doesn't find one and put it in her mouth."

"We will, Mama."

"Hi, Mom," Cat heard the children say, one at a time.

Cat glanced toward the stairs. Billie sat on the steps with a big grin on her face.

"Have you been sitting there the whole time?"

Billie walked to the couch and kissed Cat. "You're quite an arbitrator."

"I swear, those kids have given me enough practice over the past year."

Billie lowered her long frame onto the couch beside Cat.

A warm feeling erupted in Cat's chest. Sometimes, just Billie's closeness was enough to make a surge of love flow through her.

Billie waved her hand back and forth in front of Cat's face. "Hello? Anybody home?"

Cat snapped out of her trance.

"Are you all right?" Billie asked.

"I was thinking about how beautiful you are, and how lucky I am that you're mine."

Billie traced the outline of Cat's jaw with her fingertip. "I'm the lucky one."

A tiny pair of arms reached out to interrupt them. "Mama, up." Skylar stood in her playpen and raised her arms to be picked up.

Cat lifted Skylar into her arms and sat her between Billie and herself. "Did you have a good nap?" Cat suddenly stopped talking and crinkled her nose. "Uh-oh. Do you smell what I smell?"

"Pew," Billie said. "Sky, how can such a tiny girl make such a smelly mess? What are we going to do with you?"

Cat looked at Billie hopefully.

"No way."

"Rock, paper, scissors?" Cat suggested.

"Oh man, I'm no good at that game. Oh, all right."

"One, two, three, shoot. Yeah, rock crushes scissors. Round one to Cat," Cat said.

"One, two, three, shoot. Ugh. Paper covers rock. Round two to Billie. One more round to go."

Cat locked eyes with Billie. "Here goes," Cat said. "One, two, three, shoot. Oh, yeah. Scissors cut paper. I win. Billie, you're so predictable."

Cat picked Skylar up from the floor and handed her to Billie.

"I told you I sucked at that game. Come on, stinker."

Before Billie walked away, Cat grabbed the front of her shirt and raised herself on tiptoes for a kiss. "I'll get dinner started while you take care of your daughter."

"My daughter? Why is she always mine when she's made a mess?"

"Because my daughter would never do such a disgusting thing."

"Hmmm. I recall a story your mother told us about Miss Picasso Poopy Pants," Billie teased.

Cat held her hand, palm out, toward Billie. "Don't go there."

* * *

Just before dinner, Seth and Tara unveiled their Lego castle. Billie and Cat made an appropriate amount of fuss over the work of art, and it was proudly displayed on the mantle above the fireplace in the family room.

After dinner, the family retreated to the basement to watch a video. When the video ended, the children were bathed and put to bed. Cat and Billie tucked them in and kissed them good night. As they exited the last bedroom and closed the door behind them, Billie took Cat into her arms for a warm hug. They stood there for a time locked in a loving embrace.

"As much as I hate to leave this warm cocoon, you have studying to do, love."

Billie groaned. "Yeah, I know. I'll be glad when this class is over. It's been one very long year finishing my degree. I miss spending my evenings with you."

Cat smiled indulgently. "Soon, love, soon. The bar exam is a few days away. Now give me a kiss and get to work."

Billie clicked her heels together and saluted. "Yes, sir, Sarge."

Cat swatted Billie's behind as she walked into the bedroom where they'd set up a makeshift office in the corner. Satisfied that Billie was comfortably settled, Cat went downstairs to brew a pot of tea and to curl up on the couch to read. When the tea was finished, she poured a mug for herself and one for Billie. She sweetened Billie's with mint and honey and carried it up the stairs. She put it on the desk within Billie's reach then kissed her neck intimately.

"Keep that up and I'll flunk this exam for sure," Billie said.

Cat chuckled and kissed Billie on the head. "Sorry. Back to work with you." Cat paused at the door as she left the room. "Enjoy your tea." She returned to the couch and her book.

After a half hour of failing to concentrate on the printed word, Cat let her mind wander over her life with Billie. She could hardly believe more than two years had already passed since they met. Seth had just finished second grade and Tara the first, and now Billie was days away from completing her law degree. She shuddered when she recalled how they had come close to losing Billie to a gunshot wound nearly a year earlier. Cat was happy with the direction in which her life was moving. She had a good-paying, respectable job, a beautiful home, great friends, a loving partner, and three precious children. There was nothing more she wanted in her life.

* * *

Billie massaged her temples in an attempt to subdue the headache that was beginning to brew behind her forehead. She had been studying for almost three hours without a break. She sat back in her chair and flexed her neck to release the tension, then leaned her head back and closed her eyes. Her thoughts wandered to how difficult life had been for Cat over the past two years, especially with the rape. Between the psychological trauma and the pregnancy, it was nearly a year before Cat could respond to her physically. Their relationship was sorely tested in the beginning, but now held only hope and promise in the years to come. In a few days, Billie's bar exam would be behind them and life would become even better.

Physically and emotionally drained from working all day and studying for the past few hours, Billie closed her eyes and rested her head on top of her books.

* * *

Cat looked at the clock on the living room wall. It was nearly midnight. She wondered whether Billie had finished studying.

She closed her book and put it on the coffee table then went to put her tea mug in the dishwasher before heading upstairs. Cat stopped at each of the children's rooms on the way to see that they were settled in for the night. Finally, she pushed open the door to her bedroom. Inside, a soft glow came from the desk lamp in the corner. She looked lovingly at Billie, who was slumped forward, with her head on the desk.

Cat pulled the covers down on the bed, then went to Billie and gently rubbed her back. "Wake up, love, you fell asleep on the desk. Here, let me help you to bed."

Billie sat up in the chair. She opened her eyes a tiny bit and grinned. "Please, Mom, ten more minutes."

Cat chuckled. She tugged on Billie's arm. "Come on now, you know I can't carry you. You're going to have to help me here."

"You can try."

"I don't think so, sweetie. Be a good girl and give me a hand."

Billie rose to her feet and allowed Cat to lead her to the bed where she sat on the edge and teetered left to right while yawning.

Cat removed Billie's shoes and pulled her shirt over her head and tossed it to the floor. She then reached behind Billie and unhooked her bra, allowing the full breasts to bounce forward on their own accord. Cat suppressed the carnal urges that having

Billie's breasts so close to her mouth invoked. Instead, she pushed Billie onto her back and slid her jeans down her hips.

Once the jeans were discarded, Cat lifted Billie's legs onto the bed. She tried to walk away to get her a nightshirt but Billie grabbed Cat's arm and pulled her down on top of her.

"Somebody's been playing possum," Cat said. "I thought you were tired."

"I am. I only want to cuddle with my favorite lady. Got a problem with that?"

A little disappointed that cuddling was the only thing on the agenda, Cat sighed. "No, not at all. Cuddling is good."

She snuggled her head down into Billie's shoulder. *Two more days,* she thought. *Two more days and cuddling is history.*

Billie pulled the covers over both of them and kissed Cat on the temple. "Sorry, my love, but if I don't get some sleep, I'll be worthless tomorrow. I promise to make it up to you. When my exams are over, I'll make such intense, passionate love to you, you'll walk funny for a week."

Cat lifted her head. An expression of disappointment cloaked her features. "Only a week?"

"How about two weeks?"

"I'll hold you to that, dear heart."

"I'd expect no less from you."

Cat lowered her lips to Billie's and deposited several delicate kisses there.

"Good night, love," Cat said.

"Sweet dreams, baby," Billie replied.

* * *

"Tara, sit still," Cat said to her wiggly daughter.

"But, Mama, I can't see her. Can I stand on the chair?"

"Until they call Mom's name, you need to sit. When it's her turn, you can stand on the chair to see. Deal?" Cat looked at Seth, who was seated on the other side of her. "You, too, love."

With the children settled, Cat scanned the auditorium, which was filled to capacity with friends and families of the graduates.

"Leslie Marie Chamberlain," the PA system announced.

Cat nodded, giving the children permission to stand on their chairs. She had all she could do to juggle Skylar and the camera.

"Billie Jean Charland," the PA system sounded again.

"Mama, there she is," Seth said excitedly.

Tara jumped up and down on her chair and clapped her hands as Billie walked across the stage to accept her diploma and shake hands with the dean of the law school. Cat's eyes were locked on Billie as she transferred the tassel from one side of her hat to the other, descended the stage, and headed back to her seat. Cat's heart was so full of pride for Billie. Cat motioned for the children to sit after Billie had accepted her diploma. She dug a Kleenex out of her bag to dab at her eyes.

"Mama, is Mom a judge now?" Tara asked.

"A judge? No, honey. What made you ask that?"

"She's got a black dress on like judges wear."

"That black dress is a graduation robe. See, all the people who are graduating are wearing them," Cat said.

"Mom's a real lawyer now, Tara," Seth said. "She can put bad guys in jail."

Skylar wiggled relentlessly on Cat's lap. "Sky, honey, please sit still for Mama," Cat whispered in the tot's ear. She pulled out three granola bars from her bag and handed one to each child, calming them down throughout the remainder of the roll call.

After what felt like an eternity to Cat, Justin Zimmerman's name was called and the issuing of diplomas was complete. After a few parting words from the dean, the graduates rose and filed out of the auditorium.

Cat hefted Skylar into her arms. "Seth, honey, please take Tara's hand and stay close. We don't want to be separated in this crowd." Seth took Tara's hand and grasped a handful of Cat's jacket with the other. After several minutes of being stuck in a crowd that didn't appear to be moving, they broke free into the fresh air. Cat scanned the top of the crowd for Billie.

Billie heard her name before she found the source. Soon, she spotted her family. She dropped to one knee and held out her arms to the children who ran toward her. Billie enveloped them in a bear hug, lifted them, and swung them around.

Looking in the direction of the flash, she spotted Cat balancing Skylar on her left hip while trying to operate the camera with her right hand. Billie put Seth and Tara down and took Skylar from Cat's arms. She kissed her on the cheek and gave her to Seth so she could take Cat into her arms and hold her close.

"It's finally over," Billie said.

"I'm so proud of you. I love you so much."

"I couldn't have done this without you," Billie whispered. "Sweetheart, if it wasn't for you, I'd still be sitting by Seth's hospital bed feeling sorry for myself. I have so much to be thankful for. I love you with everything that I am."

Billie felt a tug at her robe and looked down to see Tara beside her with crossed legs. She bobbed up and down. "Mom, I gotta go."

Billie released Cat and scooped Tara into her arms. "Here, hold this." Billie tossed her diploma to Cat and quickly made her way to the bathroom inside the auditorium, her black robe flapping behind her.

* * *

When they arrived home, Billie unlocked the door and carried Skylar into the house while Cat grabbed the diaper bag.

The older children scooted by them into the house. "Hey, you two," Billie said. "Go change out of your dress clothes before you do anything else. And I don't want to see your good clothes thrown all over your rooms either. Fold them neatly and put them away."

"Okay, Mom," they said as they ran up the stairs.

"Does Sky need to be changed?" Cat asked.

Billie checked Skylar's diaper. "Yep. Be right back." As Billie climbed the stairs to the second story, she was nearly bowled over by Seth and Tara. "Hey, slow down. You know you aren't supposed to be running on the stairs."

Neither child responded as they continued their dash through the living room and disappeared into the kitchen. Billie shook her head and made a mental note to speak to the kids about house rules after she took care of Skylar. "All right, little one, let's change this wet diaper."

Billie changed Skylar and dressed her in a pair of shorts and a T-shirt. She went to her own room, deposited Skylar on her bed, and changed into a pair of cutoff jeans and a T-shirt. She hefted Skylar onto her shoulders and gave the giggling child a bumpy ride down the stairs and into the living room. When she reached the bottom of the stairs, she looked around at the apparently empty house and wondered where everyone was. "Cat?" she called out.

The reply came from the basement. "In the family room, love."

Billie went to the top of the stairs. "What are you doing down there?"

Cat walked to the bottom of the stairs and looked up at Billie. "The kids and I rented a movie. Come watch it with us. But grab the chips and dip first, will you?"

"Sure thing." With chips in one hand and dip in the other and Skylar still on her shoulders hanging onto her chin for dear life, Billie descended the stairs into the dark family room.

"Hey, who turned out the lights?" Billie reached for the light switch.

"Surprise!"

Billie was so startled she almost lost her passenger and the dip.

Cat rescued Skylar from her high perch and circled around to the front of Billie. "Congratulations, love."

Before Billie had a chance to reply, she was surrounded by well-wishers congratulating her on her graduation and the promotion she'd been promised upon completion of her degree.

Billie searched the crowd for Cat and glared at her. Cat winked at her in return.

A short time later, the party moved into the backyard for a cookout. As always, Jen was on hand to help. After Jen lit the grill, Billie came up behind her, tackled her to the ground, and sat on top of her. She pinned her friend's arms to the ground and leaned in close to Jen's face. "You and that sneaky redhead are in on this together, aren't you? I know you had a hand in this. You know I don't like people fussing over me."

Billie was shocked and momentarily taken off-guard when Jen kissed her on the mouth. The surprise rebuttal so startled her that she let go of her prisoner's arms. Before she knew what happened, Jen gained the upper hand and rolled them both over and was now straddling her with her arms pinned to the ground.

"Ah, exactly what's going on here?"

The two women on the ground looked up. Cat and Jen's husband, Fred, stood before them, hands on their hips, trying unsuccessfully to look angry.

Jen was the first to speak, "Umm, trying out for the World Wrestling Federation?"

"Well, don't give up your day job." Fred laughed as he helped his wife to her feet.

Cat bent over Billie who was still on her back on the ground. She offered her a hand up but suddenly found herself pinned to the ground with Billie sitting on top of her. Billie bent down and kissed her long and hard.

Out of breath, Cat panted, "What was that for?"

"Scenes of coming attractions, Red." Billie climbed to her feet and helped Cat up.

"Will the rating be PG-13 or X?" Cat darted her tongue into Billie's ear and captured her earlobe between her teeth.

Billie shuddered in reaction. "X. Definitely X. And it will be right here in front of our friends if you don't stop that."

* * *

The party was a huge success. After everyone had filled their plates and their stomachs, Jen addressed the group. She raised her wine glass and toasted Billie to wish her good luck and continued success in her job. "I know your entry into our neighborhood was a bit rocky. It took a near tragedy for us to open our minds and our hearts, but I speak for all of us when I say that we're very happy that you, and Cat, and your children are part of our neighborhood. We've grown to respect you, and your love has taught us a valuable lesson about tolerance and acceptance. You and Cat have given of yourselves countless times. You've opened your home to anyone in need, played Mr., or in your case, Ms. Fix-up, provided babysitting on short notice. The list of things you've done for this community is so long, it would be impossible to recall each one."

Jen paused to catch her breath. "What I'm trying to say is that we love both of you, and your children. And as a token of our love, and as a reward for your hard work completing your degree, everyone in the neighborhood has pitched in to send you and Cat on a one-week cruise to Aruba."

Cat and Billie were stunned. Cat wrapped an arm around Billie's waist. "You've spent the entire last year working on your degree. You deserve this, love," she whispered.

The crowd called, "Speech! Speech! Speech!"

Billie slowly rose to her feet to address her friends. "I, ah, I don't know what to say." She paused to wipe the tears from her cheeks. "You've all come to mean so much to both of us." She pulled Cat to her feet to stand beside her. "You've made our family feel very welcome here. We have a place where we can live our lives without ridicule or fear. You've truly accepted us as we are, and for that we're grateful. We're home at last."

Billie broke out of Cat's embrace, took her by the hand, and led her to the middle of their circle of friends. As she held Cat's hand, she scanned the faces of each and every guest. In a clear, but shaky voice, she said, "I had something planned for today, and it only seems fitting that it should occur in front of those we've come to love so dearly."

Billie looked around their congregation of friends again before she continued. "I want to thank each and every one of you for this cruise. I can't tell you how much this means to me... to us." She looked at Cat. "But I would like to use it, not as a gift for completing my degree, but..." Billie paused again and reached into her jeans pocket. "I'd like to use it for our honeymoon."

Several people gasped as Billie dropped to one knee in front of Cat and held up a diamond engagement ring. "Cat, I love you with all my heart. You're the mother of my children and the other half of my soul. You complete me, and I can't live without you. Will you marry me?"

Cat's eyes filled with tears. "Yes. Yes. Yes, my love. I'll marry you."

The entire backyard erupted into cheers as their friends surrounded the two very happy women and greeted them with warm hugs of congratulations.

Cat and Billie only had eyes for each other.

"Tell me what you're thinking," Billie said.

"Billie, my love for you is so intense that sometimes it hurts right here," Cat said, pointing to her chest. "I don't know how to express it. I love you so much."

Billie lowered her forehead to meet Cat's. "Well, I thought it's about time I made an honest woman out of you." She took Cat's left hand and slipped the engagement band onto her ring finger. Cat held her hand out and looked at the diamond sparkling in the sunlight.

"Cat Charland. Caitlain Maureen O'Grady Charland. I like it."

Billie frowned. She squeezed Cat's shoulders. "Cat, don't feel that you have to take the Charland name. Heaven knows you have every reason not to want it."

Cat touched both sides of Billie's face with her fingertips. "I know you kept your married name for Seth's sake, to preserve the feeling of family between you. I want to take your name for that very reason. I don't think of Brian when I hear your name. I think of you. I think of the one person I'll do everything in my power to make happy for the rest of my life."

Billie kissed her. "You already do make me happy, love. You already do."

* * *

Later that evening, while Cat sat on the couch and read a book to Tara and Skylar, Billie lay on the rug in front of the fireplace with Seth as they built a ship out of Lego blocks. Cat was distracted from her reading by Billie's foot running up and down her leg. She was convinced that she'd die of frustration before she had Billie alone to herself.

Soon, it was time to bathe the children and put them to bed. Eight-year-old Seth guarded his modesty fiercely, so he ran into the bathroom ahead of them and locked the womenfolk out. Soon, it was time for Billie to bathe Tara and Skylar.

Cat and Seth sat in the kitchen drinking hot chocolate when sounds from the second story bathroom floated down to them. When Cat went to investigate, she wasn't pleased with the water all over the walls and floors. She stood in the doorway with her hands on her hips and cleared her throat. Cat found it difficult to retain her mask of displeasure as three pairs of eyes looked at her from soap-bubble-covered faces. She crossed the room and reached for Skylar, when the next thing she knew, she was falling into the tub of water, fully dressed.

"Billie!" Cat shrieked and struggled to keep her head above the water. She finally regained her composure as she sat in the tub of soapy water. "That wasn't funny."

"Yes it was, Mama," Tara said. "You have bubbles on your nose."

Cat wiped the bubbles away and looked at the expectant faces of Billie and the two girls. She couldn't help but grin. "All right, I admit it was pretty funny, but it's late and you two need to get ready for bed," she said. "Billie, if you'll do the honors, I'll clean up this mess."

A half hour later, Cat wiped the last vestige of soapy water from the bathroom floor then made her way downstairs to secure the house. As she reached the bottom of the stairs, she realized Seth was still up and watching television in the living room. "Hey, scout, time for bed."

Cat neatened the kitchen and made her way around the first floor of their home locking doors and shutting off lights. Chiming from the grandfather clock in the living room signaled that it was nearly an hour since she asked Billie to put the girls to bed. As she climbed the stairs, she noticed it was very quiet. She and Billie normally reserved the few hours after the kids went to bed for themselves, watching television in bed, reading, or making love. On this night, she failed to see the faint glow and flickering of the television from under the bedroom door. She assumed Billie had gone to bed as well. She pushed open the door to their room. "Billie?"

"I'm here, love."

Cat saw a movement from the far side of the room as Billie, still naked from her bath with Tara and Skylar, walked toward her. Cat accepted the hand Billie extended to her and stepped into the room. Cat soon found herself pressed against the closed bedroom door and unexpectedly aroused by the intensity she saw in Billie's eyes.

"I love you," Billie said. "I want you so much, but I don't want to scare you. Promise me you'll stop me if you're uncomfortable?"

"I promise," Cat replied breathlessly before submitting to a toe-tingling kiss.

Cat allowed Billie to capture and pin both her wrists to the door, high above her head, with one hand. A small inkling of anticipation stabbed at her heart as she felt Billie's other hand circle her throat. She couldn't believe the intensity of desire that coursed through her veins. It threatened to consume her, body and soul as she surrendered her love and trust to Billie. Moans escaped her throat as Billie's tongue sought entrance into her mouth. She felt an odd excitement build within her groin as Billie pressed her into the door.

Cat was both amazed and overwhelmed at her body's reaction to this rough approach to lovemaking. The excitement that grew from within her core demanded more… more intensity… more risk. Cat struggled slightly against Billie in an effort to inflame her passions. Her struggles invoked more than she imagined.

Cat's arms fell to Billie's shoulders when she was suddenly released from being pinned against the door. Her gaze locked boldly with Billie's as she felt Billie grip the waistband of her skirt and panties and literally tear them away from her body. She gasped at the pure sensuality of the act.

Cat's breathing became labored. Her chest rose and fell in an effort to draw air into her lungs. Her heart beat rapidly as excitement coursed through her veins. She pressed her abdomen into Billie and found herself lifted higher against the door until she was at eye level with Billie. She instinctively wrapped her legs around Billie's waist as her body bore the weight of Billie pressing her into the door.

"Are you all right?" Billie asked.

Cat nodded vigorously. "Don't stop. Please don't stop."

She tilted her head against the door and moaned as Billie kissed her neck. "Oh God, Billie. I need you. Please. I need you now."

"Oh no, my love. Not yet."

Cat saw such intense passion in Billie's eyes. "My God, Billie, one look into those smoldering blue eyes and I'm saturated. You surprise me with your intensity."

"Do you want me to stop?"

"God, no! Love me. Please."

Once more, Cat looked into Billie's eyes as Billie grabbed the front of Cat's blouse with both hands and tore it open. Cat soon found her arms trapped by her sides as Billie pressed the blouse off her shoulders. Cat's breath caught in her throat and a small inkling of fear began to grow in the pit of her stomach. She fought to quell the feeling. *Calm down. Trust her. You know how much she loves you.*

"My arms. Please free my arms," she said. Billie pushed the blouse completely off and tossed it aside, exposing Cat's lace-covered breasts to Billie's gaze. Cat leaned forward and made room for Billie to reach behind her and unhook her bra. An audible sigh of relief escape Cat's mouth as the elastic prison fell away.

She pressed her breasts forward and invited Billie to explore their fullness. Her desire multiplied as Billie massaged Cat's sensitive nipples between her thumb and fingers.

"More, Billie. I need more."

Billie lifted Cat's breasts and lowered her head to meet them. Billie sucked one swollen bud into her mouth and circled it with her tongue. Cat shrieked with desire as Billie bit down lightly on the sensitive nub.

A spasm wracked Cat's body. "Billie. Oh my God. Billie, please."

Cat almost fainted when Billie switched to the other breast. Intensely sensual feelings ran through her. She grabbed two handfuls of Billie's hair and drew her closer to her breasts.

Cat writhed against Billie and tightened her legs around Billie's waist in an effort to push her heated core closer. The frustration building inside her chest was raging beyond her control. "I want you, Billie. I need you now."

"How much do you want me?"

Cat's lips and throat were so dry, she could hardly speak. "I want you with everything that I am."

"With everything that you are? What are you?"

Cat stared at Billie and allowed her intense desire to surface. Her voice was breathless as every word was an effort to voice. "I'm the one who loves you unconditionally. I'm the one who wants to make love to you every moment of my life."

Cat sensed Billie's tenuous hold on her emotions as a low growl escaped her throat. She instinctively knew Billie was holding back. "What do *you* want, Billie?" Cat could feel the tremors run through Billie.

"I want you, Cat. I want to make love to you over and over. I want to plunge into your depths and taste your sweet nectar. I want to drive you to the edge of madness and catch you when you fall back to earth. Let me love you. I love you and I need you."

Each one of Billie's declarations sent Cat closer to the edge of ecstasy. She knew she wouldn't be able to hold out much longer. "Do it. Please do it."

Billie reached around one firm cheek and plunged deeply into Cat's depths. "Oh my God. Billie. Harder, please, harder. Oh God. I'm coming! I'm coming."

Cat soared to the heights of desire as she alternately pressed herself down onto Billie's hand and into the door behind her. In the recesses of her mind, she felt Billie slow her pace as the orgasmic ripples subsided. She wrapped her arms tightly around Billie's neck as Billie pulled her away from the door and carried her to the bed. Cat pulled Billie's face toward her and gently kissed her. "I love you more than life itself," she said.

"Let me hold you," Billie said.

Cat nudged Billie onto her back and molded herself into Billie's side, with one knee resting on Billie's abdomen, her head on her shoulder, and her arm draped around Billie's waist. She felt Billie's arms surround her.

Cat stirred as her heartbeat returned to normal. She rolled over and looked at Billie. As she peered into Billie's eyes, she saw unspent desire still smoldering beneath the sea of blue. Cat straddled her. Billie circled Cat's waist with her hands. Cat slapped her hands away. "No, Billie. My turn. I'm in control now. No touching. Understand?"

Billie agreed with a nod.

Cat bent over and began her exploration. She began at Billie's eyelids, intending to kiss every bit of exposed skin. She worked her way down Billie's face and over her mouth, biting earlobes and flicking her tongue inside Billie's ears.

Billie's hands came up to circle Cat's shoulders. Again, Cat slapped her hands away. She was firm in her resolve as she scolded Billie once more. "I said no." Two could play this game. Cat impressed herself with her rough treatment of Billie.

Billie lowered her hands.

Cat continued her exploration of Billie's body. She stopped at Billie's breasts and savored the feel of erect nipples as her tongue danced across them.

Billie moaned as Cat kneaded, tasted, and suckled her breasts. Cat could feel Billie's heartbeat quicken as her hands once again violated Cat's space.

Cat sat up and looked at Billie sternly. She rolled off Billie and walked to their closet, returning with a leather belt. Within seconds, she wrapped it around both of Billie's wrists and tied it to the headboard, effectively trapping both of Billie's arms above her head. She lowered her face close to Billie's. "I didn't want to do that, but you forced me to. Don't fight me. I want you, and I'll have you, on my terms. Do you understand?"

Cat smiled at Billie's submission and resumed her savory trek across Billie's abdomen. She dipped her tongue into Billie's navel and was immediately rewarded as Billie pressed her body forward. She recognized the look on Billie's face as one of desperation and knew she'd soon lose control over the situation if she didn't act quickly. She whispered in Billie's ear, "Close your eyes, my love."

Billie complied.

For long moments, Cat did nothing but watch Billie's body language. Billie's abdomen began to gyrate and press upward. Billie's legs became restless. When Cat felt she had waited long enough, she dove deep into Billie's core. Almost immediately, Billie's muscles contracted around her fingers as an orgasmic eruption seized Billie and her entire body arched upward. The strain on the belt tying her hands to the headboard caused the buckle to break, freeing Billie's hands.

"Cat. Oh my God, Cat. More. I need more." Billie grasped large handfuls of bedspread.

Cat continued to plunge into Billie until she felt her teeter on the edge of consciousness and the spasms subsided. Cat folded Billie securely in her arms as her body relaxed. She smiled as Billie inhaled deeply and released a sigh.

"I love you," Billie said softly.

"I love you, too, with all that I am."

Chapter 22

Monday mornings. Ugh, Billie complained to herself as she turned off the alarm. She rolled back over and pulled the still-sleeping Cat into her arms. It always amazed her how Cat slept through the alarm. Not for the first time, she wondered how she managed to get out of bed by herself before they met.

Billie kissed the sleeping woman on the cheek with no response.

She kissed Cat's mouth. Still, no response.

Time to pull out the big guns. Billie reached under the blankets and ran feather-light caresses up and down Cat's arm. As Cat began to stir, she grew bolder and stroked Cat's side. Cat moaned. She trailed her fingertips up and down from Cat's hip to breast.

Cat opened her eyes and smiled. "Don't you dare."

Billie pounced on Cat and tickled her until Cat was reduced to helpless laughter.

"Stop. Please stop. I'll pee my pants if you don't let me up. Please."

"You aren't wearing any pants."

"Then, I'll pee the bed."

Billie ceased her attack and rolled off Cat. Cat climbed out of bed and ran to the bathroom while Billie reclined with hands tucked behind her head. A few moments later, Billie heard the shower. A movement from the bathroom doorway drew her attention. She watched as an arm snaked out from behind the door. The index finger crooked toward her and beckoned for her to come hither.

She didn't need to be invited twice.

* * *

As part of their normal routine, Billie got the kids ready for school and day care while Cat started breakfast. Soon, the entire family was seated around the table, enjoying a breakfast of scrambled eggs, bacon, and toast.

Cat made a trip around the kitchen table, kissed each child and wished them all a good day. "I'll see you guys this afternoon when I pick you up at the day care."

She bent down to kiss Billie, and in a blink of an eye, she found herself sitting in Billie's lap.

Cat draped her arms around Billie's neck and kissed her. "I hope you're still this affectionate after we're an old married couple."

"You can count on it."

"Speaking of marriage, you know New York doesn't allow same-sex marriage. Hell, they don't even support civil unions."

"I know. It could be worse. New York could have a Defense of Marriage Act. The fact that it doesn't is reason for hope."

"What do you mean?"

"Thirty-eight states have either a constitutional ban against same-sex marriage or a Defense of Marriage Act which defines marriage as being between a man and a woman. The fact that New York has neither means the door is open for change, and I intend to do just that, change the state's laws."

"You're kidding me."

Billie traced the side of Cat's face with her fingertips. Her demeanor became stoic. "Sweetheart, I've waited my entire life to find you. I want our love to be official. I want us to be counted among those who are committed to each other legally. I want to do everything in my power to be sure you and the kids receive as much legal protection as our heterosexual friends have. I won't rest until that happens."

"You know I'm with you every step of the way, right?" Cat promised.

"Every step of the way. Now hit the road or you'll be late for work."

"One more kiss for the road, and I'll be on my way."

*   *   *

Cat threw her car keys on the table as the kids rushed by her into the living room. "No fighting over the TV today, okay?"

"Okay, Mama."

She filled the teapot with fresh water and retrieved a cup from the cupboard. The phone rang as she turned the burner on under the pot.

"Hello?"

"Hi, baby. How was your day?"

"Hey, love. It was okay. A couple of surgeries, but overall a quiet day in the ER. We just got home from the day care. How was your day?"

"It was pretty busy in court, but relatively successful. We were so busy that I didn't have time to begin researching New York's same-sex marriage options. If it's okay with you, I think I'll stay late tonight and do some of the groundwork. Don't wait dinner for me. I'll get takeout delivered."

"Okay. Wake me when you get home."

"I love you, Cat."

"Love you, too. Bye."

* * *

Billie crept across the floor to her side of the bed and sat down gently so as not to disturb Cat. She stripped off her clothes and laid them across the chair next to the bed before she climbed in and carefully cuddled against Cat's back. She wrapped her arm around her waist and nuzzled her nose into Cat's neck. Her heart ached as she reviewed the information she'd uncovered on efforts in New York to legalize same-sex marriage.

"It must be really bad."

Billie lifted herself onto one elbow and looked at Cat. She wasn't sure whether Cat had spoken or she was hearing things.

"It must be really bad," Cat said again. "You're as tense as an iron rod."

Billie closed her eyes and rolled onto her back.

"Talk to me, love. Please don't shut me out," Cat said.

Billie opened her eyes and studied the shadows the moonlight cast on Cat's face. Bittersweet warmth filled her chest as the love she felt for this woman washed over her. "I love you."

"I love you, too, with all my heart. Please, tell me what's wrong."

"It looks like we're facing an uphill battle."

"What do you mean?"

"Well, there've been a couple of unsuccessful attempts in the past to change New York's marriage laws. In July of 2006, New

York's highest court ruled that the state doesn't have to recognize same-sex marriages."

"But you said New York doesn't have a Defense of Marriage Act."

"That's true. On one hand, there's nothing in the laws that constitutionally bans same-sex marriage, but on the other, there's nothing in the laws that actually requires same-sex marriage recognition."

"You said there were a couple of attempts. What was the other?"

"The second attempt was the most recent one. Just last month in fact. December 2009, the state senate rejected a bill that would have allowed same-sex marriage."

Cat rolled over so she was lying partially on top of Billie. "Are we going to settle for that, or are we going to fight this?"

Billie smiled. "I was hoping you'd ask that question. We do have one bit of hope to cling to."

"What's that?"

"Even though New York doesn't recognize same-sex marriages performed in New York, they do recognize them performed in other states. That is tons better than starting with laws that are totally and completely against gay marriage all together."

"That's a ray of hope. I say we go for it. We have nothing to lose and everything to gain. I'm not ashamed of our love. I want the world to know that. I want the same rights enjoyed by men and women who are married. What makes their love any more real than ours? I don't like being told that I can't legally be with the one I love. I want to fight this with everything that I am."

"It won't be easy."

Cat's smile eased the tension in Billie's chest. "I told you this once before. I don't want easy, I want you. The best things in life never come easily, and you're the best thing that has ever happened to me."

"C'mere, you." Billie pulled her in close. "I love you."

"Ditto, my love. Go to sleep. We have a lot to do tomorrow."

* * *

The next day Billie met with her supervisor, Art McDonough.

"Do you realize what you're getting yourself into here?" Art asked.

"Art, you're married, right?"

"You know I am."

"Do you love your wife?"

"With all my heart. Heaven knows we've talked enough about our respective partners. You should know by now how I feel about Marge."

"Then tell me. How would you feel if you were told that your love was invalid and that you couldn't be legally married to Marge?"

"I'd be pissed off big-time."

"Bingo." Realization visibly dawned on Art's face.

"I'm convinced," he said. "I'm on your side. I'll do anything and everything I can to help you and Cat with this."

Billie kissed him on the cheek. "Thanks. I knew I could count on you."

"Anytime."

* * *

Art worked all morning to help Billie draft a petition to the court. Late that afternoon, he insisted on going with Billie to deliver it.

"How long do you think it'll be before they react to the petition?" Billie asked as they walked toward the parking lot.

"It's hard to tell. With a petition as unusual as this one, they might deal with it right away or they might take the opposite approach and push it off until the response window closes at the end of thirty days. In any case, the actual hearing won't happen for another two or three months. The state will need time to prepare its case."

"That's not necessarily a bad thing. We can use that time to prepare our case as well," Billie said.

"True." Art held her car door open for her as she climbed in. "We'll get started on it first thing tomorrow morning."

Billie reached through the open window and shook Art's hand. "Art, you're a true friend. I can't thank you enough for your help."

Art bent down so his face was level with Billie's window. "Let me tell you a story, Billie. I had a brother, Mike, who died of AIDS a few years back. He was in a very committed relationship toward the end, and it was the first time in his entire life that I can say he was truly happy. I loved my brother very much, and the treatment he received at the hands of others, including the state, made me sick.

For him and for you, Billie, I'll help you all I can." When he finished, he wiped the corner of his eye.

"I didn't know. I'm sorry."

Art stood and took a step back. "Go home. Your family is waiting for you. I'll see you in the office bright and early tomorrow morning."

Art waved as Billie drove away.

She glanced at the digital clock on the dashboard of her car. Damn. If she didn't hurry, she'd miss Seth's Little League game. As soon as the light turned green, she stepped on the gas and sped along to her destination, arriving in time to see Seth take his position at shortstop. She spotted Cat and the girls in the bleachers and joined them, sandwiching Tara between her and Cat. Billie took Skylar out of Cat's lap and pulled each of her three girls in for a kiss and a hug.

Cat leaned toward Billie. Tara giggled as she was squished between her two mothers. "How'd it go today?" she asked.

Just then, the batter hit the ball right at Seth, who got behind it, gloved it, and threw him out at first base. Billie stood up and cheered. "Yay, Seth! Way to go. Yay!" Skylar wiggled as Billie juggled her while trying to clap.

"Billie, sit down. You're blocking everyone's view," Cat said.

"Did you see that? It was perfect. Perfect."

"You wouldn't happen to be a proud mother, would you?"

Billie looked at her sheepishly. "Is it that obvious?"

"Does Dolly Parton sleep on her back?"

Both women burst into laughter at the image.

After they'd calmed down, Cat asked Billie again, "How'd it go today?"

"Good. Art and I drafted the petition and delivered it to the court. It'll be two to three months before a hearing, which will give us plenty of time to work on our case. We start tomorrow morning."

"Art's a good friend."

"The best. He told me today that he had a brother who died of AIDS a few years back."

"Really?"

"Yeah. That's one of the reasons he's so committed to help us with this suit."

"What are our chances, Billie?"

"To tell you the truth, Art thinks we're nuts. You know the saying 'you can't fight City Hall'? Well, we're doing just that. It won't be easy, but I'm in it for the long haul if you are."

"I go where you go. You know that. Count me in."

Just then, both women rose to their feet and let out a loud whoop as Seth once more cleanly fielded the ball.

* * *

On their drive home from Seth's baseball game, Billie and Cat passed Jen on her power walk through the neighborhood. Billie pulled up alongside, and Cat rolled down the window. "Hi, Jen," she called out cheerfully.

Jen looked into the backseat. "Did you win, slugger?"

"We clobbered 'em."

"Fantastic."

"How about a cup of coffee after your walk, Jen?" Cat asked.

"Sure, I'll be right over. Got to let Fred know where I am first. You know Fred. If I'm late, he'll call out the Marines."

"See you in a while." Cat rolled up the window as they drove away.

* * *

"Hey there, neighbors!" Jen announced her arrival and let herself in. She went to the kitchen cupboard, grabbed three coffee mugs from the shelf, and poured coffee for all of them. She brought the mugs to the table then grabbed the milk out of the refrigerator and the sugar off the counter.

Billie came up behind her. "Make yourself at home."

"Don't worry, Oh Tall One, I am." She gave Billie a hip-check and nearly sent her crashing into the table.

Jen sat at the table with Billie and Cat. "So, what's up?"

"We've decided to fight City Hall," Cat said. "Billie's going after the courts to get the anti-gay marriage law changed."

"Wow!" was all Jen managed to say at first. "You know we're behind you, don't you? The whole neighborhood, I mean."

"Yeah, we do," Billie said. "Thanks."

"Hmmm," Jen mused, "you might have more of a case if you already had a joining ceremony behind you."

"How would we go about doing that without a marriage license?" Cat asked.

"There are organizations and churches in the area that will perform the joining ceremony without a license," Jen said. "It's more symbolic than legal, but I can't imagine it would hurt your case."

Billie nodded. "You might have something there. If we're already joined, we'll have a firmer basis for wanting it legally recognized. I like it."

"So, how do we find this church?" Cat asked. "I was raised Catholic, but we all know how the Pope feels about us, so that's out."

Jen took a sip of her coffee. "You leave that to me. By the way, you two have been living as married for the past two years, quite comfortably from what I can see. Why the sudden urge to go legal? Don't get me wrong, I support you completely, and I'll do everything I can to help, but why now?"

"I did some research on the whole same-sex marriage issue," Billie said. "It seems that without the legal recognition from the state, same-sex partners aren't entitled to the same rights that heterosexual married couples are. Those rights include child custody, tax breaks, control of community property, the right to make medical decisions about each other and the children, rights to inheritance, and things of that nature."

"I didn't realize that," Jen said.

"It gets worse. If Cat or I died, there would be no guarantee that the surviving partner would be able to keep the kids together or even retain ownership of our home, even though we bought it together. If we win, the state will afford us these rights and more. Unfortunately, we still won't be recognized at a federal level. It would take repealing the Defense of Marriage Act to accomplish that, but it's a beginning. We need to protect each other and our kids. That's why we're doing this."

"Those are good reasons. I totally understand," Jen said. "Again, you know I'm behind you, and I'm sure the neighborhood will lend its support as well. I wish you all the luck in the world."

"Thanks, Jen," Billie and Cat replied together.

Jen downed the last gulp of coffee, rinsed out her cup, and put it in the dishwasher. "I've got to run. I'm sure Fred is pulling his hair out trying to get Stevie and Karissa ready for bed." Jen walked around the table where Billie and Cat sat. She hugged both of them at once and planted a kiss on each of their cheeks. "Let me know if there's anything I can do for you... babysitting, organizing demonstrations. You know, the fun stuff."

Cat hugged Jen. "Jen, we love you. You know that, don't you?"

"Yeah, I do. The feeling is mutual. All right, enough mushy stuff. I hear Fred's follicles screaming. Got to go. I'll find that church and let you know tomorrow. Bye."

When Jen left, Cat and Billie looked at each other. "Demonstrations?" they said together.

* * *

A week later, Billie and Cat sat at Jen and Fred's pool enjoying margaritas and discussing the wedding with their friends.

"You two amaze me," Billie said to Jen and Cat. "It's only been a week and everything's planned... the church, reception hall, meal, band, flowers."

Jen waved a finger. "You forgot to mention the invitations. They went out yesterday."

"How'd you manage to get that much done in a week?" Billie asked.

"It helps," Jen said, "that I'm a stay-at-home mom. While your nose was buried in legal reference books most evenings, Cat and I were busy organizing and making decisions. I simply made the phone calls during the days while you and Cat worked."

"We really do appreciate the effort you're putting into this," Cat said.

"No problem."

Billie reached across the table for Cat's hand. "Do you want to ask them, or should I?"

"Go ahead," Cat replied.

"Fred, Jen, we'd be honored if you'd agree to stand up for us at the ceremony."

Jen's eyes opened wide. "You want us? Don't you have family you should be asking first?"

"I have three sisters," Cat said. "I called each of them to let them know about the ceremony, and they all volunteered to stand up for me, but I can't make myself disappoint any of them by choosing one over the other. I told them that, and they understand. As far as Billie's concerned, she's an only child."

"Besides," Billie said, "you and Fred have become our family. We love you both dearly, and we'd really like you to be our Matron of Honor and Best Man."

"I'm flattered. Yes, of course. I'd be happy to be your Matron of Honor. Fred?"

"Absolutely. Count me in."

"Great. We thought Fred could stand with me and you can stand with Cat, Jen," Billie said.

"What about other attendants?" Jen asked.

"We figured Seth would walk Billie down the aisle, while Dad escorts me," Cat explained. "Tara and Skylar would be the flower girls."

Billie leaned over the patio table and looked at the list in front of Jen. "So what does that leave?" she asked.

"The rings and clothing," Jen replied. "Have you thought about what you'd like to wear?"

"Cat and I would like to wear matching dresses if we can find two alike in our sizes," Billie said.

"I know a local seamstress," Jen said, "who can help with alterations if you can find something even close to matching. She can probably make dresses for Tara and Sky as well. I'm sure I can find something off the rack for me. The tuxes for Seth, Fred, and Doc can be rented from the formal wear outlet in town."

"Jen, what would we do without you?" Billie asked.

* * *

In the few weeks before the ceremony, Billie and Art focused their efforts on searching the state's current rules and regulations regarding marriage and drafting a petition to challenge them. The court date was exactly one month after the joining ceremony.

"We've got our work cut out for us, Art," Billie said as she read an article on the state's same-sex marriage ban.

"I told you this wouldn't be easy. Our biggest hurdle will be with the state senate. Public opinion polls are in our favor, and the New York State Assembly has passed same-sex marriage legalization bills multiple times. The New York Senate, however, is more conservative than the state assembly. Remember, the most recent legislation was defeated as late as December 2, 2009," Art said.

"That's why it's important to strike while the iron is still hot. I plan to bypass the senate and file an appeal to the New York State Supreme Court." Billie handed a hefty pile of papers to Art. "Here. You scan through these while I tackle this other pile. We need to put together a fact sheet that we can build our argument from."

"Okay. I'll focus on the historical aspects of the same-sex marriage movement, and you can look for legislative information. Deal?"

Billie sat up in her chair. Her spine cracked audibly, and she let out a sigh of relief. "That felt good." Art was penning a few notes on his yellow legal pad. "Any luck?" she asked.

"Actually, yes. Apparently, New York has a long history of civil disobedience on this topic among its elected officials. Listen to this: February, 2004, the mayor of New Paltz performs same-sex civil weddings. A week later, he's charged with 19 misdemeanor counts of solemnizing marriages without a license. Despite the charges, the mayor vows to continue performing the unions. In March, the mayor of Nyack declares that he will begin officiating at same-sex marriages and will seek marriage licenses from municipal clerks' offices. July, 2004, the mayor of Ithaca provoked a court hearing by sending marriage applications from same-sex couples to the New York State Department of Health and offered the five gay couples the backing of Ithaca's legal resources if the applications were denied. Those are from 2004 alone. It appears the general public and many of its elected officials are in our corner."

"Unfortunately," Billie said, "it's the state supreme court we have to convince. We can certainly use public opinion as an argument, but we need something more substantial to turn this into a civil rights case, not a public opinion poll."

"I think you're right. It's time to pull out the big guns and do some Internet searches. We can't use information directly from the Internet itself, but we might find something that will point us in the right direction."

"I think we should begin with the arguments used by some of the other states that have already granted same-sex marriage rights," Billie said. Within minutes of beginning her search, she threw her arms into the air. "Bingo! That didn't take long. I think I've got something."

"Let me see."

"Listen. On December 20, 1999, the Vermont Supreme Court ruled in *Baker v. Vermont* that same-sex couples are entitled under Chapter I, Article Seven, of the Vermont Constitution to the same benefits and protections afforded by Vermont law to married opposite-sex couples. The court required same-sex benefits and protections but didn't require Vermont to grant marriage licenses to same-sex couples. The law went into effect on July 1, 2000. Vermont became the first U.S. state to offer a civil union status that provided the same legal rights and responsibilities of marriage."

"Vermont, huh? They've always been a pretty progressive state. Does it say anything else?"

"Yes. A bill that would allow same-sex couples to marry was introduced February 6, 2009. The measure passed both the senate and the house but was vetoed by the governor. The very next day, the senate and the house overrode the veto, making it the first time since 1990 that a Vermont governor's veto was overridden. The law went into effect on September 1, 2009."

Billie bookmarked the web site and hit the back button to return to her previous search results.

"Look at those headlines," Art said. "Connecticut, New Hampshire, Massachusetts, Vermont, and Iowa have all legalized same-sex marriage, and Washington, D.C. recognizes it. And New Jersey and Nevada support civil unions."

"I have a good feeling about this. With this kind of trend, we're almost a shoo-in."

"Key word is 'almost.' California's a good example of what can go wrong," Art said. "It's inconceivable to me that marriage rights were granted and then taken away from same-sex couples there. And to top it all off, the state legislature ruled that Proposition Eight wasn't unconstitutional. I don't know how they're going to deal with the fact that they're denying marriage rights to some same-sex couples but are legally recognizing same-sex marriage for couples that got married before Prop Eight passed. Sounds like a discrimination suit to me."

Billie sighed. "I hear you. As much as I want to be excited about what we've discovered, I know guarantees are hard to come by. We can only present what we think is a water-tight case, based on alleged violations of our state's equal rights amendment on the grounds of sexual discrimination, and hope it floats."

*　*　*

When Billie arrived home that evening, Cat found herself unexpectedly swept up into Billie's arms and twirled around the kitchen.

"Billie! Billie, put me down," she said with a squeal.

"We found it. We've established the precedence. Now we have hope."

"Really? Tell me about it."

"Vermont."

"Vermont?"

"Vermont, Connecticut, New Hampshire, Massachusetts, and Iowa to be exact. They all legally recognize same-sex marriages.

They challenged that their denial of marriage licenses violated the state's equal rights amendment, which disallows discrimination based on sex."

Cat looked a little confused. "How does that help us?"

"Don't you see? It sets a precedent. It gives us a basis on which to argue our case. All we need to do is research our state's equal rights amendment in detail to determine whether it also disallows sexual discrimination and put a case together to show how the anti-gay marriage law violates that amendment."

"I don't understand. How can it be sexual discrimination when it applies to both gay men and women?" Cat asked.

"It's sexual discrimination because a marriage license is denied based totally on the genders of the participants."

"It sounds so easy," Cat said.

"Far from it, love, but it does give us direction and hope. What do you say we go out and celebrate at the ice cream stand?"

"Did someone say ice cream?" Cat moved out of the way in time to avoid Seth who slid into the kitchen on his knees.

"Yeah, sport. Go get your sisters, will you?" Billie asked.

"Last one in the car is a rotten egg," Cat said when all three children returned cheering to the kitchen.

Seth picked up Skylar and ran out to the car, with Tara right on his heels. Cat looked at Billie.

"Do you want to be the rotten egg, or do I get that privilege?" Billie asked.

"That would be you," Cat said as she ran after the kids.

* * *

As their wedding day neared, things became more and more hectic for Billie and Cat. Cat and Jen dealt with a thousand last-minute details, while Billie worked late every night on their court petition. Three days before the wedding, they still hadn't purchased rings.

Cat was in a panic and very short-tempered as she called Billie's office.

"Billie Charland," Billie said into the phone.

"Are you ready to go pick out rings?" Cat asked. Cat's impatience was increased by the distinct pause at the other end of the line. "Billie?"

"I'm sorry. Art and I are in the middle of compiling some important information for the hearing. I can't leave right now."

"Damn it, Billie. When do you think we're going to get these rings? After the wedding?"

"I'm sorry, but we're at a point where it would be inconvenient to stop. I'll make it up to you, I promise."

"Fine. I'll see you when you get home." Cat abruptly hung up the phone.

Billie dropped her head into her hands. "Shit."

"Trouble in paradise?" Art said.

"Yeah. She's losing patience with me working so late every evening. I feel like a real heel. Cat and Jen have worked hard on this wedding, and I can't even take a few hours to shop for rings."

"Look, Billie, if we manage to get through this one argument tonight, I think we can take the rest of the week off. Besides, the wedding's only three days away and you need time to get reacquainted with Cat. You haven't seen her in so long I'll bet she's forgotten what you look like."

"The rest of the week off?' Billie asked hopefully.

"Yes. Now get to work."

"Slave driver." Billie dove into the stack of papers on her desk.

* * *

It was near midnight when Billie made it home. When she let herself into the house, she was surprised to see a light on in the living room.

Damn. I'm in big trouble here. I can feel it. She made her way through the kitchen and into the living room. Cat was sitting on the couch working on a crossword puzzle. Billie crossed the room, knelt on the floor in front of her, and laid her head in Cat's lap. "I'm sorry," she whispered.

Instead of the cold shoulder she'd expected, Billie felt Cat's hand rub up and down her back.

"No, I'm the one who's sorry, love," Cat said. "I didn't mean to sound so harsh. I know you're trying your hardest to win this case for us. I should be supportive, not a nagging fishwife."

Billie lifted her head from Cat's lap. "I've arranged to take the rest of the week off. We'll shop for rings in the morning, and then I'm all yours. I'll help you in any way you need. All you need to do is point me in the right direction."

"Thank you. You don't know what this means to me. I love you."

"I love you, too. Never forget that."

"Never," Cat replied.

* * *

"Jen," Cat said, "spending the night apart before your wedding is for newlyweds. Billie and I have been living together for almost three years now."

"Humor me. I'm a traditionalist at heart, and besides, Billie doesn't really have any family and I thought this could be a way for Fred and me to fill that role for her."

"I hadn't thought of it like that before. You're right, of course. My parents and sisters will be here for the wedding, but Billie has no one except us and our friends." Cat hugged Jen. "Thank you for thinking of that."

* * *

Cat's three sisters and their families had come in from out of town for the wedding. On the morning of the ceremony, her sisters and mother arrived at the house to help prepare Cat. Doc opted to lend a hand at Jen's.

Cat felt very special, surrounded by her mother and sisters.

Her sister Bridget picked up a framed photograph from the living room mantel. "Is this Billie?" she asked.

"Yes. That was taken about a year ago."

"She's even more attractive in this picture than in the one you emailed to me."

"I totally agree with you."

"And she's just as nice as she is beautiful," Ida said. "She loves Tara and Skylar like they were her own."

"As far as she's concerned, they are her own, just as Seth is mine," Cat said.

"I for one can't wait to meet the one little sis finally decided to settle down with," her sister Amy said.

"Like, anyone has to be better than Shannon. She was such a loser," Drew added.

"Drew, be nice," Ida said.

"Well, duh! I mean, look what she gave up."

Cat smiled and reveled in the sense of family that filled her heart. It had been a long time since she had spent any quality time with her siblings. Even talking with them on the phone as often as she did couldn't replace actual time spent together. It seemed incredible to her that in the three years since Cat and Billie met, the opportunity hadn't arisen for Billie to meet her sisters, but all of them lived out of state. Distance and busy lives made things difficult.

"All right, one more inspection before we're ready to go," Ida said.

Cat's gown billowed around her legs. The neckline plunged between her breasts and showed ample cleavage, and the peasant-girl sleeves fell slightly off her shoulders and exposed an expanse of skin from delicate shoulders to chin. Her red-gold hair was pulled up loosely into a bun on top of her head, and tendrils of hair hung in tiny ringlets around her hairline. Around her neck, she wore a thin velvet collar with a cameo. A slight tinge of blush adorned her cheeks, and red lipstick graced her lips. The whole effect was that of a delicate southern belle.

* * *

At Jen's, things were a bit more rocky. Billie was so nervous she couldn't stand still while Jen secured the two-dozen buttons that adorned the back of her gown.

Jen circled her until she faced her. "Do I have to tie you down to do this? Hold still, girlfriend. Geesh, you're so nervous, you'd think you're getting married or something."

Billie laughed and hugged her. "Sorry. I'll behave."

While Billie stood as still as she could, she had a flashback to her childhood and of all the times her mother had reprimanded her for being fidgety while trying to brush her hair. A wave of nostalgia filled her with melancholy thoughts about her family. Her parents died in a car accident when Seth was only two, and she had no siblings. How she wished they could be here today to see how happy she was with Cat. At least she had Seth on this momentous day.

Jen finished buttoning the dress. "All right, step in front of the mirror and let's see how you look."

Billie appeared regal. Her gown hung straight down and hugged her shapely legs. The empire waist of her dress highlighted her ample bosom and drew attention to her generous cleavage. Broad, toned shoulders were left bare by the peasant-girl cut of the sleeves as long arms extended gracefully beneath them. A thin chain adorned her right wrist, and a single teardrop pearl hung from a delicate chain around her neck. Long dark tresses flowed in waves around her shoulders. A slight shade of blush accented her cheekbones, and red lipstick adorned her lips.

She pivoted in front of the mirror. "It looks great, Jen. Thank you." Billie covertly wiped a tear from the corner of her eye. At least she thought she was being covert.

"Are you all right?" Jen asked.

Billie flashed the crooked smile that Cat claimed to love so much. "Yeah. I was thinking about my parents. They would've loved Cat. I think I'm feeling a little lonely."

"You know that Fred and I are your family now, right?" Jen asked. "We'll be there for you today."

Jen's sentiments made Billie tear up more. She pulled her friend into a close hug. "Thanks, Jen. Cat and I have come to love you and your family very much."

Jen pulled back and wiped a tear from her own eyes. "Well, if it wasn't for you, there'd be no family here to support you. For that we'll forever be grateful. And by the way, we love you, too. Now, enough of this mushy stuff. We're going to be late if we don't get this show on the road."

At last, Billie was ready to go. She'd opted to leave her hair down but had endured Jen fussing with the curling iron so that her long locks flowed in gentle waves around her shoulders.

She was startled by a voice from the doorway.

"You look very beautiful, daughter."

She smiled as she recognized Doc's voice. She walked over to him and allowed herself to be pulled into his embrace.

"I know your parents would be very proud of you, Billie. Yes, I heard part of your conversation with Jen." He paused. "I know I can't replace your dad, but I'd be damned proud to try, if you'd let me."

Unable to control her emotions, Billie buried her face in Doc's shoulder. "I'd like that a lot," she managed to say.

"Time to head out." Jen walked into the room just as Billie wiped away another tear. "Damn it, girl, you're ruining your makeup."

Billie looked up at Doc and smiled. "Busted."

Doc apologized for the damage. Jen spent a few more minutes repairing it and declared them ready to go.

* * *

Cat, her mother and sisters, and the three children stood at the top of the stairs outside the church entrance to await Billie's arrival. When the car pulled in, Fred opened Billie's door and offered his hand to help her climb out.

As Billie looked up at the crowd, she caught Cat's gaze and neither was able to look away.

"Oh my, she's a goddess," Cat's sister Amy said into her ear. "No wonder you fell for her."

"Oh, yeah," Cat said.

Billie climbed the stairs and stopped in front of Cat. "You're beautiful," she whispered.

"Hey, you two, time enough for visual foreplay later," Jen said. She snapped her fingers in front of Cat's face. "Snap out of it, Cat. How about some introductions here?"

"Oh, sorry. Ah, Jen, these are my sisters, Amy, Bridget, and Drew. Girls, this is Jen Swenson, our best friend."

After a round of pleasantries, Cat positioned herself at Billie's side and linked arms with her. "Everyone, this is Billie Jean Charland, my love, my life, my everything."

"Cute, Cat. A little corny, but cute." Billie offered her hand to Cat's sisters. "Amy, Bridget, Caitlain, Drew. A, B, C, D. I get it," Billie said. "Clever, Mom," she said to Ida.

"Blame it on Doc. He needed a way to remember their names," Ida said.

Cat's sister Drew stepped forward. "Billie, we've like, heard a lot about you, not only from Cat, but from Mom and Dad as well. Seems like my sister is like, gaga over you."

"The feeling is mutual, Drew. She's pretty special," Billie said.

"My God, you're gorgeous," Amy blurted out.

"Amy!" Cat exclaimed to her outspoken sister.

"Well, she is," Amy said.

"I agree wholeheartedly, but you don't have to embarrass her like that," Cat said with a laugh.

Bridget walked forward and linked Billie's other arm in hers. "What I'd like to know is what it's worth to you to hear about Cat's mischievous childhood."

"Name your price. I'll pay anything."

"That's enough," Cat said. "It's pretty bad when you can't trust your own sisters. Bridget, get away from her before you fill her with all kinds of lies."

At that moment, Cat noticed Doc walking toward them. He put his hands on his hips. "Caitlain, are these three up to no good again?"

"When are they not up to no good, Daddy?" Cat joked.

He looked at his daughters. "All right, you little imps, off with you. Go seat yourselves. The ceremony's about to begin."

Cat chuckled as her sisters obediently followed their father's instructions.

Billie whispered in Cat's ear. "I like them. I hope we'll have some time to spend with them before they leave."

Jen positioned Seth, Tara, and Skylar at the back of the church in the order they would walk down the aisle.

"They're so beautiful," Cat said as she and Billie both became teary-eyed.

"Oh, no you don't," Jen said. "We don't have time to repair flood damage again, understand? Pack those tears back in and keep them there."

Cat's emotions welled up in her throat as she watched Seth offer his arm to Ida to escort her to her seat, thus signaling the start of the ceremony.

Tara and Skylar walked hand in hand down the aisle, each carrying a small basket of flowers. Jen followed close behind, wearing a pink gown of similar design to the brides'. She ushered the girls into a pew with Ida as they reached the front of the church, then stood at the altar opposite to where Fred was already waiting.

Cat and Billie walked side by side down the aisle. Billie's arm was linked in Seth's, and Cat's was entwined with her father's. Billie and Cat each carried a large bouquet of spring flowers in her free hand. The small church was filled nearly to capacity with friends, family, and coworkers as the quartet made their way to the altar.

After depositing their charges at the altar, Seth and Doc took their seats with Ida and the girls. Fred and Jen stood next to their friends as the ceremony began. Jen took their bouquets from them and arranged them on the altar.

The presiding minister, Reverend Christine Altman, lifted her hands out to the sides and began in a loud, clear voice. "Welcome, friends and family of Billie and Caitlain. We are here to witness this wonderful event, the joining of two people in love. Never in the history of man has there been a more personally binding ceremony than that of marriage. These two women are here today to share with you their commitment to each other. With this ceremony, they're expressing their love for each other and celebrate that love openly and with pride. Let us all join our hearts in support of these women as they express their vows of commitment to each other."

Rev. Altman looked at Billie and Cat from her position a step above them. She smiled and whispered, "Relax. Are you ready?"

When she received affirmation from both of them, she continued. "Billie, Caitlain, please face one another."

They simultaneously took each other's hands.

"Billie and Caitlain have written their own vows which they'd like to share with you. Caitlain, you may begin."

Cat looked into Billie's eyes and cleared her throat. "Billie, I've loved you for all eternity. I believe we are destined to be together through all time, through many lives, past and present. You're my reason for living, the keeper of my heart, and the other half of my soul. You're my lover and my protector. You're in my thoughts from the moment I rise until I lay my head down to sleep at night. You fill my dreams with sweet music. You lift my soul to the very heights of heaven. I'll love you until my dying day and beyond. I pledge my love and my life to you until the end of time. I love you with all my heart. I'm honored to be your wife."

Billie reached forward and wiped the tears that flowed down Cat's cheeks. Her own throat was nearly closed with emotion. She composed herself and prepared to deliver her own vows. "Cat, you came into my life at a time when I was emotionally destitute. One look at you healed my soul and lifted my heart to new heights. You've given so much of yourself to me while asking so little in return. You're everything I could ask for. You're bright, intelligent, and beautiful. You're the mother of my children and my true soul mate. You complete me. Like you, I believe our destiny was linked many years ago. For that, I'll forever be grateful. I offer to you everything that I am. I promise to love you and protect you until the end of time and beyond. You're my one true love. I'm honored to be your wife. Thank you for loving me."

Rev. Altman said, "I believe there's no doubt as to how these two women feel about each other, so without further ado, Caitlain, please present your offering to Billie."

Cat accepted the ring from Jen. She held the ring in front of her as she addressed Billie. "This ring signifies the bond that is our love. It's a never-ending circle of love and commitment. Please accept this token as your consent to be my wife." Cat slipped the ring onto Billie's finger.

Billie retrieved Cat's ring from Fred. She held the ring in her fist. "I hold our love close to my heart as tightly as I hold this ring. I'll fiercely protect you and our family. I ask you to accept this ring as a symbol of that love and protection and as your consent to be my wife." Billie slipped the ring onto Cat's finger and their hands interlocked.

Rev. Altman once again held her arms out wide. "In the eyes of this church and our God, and in the presence of their friends and family, I declare Billie and Caitlain to be joined as one for all time." She addressed both women. "You may kiss the bride."

Billie lowered her mouth to Cat's as a loud cheer arose from the church. Several moments later, they broke the kiss and fell into each other's arms.

Rev. Altman placed a hand on each of their shoulders. "There are lots of people waiting to congratulate you. Go, celebrate with your friends and family." She stepped back as Billie and Cat were devoured by the crowd of well-wishers.

* * *

Halfway through the wedding reception, Billie wished she had brought a notebook and pen to record the names of Cat's family members. Cat introduced her to so many, there was no way she'd remember them all. In the presence of good food, music, friends, and family, the party went on well into the afternoon. Billie couldn't remember the last time she danced so much and by the time the party wound down, she was dead on her feet.

She and Cat sat at the head table and enjoyed their meal as they watched their children interact with the other guests. "Look at him," Billie said of Seth. "He's in heaven surrounded by all his female cousins. He's going to be spoiled rotten, being the only grandson among eight grandchildren."

"You can blame Daddy for that."

Billie pointed to the dance floor. "Tara seems to be enjoying herself. That kid has no inhibitions at all."

"We don't call her 'Tara the Terrible' for nothing," Cat said. "She's fearless."

"Have you seen Skylar in the past half hour?" Billie asked. "I'm not sure which relative has her now."

"Mom has her over there." Cat pointed to a table on the far wall where Ida was busy showing off her granddaughter to the other partygoers.

Late in the afternoon, Billie noticed that Skylar had fallen asleep in Ida's arms, signaling the end to a very long but exciting day. By this time, the gifts were opened, the cake was consumed, and most of the guests had already left.

Billie took Skylar into her arms. "Long day, huh, lovey?" she said to the child. "Cat, we've got our first casualty here. We should probably head home."

"All right. I'll collect Tara and Seth."

With children in hand, Cat and Billie prepared to leave but found their path blocked by Jen and her army, in the personages of Fred, Doc, and Ida.

"Where do you think you two are going?" Jen asked.

"We've got a casualty here. We've got to get her home to bed," Billie replied.

"No, I don't think so," Ida said. "I'd like my granddaughter back."

Billie raised her eyebrows to her mother-in-law.

"Don't you give me that look, young lady," Ida scolded. "This is your wedding day, and the two of you deserve at least one night alone together. Doc and I will take the children home with us. You can collect them sometime tomorrow."

Doc drew Billie's attention by clearing his throat. "I've learned not to cross her when she's in this mood. Best to do as she says."

Billie saw the mirth in Doc's eyes.

"Mom, you already have a full house," Cat said.

"You let me worry about my full house, Caitlain Maureen. Your father has planned a camping expedition in the backyard with the grandchildren. It seems only fair that your three be allowed to join in the fun."

"Camping?" Seth and Tara said together.

"Can we roast marshmallows?" Seth asked.

"It wouldn't be camping without it, scout," Doc said. "And besides, you have to come. I need another guy around with all these females."

Billie looked at Cat. "Your mom used your full name. You know what that means."

"It means we're fighting a losing battle. And besides, it looks like we're outnumbered. It might be in our best interest to give in."

Billie handed Skylar back to Ida.

"Good," Jen said. "Now that it's settled, Fred and I are taking you out to dinner, after which, you two will be spending the night in the Windjammer Hotel, complete with a private hot tub."

"You and Fred have done enough already," Cat protested.

"Look, girlfriend, I already have a sitter lined up for Stevie and Karissa. Do you think I'd willingly give up a nice dinner with friends with no kids around? Do I look stupid?"

"Do you really want me to answer that, Jen?" Billie asked.

"Watch it, Tall One, or I might have to hurt you."

Billie knelt on one knee and hugged Tara and Seth. "I want both of you to be on your best behavior at Grandpa and Grammy's tonight."

"We will, Mom," they answered.

"Dad," Billie said, stopping Doc in his tracks. "The kids' car seats are in the back of our car. Help yourself to them."

Doc surprised Billie by kissing her on the cheek. "Thank you," he said.

A bit confused, Billie said, "For what?"

"For calling me Dad. That felt good."

Billie wrapped her arms around Doc. "Yeah, it felt good here, too. I love you, you know. You and Mom both."

"I know, daughter. Have a good dinner, and don't be in a rush to pick the kids up tomorrow. They'll be fine."

"Okay. See you tomorrow," Billie answered.

Chapter 23

Cat and Billie saw little of each other as the day of the court hearing drew near. Preparation for the hearing demanded more and more of Billie's time and infinite patience from Cat as she endured Billie's prolonged work hours.

The night before the hearing, Cat cuddled with Billie on the couch in the family room. Before long, the conversation turned to the hearing the next day.

"What do you think will happen tomorrow?" Cat asked.

"It's hard to tell. Either the court will dismiss it right away, in which case we'll file an appeal, or they'll be open to argument and proceed. If they agree to proceed, we'll plead our case to the judge. This is a hearing, not a trial, so it shouldn't take long to complete our argument. After that, we wait and see. Art and I have no intention of allowing them to dismiss us easily."

"Win or lose," Cat said, "we have to take Art and Marge out to dinner after this is over. Art has worked so hard for our case, we owe him that much."

"Absolutely. In the past couple of months, he's seen as little of Marge as I've seen of you. Dinner is the least we can do to thank them both."

Cat caressed Billie's forearm. "Thank you for working so hard on this for us."

"You're welcome."

"How about we retire to our bedroom so I can give you a soothing massage?"

"How can I say no to such an enticing offer?"

"Go on ahead. I need to warm the massage oil in the microwave."

Soon, Cat sat astride Billie's naked backside, rubbing the warm liquid into her shoulders.

"God, that feels good," Billie said.

Cat could feel Billie relax beneath her touch. She began at
Billie's shoulders and mapped out a direct path toward her buttocks.
Before Cat reached her destination, however, a slight snore revealed
that Billie had fallen asleep under her careful ministrations.

Cat kissed Billie's cheek. "Poor baby. You've been wearing
yourself out with this case. Sleep well, love. You've got a hard day
ahead of you tomorrow." Cat set the alarm and slipped into bed. She
snuggled close to Billie's side and pulled the covers over them both.

*   *   *

The courthouse was filled to capacity, mostly with friends and
family of Cat and Billie. Cat, Fred, Jen, and Cat's parents sat in the
front row.

Billie and Art rose to their feet in front of the defendant's table
when the judge entered the courtroom from his chambers. He
paused slightly before climbing the two steps to the platform at the
front of the room to sit behind his desk. The bailiff started the
proceedings by reading a description on the docket. "This court is in
session. First case is Docket Number D3290-4, Charland v. State,
challenging the state's anti-gay marriage law. Judge Robert
Anderson presiding."

The judge leaned forward and looked at her and Art. Billie's
stomach clenched with nervous anticipation under his gaze.

"I see we have a rather full house today. This issue has the
potential to generate a media circus, so let me begin with a warning.
This is intended to be a simple civil hearing. I won't tolerate
theatrics. Is that clear?"

"Very clear, Your Honor," Billie replied. "We're simply here
to argue a matter of civil rights. We don't intend for it to become
anything more than that."

The judge nodded. "Fair enough. Welcome to my court. As the
bailiff said, my name is Judge Robert Anderson. I've read your
complaint, Counsel, and I understand your client's position, but I
must warn you that it will be a difficult challenge. To be successful,
you must prove that the law in question is unconstitutional on the
basis of the provisions outlined in this state's constitution. Are you
prepared to do that?"

Billie rose to her full height. "Your Honor, if it pleases the
court, I would like to point out that I'm my own client. My name is
Billie Jean Charland, a practicing attorney, and I'm challenging the
laws that prohibit legal recognition of my marriage to one Caitlain

Maureen O'Grady, with whom I've been partnered for over two years and wed in a commitment ceremony one month ago. And yes, sir, I'm fully prepared to argue that this state's law against same-sex marriage is unconstitutional."

"Very well, Counsel. You may continue."

Billie walked from behind her table. "Thank you, Your Honor."

Billie had chosen to wear her black pinstriped business suit but opted to wear the matching skirt instead of the trousers. The skirt came to just above her knees and hugged her shapely thighs sexily. Simple heels accented her nearly six-foot frame. She walked across the floor and approached the bench.

"Your Honor, it's my goal to prove that this state's anti-gay marriage law, which invalidates gay marriages, violates the terms of the state's equal rights amendment, disallowing discrimination of any kind based on gender. But before I plead the facts of this case, with your permission, I would like to address two misconceptions that some factions of the public believe are typical behaviors for homosexual couples." Billie paused to scan the papers she held in her hand.

"Permission granted," Judge Anderson replied.

"Thank you, Your Honor. First, it's a common assumption that gay and lesbian individuals have a choice about to whom they're attracted. Many people believe that we're, in reality, heterosexuals who choose to be gay. The truth of the matter is that being gay or straight is an inherent part of a person's core identity. That position is readily supported by many leading physiologists and psychologists and is backed up by clinical studies. Secondly, many people believe that gay relationships are primarily about sex, and in fact, many see us as sexually perverse. Nothing is further from the truth. The vast majority of homosexual relationships are based on love, affection, and mutual attraction. Committed gay and lesbian couples are primarily interested in loving relationships. Most are loyal to their partners, are monogamous, and are committed to family and community values, as are the majority of heterosexual couples."

Billie stopped to take a drink from the glass of water on her table. She inclined her head slightly to Cat and walked back to the front of the court to continue her statements.

"Aside from the similarities to heterosexual relationships, the primary point I want to make, Your Honor, is that this case is actually based on a civil rights issue. Many rights are violated by this state's refusal to legally recognize gay marriages. Many of those are privileges enjoyed by heterosexual couples and denied to gay couples solely based on the fact that they're of the same sex. This is clearly a case of sexual discrimination, which is a direct violation of this state's equal rights amendment." Billie walked back to her table and picked up a piece of paper. Continuing, she said, "Subsets of those rights include the following:

"A variety of state income tax advantages, including deductions, credits, rates, exemptions, and estimates.

"Public assistance from and exemptions relating to the Department of Human Services.

"Control, division, acquisition and disposition of community property.

"Rights relating to dower, courtesy, and inheritance.

"Award of child custody and support payments in divorce proceedings and in the case of a partner's death.

"The right to spousal support.

"The right to make medical decisions for one's partner in the event of incapacity of the injured party.

"The right to refuse to testify against one's spouse."

Billie once again paused to return the paper to the table. She looked up to see Art directing a small nod at her. Billie suppressed a grin as she picked up a second stack of papers and faced the judge once more.

"What I've read, Your Honor, is a list of rights afforded to married couples. Nowhere in the origins of these laws does it require that the recipients of these rights be heterosexual couples. These civil rights have long been denied to same-sex couples, while concurrently being enjoyed by heterosexual couples. It's not unreasonable for gay and lesbian couples to ask for the same rights that heterosexual couples enjoy by law, especially when denial of these rights is based solely on gender. I repeat. This is clearly a case of sexual discrimination."

Billie approached the bench and handed the judge one of the two stacks of papers she was holding. While he thumbed through them, she walked back to her table and removed her jacket. She draped it over the back of her chair and resumed her argument.

"Your Honor, what I've handed to you is a copy of several arguments against same-sex marriage. It's my intent to briefly dispute each point.

"Point one. Marriage is an institution between one man and one woman. This is probably the most used argument. I present to you,

Your Honor, that the institution of slavery was also once widely accepted in this great nation but has since been abolished. I use this analogy to show how public opinion is subject to change when presented with the proper information.

"Point two. Marriage is for procreation. This argument is based in religion and has no place in state law. If this argument is to hold, marriages between heterosexual couples that are sterile or those involving post-menopausal women should also be invalid. I submit to the court that there is no law requiring married couples to reproduce.

"Point three. Same-sex households are not the optimum environments in which to raise children. Considering this society allows murderers, sex offenders, and convicted felons of all sorts to marry and procreate, I believe that exposure to mutual affection between consenting same-sex adults is significantly less damaging to children than being raised in an environment where spousal abuse and/or crime is a common everyday occurrence.

"Point four. Gay relationships are immoral. I challenge the court to produce a legal document that determines the morality of gay relationships. This belief finds its origins chiefly in religion. Since there is a distinct separation between church and state in the Constitution of the United States, there is no place for this argument in state laws.

"Point five. Same-sex marriage is an untried social experiment. I submit, Your Honor, that same-sex marriages have been in existence in Denmark since nineteen eighty-nine, as well as in Dutch communities. In nineteen ninety-five, a survey conducted in Denmark indicated that eighty-nine percent of the clergy there openly supported same-sex marriages, and that many felt such benefits as reduction in suicide, a decline in the spread of sexually transmitted disease, and a reduction in promiscuity among gays were directly related to legalization of same-sex marriages in that country. A twenty-year history can hardly be described as untried.

"Lastly, Your Honor, point six. Granting gays and lesbians the right to marry is a special right. This last point particularly upsets me. Since ninety percent of the population already has the right to marry, why should extending it to the remaining ten percent, that being gays and lesbians, be considered special? I'm appalled that this point even exists in public opinion. What we're demanding here is equal rights, not special rights."

Once more, Billie walked over to her table for a drink of water. She sought out Cat's face and saw the pride and love reflected in her eyes. Her heart filled with a renewed sense of strength and determination as she looked back at the judge. He was thumbing through the document she'd given him and furiously writing notes in the margins. After giving him a few more moments to complete his note taking, Billie continued.

"Your Honor, as you can see, the most popular arguments against same-sex marriage have no place in state law. It's my belief that anti-gay prejudice finds its origins in fear and ignorance. People aren't comfortable with the idea of two men or two women being in love. I mentioned earlier that gays are a minority. In fact, statistically, they represent roughly 10% of the population. I submit to you, Your Honor, that constitutional government exists to protect all people, including—and especially—the powerless and the unpopular minorities. The anti-gay marriage law counteracts this very reason for the existence of constitutional government. I further submit that anti-gay prejudice also finds its origins in religion. As I've argued earlier, no state laws exist defining the morality of homosexuality. That definition exists solely with the religious community. It's long overdue for religious organizations to stop using the power of government to enforce their beliefs."

Billie paused to allow the judge to absorb her reasoning. "This last argument, Your Honor, brings me to my next point. The word marriage has traditionally been reserved for two people who legally commit their lives to one another. Much of the opposition to same-sex marriage is based on the religious aspects of the marriage ceremony. I submit to the court that the dissolution of a marriage is carried out in the courts, not in the church. This further supports the fact that marriage is a legal right that is being denied to a portion of the population, the gay and lesbian community. Denying any portion of the population the same rights enjoyed by the majority is clearly a civil rights issue, not a religious one. The Religious Right has tried to turn what they see as a moral issue into one that is legally decided by the courts. I challenge the courts again, Your Honor, to produce legal documentation that determines the morality of gay and lesbian relationships."

Billie walked back to the table and leaned her backside against it. "One final argument that I would like to make, Your Honor, is that the anti-gay marriage law directly violates this state's equal rights amendment, thereby deeming it unconstitutional. This state's ERA affords equal rights to all citizens and disallows discrimination based on religion, nationality, social class, sexual orientation or expression, race, or gender. Under this amendment, all people have equal rights. What's in error here is how this state applies this amendment. This state's government will boast that gays enjoy the same rights as non-gays. I submit that this is true for all rights afforded through the legal system except those gained through a legally recognized marriage. Examples of such rights violations have already been outlined earlier in my arguments. I submit to the court that the ERA doesn't specify marital status when it talks about equal rights. Denial of marriage licenses and legal recognition of marriage to same-sex couples constitutes sexual discrimination based on the provisions of this state's ERA."

She stood to her full height and paced back and forth to make her final point. Her voice rose in intensity and volume as she made her impassioned plea.

"A question I ask the court to consider, is whether the citizens of New York State are any less deserving than the citizens of Vermont, or the citizens of Massachusetts, or for that matter, the citizens of Canada?" A frown furrowed the judge's forehead. "I understand your confusion, Your Honor. Allow me to be more specific. In October 2004, the New York State Comptroller indicated that the state's retirement system would recognize same-sex marriages performed outside New York for the purpose of state retirement and pension benefits. Shortly thereafter, the mayor indicated that New York City's pension systems would recognize domestic partnerships, civil unions, and same-sex marriages performed outside of New York's jurisdiction... jurisdictions such as Massachusetts, Canada, Iowa New Hampshire, New Jersey, Vermont, Oregon, Hawaii, Colorado, Nevada, Wisconsin, Connecticut, California, the District of Columbia, and Washington State. In February 2008, the Appellate Division, Fourth Department, ruled that same-sex marriages consummated in Canada would be recognized in New York. In May, 2008, the governor of New York directed all state agencies to revise their policies to recognize same-sex marriages performed in other jurisdictions."

Billie paused. "Your Honor, I cite these facts in order to emphasize the point that New York has become the first state in the Union that does not allow same-sex marriage yet fully recognizes and offers benefits to same-sex couples married elsewhere. I ask again—is it fair to treat the citizens of New York with less rights and less respect than citizens of other states in this great Union?

"Your Honor, when a provision like the anti-gay marriage law allows certain rights to a portion of the population, but denies those same rights to another portion of the population, based solely on the gender of that population, it's clearly a case of sexual discrimination, it's in direct conflict with the rules and statutes of the equal rights amendment, and it's thereby proven to be unconstitutional."

Billie walked back to her seat and stood behind the desk. "That, in substance, is my case, Your Honor. I request that this court take the matter into consideration with the New York State Supreme Court for final determination. Thank you."

Billie sat down and Art's hand grasped hers under the table.

Behind her, Billie heard the slow and rhythmic beat of clapping hands. Soon, the entire room had erupted into clapping and cheering. Billie sat there, eyes locked with the judge in a plea for sympathy.

It was several minutes before the judge was able to regain control of his courtroom. He asked Billie to stand as he addressed her.

"Ms. Charland," he said, "I have to admit that I'm very impressed with your knowledge and ability to plead this case. You've made several valid points and have managed to shed enough doubt in my mind about the constitutionality of the anti-gay marriage law that I, indeed, will bring it to the state supreme court. However, in no way can I guarantee that the supreme court will rule in your favor. You may be called to testify at that hearing, so I would recommend you prepare yourself for that eventuality. You and your associates will be informed of the state's decision after due process. Good day."

"All rise," the bailiff instructed, and Judge Anderson left the courtroom.

Billie dropped back into her chair stunned. She didn't expect such a positive response to her case, especially following the stern warning issued by the judge at the beginning of the session.

Art threw an arm around her shoulder and pulled her in close. "We're halfway home," he said.

Billie released a sigh of relief and lowered her chin to her chest. The resolve she had held on to so tenuously in the days leading to the hearing crumbled as tears coursed down her cheeks. She felt soft arms circle her from behind.

"I've never been so proud of anyone in my entire life," Cat said. "I'm truly humbled."

Billie pulled Cat into her lap and held her close. Her heart was pounding as her mind acknowledged the significance of what she'd accomplished.

"I did it for you, love. For us and for our children."

"I love you," Cat said.

"Hey, you two, you've got all night to do that. Right now, I think we need to go out and celebrate," Art said.

Billie looked at him and wiped the tears from her face. "Only if we stop to pick up Marge, and only if you agree to be our guests."

"Deal, partner," he replied.

* * *

By the next morning, the press had learned of the hearing and took liberties to widely publish Billie's same-sex marriage arguments and the judge's reaction to them. Letters to the editor appeared daily for several weeks, both for and against the same-sex marriage issue. What had become a personal battle quickly escalated to the public arena, and Billie became an instant celebrity. Although she welcomed public support, she didn't anticipate the strength of the opposition, including the protesters that continuously picketed her workplace.

One evening, a few weeks after the hearing, Billie, Cat, and the kids were gathered in the basement family room for popcorn and a movie. Suddenly, they heard a loud crash in the living room above them. Billie and Cat both jumped to their feet.

"What the hell was that?" Billie exclaimed.

"I don't know, but I'm going to find out," Cat said.

"No. I'll go. You stay here with the children."

"I'm not going to let you go up there alone. I'm going with you."

Billie saw the fear on Seth and Tara's faces. She knelt in front of them. "It'll be all right. We'll be back in a minute. Seth, please stay with your sisters and don't be afraid."

Seth picked Skylar up and sat on the couch. Tara sat beside him and held his hand.

Cat waited for Billie at the top of the stairs. They pushed the door open and heard angry shouts coming from the front of the house. Billie stepped in front of Cat and entered the kitchen first. As they made their way into the living room, the angry voices grew louder. Within seconds, the source of the commotion became obvious when a second crash showered them with broken glass.

Billie grabbed Cat's arm and pushed her back into the kitchen out of harm's way. In the process of protecting Cat, she stepped on a broken shard of glass and embedded it deeply into the sole of her foot. "God damn it!" She limped into the kitchen behind Cat and grabbed the dishtowel from the counter. "Cat, call 911. Hurry."

"Billie, you're hurt."

"We don't have time for that right now. Call 911. Please."

While Cat dialed the phone, Billie listened to the protests from the crowd outside.

"You fricken queers!"

"Sick bitches!"

"Dykes!"

"Perverts!"

"We don't need your kind around here!"

"Billie, who are they?" Cat asked as she dialed the police.

The 911 dispatcher answered immediately. "This is Sergeant Bickford. What's your emergency?"

"We're under attack. We have a crowd of people outside our house throwing beer bottles through the window."

"We have a lock on your address, ma'am. A police car has been dispatched. Is anyone hurt?"

"My wife... she stepped on glass from the broken window."

"Does she need an ambulance?"

"No. The bleeding appears to be under control. Please, how much longer before the police arrive?"

"They should be there momentarily, ma'am. I'll stay on the line with you until they arrive. Can I have your name, ma'am?"

Billie's attention was drawn to the basement door as it opened and Seth poked his head into the kitchen. "Is everything all right?"

Billie shot a worried look at Cat and limped over to the door. "Seth, honey, go back downstairs. Everything's fine."

"Mom, your foot's bleeding."

"I'm all right. I stepped on a piece of glass. Please go back downstairs and stay with your sisters. Mama and I will be down soon."

Cat was still talking to the dispatcher when Billie heard police sirens in the distance. "I can hear the sirens, Cat. They're almost here."

After Seth had retreated to the basement, Billie limped back to the kitchen doorway and peered into the living room once more. "They're still out there. Hopefully the police will be able to catch a few of them."

Cat covered the receiver with her hand. "Who are they? Why are they doing this to us?"

"Well, judging by the comments, I'd say this is about the civil rights hearing. Apparently, they don't take very kindly to our lifestyle."

"They obviously don't live around here. They have no right to treat us like that. We've done nothing to them."

"Ignorance breeds hatred, I'm afraid. Oh good, I see flashing blue lights. The police are here."

Cat removed her hand from the receiver to speak to the dispatcher. "The police are here."

"That's good, ma'am. Is there anything else you need?"

"No. Thank you for your help." Cat hung up the phone and joined Billie in the doorway. From their vantage point, they saw four police cars in front of their home. A sudden knock at the front door startled them.

"This is the police. Is everyone all right in there?"

Billie began to make her way across the living room, but was stopped by Cat's hand on her arm. "I'll get the door. You sit here on the couch and elevate your foot."

Not wanting to admit that her foot was throbbing with nearly intolerable pain, Billie followed doctor's orders.

Cat opened the door and allowed the police officer into their home. "Thank God you're here."

"Ma'am, I'm Officer Johnson. Is everyone all right in here?"

"We are now," Billie said from her position on the couch.

Officer Johnson entered the living room as Billie was replacing the blood-soaked towel around her foot with a clean one. "Ma'am, do you need an ambulance?" he asked.

"No. I'll be fine. I stepped on the broken glass. What the hell happened here?"

"I was hoping you could tell me. Any idea what might've caused this attack?" Johnson asked.

"Prejudice," Cat said sadly from behind them as she stood in the open doorway and watched the police gather and handcuff the trespassers.

"Ma'am?"

"Prejudice, pure and simple. These people appear to believe they have the right to harm us because they object to our lifestyle. They think because we're bold enough to fight for equal rights, that we should become targets for their hatred."

"Ma'am, are you telling me this is a hate crime?"

"I'd say that description fits rather nicely, wouldn't you, Billie?"

"Wait a minute. Billie? As in, Billie Charland?"

"In the flesh," Billie replied.

"Well, I'll be. I've been watching your case in the papers. So, what makes you think this has anything to do with that?" Johnson asked.

Billie rose and shifted all of her weight to her uninjured foot. "Well, do the words 'dyke,' 'pervert,' and 'queer' give you any clues?"

"That's good enough for me. I'll need a full description of the incident for my report. Rest assured, we'll do our best to prosecute the violators."

Over the next half hour, Billie and Cat relayed as much information as they recalled to Officer Johnson who promised them a police car would be stationed across the street from their home for the next few days to ward off further attacks.

* * *

When it was over, Cat ushered the children from the family room and saw them all safely to their beds. When she returned to Billie in the living room, she realized Billie was trying desperately to remove the shard of glass that was still protruding from her foot.

Cat rushed to her side. "Oh my God, Billie. Why didn't you tell me the glass was still in there?" She examined Billie's foot as she poked and prodded around the wound to determine how deeply the glass was embedded. Cat looked up. "Honey, we have a choice here. Either I try to get this out for you, or we can run to the emergency room."

"You try. If we go to the hospital, the first thing they'll do is stick a needle in it."

"All right. I'll be right back." Cat returned with tweezers, peroxide, steri-strips, salve, and gauze bandages. "Here, put your foot on the coffee table and try not to move."

Cat lifted Billie's foot and put a clean, folded towel under it before she doused the wound with peroxide. For the next several moments, she maneuvered the glass shard around with the tweezers until she was able to position it for extraction. Cat periodically glanced up. Billie's hands clenched the couch cushion tighter and tighter with each fraction the shard shifted. When Cat was able to completely extract the sliver of glass, another flood of warm red liquid poured from the center of the wound. She held a clean cloth firmly to the wound to stem the flow of blood. Billie's face was pale and drawn. "Sweetheart, are you all right?" she asked softly.

Billie opened her eyes and looked at Cat but remained silent. She closed her eyes once more and nodded in response to Cat's question.

Cat continued to dress the wound in silence. Before long, the bleeding stopped and Cat closed and bandaged the cut. When she finished, she cleared away the blood-soaked towels and returned the medical supplies to the bathroom. In silence, she assisted Billie up the stairs to their room where she tucked her into bed and kissed her gently on the forehead. "I'll be back in a bit, my love," she whispered.

* * *

Billie lay on the bed and stared angrily at the ceiling as she listened first to the sound of the vacuum cleaner, and then to the hammering as she envisioned Cat cleaning up the broken glass and boarding up the broken windows. Maybe this fight wasn't worth it. She didn't mean for her arrogance and pride to put Cat and the kids in danger.

Sometime later, Cat slipped into bed beside her and draped an arm over her middle. Billie rolled onto her back and invited Cat into the crook of her arm.

"Thank you for cleaning up the mess downstairs," she whispered.

"No thanks necessary. It's the least I can do."

Billie lifted her head and looked questioningly at Cat. "What do you mean?"

Cat traced the line of Billie's jaw with her fingertips. "I so appreciate what you're doing for us and our children. The least I can do is support you in any way I can."

"Cat, while I was lying here waiting for you, all I thought about was the danger this case has put you and the kids in." Billie closed her eyes and pressed her head back into the pillow for several long moments. "I'm considering dropping the case."

Cat bolted upright in bed. "You can't stop. You can't give up."

Billie shook her head back and forth. "Those people out there tonight could've hurt you and the kids. I can't..."

Cat put her hand on Billie's chest between her breasts. "You can't what? You can't take the risks? You can't see it through? No. I won't let you give up. You've come all this way... no—we've come all this way. We can't turn back."

"Cat..."

"No, Billie. This isn't about you and me anymore. This is about everyone who faces that kind of ignorant hatred. Don't let them defeat you. Don't you know you're my foundation, my strength? Don't crumble now. I need you to be strong. We all do."

Billie stared at Cat. Her brow furrowed as she fought the tears. "I'm afraid."

"I am, too. I am, too, but we can't run away from everything that scares us. What kind of example is that for our children?"

Billie trembled as emotion overwhelmed her. "You're right. I won't give up. I promise."

* * *

The next evening, Billie invited Jen, Fred, and Art over for a discussion. She briefed them ahead of time, knowing that she'd need a united force to confront Cat.

Billie watched Cat pace back and forth across the living room. "No, Billie. I'm not leaving. This is as much about me as it is about you. I'm not leaving you here alone."

"She won't be here alone," Fred said. "Art and I will be staying with her until the notoriety wears off. They'll eventually get tired of the game and leave you alone."

Cat looked at her wife. "Billie?"

"Cat, please. I promised you last night that I wouldn't give up, but I can't fight this and protect you and the kids at the same time. Please go to your parents' house. I promise it won't be for long. If you can't do this for me, do it for the kids. Please."

"Cat, honey," Jen said, "we don't know what these people are capable of. Billie's right. We need to keep you and the kids safe."

"I see I'm pretty much outnumbered here," Cat said.

"Cat, please don't look at it that way," Jen said. "We love you and we only want to keep you and the kids safe. Try not to be too angry with us."

"All right. All right. I'll go."

Billie released the breath she'd been holding and pulled Cat in close. "Thank you. I wouldn't be able to bear it if something happened to you or the kids."

* * *

Billie relaxed a little once Cat and the children were safe. In the full week following Cat's move to her parents' house, there was only one anti-gay incident. Someone wrote distasteful graffiti across the front yard fence. Billie, Fred, Art, and Jen painted over it so Cat wouldn't see it when she came home.

After a few more days, with no repeat incidents, Billie felt safe enough to insist that Art go home to his wife. He left with the assurance that Fred would continue to stay in the house with her at night.

Billie didn't dare visit Cat and the kids at her in-laws' home. She feared she'd be followed and might unknowingly disclose Cat's whereabouts to the zealots. She did, however, contact her by phone several times a day. She missed her family dearly.

The following week, Billie walked through the dark parking lot after working late into the evening. She was distracted by her thoughts of Cat and the children. When she was within a few feet of her car, she was confronted by three men. Billie looked around for an escape route, but they had her surrounded.

"Hey, lezbo, where are you going?" one of the men asked as he tapped the end of a club into the palm of his other hand.

"Don't do this," Billie said.

One of the other men pushed her from behind. "Or what?" he asked.

Billie entered a martial arts stance and braced herself for an attack.

"Oooo, look at the big, tough she-man," the third man said. "I'm so scared."

"I'm warning you. Walk away."

"Not a chance," the man with the club said as all three assailants descended upon her.

Billie quickly maneuvered herself from the center of their circle and landed a sidekick on the knee of one of the assailants. She heard an audible crack when her foot made contact.

"Ahhh! She broke my leg. She broke my fucking leg," the man wailed. The other two attackers intensified their efforts.

Outnumbered, Billie quickly lost any advantage her martial arts training may have given her. The men beat her for what felt like an eternity.

Her assailants stood over her in the dark lot next to her car. The man with the club landed one last kick to her ribs. "Let this be a lesson to you. Drop your suit. You're a sick bitch. Your kind isn't welcome around here."

Billie spat a mouthful of blood onto his shoes. "Go to hell."

The man lifted the club high into the air and landed it firmly on her head.

* * *

Billie regained consciousness near dawn. She lay on the ground for a long time, trying to gather enough strength to move. After a time, she dragged herself into the car and called Art from her cell phone.

Marge answered. "Marge," Billie said in a weak, broken voice. "This is Billie. I need Art. Please hurry."

"Billie? Are you all right? Art. Art, wake up," Marge urged her sleeping husband. "Billie, talk to me. Where are you?"

"Work... parking lot... tell Art... hurry," she said before she lost consciousness.

* * *

Art sat up in bed, struggling to full alertness. "What is it?"

"Get up, quick. Billie's hurt. We need to go to your office."

Art jumped out of bed and got dressed. Marge slipped something on, and a few moments later, they were in their car and on their way to the office. As they pulled into the parking lot, they saw Billie's car with the door open. Art found Billie unconscious across the front seat with her legs still on the outside and the cell phone still in her hand.

They loaded her into their car. Marge cradled Billie's head in her lap in the backseat as Art negotiated traffic. Within minutes, they arrived at the emergency room and Billie was wheeled into Triage. Marge provided the receptionist with what little bit of information she knew about Billie, and Art called Cat.

* * *

Cat bolted awake at the unexpected ring of the phone so early in the morning. Fear immediately consumed her. "Hello?" she said apprehensively into the phone.

"Cat. This is Art."

Before he said another word, Cat broke in. "Where is she? She's hurt, isn't she? Tell me where she is, please."

"She got beat up. She's at Albany Medical Center on Commercial."

Cat didn't even reply. She hung up the phone and jumped out of bed. She threw on some clothes and wrote a note to her mother that she'd return soon. She ran every red light and stop sign between her parents' home and the hospital. By sheer luck, she arrived there unscathed. She rushed into the emergency room, trying to look everywhere at once, and ran right into Art. He grabbed her by the arms.

"Whoa, slow down, Cat. You'll be no use to her if you don't calm down."

"Where is she? I need to see her."

Art pointed to an examination room door. "She's only been in there for twenty minutes. They'll let us know as soon as they can. Right now, you need to see the receptionist." He led her over to the check-in window.

Marge was still there, trying to help the receptionist. "Thank God, her wife is here." She motioned for Cat.

The receptionist frowned.

As soon as Cat saw Marge, she went into her arms.

"It'll be okay, Cat. I know it will," Marge said.

Cat calmed down enough to answer the receptionist's questions. When she got to the part about married status, Cat answered "married" and gave her own name as spouse. The receptionist again looked at her oddly and refused to write down the offered information.

As the receptionist finished with Cat, the emergency room doctor came out and asked to see the family of Billie Charland. Cat came forward and introduced herself as Billie's wife.

"I see," the doctor said while he walked away from her. Cat chased after him, grabbed his arm and swung him around to face her.

"I'm her wife. We've been married for two months. Tell me how bad she's hurt."

"Listen, miss. You're not her legal spouse in this state, and I can't accept that you are." He addressed the nurse. "Have Ms. Charland moved into a semiprivate room until a family member can be located."

Cat was out of her mind with anger and worry. The reality of what motivated Billie in her legal quest hit her like a ton of bricks.

By God, if she'd ever doubted Billie in this venture, she'd learned her lesson today.

Not knowing what else to do, she called her father. She hated to rely on Daddy every time she had a problem, but Billie's health was at stake here, so there was no question about swallowing her pride.

Doc arrived ten minutes later. Within moments, Cat was standing by Billie's bedside. "Oh my God, Billie." Cat almost didn't recognize Billie through the massive black and blue marks that covered her face and arms. Her left arm was set in a fiberglass cast, and her right eye was swollen shut. Cat sat down on the side of Billie's bed and caressed what she could of her face. "Billie, look at what they've done to you," she said through her tears.

"It hurts worse than it looks," Billie joked.

Surprised, Cat said, "You're awake."

"Unfortunately, yes. Did they get the license number of the truck that ran over me?"

"Art's talking to the police, but they'll want to see you as soon as you're up to it. It was the anti-gay activists, wasn't it?"

Billie nodded her head, then grimaced.

"Damn it," Cat said. "When will it end? When I got here tonight, they wouldn't let me in to see you. The doctor brushed me off when I told them I was your wife. I understand completely now what's driving you with this case. Please forgive me if I've ever wavered in my faith in you." Cat lowered her head to Billie's shoulder.

Billie reached up with her uninjured arm and stroked Cat's hair. "Shhh. It's all right. I've never doubted your love and faith in me."

* * *

Billie turned her gaze toward the door and tried to smile when Doc came into the room. "So am I going to live?"

"What did you find out, Daddy?" Cat asked.

Doc sat at the end of Billie's bed and opened the folder he carried with him. "Billie-girl, it's a good thing you've got a hard head, otherwise, they might have killed you."

Billie chuckled and winced at the movement. "Please don't make me laugh. Hurts like hell."

"Sorry about that. So, the extent of the damage is as follows: broken left arm, three broken ribs, one on the right and two on the left, slight concussion, several cuts, abrasions, and bruises, including one very swollen eye," he said. "The good news is there don't appear to be any internal injuries so you won't need to be here for long."

"When can I go home?"

"Tomorrow should be soon enough," he said. "And you'll be coming home with me. No arguments, understand? If you argue, I'll send Ida after you."

"Please, no! Not that." Billie chuckled and winced again.

A knock at the door interrupted their wordplay. It was a uniformed police officer. "Is this Billie Charland's room?"

Doc met the officer at the door. I'm Doctor O'Grady, Ms. Charland's physician."

"Is it possible for me to have a word or two with Ms. Charland?" he asked.

Doc looked at Billie. "Are you up to it?"

"Sure, come in. Have a seat."

"Make it short, Officer. As you can see, Ms. Charland should be resting."

"I will, sir. Thank you."

Cat moved to the other side of the bed. Doc stood in the background.

A half hour later, the officer had a full account of the attack, including a detailed description of Billie's assailants, and that she might have landed a lucky kick to one of their knees, probably breaking it.

The officer rose to leave. "Thank you, Ms. Charland. We have a good idea who did this to you. Do you think you can pick them out of a police lineup?"

"Absolutely."

"Good. I'll be in touch within the next couple of days. Until then, I hope you recover soon." The officer stopped at the door. "On a personal note, ma'am, I want you to know that I've been following your case, and I think you have a lot of courage and conviction for doing this. I hope you win."

"Thank you, Officer, I appreciate your support." When he left, Billie smiled at Cat. "That is one of the many reasons this is worth all the effort."

Chapter 24

Several days later, Billie sat behind a two-way mirror and watched as six men were ushered into the room. Upon command, they turned left, right, and back to center.

"Do you see any of your assailants in this lineup?" the detective asked.

"Numbers two, three, and six," Billie said. "I'm the reason number six is using crutches. How did you find them?"

"We've been watching the group they belong to for a while. Based on your tip, we interviewed the one on crutches, and with a little pressure, he cracked and opted for a plea bargain in exchange for supplying information about his fellow assailants."

"I'm happy these three are off the street, but I can't help but wonder if there are more waiting in the wings to take their places."

"We have it on good authority that one of these three is the primary ringleader. We're hoping they'll lose their momentum with their leader behind bars."

"One can only hope, Detective. One can only hope."

For the next three weeks, Billie, Cat, and the kids stayed at Doc and Ida's house while Fred kept an eye on things at home. As predicted, since the arrest of the three assailants, all anti-gay activity ceased. After much discussion, Billie and Cat decided it was safe enough for their family to move back home.

As soon as they returned, Billie went back to work, still sporting ugly looking bruises, wrapped ribs, and the cast on her arm. She carried her full workload even though she was urged to work part-time for a while.

On her fifth day back, she received a letter from the court, delivered to her office. She turned the envelope over and over in her hands, afraid to open it. She put it on her desk and sat down. With her hands placed on the blotter on either side of the envelope, she stared at it for long moments before she picked up the phone and dialed the hospital. Soon, Cat answered.

"Caitlain Charland."

"Hey, love."

"Billie. What a surprise. Is everything okay?"

"We'll know in a few minutes. I received a communication from the court."

"It's about time. The court hearing was nearly a month ago. What does it say?"

Billie could hear the nervous tenor in Cat's voice. "I don't know. I haven't opened it yet."

"Well..."

Billie picked up the letter and slipped the blunt-edged opener under the corner of the flap. Slowly, she ran it down the length of the envelope and extracted a single page.

"What does it say, Billie?"

Billie unfolded the letter. "It appears to be from Judge Anderson."

"Read it to me."

"Dear Ms. Charland. I generally do not take liberties to communicate directly with attorneys who argue cases in my court, but I was duly impressed with your ability to argue your case. It appears that you've done your homework, Ms. Charland. I had your entire testimony transcribed and submitted to the New York Supreme Court. The facts and arguments posed in my court indicated to me that your case had merit, and hence I have made myself an advocate and have lobbied for it to be moved to the top of the docket. The Court has spent the past three weeks deliberating and is now ready to render a decision. In no way will I guarantee the outcome of this case, Ms. Charland. That is for the Court to decide. With that in mind, you will be summoned to attend the session in which the decision shall be rendered. That session is scheduled for next Monday. Yours truly, Judge Robert Anderson."

Billie's hands shook as she lowered the letter to her desk. A long silence permeated the air.

"Billie? Are you there?"

Cat's voice snapped Billie out of her trance. "I'm here."

"What does it mean?"

"It means, in three days the direction of our lives will be decided."

* * *

Later that evening, after the children were in bed, Billie reclined in a tub of hot water with her fiberglass-clad arm on the rim of the tub. Cat sat between her legs with her back resting against Billie's chest.

"Are you sure I'm not hurting your ribs?" Cat asked.

"No, love, I'm fine. More wine?"

"Sure, fill'er up." Cat held her glass up as Billie grabbed the wine bottle off the shelf next to the tub and filled their glasses.

"So the decision is Tuesday, huh?" Cat asked.

"Yes. I'm so nervous my stomach is doing flip-flops."

"Is there anything I can do to take your mind off of things?" Cat asked.

"You could wash my hair for me."

"You want me to wash your hair?"

"Yes. Heck, the cast seems like a good excuse to get you to run your hands all over my body."

"Let me clue you in on something, love. You don't need an excuse."

Cat reached for the shampoo. "Under," she said, and Billie sank below the water and resurfaced.

She fell into a nirvana-like trance as Cat massaged her scalp. "I'll give you two hours to stop that."

Cat removed the showerhead from its brace and held it above Billie's head. "No, I don't think so. I have other plans for you to fill the next two hours."

"Oh goody!" Billie exclaimed as she struggled to climb out of the tub.

* * *

Billie kissed Cat for good luck before she entered the supreme court judicial hearing at nine o'clock on Tuesday morning. She was so nervous she was visibly shaking. She closed her eyes for a moment to calm herself. "Thank you for being here with me, love."

"I wouldn't be anywhere else. This is as much about me as it is about you."

Billie took Cat's hand and led her into the judiciary hearing where they sat in the back of the room. Within minutes, their case was called to the docket. Billie stood and stepped into the aisle then paused and looked at Cat.

"Billie, what are you doing? Go," Cat urged.

Billie offered Cat her hand. "Like you said, this is as much about you as it is about me. Come with me." Billie interlaced her fingers with Cat's and led her down the aisle to the bench.

The session chair, Judge William Reinhardt, addressed Cat and Billie directly. "Which of you is Ms. Billie Jean Charland?"

Billie took a step forward. "I am, Your Honor."

"And who's this with you, Ms. Charland?"

Billie took Cat by the hand. She pulled Cat forward and wrapped a protective arm around her shoulder. "This is Caitlain O'Grady, and I'm proud to call her my wife, Your Honor."

"I see. Well, Ms. Charland, you've caused quite a stir in this court. You see, several of us on this panel don't believe in same-sex marriages."

Billie grabbed Cat as she stepped forward, and gave her a warning look not to say anything.

"Like I said, Ms. Charland, not all members of this panel agree with the concept of same-sex marriage. We do all agree, however, that every citizen in this great country deserves equal rights and equal consideration under law, and that every citizen in this state should receive fair and equal treatment relative to the other citizens of this country. Thanks to you, we now know laws exist in our state that could be deemed as discriminatory on the basis of gender. Also thanks to you, those laws have been ruled unconstitutional and will be stricken from our books. Congratulations, Ms. Charland. You've won your case, and our fair state will be much better for it."

"Does this mean we can apply for a marriage license without denial?" Cat asked.

"Yes, ma'am, that's exactly what it means. Your union will be legally recognized by the state with rights equal to heterosexual couples, effective one month from today."

Cat began to cry. She wrapped her arms around Billie's neck. "By God, you did it, love. You did it."

"No, Cat, we did it. We did it together." Billie turned to address the court. "If it pleases the court, I wish to express our sincere gratitude with respect to your open mindedness and for doing what you know is right."

"No, Ms. Charland," Judge Reinhardt said. "We thank you. We pride ourselves in governing over a fair and just state. You showed us where the law was in error and gave us the opportunity to correct the situation."

"I just want you to know, sir, that I appreciated the opportunity to present our case."

"No thanks necessary. By the way, your injuries…"

"My injuries were administered by those not as open minded as yourself, Your Honor."

"Well, I apologize if our laws contributed to your pain."

"Your Honor, sometimes even laws don't stop the homophobes, but thank you for your concern." She took Cat's hand, and together, they left the courtroom.

* * *

One month later, Billie and Cat exited the chambers of Judge Robert Anderson with wedding certificate in hand. They posed for several press photographers and gave statements for the paper. Afterwards, Billie and Cat, along with their children and Jen, Fred, Marge, Art, and Cat's parents, rode in the rented limousine to the airport. Billie and Cat were scheduled to catch a plane to Florida to board the cruise ship to Aruba. It was long past due for them to go on their honeymoon.

"Promise me you'll be good for Grandpa and Grammy while we're gone," Billie said to the kids. Several hugs and kisses later, Billie and Cat boarded the plane. After they were in the air and the seat belt sign was off, Billie excused herself to use the restroom. On her way back to her seat, she saw an attractive male passenger chatting with Cat. She heard Cat introduce herself as Cat Charland. The pleasure of hearing Cat use her name was overwhelming.

"Are you traveling with someone?" the man asked.

"As a matter of fact I am, and here she is," Cat replied as Billie reached them. "Billie, this is James Shepard. James, this is Billie Charland, my wife."

"Er… ah… nice to meet you, Billie. Ah… maybe I'll see you later. Bye," James said as he scurried away.

"Well, Mrs. Charland, do you always scare nice young men away?" Billie asked.

"You'll pay for that, Billie. Be afraid. Be very afraid."

"Oh, I'm counting on it, Mrs. Charland. I'm counting on it."

Part V:

What's In a Name?

Chapter 25

Autumn arrived and the children returned to school soon after Cat and Billie came home from their Aruba honeymoon. Seth was starting third grade, and Tara was entering second grade. The trees donned coats of many colors as the evening temperatures cooled.

Billie and Cat spent the autumn evening cuddled together in the family room as they sipped tea and watched the red-orange glow of the fire. A yawn broke the spell.

"Are you tired, love?" Billie asked.

"No, not really, just relaxed." Cat snuggled even closer to her.

Billie tightened her arms around Cat. "This is nice."

"Hmmm."

She kissed the top of Cat's head. "Are you happy?"

"Very."

"Me, too. I love you, you know."

"I love you, too, with all my heart."

The women sat in companionable silence, once more captivated by the fire before them.

"Did you notice that Tara was acting funny tonight?" Cat asked.

"She was a little quieter than usual, now that you mention it. Did she say anything to you?"

"No, and that concerns me. You know how verbal Tara usually is when she has something on her mind. I'm a little worried about her."

"Well, let's see how she is in the morning, and if she hasn't snapped out of it, we'll take her aside and talk to her after school."

"All right." Cat sipped her tea.

Billie changed the subject. "God, I can't believe Christmas is a little more than two months away. Where does the time go?"

"I know. We have a ton of shopping to do," Cat said.

Billie groaned.

"What's the groan for? You know you like buying toys for the kids. I remember our last shopping trip. I had to drag you away from the Sony PlayStation display so the other shoppers' children could play with it."

"Well, it's more fun than shopping for clothes and other gifts."

"Don't be such a Scrooge. Christmas is only once a year. It doesn't kill you to shop with me."

"Bah, humbug," Billie said teasingly.

She kissed Cat. "What do you say we turn in?"

"Sounds good to me."

"Go on ahead," Billie said. "I need to take care of the fire first. I'll be along in a few minutes."

Billie grabbed the poker and shifted the remains of the wood around so that it would reduce to ash faster. She knelt on one knee and stared into the fire. She wondered about Tara's attitude that evening. Tara hadn't been herself since she got home from school.

Billie poked at the fire and thought about how far her family had come in three short years. Tara was only four when she and Cat met, and now she was seven and already in second grade. Billie shook her head and realized Seth, at nine years old, was just a year away from his pre-teen years. Skylar was almost two and a half. It seemed like yesterday that Cat was pregnant and Billie was pushing Seth across the park in his wheelchair. Where had the time gone?

Soon, the fire was low enough to be left safely unattended. Billie turned off the lights and went upstairs to discover Cat already asleep, curled up in the center of their bed. Billie smiled at the sight as she removed her own clothing and slipped in behind her. She took Cat into her arms and molded herself around the sleeping woman. She joined Cat in slumber as a blissful silence fell over the household.

* * *

"Billie, are the kids up yet?" Cat called from the bathroom.

"Seth's in the shower, and Skylar's dressed and watching cartoons, but as usual, Tara's dragging her feet getting out of bed."

"I'll be finished here in a minute, then I'll get breakfast started."

"If anything will get Tara out of bed, it's food. I'll go nudge her again," Billie said.

Moments later, Billie returned to their bedroom carrying Tara in her arms. Tara's head was lying on Billie's shoulder.

"It looks like we have a sick little girl here, Mama." Billie winked at Cat to indicate the less than serious nature of the illness.

Billie hid a smirk as she watched Tara do her best to don a sickly look when Cat felt her forehead.

"Hmmm, no fever. Where does it hurt, honey?" Cat asked.

"Everywhere," Tara said.

"That sounds pretty serious. Maybe I should call the doctor," Cat suggested. Billie struggled to hide a grin.

"No, Mama, I'll be all right, but I think I need to stay home from school today."

"I don't know. You've got to be pretty sick to stay home from school," Cat said.

Billie caught her eye and mouthed to her that she'd call in and stay home with Tara and Skylar.

Cat felt Tara's forehead once more. "All right, love. Maybe you should stay home." She looked at Billie. "Mom, can you stay home with her today?"

"Sure. I'll call in and take the day off," Billie said. "Tara, seeing as you're so sick, you'll have to stay in bed all day. We'll want to make sure you're well enough to go to school tomorrow. I'll be right back," she said to Cat. "Right after I put Tara back to bed."

Billie returned to Cat and enveloped her in a bear hug from behind. Cat swung around in Billie's arms. "Make it tough on her. I don't want her to get the idea that she can take a day off from school whenever she feels like it."

"Don't worry about that. She'll be begging to go to school tomorrow. Anyway, I thought maybe I could get her to tell me what's bothering her. It could have something to do with her reluctance to go to school."

"Good idea." Cat modeled her new outfit. "How do I look?"

"No scrubs today?"

"I'm not scheduled for any surgeries today. I have a staff meeting this morning and tons of office work to catch up on. I thought it would be refreshing to wear something other than those shapeless scrubs for a change. So tell me. How do I look?"

Billie wrapped her arms around her and nibbled at her neck. "Good enough to eat."

Cat pushed Billie away. "I'll take a rain check on that offer. Right now, I'd better start breakfast before our children call a mutiny."

* * *

"Mom, it's not fair," Seth said.

Billie took Seth the by shoulders. "Look, honey, your sister doesn't feel good, so she needs to stay home. Would you rather be sick so you can stay home, too? Believe me, Tara won't be enjoying herself today."

"I guess not," he said. "But it still isn't fair."

Billie wrapped Seth in a hug and kissed him on the cheek. "Sometimes life isn't as fair as we'd like it to be, but it usually works out in the end. Now, where's that cute smile I love so much?"

Seth displayed his dimples as he smiled.

She tweaked his nose. "That's my guy."

Billie took Seth's lunchbox and added a package of cookies from the pantry. She handed it back to him and winked. "Don't tell anyone."

"Never."

"Good. There's your bus. Have a great day. And remember to get on the bus that will bring you home instead of to the day care after school, all right?"

"I'll remember, Mom."

Billie stood in the front window, watched Seth board the bus, and turned her attention back to Skylar. She knelt on the floor next to Skylar's highchair and kissed her on the nose. "Hey, sweetling. Are you about finished with your breakfast?"

Skylar picked up the oatmeal bowl and licked the bottom of it. "More?" She handed the bowl to Billie.

Billie chuckled. "I know where Mama got that pathetic baby-girl face... from you." Billie spooned a little more oatmeal into the bowl and drizzled maple syrup and milk into it. "Stir it up first, Sky."

As Skylar finished her breakfast, Billie walked quietly up the stairs to Tara's room and peeked around the corner. She saw Tara sitting in the middle of her bed playing with her dolls. Billie backed up a few steps and intentionally made a little noise to warn Tara of her approach. As she expected, when she entered her room seconds later, Tara was under the covers. The blankets on her bed looked rather lumpy.

Probably the dolls, Billie thought.

She felt Tara's forehead. "Still no fever. Are you hungry?"

"Yes," Tara said in a faint voice.

"Well, you'd better eat light. We don't want you to get sicker."

Tara frowned.

"I'll be right back, sweetie," Billie said.

When she returned to the kitchen, she saw that Skylar had finished her oatmeal.

Skylar reached out her arms to Billie. "I all done, Mommy."

"Sky-Baby, you have more cereal in your hair, ears, and on your clothes than in your stomach. Hold on a minute, sweetie, while I get breakfast ready for your sister." Billie scooped a small amount of cottage cheese on a plate along with a sliced apple and a piece of toast for Tara. Although it was nutritional, Billie knew it was definitely not what Tara would prefer for breakfast.

She walked over to Skylar. "Okay, rug rat," she said. "You need a bath. Up you go." Billie lifted Skylar from her high chair and cradled her in her arms.

Billie ducked, but Skylar rubbed her small oatmeal-covered hands on both sides of Billie's face, as well as sliding them up and down her arms. "Mommy take bath, too?"

"Looks that way," she said with a helpless laugh.

Billie climbed the stairs to Tara's room while she balanced Skylar on one hip and the plate of food in one hand. She pushed the door open with her hip in time to see Tara scurry under the covers. Billie pretended not to notice. She put the plate of food on the nightstand.

"Your sister needs a bath, love," she said to Tara. "You can see she's made quite a sticky mess out of me as well, so I think I'll fill the tub with bubbles and join her. Eat what you can then lay down and rest. I'll be in to check on you after our bath."

Billie left the door to Tara's room open as she went across the hall to the bathroom and filled the tub with warm soapy water. She undressed Skylar and sat her in the tub as it filled. Skylar began to splash around. Billie removed her own clothes and climbed in behind her, and soon they were splashing and making funny hairdos, beards, and mustaches with the soap bubbles. Every now and then, Billie glanced at Tara's room to catch her lying on the floor, a wistful look on her face. After nearly an hour, the water was cool, so Billie pulled the plug and ran the shower over both her and Skylar to rinse the soap from their bodies and hair.

Billie climbed out of the tub and toweled herself dry then wrapped a large towel around herself. She reached for Skylar, wrapped a thick soft towel around her and lifted her out of the tub. Skylar stood on the bath mat while Billie dried her off. No sooner was she dry than she took off running out of the bathroom and down the hall to her room.

"Oh no! Naked baby. Hurry, catch her," Billie yelled as she ran after the giggling child. This was a favorite after-bath game of hers and her daughters'. She'd chase them into their rooms, catch them, throw them on their beds, and tickle them until they gave up. Only then would they consent to getting dressed. More than once, Billie worried about how old they'd be before they outgrew this game. She didn't think a teenage Seth would appreciate seeing his sisters run through the house naked.

As Billie chased after Skylar, she saw Tara run quickly back to her bed from where she had been sitting in the doorway. Billie wondered whether she was wishing yet that she'd gone to school.

After both she and Skylar were dressed, Billie settled her on the couch in the living room to watch Barney while she checked on Tara. Tara once again was reclining against her pillows, covers pulled up to her chin.

Billie noticed that Tara had eaten the apple and about half of the toast but hadn't touched the cottage cheese. She sat on the edge of Tara's bed and brushed a couple of stray locks off her forehead. "It's understandable that you're not very hungry."

"Not for cottage cheese," Tara said. "Maybe for pancakes, though." Billie nearly laughed out loud at the pathetic puppy-dog eyes Tara turned toward her.

Instead, Billie kissed her on the head. "Oh no, my love. Pancakes are a bit much for someone who's sick. How about a glass of warm milk instead?"

"Can I have chocolate in it?"

Billie didn't have the heart to say no. "One hot chocolate, coming up." Billie rose to her feet. "You stay here in bed and get some rest. I'll be back with your hot chocolate as soon as it's ready."

Billie returned to the kitchen, barely able to keep the grin off her face. While the hot chocolate was warming, she cleaned up the breakfast dishes and washed the mess from the table and high chair. When the milk was ready, Billie poured it into a plastic travel mug and took it to Tara.

Billie spent the majority of her morning loudly playing with Skylar, loud enough for Tara to hear. She checked on Tara often enough to keep her running back to her bed several times an hour. Billie noted that after about two hours of this, Tara gave up and stayed in her bed.

Billie brought lunch to Tara after she fed Skylar and put her down for a nap. She put the tray of food down on the nightstand beside Tara's bed and felt her forehead for the five-hundredth time that day. "Still no fever. That's a good sign."

Tara was forgetting more and more often to act sick as she broke out into a big smile at the sight of the food Billie brought. After her light fare at breakfast, Tara was hungry and it didn't take her long to eat everything on the tray. Billie smiled again and collected the dirty dishes. "Tara, I'm very proud of you. You must be feeling better. You ate everything on your tray."

"Do you think I'm good enough to have cookies for dessert?"

Billie assumed a skeptical look. "I don't know. Maybe we should wait until this afternoon to decide. Let's give your stomach a chance to digest what you ate before eating anything else, all right?" Billie picked up her half-empty glass of hot chocolate and handed it to her. "Here, finish up."

Tara drank the milk and handed the glass back to Billie, a scowl etched firmly across her brow.

"Thanks, sweetie." Billie kissed her cheek and pulled the covers up higher around her neck. "I'll be back after I clean up the lunch dishes." When she finished washing the dishes and the countertops, she folded the dishcloth over the edge of the sink and rested her backside against the cupboard. Boy, this babysitting was hard work. All of this running around, back and forth between the kids. Phew, she was beat.

* * *

Tara sat with her back against the headboard and her arms crossed in front of her when Billie returned. Billie stopped in the doorway and watched her for a few minutes. For the hundredth time she marveled at how much Tara looked like Cat.

Billie noted the guilty expression on Tara's face as she looked up. Billie continued to lean against the doorframe as she waited for her to make the first move.

"Mom, can I talk to you?"

Billie walked over and sat next to Tara on the bed. She leaned her back against the headboard and crossed her legs on the bed in front of her. "Sure, honey, what's up?"

Tara leaned against Billie. "I'm not sick."

Billie smiled and looked at Tara. She lifted Tara's chin with two fingers. "I know."

Tara's eyes grew large. "You know?"

"Yeah. Do you want to tell me the real reason you didn't want to go to school today?"

Tara looked at her hands in her lap. Several moments passed with no response.

"Tara?" Billie prompted.

Instead of answering her question, Tara surprised Billie by asking one of her own. "Mom, do you love me as much as you love Seth and Sky?"

Billie was floored by the question. She pulled Tara into her lap, one leg on each side so they were facing each other. Billie lifted Tara's chin to look into her face.

"Tara, I love you with all my heart. Yes. I love you as much as Seth and Sky. Sweetheart, why would you ask such a question?"

"At school, we're starting this Christmas project and we had to write the names of our brothers and sisters and moms and dads down to make cards." Tara paused, as though not sure how to continue.

"Go on."

"Some of the kids at school laughed at me 'cause I have a different name than everyone else." She began to cry.

"What do you mean?"

"How come my last name is O'Grady, and Seth and Skylar and you and Mama have Charland for a last name?"

Billie was dumbfounded. She'd never given Tara's lone-name status a thought. It suddenly occurred to her how that might look to Tara. Her heart broke. "Oh, Tara, sweetheart." She pulled the crying child to her chest and held her close. Tara sobbed into her shoulder.

"The other kids said that you and Mama aren't my real parents. They said I'm adopted."

Billie pulled Tara away from her chest to look into her face. "Tara, listen to me. You're not adopted, do you understand? Mama is your real mother. Sweetheart, you look exactly like her, and your sister looks like you, too. You belong to Mama and me, I promise."

Tara rubbed her eyes and looked at Billie. "Are you my dad?"

Billie stared at her. God, where was Cat when she needed her?

She took Tara's face in her hands. "Tara, it takes a man and a woman to make a baby, right? That was explained in the book Mama bought that we read to you and Seth, remember?"

Tara nodded.

"Well," Billie continued. "You know that Mama is your real mother, right?"

Again, Tara nodded.

"And you know that I'm not a man, right?"

Once again, Tara nodded. "So you can't be my dad."

"No, honey, I'm not your dad." Billie's voice was tinged with regret.

Tears once again rolled down Tara's cheeks. "Who is my dad?"

Billie pulled her close and kissed her head. She let Tara cry for a few minutes until she had calmed down. Once again, Billie held her at arm's length.

"Tara, before you were born, Mama and her partner Shannon wanted a beautiful baby girl, so they went to the doctor and the doctor helped them to have you."

"Is the doctor my dad?" Tara asked.

"No, he isn't," Billie said. "I'm not sure who your dad is. What's important here is that you have two parents who love you very much."

"Do you want to be my dad?"

Billie shifted Tara onto her lap. "I want that more than anything else in my life right now, love."

Tara leaned her cheek against Billie's chest.

It wasn't long before Tara fell asleep in Billie's arms. Not wanting to disturb her, she slid down onto Tara's bed and stretched out so that Tara was lying on top of her, using her whole body as a pillow. Physically and emotionally exhausted from their ordeal, both of them were soon fast asleep.

* * *

Billie and Tara barely woke in time to meet Seth's bus at the end of the driveway.

"Do you have homework?" Billie asked as Seth dropped his school bag on the floor near the kitchen door.

"Yeah, a little."

"I'll give you a hand with it after dinner." Billie wondered if something was bothering him.

She dropped down to one knee in front of Seth and touched the side of his face. "Are you all right, honey?"

Seth shifted from foot to foot. "I got in a fight at recess today." Billie's eyes narrowed as she waited for Seth's explanation. "Some kids made fun of Tara, so I decked them."

Billie tried very hard to hide a grin. She cleared her voice. "What did they say about her?"

"They said she was adopted and that she was a bastard. Is that true?"

Billie was shocked at Seth's choice of words. She pulled out a kitchen chair and sat down. Seth sat on her knee. "Seth, Tara isn't adopted. Mama is her real mother. Those kids were being mean." She kissed him on the forehead. "It was very brave of you to defend your sister."

"She'd do the same for me."

"That she would." Billie chuckled as she thought about how feisty Tara was and remembered the boy she punched in the eye at the day care years earlier when he made fun of Seth's handicap shortly after his brain surgery. She looked at Seth. "How about a treat and a game while we wait for Mama to get home?"

"What kind of game?"

"Why don't we have some cider and donuts, and we'll all decide together."

"Okay."

"Good. Get your sisters for me, will you?"

As Seth ran to collect his sisters, Billie dropped her head to her arm on the table and groaned. She and Cat would have a lot to talk about tonight.

* * *

Cat came home to the sound of screeching and laughing coming from the family room in the basement. She dropped her coat and purse on the kitchen table and went to investigate.

She sat on the bottom stair and watched as Billie tied herself up in knots with Seth and Skylar wrapped around and under various body parts. Tara sat cross-legged a few feet away and yelled, "Right hand on yellow!" All three of them picked up their right hands and fell into a heap on top of the Twister mat, with Billie on the bottom. Tara jumped up and dove right on top of them. The kids did a little victory dance around Billie who was still out flat on her back while Cat clapped her hands and gave a little curtsey to the victors.

"Congratulations, my brave knights. I see you've slain the dragon," she said, pointing to Billie.

Seth put one foot on Billie's stomach and said, "That we have, oh fair maiden."

"Well, Sir Seth," Cat said, "would a kiss from the fair maiden do as a reward?"

"You bet," Seth said as he accepted Cat's kiss and hug.

"Hey, what about Sir Tara and Sir Sky?" Tara said.

Cat dropped to her knees and opened her arms to her daughters. "Oh, heavens, we can't forget them, can we?"

Skylar jumped up and down and clapped her hands. "I wanna play again."

Cat chuckled. "Why don't you three brave knights play again, while I talk to Dragon Lady here." Cat offered her hand to Billie and helped her up from the floor.

"We've a lot to talk about," Billie whispered.

Cat raised an eyebrow.

"Tonight," Billie said. "After the kids are in bed."

Cat could tell by the tone of Billie's voice and the look on her face that it was serious. She nodded and allowed herself to be pulled into another hug.

Billie pushed Cat back to arm's length. "Wait a minute here. Dragon Lady?"

"Oops!" Cat flew out of Billie's arms and up the stairs, with six feet of fire-breathing dragon right behind her.

* * *

"They told her what?" Cat demanded loudly.

Billie sat on the bed, feeling very out of control of the situation, while Cat paced back and forth across their bedroom. She always knew that Cat had a temper when riled, but she'd never seen it quite this bad before.

"They told her she was adopted," Billie said again.

"Why those little bastards. If I get my hands on them…"

Billie stood and caught Cat on one of her many passes by the bed and held her close. "Honey, calm down. This isn't going to solve anything. Please."

Cat pushed out of Billie's embrace. "All right. I'm calm." She walked a few feet away and swung around. "What brought all this on?"

"Tara's class was working on a Christmas project to make cards for each family member. The first thing they had to do was list the first and last names of everyone in their family—"

"Don't tell me. Her classmates noticed that her last name was different from the rest of us."

"Exactly."

"Why those insensitive little brats. I'm going to school tomorrow and—"

"No, you're not."

"What do you mean, I'm not?"

"What I mean is that you don't need to worry about the kids picking on Tara again. Seth took care of it."

"Seth?"

"Yes. Apparently a few of the kids were bad-mouthing Tara at school today, so Seth decked them at recess."

"Our Seth? Our mild-mannered son?"

"Yep," Billie said proudly.

"Billie, you know that's not funny. I hope you discouraged him from fighting in the future."

"No, I didn't. In fact, I told him that I was proud of him for defending his sister."

"Oh God. What am I going to do with you two?"

"The question is what are we going to do about this whole situation?"

"First, I have to convince Tara that she isn't adopted," Cat said.

"I've already done that. In fact, we had a long talk today about moms and dads."

Cat frowned and Billie said, "Maybe you'd better sit down and I'll tell you all about it."

They sat on the side of the bed, facing each other. Billie took Cat's hands in hers. "She asked me about her father, and I told her about Shannon."

"You what?" Cat jumped up and walked a few feet away. "Damn it, Billie."

"Will you calm down and get your ass back over here?"

Cat sat down again. "What did you tell her?"

"Let me start from the beginning. She asked me if I loved her as much as I love Seth and Skylar."

"Why would she ask a question like that?"

"I think she was trying to justify why they had my last name, but she didn't. She told me about the confrontation at school, the one about being adopted. It pretty much mirrored what Seth said. I think I nipped that in the bud." Billie paused to organize her thoughts. "This is where it gets sticky. She asked me if I was her dad."

Cat's eyes opened wide. "How did you handle that question?"

"Well, I mentioned the book you picked up. You know, the one about talking to your kids about sex?"

Cat nodded.

"I reminded her that it took a man and a woman to make a baby. It didn't take her long to realize that I couldn't be her father because I wasn't a man, so she asked me who her father was."

A variety of emotions played across Cat's face.

"What did you tell her?" Cat asked. Billie heard the apprehension in Cat's words.

She squeezed Cat's hands tighter. "I told her that you and your partner Shannon wanted a beautiful baby girl, so the doctor helped you have her." She looked intently at Cat to gauge her reaction. Cat appeared to be relatively calm, so she continued. "She then asked me if the doctor was her father, and I told her he wasn't and that I didn't know who her father was."

"How did she react to that?"

"She didn't seem to care one way or the other. What she really wanted to know was if I wanted to be her dad," Billie said.

"How do you feel about that?" Cat asked.

"How do I feel? How can you even ask that?" Billie said sharply. When she saw she'd hurt Cat's feelings, she added, "The real question is when do we start adoption proceedings?"

Cat smiled through her tears. "Right away, love. Right away."

Chapter 26

Billie went to work the next morning with one goal in mind—
to determine what it would take for Billie and Cat to officially adopt
each other's children.

Around noon, Billie was in the archives room, searching
through documents on adoption and family laws, when Art
McDonough poked his head in.

"Hey, Charland," he said. "I'm calling in an order for lunch.
Are you interested?"

Billie looked up from the dusty law volume. "Sure. Ham and
cheese on rye, with mustard, and a diet cola."

Instead of leaving to place their order, Art walked farther into
the room. "What are you researching?"

Billie turned the volume around and showed Art the cover.

"Family law, huh? I wondered when you'd get around to that."

Billie raised her eyebrows at him.

"Well, it does seem like a natural next step," he said.

"The more I look into this, Art, the more I realize this is
something we need to do to protect the kids. Among other things,
legal adoption will guarantee all three children an equal share in
inheritance rights, financial support from one or both parents in the
form of child support in the event of divorce or separation, and
rights to health insurance and benefits from both our employers. It
also gives both Cat and me the right to make legal decisions about
the children, such as those surrounding medical or educational
issues, and the right to social security benefits. I didn't realize how
many risks we've been taking over these past three years by not
adopting each other's children."

"Need any help?"

"I've spent the entire morning looking the process over. It
appears to be pretty cut and dried. Thanks to our new same-sex
marriage law, adoption of children among same-sex couples won't
be a problem."

"Well, the two of you are legally married, and the kids have been living in a family environment with you for the past three years. That should at least help speed the social study part of the process."

"Social study?"

"Yeah. The judge will choose someone to investigate you and Cat. An appointed agent will visit your home and interview both of you, your friends, and maybe even the kids," he explained. "I know it feels like a personal intrusion, but it's in the best interest of the children. Don't worry about it. With the support of your friends and family, including yours truly, you'll have no problem."

Billie groaned at the thought of her privacy being invaded but, at the same time, inwardly acknowledged that the children were worth whatever they had to go through to make things legal.

"Thanks for the support, Art," she said. "I really see only one potential hitch in this process."

"What's that?"

"Before we legally adopt each other's children, Brian, and Cat's ex-partner, whose name by the way is Shannon Manning, will have to legally give up their rights to the children. Once that's accomplished, it's basically a matter of paperwork and formalities in court."

"And if they don't willingly give up their rights?" Art asked.

"Then we'll petition the court to terminate their rights based on abandonment, failure to support, and possible moral corruption."

"Ouch. You're one nasty bitch," he teased.

"You don't know the half of it. Mess with my family, and you'll see how nasty I can get."

"No, thank you. I think I'll stay on your good side if that's okay with you. I'll go order us some lunch and come back to help you fill out and file the forms."

"Thanks, Art."

* * *

While they ate lunch, Art and Billie discussed how they were going to serve papers on the other two parents.

"Brian's in jail, so you know exactly where he is. Do you know where Ms. Manning is?"

"I've no idea, but Jimmy might be able to find her. Cat kept track of her for the first year or so after they split. I think Cat said she transferred her residency to a Texas hospital, but she might've relocated from there. We don't talk much about Shannon. She deserted Cat and Tara when Tara was only two."

"Is her name on Tara's birth certificate?"

"That's a very good question. I'll have to ask Cat. I do know that she legally adopted Tara, so even if she's not on the birth certificate, we'll still need to serve papers."

"I think the best way to serve them is by having the local sheriff personally deliver a certified summons. That way, we'll be sure they receive them," Art said. "If we have proof that they received the summons, and they choose to ignore it, they'll lose their rights by default. If they contest it, we take it to court."

Billie grinned at her partner and friend. "We?"

"I almost feel like they're part of my family, too. They do call me Uncle Art, after all."

"That, they do, my friend."

"All right. Let's get started on these forms."

* * *

On her way out, Billie stopped at the criminal law office to see Jimmy. She found him in his cubical, reading an article on the Internet. She put her arm around his shoulders. "Hi, Jimmy, old buddy, old pal."

Jimmy looked up. "I know a favor request when I hear one, missy. What can I do for you?"

Billie adored Jimmy. He was very much a small town lawyer and still wore plaid suit coats and a bow tie to work. Nearly retirement age, he was a comforting fixture around the office. He did his job well and thoroughly, and despite his age and constant grumbling about the newfangled Internet technology, he mastered it in no time and provided an invaluable service to Billie and the rest of the firm with his surfing skills.

"Jimmy, I need to find someone. Her name is Shannon Manning. She'd be around thirty-six-years old. She began her medical residency here at Albany Medical Center then transferred to a Texas hospital five years ago. She's most likely a doctor, but I don't know what her specialty is. Do you think you can help me out?"

"That shouldn't be a problem. You said she left about five years ago, huh?"

"Correct."

"This is personal, isn't it?"

"Yes it is."

"Give me a minute, missy, and I'll have an answer for you."

Jimmy's fingers flew over the keyboard as he entered pertinent information into his favorite people-search website.

"Got it! Dr. Shannon Manning, Riverside General Hospital, Houston, Texas. Specialty: Pediatrics."

Billie looked over his shoulder at the picture that was displayed on the screen. *Hmmm, she's very attractive.*

"Could I ask why you're looking for her?"

"Sure. Cat and I are trying to legally adopt each other's kids, and we need her to relinquish her rights to Tara."

"I see. So I assume you'll need an address?"

"Yes, that would be great."

"Sure. Here, let me print it out for you."

Jimmy handed Billie a sheet of paper complete with a name, address, phone number, and photograph of Shannon Manning.

Billie kissed his cheek. "Thanks, Jimmy, I owe you one."

* * *

Billie arrived home as the family was sitting down to dinner. Cat met her at the kitchen door and stood on her tiptoes for a kiss.

"I have a few forms for you to fill out, and some news to discuss with you later," Billie whispered.

Cat took Billie's face between her hands. "Bad news?"

"Not really. We'll talk after dinner."

Billie made her way around the table to kiss and hug each child then helped Cat bring dishes to the table. Soon, she sat in front of her filled plate and listened to the kids chatter about school.

After dinner, the children went into the living room to play while Cat and Billie worked together to load the dishwasher. Before long, Billie trapped Cat between her own body and the kitchen counter. She lifted Cat onto the counter top, stood between her legs, and nibbled on Cat's neck.

"God, that feels good," Cat said.

Billie froze as a sound came from the other room. She casually turned around so that her back was to Cat, and leaned against the counter while Cat's arms circled her neck and came to rest in front of her above her breasts. Cat rested her chin on Billie's left shoulder.

Seth came into the room.

"Mama, can we have some milk and cookies for dessert?" he asked.

"Sure, honey," Cat said, "but not in the living room. Why don't you go get your sisters while I pour some milk for you."

"Tara, Sky, milk and cookies in the kitchen," Seth yelled.

"I could've done that, scout," Cat said as Billie chuckled.

When the kids finished their dessert, they retreated to the family room to watch a Christmas special on TV.

With the kids out of earshot, Billie took Cat into her arms. "Finally, we're alone."

"Yes. And now that we are, what is it that you've got to tell me? You're strung as tight as a bowstring. Out with it."

Billie led Cat to the kitchen table. "Sit," she said.

Cat did as requested. Billie pulled two mugs out of the cupboard, added mint-flavored tea bags to them, and put the teapot on the stove to heat.

"You're scaring me," Cat said. "Tea is a comfort food. What's wrong?"

Billie reached for Cat's hands. "Well, there's good news, and somewhat of a complication. Which do you want to hear first?"

"The good news."

"All right. The good news is that the adoption process is rather simple once we have the proper forms filled out. The fact that we're legally married and have been living as a family for several years is a real benefit. I also think we need to discuss this with Tara and Seth before I file the forms. Maybe after their program tonight, we can put Sky to bed and sit down with them."

"All right. What's the complication?" Cat asked as the teapot began to whistle.

Billie rose to prepare their tea. She added honey and a drop of milk to the mugs and stirred before she carried them to the table and put one down in front of Cat.

Cat lifted the cup to her mouth and took a sip. "Oh, this tastes good. Thanks. Now, enough stalling. Spill it."

"Well, one of the requirements for a hassle-free adoption is that the other legal parents have to relinquish their rights to the children. In other words, we need them to sign forms agreeing to give them up."

"And what do we do if they refuse?"

"We file a termination of parental rights suit against them based on abandonment and failure to support," Billie said. "It could get messy, but with Brian's criminal record, and the fact that

Shannon deserted Tara, we have a very good chance of winning that argument."

Cat wrapped her hands around her mug. "That's not so bad. So we may end up with a fight on our hands, but one that we can win. I can deal with that."

Billie smiled at her confidence and determination.

"There's just one issue, Billie. I don't know where Shannon is."

"That won't be a problem. I've already located her. She's a pediatric physician at Riverside General Hospital in Houston, Texas. I even have a home address for her." From her briefcase, Billie pulled out the computer printout Jimmy had given her. She handed it to Cat.

Cat looked at the picture of Shannon. "Wow. Any idea how old this picture is?"

"No. Why?"

"She's changed significantly since the last time I saw her."

"How so?"

"I don't remember her being this attractive," Cat said. "It's a pity beauty is only skin deep."

Billie rubbed Cat's back. "I'll file the forms tomorrow. Let's hope that things go well and she agrees to sign them. If she doesn't cooperate, she'll be called here to attend the hearing. If she doesn't respond, she'll automatically relinquish her rights. If she does respond, she'll either sign the forms or fight the adoption. If she fights, it will get nasty."

Cat looked at Billie. "Nasty? Why?"

"Because if she fights the adoption, I plan to petition the courts to force termination of parental rights based on desertion and nonsupport. If that happens, it could have social and professional consequences for her career. It might also mean a face-to-face confrontation with her. Are you sure you want to do that?"

"File the forms. I need to protect the children more than I need to protect her."

Billie kissed Cat on the head. "Now that it's settled, let's go watch the Grinch steal Christmas."

* * *

After the Christmas show ended, Billie invited the kids to play a game of Chinese checkers while Cat put Skylar to bed. The kids sat on the couch and Billie on the ottoman opposite them, with the coffee table holding the checkers game between them.

"Mom, is everything okay?" Seth asked as they arranged the marbles on the board.

Billie smiled at his perceptiveness. "You're too smart for your own good, Seth Michael Charland," she said as she ruffled his hair.

"You usually don't let us stay up past our bedtime on a school night."

"Relax. Everything's fine. Mama and I have something we want to discuss with you and Tara. That's why you didn't follow your little sister up to bed."

As though on cue, Cat returned to the family room and sat with Billie on the ottoman. The checkers game was forgotten.

Cat leaned forward. "Seth, Tara, Mom and I want to talk to you about adoption. Do you know what that means?"

Tara tensed.

Billie saw the panic in Tara's eyes and reached out to take her hand. "Tara, honey, remember our talk yesterday?" She continued after receiving a nod. "We want to know how you and Seth would feel about me adopting you and Skylar, and Mama adopting Seth. That would make both Mama and me your real parents, just like you wanted, sweetheart. Mama is already your real mother, and I'm Seth's real mother. If I adopt you and Sky, and Mama adopts Seth, then we'll both be your real mothers. Understand?"

"Cool," Seth said.

Tara smiled. "Yeah, cool."

Cat and Billie looked at each other and grinned.

"In that case," Cat said, "off to bed with you both. School tomorrow." After extinguishing the fire, Billie followed her family upstairs and helped Cat tuck the children in. They met in the hallway outside Skylar's room where they fell into each other's arms.

"If the rest of this adoption issue goes that well, we'll be on easy street," Cat said.

"They're worth whatever it takes to make it legal. I hope things go well, but we need to prepare for a fight if it comes to that," Billie said.

"Well, let's hope it doesn't. Are you ready to call it a night?"

"No," Billie said. "I'm ready to take you to bed, though." She raised her eyebrows up and down suggestively.

Billie watched that little wrinkle she loved so much appear above the bridge of Cat's nose when she smiled. She pushed their bedroom door open and allowed Cat to enter before her. Billie lowered Cat gently onto the bed and laid her tall frame over her.

"Have I told you yet today how much I love you?" Billie asked.

"You tell me every time you look at me."

Billie traced Cat's jaw line with kisses and worked her way slowly toward her ear to take the sensitive lobe between her teeth. A moan escaped Cat's throat as Billie's tongue flicked into Cat's ear. A shudder of desire rocked Cat's body as Billie kissed her way down the length of Cat's neck to the base of her throat and pointed her tongue to dip into the little indentation between her collarbones.

Billie lifted the hem of Cat's shirt and pushed it upwards and over her head, exposing the supple flesh beneath it. She ran her hand across Cat's face, down her neck, and between Cat's breasts. "You're so beautiful," she whispered hoarsely.

"You make me feel that way, Billie. I feel so loved and safe in your arms. Thank you."

Billie lowered her mouth to Cat's chest and left a trail of kisses from between her breasts to her navel. Sensuous lips flitted across taut abs, causing Cat to suck in her breath. Billie's desire was heightened by the deep guttural moan that escaped Cat's throat as Billie's tongue slipped into her navel.

Billie shifted her weight slightly to allow access to the button on Cat's jeans. She slowly lowered the zipper and slid her hand inside the waistband and down one of Cat's legs under the denim material.

Cat grabbed Billie's head by two handfuls of dark hair and kissed her.

"Patience, my love," Billie whispered as she felt Cat's desire rapidly escalate. Billie rose to her knees and slid Cat's jeans and socks off and threw them onto the floor.

Billie sat back on her heels and looked at her wife clad only in lace bra and panties. Her own desire rose as she let her eyes feast on the beauty before her. Well-toned, but shapely legs, hipbones protruding slightly above a flat stomach, full breasts, delicate neck and shoulders, slightly muscular arms. A shudder ran through Billie as she fought to control her own desire. "God, Cat, what you do to me."

"Off," Cat said. She pushed at Billie's shoulders.

"Huh?"

Cat could see the confusion on Billie's face. "I said, off. Take these clothes off. I want to feel you."

Billie climbed off Cat and stood by the side of the bed where she began to remove her clothing.

Cat stopped her when she too was clad only in her bra and panties. "Come here."

Once more, Billie lowered herself over Cat and they kissed.

"It took all the control I had not to throw you on the table and ravish you in front of the children at dinner tonight," Cat said. "That crooked smile of yours makes my heart do flip-flops."

Billie smiled crookedly at her.

"Oh God." Cat groaned as she once again pulled Billie's head down by two handfuls of hair. This time, there was no denying her. She locked legs with Billie's and flipped them over, successfully putting herself on top. She quickly straddled her wife and sat on her abdomen. She proceeded to run her hands down her own body in a sensuous display that she knew would drive Billie crazy.

Billie grabbed Cat around the waist.

"Oh no, not yet." Cat grabbed Billie's hands and pinned them above her head. Cat leaned over and allowed her hair to fall forward to frame their faces. While maintaining her hold on Billie's hands, she kissed her passionately, thrusting her tongue deep into Billie's mouth.

Cat let go of Billie's hands and reached under her to release the catch on Billie's bra. She heard Billie moan as the garment fell away. Cat threw the bra aside and cupped the fullness with both hands and rubbed the nubs into attentiveness with her thumbs before she feasted on them with her mouth.

"Oh my God, Cat." Billie arched her chest closer.

Cat reached back to release her own breasts from their lace prison then leaned over until her breasts contacted Billie's.

Billie grabbed two handfuls of Cat's breasts and brought them to her mouth.

The pile of clothes on the floor grew higher as their panties joined the fray. Lost in the rush of sensation, Billie physically turned Cat around so that they could each feast on the other, delving deep into the core of their very beings as they both descended into oblivion.

When it was over, Billie urged Cat to turn around and lay beside her. She wrapped her arms tightly around Cat and kissed her tenderly, blending their essences together.

"I love you," Billie said.

"I love you, too," Cat replied and drifted off into dreamland.

Billie lay there for a few more moments. She thought about the adoptions and about everything they had to gain... and lose. Until Jimmy produced the picture of Shannon earlier in the day, Billie hadn't realized how attractive she was. Concern filled her heart and mind—concern that Cat's attraction might be rekindled when she saw Shannon again. Billie closed her eyes and sighed. *Stop thinking that way, Billie. Cat loves you. Trust her like you want her to trust you.* She willed herself to relax until she joined Cat in peaceful slumber.

Chapter 27

Billie's first priority the next morning was to file the voluntary termination of parental rights forms for all three children. She estimated that Brian and Shannon should receive the forms within two to four days. Those were the longest four days of her life.

Brian's response came through his lawyer. In a statement read to Billie over the phone four days after filing the forms, his lawyer quoted him as saying, "There's no way in hell I'm going to give up my children to a couple of friggen dykes."

Billie was so angry she hung up the phone on him. She grabbed her coat and car keys, stormed out of the office, and drove fifty miles to the correctional center where Brian was incarcerated.

She pulled into the parking lot of the jail and announced herself to the guard at the desk. Since it was an unplanned visit, she was asked to wait while they notified Brian that she was there. Soon, the guard returned and escorted her to a locked room that contained only a table and two chairs. She paced back and forth while she waited for Brian to be brought to her. She had to consciously restrain herself as he walked across the room and sat down on one of the chairs. The guard stood inside the room near the door.

She walked boldly to his table and put the forms in front of him. She rested her hands on the edge of the table but didn't sit down, giving her a height advantage over him and requiring him to look up at her.

"Brian," she said in a calm voice, which belied the storm raging inside of her, "I'm only going to ask you this once. Please sign these release papers. If you care at all about Seth and Skylar, you'll sign them."

Brian smiled and said, "Go to hell, bitch."

"Have it your way," she said calmly. In reality, she wanted to rip the bastard's head off, but losing control would only hurt her case, so she gathered up the forms and walked to the guard who let her out before leading Brian back to his cell.

Billie sat in her car for several long moments before she was calm enough to drive. "All right, Brian," she said out loud. "You want to play hardball, asshole? We'll see what Mommy and Daddy have to say about this."

Brian's family was wealthy and relatively influential in the community. They were also very socially conscious about appearances. Billie intended to plead her case to them and hoped they'd strong-arm Brian into signing the papers. If they refused to cooperate, she planned to go to the press with her story.

A half hour later, Billie sat in the parlor while she waited for Mrs. Charland to appear. Soon, a well-coiffed, matronly woman with an air of superiority waltzed into the room.

"Billie, how nice to see you," Mrs. Charland said.

Billie wanted to wipe the saccharine smile right off her face. "Mrs. Charland," Billie said.

"What may I do for you, dear?"

Any self-respecting grandmother would ask about her grandchildren first, you bitch. Out loud, she said, "Mrs. Charland, I've come to request your help in a very delicate matter."

"And what would that be?"

"I want you to convince Brian to give up his parental rights to both Seth and Skylar."

Mrs. Charland frowned. "Skylar?"

Billie tilted her head slightly to the right. "You don't know about Skylar?"

"No, I'm afraid I don't."

Billie ran her hand worriedly through her hair. "Mrs. Charland, Skylar is your granddaughter."

"I wasn't aware that I had a granddaughter."

"I know you're aware of why Brian is in jail. After all, you spent a significant amount of money trying to keep him out of there." Billie paced back and forth a few times before she stopped and addressed her ex-mother-in-law once more. "Skylar was conceived during the rape. Brian is her father. Apparently, Brian never let you in on that tidbit of information."

"I'm sorry, Billie. I know Brian has caused you a lot of emotional trauma over the years. I'm sure you have many reasons to hate him."

Billie inhaled and released her breath slowly. "I've tried very hard to put the past behind me. I have a wonderful wife and three fantastic kids, and all I'm trying to do is to protect them and surround them with as much love and stability as possible. That's why I'm here, to ask you to encourage Brian to give up his parental rights to these two children so that my wife and I may adopt them. We've all been living quite happily as a family for three years, and we wish to make them legally ours. Both of ours." Billie opened her briefcase and retrieved the forms Brian had refused to sign. She handed them to Mrs. Charland. "Here are the forms. For your grandchildren's sake, I urge you to do this for them."

Mrs. Charland looked at the forms as she spoke. "Do you really expect Brian to listen to me?"

"I expect you to use your great influence over him, yes. I also expect you to be motivated by the desire to keep this procedure as quiet as possible," Billie said as she allowed the subtle threat to hang in the air.

Billie watched Mrs. Charland's jaw clench as the threat hit home. "I'll see what I can do. You should be hearing from Brian's lawyer shortly."

"Thank you, Mrs. Charland." Billie prepared to leave. She stopped near the doorway and opened her briefcase. "By the way," she said as she fished around inside, "Seth and Skylar are very beautiful children. You'd be proud of them." She handed her a recent photograph of the three children.

Mrs. Charland accepted the picture and studied it carefully as her eyes misted over. Billie turned and walked out the door.

Billie couldn't believe how pumped she felt over the encounters with Brian and her ex-mother-in-law. God, it felt good holding that threat over the old hag. The adrenaline still flowed out of control that night when she went home and recounted the events to Cat.

Two days later, a large envelope appeared on Billie's desk with termination of parental rights forms completely filled out and signed by Brian for both children.

*   *   *

"God, I'm beat." Billie carried an armful of Christmas presents into the house and collapsed on the couch.

"Gee, let's see, three hours of shopping and you're still alive. Imagine that," Cat teased.

"You should've let me stay in the arcade while you shopped. Maybe I wouldn't be in such a foul mood."

"You're such a big baby sometimes. Christmas is less than two weeks away, and we're almost finished with our shopping. Trust me, you'll survive this. Husbands and wives all over the world do this every year."

"What do you mean, almost finished?" Billie gestured toward the multitude of packages around them. "I thought this was the last of it."

Cat walked to the couch behind Billie and kissed her on top of the head. "We only need a few more things. It won't take long. Now, how about helping me hide these so we can collect the kids from Jen's?"

Billie hated it when Cat bribed her with kisses. She always lost that battle. She grabbed several bags of gifts to tote downstairs into the storage room. Once all of the packages were stowed away, Cat called Jen to let her know they'd be there soon.

* * *

"Look, the kids are building snowmen," Billie said as they neared Jen and Fred's house.

"Mom! Mama!" the kids hollered as Billie and Cat stepped through the gate.

Cat put her hands up. "Don't you dare."

Without hesitation, the children tackled her into a snow bank.

Billie's attention and laughter was focused on Cat, so she didn't expect the snowball that hit the back of her head. She swung around and saw Stevie running away. "Why you little stinker." She quickly picked up a handful of snow and made her own weapon to throw back at him.

Soon, the front yard erupted into a full-fledged snowball fight.

Billie turned around when she heard her name called out. A snowball struck her in the middle of her chest.

"Bull's-eye." Jen clapped her hands.

"Hey! Where did you come from?" Billie asked.

"I heard the commotion in the front yard and it looked like fun. I grabbed my coat and gloves and joined the fray, with Fred right behind me. I haven't had a snowball fight in years. I'd forgotten how much fun it is."

After about a half hour, four very wet and tired adults called a truce while the children continued to play.

"I'll put on a fresh pot of coffee then we can chat," Jen said as they retreated to the warmth of the house.

"Thanks for watching the kids, Jen," Cat said. "We've just about finished our shopping."

"Key words, 'just about,'" Billie said. "That means at least one more trip to the battlefields."

"I hear you," Jen said. "Shopping at Christmas time is a royal pain. Rude shoppers, no parking, long lines. I try to get most of my shopping done early for just those reasons, but every year, it seems I forget something and have to brave the mall."

She poured coffee for all four of them. "So how're the adoption proceedings going?"

"They're going much better, thanks to Big Bad Billie, here," Cat said. "Brian refused to sign the release papers for Seth and Sky, so Billie discussed the potential for a press disclosure with Brian's mother. As socially-conscious as she is, that would be like the kiss of death to her, so we're assuming she pressured Brian into signing them."

"We're still waiting for Cat's ex to respond," Billie added. "We do have a question for both of you, though. Part of the process is a social study. The judge will appoint someone to basically do a personal background check on us and to visit our home. They'll also want to interview friends and family."

"You don't even need to ask, girlfriend. We'd be happy to," Jen said.

A noise at the door drew their attention to Skylar. "I cold," she said.

As Cat attended to Skylar, Billie took advantage of the opportunity to drag Jen into the living room. "Jen, I need help."

"Let me guess. You don't know what to get Cat for Christmas, right?"

Billie drew her eyebrows together in a feeling of hopeless despair.

"All right. I'll help, but you're going to owe me big time for this one, got it?"

"Anything," Billie said.

"We'll have to do this while Cat's at work. Can you take a break about midday on Monday?"

"Sure."

"I'll meet you at the food court in the mall at twelve-thirty."

"Twelve-thirty on Monday. Got it."

"What are you two plotting?" Cat asked when she walked into the room.

Billie put her arm around Cat and led her back to the kitchen. "Oh, nothing," she said as she winked at Jen over Cat's head.

* * *

On Monday, Billie met Jen as arranged and spent two hours shopping for Cat. Billie purchased several nice items, including a very sexy teddy and garter belt ensemble from a fancy lingerie store. She thanked Jen a thousand times as they walked to her car.

"Just remember," Jen said. "You owe me for this."

"Big time, Jen." Billie hugged and thanked her once more before they parted company and she returned to work.

Billie sat at her desk and noticed the light on her answering machine was blinking. She was undecided as to whether to listen to it or not.

Art poked his head into her office. "Your phone's been ringing off the hook. You'd better check that. It might be important."

Billie punched in her password and waited patiently for the canned phone mail introduction to finish then pushed the number three to listen to the message. It was from Cat.

"Billie, you're not going to believe this. I got a call from Shannon. Call me back when you get this message."

Billie was on the phone in an instant.

"Hey, love. Thanks for calling me back."

"So she contacted you, huh?"

"Yes. She called me at work. Talk about being surprised."

"I don't like the sound of this. She should've contacted us through her lawyer."

"What difference does it make?"

"I just don't want to screw this up on technicalities. Did she say anything about the adoption papers?"

"Kind of. She mentioned that she received something in the mail from someone named Bill Charland. Obviously she thinks you're a man, and most likely my lawyer."

"You didn't talk details with her about the adoption, did you?" Billie asked.

"No. She was in a hurry, so she called to say she wanted to meet with me."

Panic settled in the pit of Billie's stomach.

"I'm not sure that's a good idea. She should be working through her lawyer."

"I've no reason to fear her. She wants to talk over coffee. I don't see anything wrong with that."

Billie fell silent.

"Talk to me. You aren't feeling threatened by her, are you?" Cat asked.

"We'll talk about this when I get home."

"No, we'll talk about this now. I've told you before that you need to trust me. It sucks that you apparently don't."

"So when's this little rendezvous supposed to happen?" Billie asked sarcastically.

"Rendezvous? You make it sound dirty. Coffee. We're just having coffee."

"When?"

"She's going to be at a convention about a half hour from here in two days. She wants to meet for coffee beforehand."

"I'm going with you," Billie said.

"There's no need for you to go. I'll talk to her about the adoption. I'm sure she'll be reasonable."

"You don't know that. You said she petitioned the court for custody when you two split. Maybe she'll see this as an opportunity to get Tara back."

"You're being ridiculous."

"I prefer to think of it as being cautious."

"Call it what you will. I'm going to meet her for coffee, alone. If she's uncooperative, you can have a shot at her."

A shot at her? I'll do more than shoot her if she tries anything stupid.

* * *

Two days later, Billie paced back and forth across her office as she waited for Cat to call her with an account of her meeting with Shannon.

Art stood in the doorway of her office, drinking a cup of coffee. "You're going to wear a hole in that carpet if you keep pacing, Charland."

"I can't help it. I'm worried about her."

"No, you're not."

Billie stopped short. "What do you mean?"

"You're worried about Manning. Or better yet, you're worried about Manning's effect on Cat."

Billie sat down behind her desk and dropped her head into her hands. "You're right. You're absolutely right." She looked up at Art. "She was with that woman for four years. From Cat's account, she was madly in love with her. Christ, she had a child for her at age twenty-two, right at the start of her medical residency, because Manning thought it was a good idea."

Art walked over to Cat's desk and sat on the corner, facing her. "There had to be a reason they split. Don't you think that reason might still be valid?"

"That's the problem. Cat has no idea why she left. She's told me before that there's this nagging feeling in the pit of her stomach sometimes because she doesn't understand what went wrong. Don't you see, Art? She still thinks about her, even to this day. She's still vulnerable. What if Manning takes advantage of that vulnerability?"

* * *

Cat pulled into a parking space very near to the coffee house where she had planned to meet Shannon. She climbed out of the car and deposited several coins into the meter then smoothed the wrinkles out of the corduroy blazer she was wearing over a button-down shirt, blue jeans, and high-heeled boots. She slung her purse over her shoulder, walked the half-block to the coffee shop, and went inside.

"Good morning," Cat said as a waitress met her at the door. "I'm meeting someone here." Cat quickly scanned the room. "But I don't see her yet."

"Would you like to have a seat while you wait?" the waitress asked.

Cat followed the waitress to a table in the front window. She sat down and spread her napkin across her lap, then looked up. Directly across from the coffee shop, a tall, slim woman with short-cropped blonde hair stepped off the curb to cross the street. She was dressed in a well-tailored, double-breasted business suit with a form-fitting skirt that fell to mid-thigh. Her long legs were covered with suntan hose, and she wore open-toed, high-heeled shoes. Perched on her turned-up nose sat rectangular-shaped eyeglasses.

Cat felt as though she'd been punched in the stomach. "Oh my God," she whispered.

Shannon waved to her through the window before entering the café. "You haven't changed a bit," she exclaimed as she walked over and wrapped her arms around Cat.

"Well, I can't say the same for you. You're gorgeous," Cat replied without thinking.

"Thanks." Shannon sat down opposite Cat. "I was kind of frumpy back in the days of our residency."

"Not even Sandra Bullock would look good in hospital scrubs," Cat joked.

"You have a point there." Shannon folded her napkin across her lap as the waitress approached. "Two coffees, black for me, cream and sugar for her," Shannon said.

"You remembered how I drink my coffee."

"I remember a lot of things about you, about us. So, tell me about yourself. What have you been up to?"

"I finished my residency four years ago and became certified as an anesthesiologist."

"Anesthesiologist, huh? Do you like it?"

Cat sipped her coffee. "Very much. There's something comforting in knowing you're keeping someone stable through life-saving surgery. I also work in the ER when I'm not scheduled to assist in a surgery."

"Eww. The ER can be a ghastly place to work."

"Sometimes, but it can be exciting and rewarding as well."

Shannon leaned forward. "I've set up a lucrative practice in pediatric medicine. My client base has grown so much in the past three years that I've had to take on partners."

"Do you like working with children?" Cat asked.

"Not especially, but there's good money in it. If there was one thing I learned from you, Cat, it's that parents will do anything for their kids, including paying hefty medical bills."

Cat sat back in her chair. "You've got to be kidding me. You chose pediatrics only because of the income potential?"

"Of course. Why else? Why do you do it?"

Cat shook her head in disgust. "I do it to help people, Shannon. That's what a doctor's supposed to do."

"I help people, too. I just get paid handsomely for it."

Cat put her napkin on the table. "You know, Shannon, you're not at all like I thought you'd be. What happened to the loving, caring, sensitive woman who loved children?"

Shannon looked directly at Cat. "She had her heart broken when you took her daughter away. And now you're trying to do it again."

Cat was caught momentarily off-guard. "I didn't take her away from you, Shannon. You walked away from her."

"Only because you threatened to have me arrested for kidnapping. And now, sweet girl, you want me to hand her over to you, lock, stock, and barrel so you can play house with someone else."

"I didn't ask you to leave, Shannon. You walked out on me. And while we're talking about that particular subject, exactly why did you do it? Why did you leave? For the life of me, I can't figure that one out."

"I left for greener pastures. Less responsibility, more freedom, more excitement. Two years of playing mommy wore thin. It can be rather confining at times, don't you think?"

Cat felt the anger rise in her chest. "If you didn't really want her, why did you file for joint custody?"

"I had my reputation to think about. Who in God's name would hire a pediatrician who didn't like children? Fighting for my daughter surely had to prove I was a good mother. Yes?"

"Did you plan to abandon Tara after you opened your practice? Is that it?" Cat seethed with anger.

"Something like that. So, that leads me to this little surprise I received in the mail from some lawyer named Bill Charland. What's it worth to you, Cat?"

Cat slammed her hands down onto the table and rose to her feet. "What's it worth to you? Is it worth your reputation? My lawyer's name is Billie Charland, not Bill, and she happens to be my wife. We're fully prepared to drag you through the courts for child abandonment and desertion if you don't agree to sign those papers. And if you have any plans to extort money out of us in exchange, we'll absolutely go public with this and your precious little reputation won't be worth shit. Do you understand?"

Cat threw a ten-dollar bill onto the table and pushed her chair in. "We'll start the proceedings against you within a week if we haven't received the papers releasing your rights to Tara by then. Don't underestimate me, Shannon. You'll be sorry you did."

Chapter 28

Cat paced the floor as she recounted her conversation with Shannon for Billie when she returned home. "I can't believe I fell for that line of shit when I met her ten years ago," she ranted. "How could I be so naive?"

"You were in love. It may sound corny, but there's truth in the saying, 'love is blind.'"

"Damn it. I feel like such a fool. For the past five years, I've been blaming myself for our breakup. I've been wondering what I did wrong, wondering if I was repeating the same mistakes with you, and all along it wasn't even me. She was only trying to advance her career at any cost. She never once apologized for hurting me. Not then, and not now. Even today, I got the impression she felt justified in her actions. I have no idea whether she even felt bad about hurting me. She just moved on and left me wondering why."

Billie stopped Cat in mid-pace. "I'm proud of you for standing up to her. I'm glad I wasn't with you. I probably would be sitting in a jail cell if I'd been there."

"When I think," Cat said, "of what it would've done to Tara psychologically if Shannon had left when she was older, I want to scream. How dare she use Tara for her own gain? All along, she was using us to build a reputation for herself as someone who loved children enough to devote her life to pediatrics. No wonder she suggested out of the blue that we get pregnant. How cold and manipulating can a person be? All along, she planned to discard us when we'd outlived our usefulness."

Billie released Cat and sat on the couch. She appeared somewhat unsteady on her feet.

Billie rubbed her forehead above her right hairline then patted the couch beside her. "Come sit with me."

Cat curled up at Billie's side. "Do you have a headache, love?"

298

"Yeah. They've been coming and going for a few days. I'm sure it's the stress of this adoption thing."

"Maybe we should have it checked out."

"No. They're not that bad. A couple of painkillers will take care of it. So, back to Shannon. Did she give you any indication that she'd sign the adoption papers?"

"She didn't have them with her when we met, and quite frankly, we didn't have a chance to talk about it civilly like I'd hoped."

"Damn. I hope she doesn't give us a hard time about it."

"Billie, I'm totally prepared to drag her through the mud if we don't hear from her within a week. I basically told her that would happen if she didn't sign the papers by then."

Billie grinned. "I wish I could've been there. I bet you look cute with your claws out."

* * *

Billie slept through the alarm the next morning and had to rush to get ready for work. "Geesh, Cat. I don't understand why I didn't hear the alarm. I never do that."

"It happens, love." Cat handed Billie a travel mug of coffee for the road. "Didn't you take a sleep aid last night? Maybe that's the culprit."

"You might be right. I took one of those fortified painkillers with a sleep aid in it to get rid of the headache I had last night."

"How's your head this morning?"

"It feels fine. It appears I needed the sleep."

"Good... kisses," Cat said as she stood on tiptoe to receive her kiss. "Now hit the road, Jack. You're late for work. Me, too, as a matter of fact. I'd better get my butt in gear as well."

"I'm going. Love you. I'll see you tonight."

"I love you, too, sweetie. Have a great day."

"You, too," Billie called on her way to her car.

* * *

Billie was an hour late by the time she made it to the office.

"What's the matter, Charland? Did Cat not let you out of bed this morning?" Art teased.

"Very funny. I slept through the alarm."

"Didn't Cat hear it?"

"Cat never hears it. She'd be late for work every day if I didn't wake her up. Needless to say, I wasn't the only one rushing to get out of the house this morning."

She carried her coffee mug into her office. An envelope addressed to Bill Charland was sitting on her desk. "Well, I'll be," she said out loud. "Hey, Art. When did this envelope arrive?"

Art poked his head into her office. "First thing this morning. An overnight courier delivered it. Whatever it is, it must be important."

Billie inserted her little finger inside the edge of the flap and slid it along the length of the crease until the top was torn open. She extracted a single piece of paper with a sticky note attached to it. The paper read, "I, Shannon Manning, hereby relinquish all parental rights and responsibilities for one Tara O'Grady, born April 21, 2002, to Caitlain M. O'Grady. I've signed this document in good faith and without coercion." Billie verified the notary public's seal to confirm it was a legal and binding document. She looked at the sticky note attached to the form. "Bill, or Billie, or whatever your name is. Take care of Cat. She's good people. I know firsthand that when she loves, she loves completely. You're a lucky woman. Don't ever forget that. Shannon."

Billie's vision became blurred with tears as she read the note again. *Don't worry, Shannon, I won't forget. I promise.*

* * *

A week later, on Christmas Eve day, Cat and Billie stood before Judge Maria Rocque, surrounded by their three children, Cat's parents, and their dear friends Jen, Fred, Art, and Marge.

Judge Rocque rose from her seat and walked around the bench to stand in front of Billie and Cat and the children. She touched each child on the head as she walked by. "Billie and Caitlain, I can see that the children are very much loved by both of you, and it's obvious to me, the love they feel for you as well. I've long been a proponent of two-parent households, but I'm not so naïve as to believe that those parents must be a man and a woman. Children need love. They need to be protected, nurtured, and provided for. They need to know they're safe and secure. From what I've seen personally during our interviews, and through the testimonies of family, friends, and colleagues, these children have all that and more. So, without further ado, I declare that Billie Jean Charland and Caitlain Maureen O'Grady Charland will be the legal parents of

Seth Michael Charland, Tara Marie Charland, and Skylar Jean Charland. You are now a family in name as well as in love."

Billie locked eyes with Tara and mouthed the words "Tara Charland" to the seven year old.

Tara grinned from ear to ear.

* * *

That evening, Cat, Billie, and the children huddled together on the couch in the family room. Tara was curled up tightly in Billie's left arm. Seth's head was lying in Cat's lap while she brushed corn-silk-colored locks off his forehead. Skylar sat huddled between her two mothers eating popcorn. They were watching the tail end of a Christmas show they'd rented.

"Okay, rug rats, off to bed with you. Santa won't come until you're sleeping," Billie reminded the kids as the credits rolled.

"Yay, Santa," the children yelled as they ran toward the stairs.

"Don't forget to brush your teeth," Cat said. "I'm right behind you."

Halfway up the stairs, Tara stopped and returned to Billie, who was tending the fire in the fireplace.

Cat stopped as well and sat on the stairs.

Tara walked up to Billie and wrapped her arms around her neck. "Mom?" she said.

Billie slipped her arm around Tara's waist and lifted her to sit across her bent knee. "Yes, love?"

"Will Santa still find me?"

Billie was a little confused. "Sure he will. Why do you ask?"

"Well, my name isn't Tara O'Grady anymore. What if he can't find Tara Charland?"

Billie kissed her on the cheek. "Listen, love, Santa knows you and loves you, regardless of what your last name is, just like Mama and I do. Changing your name doesn't change who you are here, inside," she said as she pointed to Tara's chest. "You might have a new name, but you're still Tara, and nothing will change that. Santa knows that. He'll find you, sweetie, I promise."

Tara kissed Billie full on the mouth. "I love you, Mom. Good night." Tara hopped down off Billie's knee and headed for the stairs once more.

"'Night, sweet pea. I'll be up for good-night kisses in a few moments," Billie said as Tara ran up the stairs.

Cat descended the stairs and walked across the room toward Billie. Billie rose to her full height and pulled Cat into her arms.

"Merry Christmas, love," Cat said.

Billie's voice shook with emotion as she spoke. "This is the best Christmas I've ever had in my entire life. I'll never regret making this commitment, Cat. All I've ever wanted I have right here within these walls. My wife, my children, my family. Merry Christmas to you, too, sweetheart," she said and lowered her head to claim her wife's lips.

Photo Credit: Song of Myself Photography, Provincetown, MA

About the Author

Karen D. Badger was born in Vermont. She is the second of five children raised by a fiercely independent mother who, in addition to being the strongest influence in Karen's life, is also one of her best friends. Karen holds a BA in Theater Arts and Elementary Education and a BS in Mathematics. She is a Semiconductor Engineer with 32 years of experience behind her and plans to continue that work as long as it remains challenging.

Family is the most important and rewarding priority in Karen's life. Her sons, Heath and Dane and their beautiful ladies, Kacie and Daisy, are at the center of Karen's universe. Heath and Kacie have expanded that universe with three gorgeous grandchildren who are the apples of their Nona's eye. Kyren, at nearly five years old, is very protective of his two sisters Ariana, who is three, and Ellie, who is one.

Her life wasn't quite complete until she met the love of her life, Bliss, at the 2007 Golden Crown Literary Society's annual Writers' Conference in Atlanta, Georgia. They currently live in Vermont and enjoy kayaking, camping, and motorcycling in the Green Mountain State. They also spend time working on their homes, which seem to be in a constant state of renovation, in New Mexico and Vermont.

Karen D. Badger, better known to her online fans as "kd bard," is the author of *On a Wing and a Prayer* and *Yesterday Once More*, winner of the 2009 Speculative Fiction Golden Crown Literary Society Award. Her third book, *In a Family Way*, is the first installment in *The Commitment* series. All of Karen's books are published by Blue Feather Books Ltd.

Karen is currently editing the second book in *The Commitment* series, *Unchained Memories*.

Coming soon from Blue Feather Books:

Come Back to Me, by Chris Paynter

Author Angie Cantinnini's agent convinces her she must use a pseudonym if she hopes to land a contract with a mainstream publishing company—especially since the protagonist of Angie's novels is a hard-boiled male detective. Neither Angie nor her agent anticipates the raging success of the series of books or the mountain of wealth that accompanies each new release.

As a best-selling author, Angie should be delighted with her Bohemian life in Key West, but happiness is elusive because it's her alter-ego, Zach England, who's receiving the accolades, while Angie is relegated to anonymity.

Meryl McClain, the recently hired book review editor at the prestigious *New York Banner*, wants to make a strong first impression with her readers, so she picks Zach England's latest novel for her debut column. She offers a scathing critique, unaware the real author behind the pseudonym is her long lost true love, Angie. Heartrending choices separated the lovers eleven years earlier.

Seeing Meryl's review overwhelms Angie with feelings she thought she'd laid to rest years ago. This stroke of Fate beckons them to reunite, but Angie's secret identity and Meryl's struggle with a childhood trauma conspire to keep them apart.

Torn from a shared moment in their past, the words *Come Back to Me* have haunted the two women for more than a decade. Is it too late for Angie and Meryl to choose love again?

Canyon Shadows, by KC West and Victoria Welsh

Archaeologists Kim Blair and PJ Curtis, newly married both in ancient days (thanks to time travel) and in modern times, are eager for some privacy and relaxation. They set up housekeeping on Kim's ranch near Santa Fe, New Mexico. Though idyllic in nearly every way, their domestic bliss becomes tedious, and the Land of Enchantment seems too tame after the action-packed adventures Kim and PJ experienced in Arizona, Wales, and Greece. Then a visit from an Amazon spirit guide forces them to refocus on their destiny and warns them of unexpected danger and heartache.

While PJ is away on a business trip, someone breaks into the house on the ranch. Kim's trusted wolf-dog, Pup, is injured and Kim disappears. Few clues exist, but PJ finds the one most likely to reunite her with her beloved Kim. PJ must risk everything to rescue her spouse from a desolate canyon hideaway.

In this fourth book of the West and Welsh "Shadows" series, Amazon shaman meets Navajo medicine woman in a gripping saga. PJ and Kim combat unspeakable evil, face overwhelming physical and mental pain, and strive valiantly to restore the harmony they so treasure. They've said they'll love each other forever and always, but just how long is that? The answer is a matter of life or death, and lies in the Canyon Shadows.

Staying in the Game, by Nann Dunne

A serial killer has every college in the area on tenterhooks. When Shelley Brinton switches to Spofford College and acts mysteriously, her softball teammates jump to unnerving conclusions. Angela Wedgeway cautions everyone that Shelley should be considered innocent until proven guilty, but her words fall on deaf ears.

The group decides to shadow Shelley each night, and to Angela's dismay, their case against Shelley gets stronger and stronger. Everyone is shocked when the truth comes out, and Angela receives the worst shock of all. Who is Shelley Brinton? What dark secret drives her? Is Angela's life in danger? The answers astound everyone involved.

Coming soon, only from

Bluefeatherbooks
L I M I T E D

Make sure to check out these other exciting Blue Feather Books titles:

Tempus Fugit	Mavis Applewater	978-0-9794120-0-4
In the Works	Val Brown	978-0-9822858-4-8
Lesser Prophets	Kelly Sinclair	978-0-9822858-8-6
Possessing Morgan	Erica Lawson	978-0-9822858-2-4
Merker's Outpost	I. Christie	978-0-9794120-1-1
Whispering Pines	Mavis Applewater	978-0-9794120-6-6
Diminuendo	Emily Reed	978-0-9822858-0-0
The Fifth Stage	Margaret Helms	0-9770318-7-X
Journeys	Anne Azel	978-0-9794120-9-7
From Hell to Breakfast	Joan Opyr	978-0-9794120-7-3
Detours	Jane Vollbrecht	978-0-9822858-1-7
Possessing Morgan	Erica Lawson	978-0-9822858-2-4

www.bluefeatherbooks.com